IRENE RADFORD

GUARDIAN OF THE TRUST

Merlin's Descendants:

Volume Two

DAW Books Presents
the Finest in Fantasy by
IRENE RADFORD:

Merlin's Descendants:

The Dragon Nimbus:

The Dragon Nimbus History:

IRENE RADFORD

GUARDIAN OF THE TRUST

Merlin's Descendants:

Volume Two

DAW BOOKS, INC.

DONALD A. WOLLHEIM, FOUNDER

375 Hudson Street, New York, NY 10014

ELIZABETH R. WOLLHEIM
SHEILA E. GILBERT
PUBLISHERS

http://www.dawbooks.com

MAGNA CARTA translated in Albert Beebe White and Wallace Notestein, eds., *Source Problems in English History* (New York: Harper and Brothers, 1915)

Jacket art by Gordon Crabb.

Map by Michael Gilbert.

DAW Book Collectors No. 1145.

DAW Books are distributed by Penguin Putnam Inc.

Book designed by Stanley S. Drate / Folio Graphics Co. Inc.

First printing, March 2000
1 2 3 4 5 6 7 8 9

DAW TRADEMARK REGISTERED
U.S. PAT. OFF. AND FOREIGN COUNTRIES
—MARCA REGISTRADA
HECHO EN U.S.A.

PRINTED IN THE U.S.A.

This book is dedicated to my husband Tim.
I trust him to love me as much as I love him.

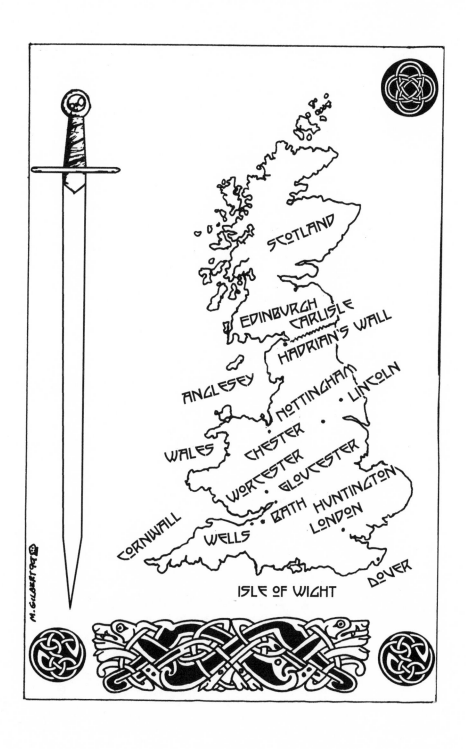

M. GILBERT

SCOTLAND

EDINBURGH
CARLISLE
HADRIAN'S WALL

ANGLESEY
NOTTINGHAM
LINCOLN

WALES
CHESTER
WORCESTER
GLOUCESTER

CORNWALL
BATH HUNTINGTON
WELLS
LONDON

DOVER

ISLE OF WIGHT

Author's Notes

Literature and Hollywood have made several fortunes portraying King John as the epitome of evil. From Sir Walter Scott to Kevin Costner, John Plantagenet looms as an evil conspirator, lover of torture, and greedy tyrant. I discovered an entirely different man in my research.

Like some politicians of our day, the good accomplished by this political and military leader is forgotten in the face of his mistakes.

Certainly John committed some atrocities. The incident of hanging twenty-eight Welsh hostages in 1212 is true. Lady Neville's offer of one hundred chickens for the privilege of sleeping with her own husband rather than the king is documented. He earned the animosity of those who should have trusted him most—his own barons. He preferred the company of commoners and mercenaries to his peers. And he alienated the church, the single most powerful entity in the western world at the time.

In today's parlance I would call John paranoid. His entire life was marred by reaction after extreme reaction to suspicion and fear. Throughout his reign he operated under the philosophy of "betray others before they have the opportunity to betray me." He could have learned this attitude as a survival mechanism very early in life. He grew up with three very ambitious and ruthless older brothers. They declared war on their father and each other. Their mother, Eleanor of Aquitaine, was often the instigator and focus of these disputes, pitting father and sons against each other in bitter power plays. Love and nurturing do not seem to have been a part of that volatile household. Or perhaps, as I have portrayed, John's paranoia grew under the influence of another. The truth may never be known.

John's reign is also marked by many great advances in political science. John loved the day-to-day details of running a kingdom. He loved the law and was an educated and fair jurist. He also made certain the day-to-day details of life as well as his judgments were recorded. We know the lives of previous kings from their chroniclers, men who kept journals and were often tainted by prejudice. Few chronicles of John's reign survived. But we do have copious records of the minutiae of John's life and career. The immense bulk of these records became too cumbersome to cart around in the baggage train. So a central chancery, or archive, was established in London to house the documents. Learned men were hired to study and guard them.

John also established a central exchequer, or treasury, in London. Prior to this, the king, or his chancellor, carried the bulk of the treasury along with the baggage on the king's progress throughout the country. John may have lost the crown jewels while fording a river in spate, but his treasury remained intact. Yet as the economy grew more and more toward coinage and depended less upon consuming tithes of food, wool, or horseflesh on the spot, the treasury, too, became too bulky to carry around.

With a central exchequer, those with legitimate and authorized expenses could be reimbursed directly from the treasury and not have to wait on a whim of the king.

John had no home as we know it. He, like his ancestors, lived an itinerant life, demanding hospitality of barons and of a dozen or so royal residences kept in readiness for the court.

One comment that keeps recurring among my readers is that the proper address of a king/queen is "Your Majesty," for a prince/princess "Your Highness," for a duke "Your Grace," and "Milord or Milady" for lesser nobility. Majesty is an invention of the Tudors almost three hundred years after King John. The Tudor claim to "majesty" was through a bastard line at that. I guess they felt they had something to prove.

I have taken a few liberties with the strict time line of history in this book. Eustace de Vesci and Robert Fitz Walter did declare their followers the Army of God. John did promise to go on Crusade and make England a papal fief. But not until the civil war that followed the Magna Carta in 1215. The issues of this civil war are incredibly complex, and I condensed many of them to fit the book for dramatic effect.

Reading the Magna Carta the first time can be disappointing. It is not a declaration of the rights of man. It is rather a peace treaty between John and his barons, based upon economics. The common man had very little to do with it. On second reading it becomes more interesting, indeed a fascinating peek into the priorities of the barony of the period. It also gives hints about some of John's shortcomings as a king. I have tried to address most of the petitions in some context within the story. Many of the clauses are just too complex or speak of issues that arose during the civil war between John's reconciliation with the church in 1213 and the signing of the Magna Carta in 1215. The translation of this document at the end of the book is available on the internet at www.fordham.edu/halsall/sbook.html Paul Halsall, editor.

Many thanks to Alan Lupack, Curator, The Robbins Library, University of Rochester for his insight into the Robin Hood legends.

Hourglasses, sundials, and candles marked with an estimated burn rate were the only timepieces available to most people. Commoners rarely had access to these. Church bells marked the passage of time. They rang for each of the eight services, or offices, of the day. Prime came at dawn, followed by Terce at midmorning and Sext at noon. Midafternoon was called Nones, followed by Vespers at sunset. Compline was a normal bedtime and Matins rang in the next day at midnight. For the truly dedicated and those who lived within cloisters Lauds came in the wee small hours of the morning. Roughly three hours passed between each service, but during summer and winter when the sunrise and sunset shifted, so did the hours of the day.

If you are looking for a bibliography, may I suggest *King John,* W.L. Warren, University of California Press, 1961; *Who's Who In Early Medieval England,* Christopher Tyerman, Sherheard-Walwyn, 1996; *Daily Living In The Twelfth Century,* Urban Tigner Holmes, Jr., University of Wisconsin Press, 1952. My bookshelves overflow with other volumes I referenced, but these are the three I relied on most frequently.

Any mistakes you may find in interpreting these learned scholars are mine.

In the Cast of Characters I have tried to lump people together in groups by family or association. Not every person in the Cast of Characters appears on stage in this book, but their presence is strongly felt and often mentioned. Real people are denoted with an "*" in front of their names. Two characters fall into the realm of myth. Scholars argue continually about their place in history as merely myths or real people. They get a "?" in front of their names. You, my dear reader, have the privilege of deciding for yourself their place in history and literature.

As always, there are people to thank for their help in putting together a project of this magnitude. First off, my husband, Tim, gets virtual and real hugs for his patience in putting up with me, as well as his assistance on our research trip to Britain. He took wonderful photographs, navigated, and organized the itinerary while I was pounding away at a deadline. Let's add my son Ben and his lovely wife Yukari for their unending support and encouragement when I hit the "muddle in the middle blues." Big brother Ed, was always willing to walk beside me as I thrashed through a plot problem. My other big brother, Jim, (he's the political scientist in this odd family) offered me some interesting insight into the politics of the period.

Family is wonderful for helping a writer get through a book. But other writers and readers are essential. Karen Lewis and Beth Gilligan were always only as far away as my telephone for ideas, logic, research, and for critical reads of the mess of a manuscript. Thanks to them, it is less of a mess. Thanks also to Mike Moscoe for his vast knowledge of church ritual. Sharan Newman gets extra points for keeping me honest on many historical details.

Then, too, artist Gordon Crabb needs to be remembered for his images that inspired several scenes.

My editor, Sheila Gilbert, cannot be left out of any list of thank yous. She believed in me and bought this book before I knew for certain I had the skills to write it. Her careful guidance and friendship made it all possible.

Most of all I need to thank Carol McCleary of the Wilshire Literary Agency. Agent, best friend, stern disciplinarian, nurse, business associate: she is what I need when I need it most. I could not have gone this far in my career without her.

And so I hope, Dear Reader, that you have as much fun with this book as I did. I learned a lot about the law and about justice. I learned a lot about writing. I also learned a lot about trust—trusting myself, trusting others, trusting my faith, and trusting my dog—or cat since I am down to only one pet (familiar, companion) these days.

Irene Radford
Welches, Oregon

CAST OF CHARACTERS
* denotes historical figure.

Lord Henry Griffin, Baron of Kirkenwood: 1127–1208. Took the cross for the Second Crusade 1147–1149. Descendant of Merlin and Arthur. Carries the legendary title of the Pendragon.

Resmiranda Griffin: (Ana) 1191–? Only child of Sir Brian de Griffin and Mathilde. Great-niece to Lord Henry Griffin.

Carlotta, Lady Griffin: 1136–1199. Witch of Welsh origins, wife of Henry Griffin.

Diddosrwydd: Uncle Henry's wolfhound, name means shelter, safety.

Mathilde, Lady Griffin: 1177–? Resmiranda's mother.

Brian de Griffin: 1175–1218. Resmiranda's father, always off at war or tournament.

Richard Plantagenet: 1157–1199. King of England 1189–1199. Third son of Henry II and Eleanor of Aquitaine. Absent from England on crusade 1190–1194.

John Plantagenet: 1167–1216. King of England 1199–1216, youngest son of Henry II and Eleanor of Aquitane.

Isabelle d'Angoulême: 1188–1246. John's queen, his second wife, and mother of his five legitimate children.

Prince Henry: 1207–1272. King of England as Henry III 1216–1272. John and Isabelle's oldest child and heir to the throne.

Arthur of Brittany: 1187–?1203. Posthumous son of Geoffrey, Henry II's second son, and Constance of Brittany. Born after Richard I ascended the throne. By laws of primogeniture, he should have inherited the crown from Richard. He disappeared after John assumed the crown. His fate is a matter of great conjecture.

Radburn Blakely: 1166–? Lord of Nigel Burn, illegitimate half brother to King John. Grandson of Tryblith, the demon of chaos.

Tryblith: Demon of chaos.

Sir Edmund Fitz Gyr: 1162–1208. Marcher Lord in charge of Mendip Mor Castle.

Lady Hillary: 1166–1208, his wife.

Newynog: Resmiranda's wolfhound, daughter to her great-uncle's hound, both descended and named for Wren's hound in *Guardian of the Balance.*

Joseph: Page in the Fitz Gyr household.

Hugh Fitz Chênenoir: 1174–? Knight, former mercenary for King John. Holds land in wardship to his stepson.

Archibald of Lea (Archie): 1173–1220. Hugh's sergeant at arms.

Orage: French for Thunderstorm. Hugh's destrier.

Ardyth, Lady Bellecôte: 1170–1204. Hugh's first wife, widow of Robért, and mother of young John (Johnny). King John arranged the marriage to Hugh against her wishes.

Baron Robért de Bellecôte: 1167–1201. One of King John's men who invades Kirkenwood. Accused of betraying Henry Griffin's son in the Holy Land during the Third Crusade. Ardyth's husband and father of Johnny.

John Bellecôte, Baron of Bellecôte, (Johnny): 1202–1209, Sir Hugh's stepson.

Walter Geoffrey de Chancell: ?–1208. Killed by Hugh in skirmish. Mercenary now attached to William de Briouze.

William de Briouze: ?–1211. Gaming partner and confidant of King John. Later hounded into exile and his family killed by John.

Peter des Roches: ?–1238. Bishop of Winchester 1205–1238, Justiciar 1213–1215, loyal to King John. Remains in England after Interdict and Excommunication.

?Arthur Pendragon: Legendary king of ancient Britain. Probably reigned around 500 AD.

John Howard: Innkeeper of Wells.

Stephen Langdon: 1165–1228. *Pope Innocent III's candidate for Archbishop of Canterbury. Chief negotiator in developing the Magna Carta.

Father Gerard: Priest accused of murder and the center of a controversy—does he come before a clerical court or a criminal court?

Sir Arundel: 1173–1216. Justiciar of Bath.

Lorenz Casale: Glass merchant from Venice.

Sir Nigel Marchand: Knight of Sir Hugh's acquaintance who holds lands through the Bishop of Worcester.

Lady Sigrid: Sir Nigel's wife.

*Petit: John's valet.

*William: John's bathman.

Fantôme: 1192–? Radburn's servant and pet assassin; has magic inherited from Nimuë.

Father Truman: hereditary priest of Kirkenwood.

*William Marshall, Lord Marshall of England: 1147–1219. Foremost knight of all Europe, intensely loyal, very wealthy and powerful. Served King Henry II, his eldest son—the Young King—Richard I, King John, and John's son Henry III. Primary general for King John during the civil war 1212–1216. Became regent for John's son, Henry III, despite his great age.

*Ranulph, Earl of Chester: 1170–1232. John's chief supporter among the barons. First wife was Constance of Brittany. Put her aside and remarried.

Daffyd: Steward of Kirkenwood.

Brigid: Daffyd's wife and Resmiranda's maid.

Sir Simon: Knight of Resmiranda at Kirkenwood.

Lady Hilda: Sir Simon's wife. Horseface Hilda acts as chatelaine of Kirkenwood in Resmiranda's absence.

Sir Andrew: Knight of Hugh and a friend.

Lord Silvester: Minor lord of Lincoln.

?Robin Locksley, Earl of Huntington: Host to Resmiranda while she hides and is supposed dead.

Robert, Marion, Meredith, Will, and Tobin: Robin's children ranging in age from 14 to 5.

Father Adrian: Priest of Huntington

*William Longsword: c. 1150s–1226. Earl of Salisbury. King John's illegitimate half brother.

*Hugh Neville: One of John's gaming companions. John had a legendary affair with his wife.

*Joan Neville: His wife, first name unknown in my research.

*Brian Delisle: Henchman of John.

Sybella Delisle: His wife.

*William Brewer: Henchman of John.

*John de Grey: ?–1214, Bishop of Norwich 1200–1214, John's secretary, and candidate for Archbishop of Canterbury.

Henrietta Carlotta Griffin: 1209–? (Hetty) Resmiranda's daughter by King John.

*Robert Fitz Walter of Dunmow and London: ?1170–1235. Prime instigator in the rebellion against King John 1212–1216. He surrendered valuable castle of Vaudreuil to Philip of France, and John refused to pay his ransom. Fitz Walter never forgave John. Violent temper, air of a fanatic.

*Eustace de Vesci of Northumberland: 1169–1216. Second only to Robert Fitz Walter in the rebellion. A cautious man, careful of his money. Never got deeply in debt to the king, but stood surety for others. His wife—a bastard daughter of David of Scotland—had an affair with John. Typical northerner, insular, hated influence from the south.

*Llewelyn: Prince of North Wales. Married to **Joan, King John's illegitimate daughter.

Sir Kendric of Southwark: Former mercenary, royal knight assigned to guard Kirkenwood in Resmiranda's absence. Loyal to John.

Deirdre: Crone who baptizes Hetty.

Coffa: Remembrance, the wolfhound pup Resmiranda gives to Hugh.

*Pandulf Masca: ?–1226. Papal legate who negotiates John's reconciliation with the church.

Prologue

Kirkenwood Grange, near Hadrian's Wall. Spring in the Year of Our Lord 1199. The tenth year of the reign of our beloved King Richard Coeur de Lion.

HENRY Griffin, eighth baron of Kirkenwood, listened to the irregular rhythm of his heart. *Thump, thum, thum. Kathump, thum.* Consciously he slowed and steadied his breathing. He needed control over himself if he hoped to save Lotta.

Thump, thum, thum. Kathump, thum.

Nothing worked. His heart knew that part of him would be ripped to shreds if he let Lotta die tonight. He had to save her.

"Come, Resmiranda." He held out his hand to his great-niece. Her childish fingers, sun-browned and toughened by hard work in the herb garden seemed pure and innocent entwined with his own. The smoothness of her skin contrasted sharply with his, wrinkled and spotted with age and not so innocent anymore.

The world had turned upside down, and he had failed to set it right again. More than fifty years of harmony he had shared with his beloved Lotta. He didn't know how he could go on without her.

Nothing would ever be right again without her.

Thump, Kathump, thump, thummmmmmmm.

A tear escaped his eyes. He tried to sniff it back, but more followed.

Resmiranda wiped away the tears gently with a piece of embroidered linen that showed smudges from her latest foray into the herb garden.

"Do not be afraid of death, child," Henry whispered. He gulped

1

back his tears, trying to convince himself as well as this precious child. "Death is a part of life, a transition that comes to us all. Sometimes we need to postpone it a little, though. Aunt Lotta's work on this earth is not yet done. She needs to live just a little longer. Would you help us do that?"

He'd tried desperately to save his wife from that transition to death and heaven. But he couldn't do it alone. Not even the presence of Diddosrwydd, his wolfhound familiar, had given him the talent and strength to work this ancient spell, handed down through the family for more generations than he cared to count.

Thump, kathump, thum, thummm.

Lotta had taken to her bed only yesterday. The day before she had filled Kirkenwood Grange with laughter as she scattered newly picked flowers into the floor rushes. Each step brought the fragrance of spring and fresh air.

Today the stink of sweat and fear and fever replaced the flower scent he usually associated with his wife.

Yesterday she had shouted with triumph as one of the serving maids brought a new son into the world. She'd scolded Cook only a little for scorching one side of the roast while he wrung his hands waiting for his son to bellow his displeasure at his abrupt entrance into this world. Another transition. One of joy, not sadness.

Lotta always made sure the entire grange celebrated the joy of life. What would they do without her? What would *he* do without her guidance, her steady will keeping him from giving in to the violence in his nature?

Even now his hands trembled with the need to lash out at something, someone. He clenched them tightly, until Resmiranda squealed a little protest at the intensity of his grip on her hand. Her fragile little hand, not a sword hilt. He'd put his soldiering days behind him over fifty years ago, when Lotta came into his life and showed him a different way of living. Still his need for violence haunted him.

He gulped and forced himself to continue what he'd started.

"I have to wash my hands before working magic, Uncle Henry," Resmiranda insisted. She tugged free of his grasp and darted to the ewer and basin on the side table. Happily she splashed water over her hands and face. Just like the puppies she so loved, she slapped the collected water in the basin before returning to his side. Her wet hand slipped into his easily.

Mathilde, her mother, scowled at her and counted three more prayers on her beads.

"Aunt Lotta is a crone—an older wisewoman," Henry explained, more to his nephew's wife than to Resmiranda. "Your mother, counting her prayers in the corner, is a matron. And you, little Resmiranda, are yet a maid. Together the three of you can build the great healing magic." At eight, the child manifested a wonderful understanding of arcane rituals. Mathilde, her mundane mother, hid from all references to magic.

Resmiranda stood behind him and squeezed his hand in understanding. He gently squeezed back, acknowledging her acceptance of the task before them.

Thump, thum, thump, thum. His heart beat in a rhythm nearer to normal. He took a deep, steadying breath.

They stood there for a long time, watching Lotta breathe. She had wasted away so much in only two days, she barely made a bump beneath the blankets and counterpane. Her gray hair spread out across the bolster looked dull against the white bedding.

Henry held the memory of the setting sun glinting off her rich black tresses, giving them deep blue highlights as she spun in place before the Beltane bonfire, nude and at home. He remembered the heaviness of her breasts, the slight rounding of her belly, the joy of joining with her that night. . . .

Her hair had seemed a silken mantle fanning out around her head as she lay beneath him. The blue highlights within it seemed almost like the halo of a saint. The saint who had given him back his reasons for living. He had wept with joy.

She had been a young girl their first time together, barely old enough to marry. They had conceived their first child that night.

To him she would always be that beautiful young girl, full of life and love for the world and all who dwelled within it.

He still hardened with need every time he looked into her beautiful blue eyes.

Thump, thum. Holding his memories in his heart steadied him.

"Resmiranda," Aunt Lotta whispered hoarsely. "Place your hand upon my chest. I need your strength." Her cough deepened.

Henry didn't like the terrible rattling sound. Resmiranda cringed away from it, too.

Thum, kathump. His heart skittered again in fear.

"Put your hand here, Resmiranda." Henry guided her flattened palm atop Lotta's shift, just above her shrunken breasts. He kept one hand on the child's. Pulsing green light outlined Resmiranda's tiny hand. Good. The magic had begun. "And you must hold my other hand, Mathilde." He beckoned Resmiranda's mother closer.

"I do not like this, Lord Henry." Mathilde sidled nearer, hesitant, chin quivering. She ran her gold-and-ivory prayer beads through her fingers much too rapidly to actually recite any prayers. "Father Truman should be here. He should offer prayers for her soul. Only through a priest and the blessed saints can we request the miracle of healing."

The golden cross of the prayer chain glinted in the flickering candlelight. The etching had been worn almost smooth over the generations. Mathilde used her wedding gift so much, she might have to replace the beads soon. They'd been new only two generations ago.

"Take my hand, Mathilde. Why would God give my family this special talent if not to use it? We seek to heal, not to harm."

"Sometimes we are given tests. *Not* giving in to the temptation to use 'special' gifts can sanctify our souls," Mathilde replied.

Henry wanted to scoff at her objections. "Being afraid of God-given talents is a sin as well. Come. Join us and learn that we do not abuse our gifts. We use our powers only for good." He grasped the young woman's hand, prayer beads and all. She didn't pull away. Not yet anyway.

The vibrations of Lotta's uneven breathing tingled through Resmiranda's palm up into his arm to become a ringing in his back teeth. His heart found the rhythm of the growing power.

Mathilde tried jerking her hand away with a gasp of surprise. Henry strengthened his grip on her, not caring that the delicate bones seemed to shift beneath his fingers.

Resmiranda looked puzzled but did not withdraw. Diddosrwydd thumped her tail and laid her huge head upon Resmiranda's foot. The dog offered her own strength to the spell, a substitute matron should Mathilde balk. Not a perfect substitute, but perhaps enough to complete the chain of power.

"Now think about warmth and calm, Resmiranda," Henry whispered. Hers was the greater talent and strength at the moment. He was only a catalyst and guide. "Picture in your mind how evenly and smoothly you draw breath in and let it go. Breathe deep." His voice took on a chanting quality. Resmiranda breathed in rhythm with his words. His heart settled into the same even cadence. He repeated his instructions in Welsh, the language of their origin.

He closed his eyes and listened to the fire sputter in the rushlights, to the rain on the roof above them, to the soft shift of stone and earth as the stone foundations settled into the earth just a little. When he knew all of them were breathing in harmony, how the dog Diddosr-wydd joined them with her own rumbling moans, and the world cir-cled around them in the rhythm of their lives, he spoke in Welsh again. "Picture in your mind, Resmiranda, how the air goes into Aunt Lotta's chest, circles around, and leaves again. See it in your mind. Follow it through the cycle. Breathe in, breathe out.

"See in your mind that Lotta breathes as deeply, as evenly as you do. Nothing blocks the air in her body. Nothing slows it down. Smooth and even."

Resmiranda's hand grew hot beneath his. The rattling vibrations in Lotta's chest faded to a smoother passage of air. Henry seemed to rise above his body, looking down on himself, Lotta, Resmiranda, and her mother. A bright green glow pulsed outward from their joined hands to envelop his wife in healing.

Witchchild! The word echoed through Henry's mental and physi-cal ears, jolting him out of rapport with the great healing magic that connected him to the three women. Pain assaulted his senses from the abrupt severance of the spell. They needed to ground and close before the magic backlashed and undid all the good they had achieved so far.

Shouts and the clash of metal echoed in the Hall. What? Who would dare?

Why hadn't Diddosrwydd warned him of the invasion?

The answer came to him even as another soldier yanked him away from Lotta. Diddosrwydd had been caught up in the massive healing energy along with the rest of them. The peaceful green aura surround-ing the spell might well have lulled the awareness of the sentries on duty as well.

Henry reached for the sword that had not ridden on his hip in over fifty years.

Armed men rushed into the room. Automatically he noted black braies, black chausses, and chainse covered in expensive black chain mail. Huge black helms covered their faces. No crests identified them.

Henry couldn't read their eyes as they kept long swords leveled and their knees bent, ready to spring into action with their weapons.

Momentarily blinded by the backlashing spell, he clutched his temples, trying to stop the white-hot metaphysical knives from penetrating his eyes. He had to think, had to react. "Where is my sword?"

Lotta!

A soldier's work-hardened hands wrestled Resmiranda and her mother from his side. Mathilde escaped to the corner. Resmiranda jerked and tried to pull away from her restraints. When that failed, she kicked the man's shins repeatedly. With no effect.

Diddosrwydd growled once, then snapped her massive jaws at an attacker. Her victim howled in pain.

Henry opened his eyes just in time to see a sword descending upon him. He grabbed the only weapon at hand, the branched iron candlestand. He whipped the post around in a flying arc as if it were a quarterstaff. Not his favorite weapon.

"*Jesu*, where did she hide my sword all these years!"

The mailed soldier reared back from the molten wax and flickering flames. He tripped over Diddosrwydd who menaced another soldier's throat.

A fifth man drove his sword at the dog. At the last moment the great beast twisted her head to snap at the danger from behind. The sword missed her, penetrating her victim instead. But he was already dead.

The passing of the soul tore Henry's mind to shreds. He fought to regain control. Lotta had taught him to revere all life, share life with all. She had also taught him to guide souls through the pain of death and know the diminishing of himself at each life lost prematurely.

Diddosrwydd felled her next attacker with one lunge.

Henry shook all over, trying desperately to regain something of his warrior youth.

Resmiranda broke free of her captor, dropping to her knees. She retched and clutched her head. Her eyes glazed in pain. The deaths affected her as well.

Run, child. Run for your life!

Mathilde pressed against the tapestry-covered walls near the corner as she muttered her prayers. She brandished the precious beads as if they would protect her from the man who approached her, sword drawn, a feral snarl on his lips and in his eyes.

"God's wounds!" Henry whispered as he instinctively fended off yet another attacker. Mathilde blocked the only escape from this chamber, though she didn't know it. The main doorway was filled with yet more invaders.

Lotta nearly sat upright, teeth bared, eyes bulging. Blood dribbled from the corner of her mouth.

"NO!" Henry screamed. "Lotta, Lotta, my love, don't leave me." He cast aside the candlestand and flung himself across the richly embroidered counterpane, shielding his wife's slight body from whoever had invaded his home and his private chamber.

An officer entered the chaotic room. The crest of a boar and a unicorn rampant facing each other on the wine-red tabard over his mail announced his claim to nobility. He grabbed Resmiranda by the shoulders, pulling her up from her crouch.

Henry didn't need to see the man's face to know his family, his history. "Bellecôte! Traitor," he screamed. "You betrayed my son and left him to die in a Saracen prison." He reached for the candlestand again, ready to kill the man, knowing his own sanity would flee with the act. What need had he of his mind or his soul if Lotta died?

"Enough," a new man said. He kicked the wrought-iron stand aside with his white boots. He wore only white. White surcoat and boots. White cotehardie. White-blond hair and pale, youthful skin. Clean shaven. But a black shadow crowded around him, part of him. The Black One of legend.

"But you are too young to be he," Henry whispered.

The Black One sneered at him.

A piece of Henry died.

A measure of quiet and order settled about the room.

Witchchild! The thought projected around the chamber loud enough for anyone to hear.

The Black One's pale eyes gleamed with triumph as he spied Resmiranda. Avarice replaced the triumph.

Resmiranda took one step toward him. She snuffled back her tears, innocently trusting the false light created by his white clothing.

"No!" Henry lunged for him, hands reaching to encircle his neck.

"Ease off, old man. In the name of King John, we mean you no harm." Bellecôte held him back.

"More treachery. Has John tried to usurp the crown again from his brother? I would expect you and your family to side with John Lackland," Henry spat.

"Richard is dead. John is king." The Black One held his hand toward Resmiranda. "Come, Little One, you and I belong together. You can feel it as well as I."

Resmiranda stared at him. Then she scrunched her face in puzzlement.

"Why are you here?" Henry stepped between the man and his great-niece. He risked looking at the bed. Lotta lay quiet now. Too quiet. His muscles itched to rush to her. He dared not move until he knew what these men demanded.

"King John has need of troops and money. You owe him both." The Black One shifted his gaze to Diddosrwydd who stood between him and the bed, growling softly.

"Such a request could have been made peacefully," Henry said quietly. He shifted his gaze about, assessing his chance of grabbing Resmiranda and fleeing through the secret passage.

"Your pack of wolfhounds and your peasants menaced us from the moment we entered the village. We expected resistance within the grange and prepared for it," Bellecôte replied and shrugged, dismissing a few deaths as lightly as if the victims were vermin.

"And what of Arthur of Brittany? John's nephew by his *older* brother Geoffrey. By right of primogeniture, established by King Henry II, Arthur of Brittany is next in line to the throne. Surely Richard named the young man his heir?" Henry insisted.

The Black One ignored the question as he eased half a step away from the dog. But that brought him closer to Resmiranda.

"Did you state your mission to the sentries in the village? Or did you enter with swords drawn, creating resistance because you expected it—or wanted it. You should have presented John's request politely, in writing as required by law." Henry needed to shift the Black One's attention away from Resmiranda. Why had his mind shouted *Witch-child* with triumph, as if the girl were his true quest and not King John's mission?

"Your sentries are absent. The grange appeared abandoned. We entered without challenge to find the entire household asleep at their tasks," Bellecôte explained. "After the fight in the village, we had reason to suspect ambush."

A strange smile lit the Black One's eyes.

Black magic! Magic of the foulest kind had sent the household to sleep. You set the spell to lull the suspicions of your underlings, Henry thought. He should have known the Black One would blithely invoke those powers to achieve what he wanted.

He wanted Resmiranda.

"We feared mischief and found it with your demon magic!" Bellecôte crossed himself. "You put your entire household to sleep rather than allow them to fight your foul spells."

Mathilde nodded and repeated Bellecôte's gesture. She seemed more enthralled with the invaders than concerned for her daughter.

"You interrupted . . . Lotta . . . my wife . . ." Henry stammered, daring to glance once more at his beloved. He had to see, had to know. . . . He knelt beside the high bed, reaching to hold Lotta's hand one more time.

"Stay where you are, Griffin!" Bellecôte warned. "We'll suffer no more of your witchcraft."

Lotta opened her eyes a little. Rheumy tears brightened them.

She lived!

"I love you," she whispered, barely audible. A great rattling breath escaped her tired lungs. She grew rigid a moment and collapsed within herself, all traces of her life gone.

"I love you, Lotta," Henry sobbed.

"You've killed her with your magic!" Bellecôte yelled, crossing himself three times in rapid succession. Then he yanked Henry up from his kneeling position, fist ready to slam into Henry's face.

Henry ducked, breaking the man's grip on his shirt.

"Get Resmiranda to sanctuary," Henry shouted, looking directly into Mathilde's bewildered eyes. He used the scattered remnants of his magic to compel her to move. "Take her now!"

He returned Bellecôte's wild punch. His fist landed in the man's jaw with a satisfactory crunch.

"Get the girl. Don't let her escape," the Black One yelled.

Henry saw swift movement out of the corner of his eyes.

The ancient family prayer beads flashed in Mathilde's hands. Then an armored stranger held them. Henry grabbed the familiar Celtic cross away from the man with his mind. He made it tangle in Resmiranda's fingers.

"Hide, Resmiranda. Don't let them turn you away from the light," Henry shouted.

Mathilde stubbornly stood before the secret exit. She clasped her hands in prayer and closed her eyes to the chaos in the chamber.

Resmiranda stared at the Black One, entranced, her hands reaching out to him in a compulsion imposed upon her by the evil descendant of Tryblith, the demon of chaos.

Witchchild! The word rang through Henry's mind. Then a solid fist hit his jaw. Stars pricked his eyelids. Blackness crowded his vision.

Chapter 1

Mendip Mor Castle, the Mendip Hills near the Welsh border, England, May, in the Year of Our Lord 1208. Ninth year of the reign of King John.

"SHUSH, no need to alarm her," Lady Hilary whispered to Sir Edmund as I descended to the hall from the sleeping apartments on the top floor of the tower keep.

What news would alarm me? Who had found me?

I'd seen death and destruction in my dreams. I knew the dreams told the truth, but past or future, my home or another's, I did not know.

Holy Mother! I did not want these visions that haunted me. I'd spent endless hours on my knees praying God would release me from them. Still they came when I wanted and needed them least.

I surveyed the occupants of the Hall—most of the inhabitants of this isolated castle. All activity centered around the Hall, the only room large enough to accommodate more than three or four people. But except for meals I kept to my room, a tiny alcove set into the wall of the keep behind the lord's bedchamber. I could not expect servants to serve me separately. They had enough work to do. Nor could I hope to receive my food anywhere near warm in any room but the Hall, directly above the ground-floor kitchen.

I proceeded to the side table to wash my hands, pretending I had not heard Lady Hilary. I gnawed my lip, wondering at the dire news Lady Hilary chose to hide from me. A page poured lavender-scented water over my fingertips, more ritual than cleaning. The warm water felt like silk on my skin and eased the tension in my fingers after a day spent plying my needle and waiting for the return of one of my messengers. I said a brief prayer as I relished the play of water over my hands. The sweet flowery scent reminded me of better days. The sparse amenities of this defensive outpost did not boast enough open space for a garden or free-flowing spring. Any flat area within the palisade belonged to training ground for the soldiers. Open ground beyond the protective walls belonged to the Welsh mists, *dieflyn*, ghosts, and raiders.

Food, clothing, spices, everything had to be imported into Mendip Mor from the town of Wells three hours' hard ride away—half a day or more by cart. In bad weather the steep track became a roaring stream, and we were cut off.

No one should be able to find me here. What did the lord and lady of the hall have to hide from me?

I made a pretense of drying my hands. Then I thanked the servant with a nod and turned back to the high table. Sir Edmund considered his table "high" only because it rested perpendicular to the trestles set up for the rest of the household, and not because it rested on a dais to honor the lord's family.

I plastered a smile on my face. A false one, but I could not let this good and gentle lord and his lady know I had overheard them. Safety lay in silence.

Two months I'd been here in this old and crumbling castle on the edge of nowhere. Two months and not a word from home. My messengers had not returned.

I had thought my years of running from convent to convent, always one step ahead of anonymous searchers, had ended last year. My relatives had made peace with King John. I went home. I stayed there but a brief time.

Two months ago the remnants of my family had sent me running again. Now I resided with Edmund Fitz Gyr, a minor marcher lord who obeyed his king.

Newynog, my half-grown and half-trained wolfhound pup, pressed against my legs with a soft whine. She had been a gift from the family almost as soon as I had walked through the gates. She knew the evening repast awaited us. She was hungry even if I wasn't. But then, her name meant "hungry" in the old tongue. I clasped the thick ruff of fur around her neck and tugged in rough affection. She turned her head back toward me, tongue lolling in doggy laughter, drool catching in her beard.

If any of my unease penetrated her senses, she did not convey it back to me.

Keeping the dog close beside me, for strength, for companionship, for courage, I approached the high table and made my curtsy to Lord Edmund. In another time and place, my family would outrank him and I'd not need anything but a polite nod. But now . . . my family was scattered, our honors, titles, and our lands left open to the man with the biggest bribe to the king.

Newynog plunked herself down beside my accustomed bench to Lord Edmund's left—the lord could afford a chair for himself. Lady Hilary already sat to his right on another bench. She had padded hers with a cushion. They shared a bread trencher for the meal. I was privileged to eat from one by myself. A rare treat in a castle that boasted few luxuries and was overcrowded with armed men. But the respect Lady Hilary hoped to show me with that lonely trencher also set me apart from the populace contained within these stout walls.

The men who made up that populace streamed into the one large room of this remote bastion overlooking the Severn River and the Welsh border. I welcomed their stern prowess if not their sweaty closeness and foul manners because I knew they would defend this castle and therefore me with their lives. Few enemies could hope to storm the motte and bailey arrangement of this castle protected by these veterans—if they could find Mendip Mor even with a map.

Servants brought the bread trenchers and the pots of stew to ladle into them. Tough mutton again, made chewable by long hours in the pot with onions and turnips. Poor peasant fare, but all that Mendip Mor could provide. I dug my silver spoon from my scrip, as did the lord and the lady. Most of the men made do with their own carved wooden utensils.

Newynog thumped her tail, letting me know she was willing to share my meal with me. I scratched her ears in reply.

When Lord Edmund and Lady Hilary reached for their wine cups after eating almost half their meal, I dared probe for what troubled them. "Did any couriers arrive today?"

"No, Lady Ana. No messages arrived," Lord Edmund said, looking anxiously to his wife. The gray streaks in his beard looked whiter, more pronounced than usual. The worry lines about his eyes deepened.

"I thought I heard a rider approach just after noon," I said. I continued to watch him for more evidence that he lied, or at least did not reveal the entire truth.

All the men below us at the long trestle tables looked at each other, at the floor, at the high ceiling, anywhere but at me.

"A horse returned to our stables, but the rider was dead," Lady Hilary whispered. Perhaps she thought the news less dangerous coming from her than from her warrior husband.

"Who was the rider?" The tiny bite of stew I had managed to eat lodged in the back of my throat. I swallowed deeply, trying to force it down rather than have it come back up and disgrace me.

"The messenger I sent out three days ago." Lord Edmund's words rang around the suddenly silent room.

"Three days. He hadn't time to . . . Did he still carry the missive I gave him?"

"No, Lady. His saddlebags had been emptied, his weapons stolen along with his life." Lord Edmund patted my hand. Lady Hilary fussed with her veil, a habit that revealed her distress. The fine murrey-colored linen was always crumpled.

"How did he die?" With my free hand I groped for Newynog. She scrambled to her feet and rested her heavy head upon my thigh. A little whine of sympathy escaped her throat.

The alarm bell tolled long and sharp from the watchtower. Fear raced up my spine along with the atonal peal.

"Raiders!" The sentry's shout echoed around the compound.

Newynog growled, nudging me off of my bench with her massive head. She herded me to crouch beneath the table as if I were merely a lost sheep.

"Raiders!" The shout came again, followed sharply by the clash of arms and the scent of smoke.

I looked around for answers, for an escape. Welsh raiders? I would rather face them than the enemies who sought me.

People rushed around me in confusion. Soldiers overturned benches and trestle tables in their haste to reach their arms. Shouts echoed from the bailey. The sound of a battering ram splintering the gate. Lady Hilary gathered her few ladies to her and retreated to the solar. I dared not lock myself into the room with only one exit.

Lord Edmund grabbed a sword and an ax from the stacks of arms against the wall. He led his men toward the bailey and defense of the walls.

I huddled beneath the table, near frozen with indecision.

Screams of wounded men rose and fell in undulating waves. The scent of blood and death followed.

And smoke. Thick and oily.

These raiders would burn us into the open if they could not kill us first.

Lord Edmund and a cohort of men backed into the Hall, fighting every inch of the way. The raiders pressed him hard, numbering at least three to one. I couldn't see much beyond the sagging door other than more and more black-clad strangers.

A man in black mail grabbed Lord Edmund from behind. He held a long knife to my host's throat. Monsieur Black muttered something.

"Never!" Lord Edmund shouted.

Monsieur Black slit his throat without further hesitation.

I gagged as blood drenched them both. A piece of my mind shared the moment of death. My heart stuttered in its rhythm, trying to stop in empathy with the dead man.

Lord Edmund sagged and dropped to the floor. Lady Hilary screamed from her place on the stairs, frozen in place at the horror of her husband's death. Her voice reached a high note in discord with the still pealing alarm bell. Her veil tore under her twisting fingers.

I shouted a stream of liquid syllables at the raiders. None of them even looked up to attend my orders in Welsh.

These men did not hail from Wales.

Another raider, also cloaked in black, cut off Lady Hilary in mid-scream with a pristine dagger across her throat. I couldn't read her attacker's eyes. Black chain mail and helm shadowed his entire face, hiding him from my vision, one more shadow among a swarm of hideous shadows.

They had attacked at twilight, the time of decreasing visibility. The time when otherworldly powers were at their greatest.

I stood up and froze beside the remnants of our evening meal, too frightened and horror-struck to move. Where could I go to escape these blood-crazed raiders who murdered blatantly but didn't stop to strip the lord and lady of their gems or rich clothing? Who were they that they burned and murdered but did not loot or rape?

Trained assassins. The thought sent sharp pains across my temples.

Newynog pushed me from behind. I stumbled over the body of the young page who had nervously poured the wine at the high table. The knife wound in his neck appeared like a grisly extra smile.

"Joseph," I gasped.

Newynog grabbed my wrist between her massive jaws. The slight prick of her teeth on my skin roused me enough to scramble to my feet. She could have crushed the bones of my arm with a single bite—or taken the hand off. All she wanted was my attention.

Blinded by my tears and not knowing where to go, I followed my dog. She knew the way. She knew the escape route and the plan we had formed within hours of our arrival, an old habit I had hoped not to need again. I closed down my thoughts, my senses, deferring to my dog's good judgment. I couldn't tell past from present, myself from my enemy.

"Call off your dog, girl," Sir Hugh Fitz Chênenoir commanded the plainly dressed young woman in the corner of a dark storage room.

No response. She stared straight ahead. The huge wolfhound growled, drool dripping from its bared teeth.

"Here's a crossbow, Sir Hugh. Kill the dog. It's the only way to get to the girl!" implored Archibald of Lea, Hugh's sergeant at arms. He held his sleeve over his mouth and nose to block out some of the acrid smoke.

"No. I prefer the beast and the girl alive." Hugh coughed out the thick foul-smelling air. They had to hurry.

"Call off your dog, so we can rescue you!"

Still no response from the girl.

He searched the dark recesses of the remote cellar room for an idea. Torchlight from a single brand behind Hugh hid more than it revealed. A tiny crack of smoky light filtered in from a grate in the ceiling near the wall. It illuminated the maid kneeling in a puddle and the huge growling wolfhound in a frozen tableau.

The young woman looked as if she'd been buried in the snow. Face pale, simple gown washed nearly free of color. Unmoving. She didn't twitch so much as an eyelash, keeping one hand tangled in the dog's bristled ruff. The other clutched worn prayer beads. Gold on the Celtic cross glinted in the meager light.

In the midst of all this death and destruction, why had she alone survived? *My dearest friend in the world died a hideous death today. He should have lived and you died.*

He swallowed the emotions that clouded his judgment. "I don't like mysteries. And you, young woman, hold the answers to this puzzle." Hugh took a step forward. The dog bared its teeth. Hugh stopped.

Movement danced around the edges of his peripheral vision. He turned his head sharply. Nothing. The dog didn't react to it. Probably just a rat fleeing the fire in the castle above. His men had battled fruitlessly for hours to save Mendip Mor Castle from the flames. They were losing the battle. Edmund's home would be his funeral pyre. *It wasn't supposed to happen this way!*

The sense of movement flickered again, just out of his visual range.

Wouldn't a rat flee outward where it could feast on the blood of the many dead in the Hall and the bailey?

A roof timber crashed somewhere above this deep room. The girl's fingers spasmed within the dog's neck fur. The beast turned its giant head toward her. Its growl turned to a solicitous whine.

Too many times Hugh's own hunting dogs had done the same thing, protecting him when the old wound in his thigh flared up and brought him low. When he was vulnerable from pain and fatigue, he sometimes imagined his dogs communicated with him.

Bah! The mists of the Welsh marches always made practical men see imps and demons, witches and fairies. He didn't have time for such fancies. His friend was dead and this young woman would follow him shortly if they didn't get her out of here. But first he had to get past the dog.

"The dog is the key to saving the girl, Archie. If we kill it, her mind will shatter and so will the answers to my questions," Hugh told his sergeant. He knew that statement for the truth at the same moment he dismissed the superstitious fears that raised goose bumps on his arms.

"We have to get her out of here, Sir Hugh," Archibald said. "Mendip Mor Hall is burning, and that dog won't let us near the girl. Kill it, or condemn her and her answers to a fiery death." The sergeant looked around the damp cellar nervously. Heat from the fire began to penetrate to this depth. None of them wanted to become trapped

down here if the castle collapsed. These old motte and bailey construc-
tions weren't meant to shoulder the weight of thick stone walls. At
least when the original wooden structure had been converted to stone,
the builders had dug two levels of cellars for the foundations in hopes
of anchoring Mendip Mor closer to bedrock.

Smoke hindered his breathing. Hugh's mind tried to panic and
force him to run from danger. He thought he saw another dieflyn—
one of the Welsh imps of earth, air, fire, or water that tormented
honest men—floating in the smoke, tickling his nose and teasing his
other senses.

He had to get out of here before he succumbed to insanity and
started talking to the imaginary imps.

"Take the men above, now. Clear the castle of all who still live
before it collapses. I'll bring the girl up," Hugh ordered.

"Are you sure?" Archie asked. He and the three men behind him
stiffened at the thought of abandoning their lord.

"Go. Get the rest of our men out of here. Send a rider to King
John. Tell him that we surprised Welsh raiders. The villeins ran at first
sight of us." Melted into the mists was a better description. "Tell the
king . . . tell him that nothing has been stolen. But every person in
the household has died at the hands of the raiders."

"Not all are dead, Sir Hugh."

"His highness need not trouble himself with one peasant maid
who cannot keep the hem of her bliaud clean and a hunting dog."
But why would a peasant maid clutch a *golden* cross and beads so
possessively? Her modern bliaud and veil had been a fashionable wat-
chet color, not a likely cast-off from lady to maid, even with the damp
stain on the hem. And why would a noble hunting dog protect the
girl unless she was high born?

Too many questions plagued him. Questions that only this girl
could answer.

"Very well. I'll leave you the crossbow." Archie placed the weapon
on the floor by Hugh's feet. Then he turned on his heel, barking
orders as he hastened toward the exit.

When the sound of the men's footsteps and their deepening
coughs from the smoke retreated beyond his hearing, Hugh drew his
sword.

The dog bared its teeth. Another growl erupted from deep within
its throat.

"I'm not going to use it, pup," Hugh reassured the animal.

The beast didn't believe him.

Slowly Hugh knelt, depositing the sword in the musty straw. Beside the long sword he placed his dagger, the only other visible weapon on him. The dog couldn't see the blades secreted in his boot and up his sleeve.

"See, pup, I'm leaving the weapons where you can see them. I won't hurt you or your mistress." *Unless she gives the wrong answers.* Hugh stood up again, holding both hands out to his sides, palms up.

The smoke thickened and swirled in the air currents. The dog sniffed briefly in Hugh's direction, then turned worried eyes back to the maid.

"Will you help me get her to safety, pup?" Hugh took one cautious step forward.

The dog whipped its head back to Hugh, ears pricked in alertness. But it didn't bare its teeth again.

He wears the crest of a traitor. The unicorn and boar rampant on a wine-red tabard. The jewels that mark the eyes and hooves were stolen from us. How can we trust him?

The fire comes ever closer. We are desperate. We must trust him. But only until we can flee again.

We can truly trust only each other. We must protect each other as no others can. We must guard our secrets well from man and from God.

Chapter 2

"COME, pup, let me carry her to safety," Hugh urged, trying to keep his voice calm and patient. "You can lead the way. I'll need you to help, pup." Two more steps.

The dog's ears dropped. It whined in a pleading tone.

"Fine, pup. I'll carry her. You lead the way. May I retrieve my sword?" Hugh's hand itched to hold the blade again. He couldn't take a chance on leaving it behind.

The dog growled again.

Hugh froze in place. "I'll not use the sword."

The dog relaxed.

Another timber crashed above. A man's screams filled the air almost as thick as the smoke.

"*Merde*," Hugh swore through his teeth. He prayed his men could rescue any of their fellows who had fallen victim to the burning Hall.

"We're out of time, pup. Let's go." In one swift movement he threw the maid over his shoulder and retrieved his weapons.

The dog bounded out of the storage room, barking furiously for Hugh to follow.

The girl weighed almost nothing, but her limp body threw off Hugh's balance. Awkwardly he threaded his way toward the center of the castle, limping only a little more than usual. The old wound in his thigh protested the climb up the twisted stairway. His shoulders bumped the stone walls at every other step. They felt hot to the touch. The fire was spreading.

He coughed out smoke at the entrance to the undercroft. Wooden walls divided the area into a maze of rooms. His eyes burned. He stumbled in the darkness. Heat radiated from the wooden floor of the hall above him. The cellar smelled of scorched flour and burning pig hide.

Embers glowed along the ceiling timbers. He thought he saw red fire imps dancing there. He ignored the taunting dieflyn.

No time to climb higher to the main doors. This cellar must have some kind of window or open door that allowed light to filter down to the girl's hiding place—he was convinced she and the dog had hidden there rather than been imprisoned by Lord Edmund. The window would be on the wall that faced the bailey rather than the exterior of the castle. Where?

"I don't like mysteries, girl. When we escape this mess, you'll tell me all."

Never!

Did he imagine that panicked voice sounding in his head? No time to ponder this. He needed to get out. The smoke thickened with every breath.

He turned in place, trying to orient himself to the girl's hiding place, the stairway, and his current position.

Smoked swirled in the draft coming from his right. He turned and headed in that direction, praying the air currents and the dieflyn hadn't twisted the breeze in some bizarre way.

"Dog, where are you?" he called, realizing he hadn't seen the animal since it climbed the stairs ahead of him.

A sharp bark to his left.

"Where?"

Two more barks, more urgent this time.

"Do you point out the exit or do you need rescue?"

"Sir Hugh!" his sergeant called, from the same direction as the dog. "Follow the dog, Sir Hugh."

Hugh coughed out more smoke. His eyes burned and filled with tears. Nearly blind, he ran in the direction of the voice and the frantic barking.

Behind him a ceiling timber erupted in flame. He ran faster. A wall of fire pursued him. He thought he heard impish laughter within the flames. He wanted to stop and join the hysterics of the imps.

The dog yipped again. Hugh clung to the frantic barking of the dog like a lifeline to his sanity.

The smoke lightened ahead. He lengthened his stride. His breathing grew more ragged. The girl weighed more heavily on his shoulder. His scarred leg weakened and twisted beneath him.

He stumbled, tripped, and fell headlong against the dirt.

Before him rose a solid wall of stones with a tiny window near the ceiling. The fire roared closer. He struggled to his feet, covering his mouth and nose with the damp hem of the girl's skirt to keep from breathing more smoke.

He was surrounded by fire and stone.

Trapped.

Within the writhing smoke, the stones began to vibrate. Fire imps danced along the cracks between blocks. Chunks of mortar rained down on his head. Hugh ducked, trying to shield the girl.

Suddenly the wall exploded outward into the bailey. He ran a circuitous path through the rubble. Seeking tentacles of flame licked his heels.

The dog bounded forward in a joyous greeting to him. His men circled the dead bodies of Lord Edmund and Lady Hilary. Someone had covered up the hideous extra smiles of their slit throats.

A traitor's death.

Hugh refused to believe his old friend capable of betraying anyone. Not Edmund. Never Edmund, much less sweet and naïve Hilary.

Oh, Edmund, you were the only one I trusted to foster my boy. Why did you have to die? Why? He screamed in his mind. *You tutored me, Edmund. You helped me when no one else would. You saved my life. And now you are dead while this unknown peasant girl lives.*

Darkness crowded my mind. shielding me from the fire and death I knew raged around me.

I drifted on a sea of memories. Many bad ones. Too many. I had survived my memories. I wasn't certain I or my secrets could survive the present.

I could not avoid my memories, just as I could not avoid my dreams of portent. I had to follow them through to the end. I skittered past other dreams of destruction and counted my prayers on the beads. I concentrated on the Holy Mother . . . on my mother. How often had I seen her without tears? Not often. One time in particular . . .

Mama held a roll of parchment upside down. She had never learned to read the squiggles of black ink that magically jumped out at me in the form of words.

I couldn't remember not being able to read. Whenever I could escape the solar and the endless needlework, I sneaked peeks at the many scrolls that housed the family archives.

The older information fascinated me more than the modern. I wove improbable, fantastic stories around my ancestors. Of Arthur Pendragon and his companions who sat in council at the Round Table, of his magical sword Excalibur, his lady love . . . his one true love and not the unfaithful one the wandering minstrels sang of.

Ever since I'd seen my first faery, I knew magical adventures awaited me.

The night before the letter arrived for Mama, I dreamed that great sadness would come to her that day. My dreams never lied.

Mama's sweet but bewildered face filled my heart with love for her. Though I was but six or seven at the time and she my mother, I protected her from the many things about our home she did not understand. I know now she'd been young, frightened, different from the sprawling and energetic northern clan. My childish perspective saw only the trouble that haunted her pale blue eyes.

"Papa will not be home by Michaelmas," I interpreted the words on the page for her. "Perhaps by Christmas. He hopes to win many tournaments and bring home many ransoms."

"Why does he leave me here alone? He is the heir now. Many of his relatives have died. He needs to come home. He has abandoned me to the mercy of pagans!" Fat tears fell down Mama's pink-and-white cheeks. But crying never reddened her pale blue eyes, or made her skin blotchy. Mama looked more beautiful when crying than when she sat in repose.

"You aren't alone, Mama. I love you. I'll take care of you."

She hiccuped and sniffed, blotting her tears with her snowy white veil. The gold-and-ivory prayer beads dangled from her wrist. She was never without them.

"I love you, too, my Ana. One day you and I will be free of this place and the ungodly relatives your father so blindly trusts our welfare to."

I didn't understand that statement, so I did what I could to make it all better.

"Mama, look what I brought you." I thrust my offering toward her, hoping she wouldn't see my grubby hands and make me wash them before she accepted my gift. I scrunched down so that my bliaud would cover my muddy bare feet.

"Flowers. How sweet, Ana." She wrapped her hands around my dirty fingers before I could soil the elegant needlework in her lap, but she didn't banish me and the flowers directly to the bathtub. I would have liked that, but now was not the time.

"Did you ask permission to pick flowers from the special garden?"

"Yes, Mama," I stated proudly. None of the servants and few of the family were allowed within the walled garden tended by the lord and lady of the grange. "I chose magical flowers, Mama. See, there's rowan for protection against all of your fears. And I picked betony for love. I do so love you, Mama. And Jacob's ladder to heaven for happiness."

I frowned slightly at the extra yellow flower I hadn't really intended to add to the group. "The wild endive is for . . . is for . . . so you can figure out why you are always so sad. And rosemary for remembrance, 'cause I want us to remember Papa, the way he was the last time he was home. That was Yule and we were all so happy then." Papa had come home from King Richard's war free of wounds, rich with silver pennies—he gave me one—and blessed by the king's favor.

But he had gone off to tournaments and another war before Lent. I was having trouble remembering what he looked like.

"You must remember to call the season Christmas, Ana, not Yule. We are Christians and we celebrate the nativity of our Savior and Lord. Only godless pagans remember Yule." Mama's voice remained gentle though her mouth pursed in an expression of disapproval. She fingered her gold-and-ivory prayer beads silently. The cross with the circle connecting all four arms was older than the beads by centuries.

"We must remember our parents and grandparents and all the things they knew back to the beginning. That's why we write down everything in the family book. We have to use the old names for things as well as the new ones." I parroted my lessons from Papa's older relatives.

"I know, my sweet. I know you love your father's family, but they are old and sometimes they forget that we live now and not hundreds of years ago. Our Savior is all we need to know now. Sometimes this clan forgets the true church."

That confused me. Everyone, aunts and uncles and cousins to the third degree—even the bastards, whatever that meant—attended mass every morning with Mama and me. They confessed to Father Truman and accepted the sacred bread from his hands. They also introduced me to the faeries who lived nearly forever and never forgot anything.

Mama never referred to my relatives by name, only by title or a contemptuous "them."

"Should I give the Lord and Lady the rosemary so they will remember to call Yule Christmas?"

Remember . . . remember . . . remember.

I would always remember the death my relatives faced when they learned the cost of remembering too much. Dream or no, I had watched them die as if I stood in the same room with them.

As I had stood in the same room with Lord Edmund Fitz Gyr and Lady Hilary when they were murdered. How could I forget the blood spurting from Lord Edmund's death wound? How could I not feel their deaths as if they were my own?

Everything I saw, heard, smelled, and thought reminded me of the weight of the burden I carried within my mind.

A notorious traitor had found me. The man wore a wine-red surcoat with the boar and unicorn rampant. He would sell me to my enemies for another title, a strip of land—for the fun of it.

Cold hatred roiled within me when I saw that crest. The Bellecôtes had hated my family for many generations. I needed to perpetuate the feud, to blame my rescuer for every ill that had befallen my clan for six generations of decline.

But I could not kill the man myself. To do that would be to murder myself at the same time.

I had to escape. How could I run again when my mind seemed divorced from my body?

Where was I?

We know how to snatch the information from The Traitor's mind. We know how to make him think he sees us sleeping on this pallet while we flee with the shadows.

Never. I would never succumb to Satan's temptation to use my talents for personal gain.

My memories faded for a time. Perhaps I slept.

Blood. Lord Edmund's blood. Death. Lady Hilary with her head lolling crookedly from her slit throat. Blood, so much blood. The roof of Mendip Mor Castle collapsing. Blood. Fire. Smoke. Hard hands reaching for me. Blood. Death. Fire. The unicorn and boar rampant on a bloody field drifted over the whole. Sapphire eyes on the unicorn and emeralds for the boar's winked at me in glee at all of the death. The diamond hooves on the unicorn ripped at the flesh of my friends.

I awoke from the dream with a start. Memory, not dream. My heart beat too rapidly. I couldn't breathe.

Holy Mother, help me!

Come to me, my bride.

I sensed safety, warmth, peace in that voice. But underneath the allure lay the hard and brittle edge of compulsion.

Was the voice in my head a dream or real? I could not tell for certain. Too often my dreams *were* real.

I fought it. Tricks learned from my relatives provided me with the means to build a wall in my mind that shut out the voice.

Darkness enfolded me. Smoke clogged my nose, oily, almost sweet, cloying. I gagged on the smell of the funeral pyre. Sweat soaked my chainse and my skin, trapping the hideous smoke. I could never scrub off the smell of stinking death.

The night breeze chilled me, made my breasts shrivel and my toes curl. The time for escape had come.

My prayer beads tangled in the fingers of my left hand. My right hand clenched, seeking Newynog. I frantically searched the area around me; felt only rough blankets and dirt.

Newynog! I screamed within my mind as I sat up abruptly. I couldn't trust my voice. Sound might betray us once more.

I had to escape now. Where could I go?

Newynog!

Witchchild! came the reply from my memory. Only witches communicate with soulless animals. Mama and the nuns who raised me had beaten that lesson into me repeatedly.

Dizziness assailed my senses. I rubbed my temples with my fingertips, unmindful of the gold-and-ivory beads I still clutched. The filigree decade beads rasped against my skin and tangled with my unbound hair.

A soft whimper to my right.

Newynog! Beloved. Where are we? I grabbed for her and stared straight ahead in the darkness. *Where can we go?*

"She's awake," The Traitor said from a few paces away. I didn't need to see the boar-and-unicorn crest on his surcoat to recognize him by his voice.

I shrank away from him. Newynog crowded close against me, keeping herself between me and The Traitor. Her tremendous weight against my chest nearly knocked me back onto the blankets. I remained rigidly upright, frozen in fear.

We must go home. But we have never had a home.

We will make a new home together. A place where our enemies cannot and dare not look.

Our enemies will find us anywhere. They do not respect the laws of sanctuary. The usurper seeks us still.

Holy Mother, help me keep my secrets safe! If the usurper finds the cache, all will be undone.

I sensed more bodies coming close. A bit of light outlined them in shadow. Armed and armored men. Newynog growled, baring her teeth. The men backed off. Not far enough to suit either my wolfhound or myself.

They blocked the exit to a richly appointed pavilion. Several braziers radiated heat and soft light. Rich tapestries separated the tent space into small rooms. Camp furniture was strewn about for the convenience of the owner.

Camp furniture, the property of a soldier not a lord. Bellecôte The Traitor should have an entire household of furniture in his baggage train, not this practical and very portable stuff. Where was I?

"All of you, get out of here," The Traitor ordered. His voice remained soft as if he did not wish to startle anyone.

I heard a rustle of cloth. Senses I shouldn't trust told me that fewer bodies crowded the space around me. A cool draft penetrated to my skin, gentler than stone-chilled drafts in the keep. With the breeze came the soft chirp of night insects. We must be in a pavilion within the bailey of Mendip Mor, below the steep motte of the keep. The wooden interior of the tower had succumbed to the fire. I had heard the beams crashing and felt the heat through the stones of the cellar.

Newynog continued growling. Her body vibrated beneath my clasping fingers.

One man remained. He moved into my field of vision, keeping a crossbow trained on Newynog.

"I said 'get out,' " The Traitor said, more harshly than before.

"But the dog, Sir Hugh, it's a wolfhound. It will rip out your throat easier than a wolf's," the armed man protested.

"It's but a pup. I can handle it. As long as we don't threaten the maid, the dog will do us no harm." The Traitor spoke softly, soothingly, holding an empty palm out to Newynog. He didn't challenge her by gazing directly into her eyes.

He knew dogs. Part of me wanted to trust him. But I knew better. He was a Bellecôte and a traitor.

I wished he would move closer so that I could see him, read his eyes. But he remained off to one side. I could see only his hand.

No other part of my body responded to my urging to *MOVE*. I continued staring straight ahead.

We have to escape. Tonight.

The Traitor and his sergeant with the crossbow watched Newynog and me too closely.

I remained rigid and unmoving.

If I sprang forward with all the speed I could muster, perhaps . . .

I remained rigid and unmoving.

I was trapped by the men, trapped by my secrets, trapped by my body.

Chapter 3

"I'VE never seen anything like this," Hugh's sergeant at arms exclaimed. "She breathes and her pulse beats strongly in her throat, yet she stares as if dead. And her muscles are as stiff and unyielding as the rigor of death. Is she bewitched?

"In a way. She has bewitched herself into this state," Hugh replied. "I've seen this before, among mercenaries and crusaders. After a vicious battle or bloody siege, some men become so horrified by what they have done that they cannot live. But the escape of death eludes them. So they retreat into this false death. The king's physician calls it *catatonia.*"

"Do you suppose she betrayed Lord Edmund and the guilt has brought her low?"

The girl began to twitch and tremble. Her arms shook so violently she thrashed and flailed about, striking at herself and the dog. Archie trembled as well, waving the crossbow around dangerously. Hugh wrapped his arms around the young woman's shoulders, holding her close against his chest.

Even in her rigidity, she seemed to fit there as if she belonged with no other man.

The dog growled briefly.

"I won't hurt her!" Hugh growled back. They stared at each other a long moment, then both leaned against the maid, trying to warm her and calm her trembling muscles.

Still she shivered.

"Sir Hugh, she responds to the accusation of betrayal but nothing else!" Archie continued to wave the crossbow as if trying to aim around Hugh.

"If she had betrayed Lord Edmund, why did she remain within Mendip Mor to be caught in the death trap? No. She reacts to the betrayal for a different reason."

He couldn't let anything happen until she told him all she knew. Only she knew why Edmund and Hilary had died so vilely. Only she could give him the means to vengeance.

Once sworn to protect her, he could not allow anything to hurt her—not even himself.

He gently brushed a tangled curl off her face and behind her ear. Her shaking eased a little. The dog whined and laid her head in the maid's lap, like a unicorn paying homage to a virgin.

"Lord Edmund and Lady Hilary gave their lives for her. I need to know why. I need to know who she is." He dismissed the unicorn allusion. If she were so innocent, then why had she hidden? How had she known when and where to hide?

"Not likely to get answers from her while she stares blankly like a dead woman. And the castle has burned without leaving any clues or records," Archie spat. "I say we send her to some convent infirmary and be done with it."

The trembling maid quieted a little.

"No. She stays with me. I found her. I must protect her." He paused a moment, allowing his oath to sink in. Then he continued, "I don't like mysteries. Secrets and puzzles and word games have a habit of reaching out and biting you in the backside when you least expect it. I want the truth and I want it now, before more of my friends die."

"Sir Hugh?" a soldier called from the doorway of the pavilion. "Sir Hugh, the pickets report movement around our perimeter. They fear we are being watched."

Archie crossed himself. "These hill mists hide ancient ghosts and evil sprites. Tell the men to build the fires higher."

"No," Hugh barked, disengaging himself from the maid. "Bigger fires will only blind our men to what transpires beyond our lines. If the raiders lurk, watching for an opportunity to strike again, we must be able to see their approach—likely just before dawn when our watchfulness is lowest. Wake up the men now and start feeding them. Let the fires die down for better visibility. I want the baggage packed and the horses saddled to ride at the first bird chirp."

"But, Sir Hugh, the mists are not natural. The men fear . . ." The newcomer crossed himself and looked over his shoulder.

"I don't believe in ghosts and demons. Those are flesh-and-blood men out there, stalking us. We ride early and long. King John is likely to be at Worcester. We'll catch up with him within two days, three at the most."

"And the girl?" Archie gestured with his trusty crossbow.

"She comes with us. One way or another, I'll avenge Lord Edmund's death. But I have to know who and why first." Hugh slammed one fist into the other. The maid cringed from the sound but made no other move.

"Easy, *ma petite*. Rest easy. I'll protect you," he coaxed some of the trembling from her as he often did with his son when a nightmare woke the boy. "King John might recognize her," Hugh continued. Something about her reactions made him taunt her with possibilities. Maybe she'd reveal clues without being aware of them. "His Highness might have some idea why raiders only murdered and burned, then fled at the first sign of opposition. I can only guess that they searched for something . . . or someone."

Her trembling began again, much worse than before. Her teeth rattled against each other. The prayer beads clattered together. Her neck swayed back and forth in a parody of negation.

"Maybe we'd best just take her to the nearest convent and let the good sisters care for her," Archie grumbled.

Her trembling ceased immediately.

"Interesting." Hugh moved into her direct field of vision. He cared not that he wore only a shirt that revealed most of his chest and legs. Modesty had no place on the field of battle.

She didn't shift her gaze, but he sensed that she surveyed him closely. What did she see? Did he come up lacking?

Hastily he closed the shirt ties at his throat and made sure the fine linen hadn't ridden up to his bum during his restless sleep.

The dog appraised him as well. She opened her mouth and let her tongue loll. Hugh caught a whisper of humor in the wolfhound's expression.

Nonsense. Dogs didn't laugh. In a moment he'd be seeing ghosts and demons as well.

"There is a Gilbertine convent not far from here," Hugh said, testing the girl again.

She remained as still as ever.

"What about the Cistercians two leagues farther," Archie suggested.

Her eyes brightened just a little. And was that a slight easing of the tension in her shoulders? She wanted to go to the Cistercians. For some reason the hard physical labor and long hours of silent study within the cloister dictated by that order appealed to her. The Gilbertines led more open lives, moving and working with the populace. She'd accept that but preferred the other.

"No, I think not the white-robed sisterhood for you, *ma petite,*" Hugh replied. He needed her to react. Maybe if he could provoke her enough, she'd break free of this catatonia and answer his questions. "We'll take her to King John and let him worry about her."

A tiny whimper of protest escaped her lips.

Worcester Castle

Radburn Blakely waited outside King John's private solar, listening. It was an old habit he saw no reason to break. Best to scout the territory before entering.

"Isn't it time, Highness, that you gave Lord Radburn Blakely a task to complete away from court?" William Brewer, one of the king's favorite companions, asked quietly. The chink of coins dropping suggested he toyed with his gambling stakes.

What else would John be doing with Brewer at this time of night? Radburn asked himself with a sarcastic smile.

He risked peeking through the curtained doorway at the cozy scene of the king and three companions gathered around the dice table beside the fire.

"Yes, Highness, these past three days of peace without your half brother's constant goads have worked wonders on your temper and the mood of the entire court. Even the queen smiles more when he takes his magic elsewhere," Brian Delisle added. The high-pitched whine in his voice dropped to petulant, as it always did when he lost at dice.

"The queen is most lovely this week, isn't she?" King John smiled and looked around the room as if he expected Isabelle d'Angoulême to appear. She didn't come to her husband's side often since the very difficult birth of her first son, Prince Henry, last year. At this time of night she was most likely asleep with all of her ladies forming a tight barrier against the king's intrusion.

The entire court knew that John might soothe the ache in his loins with other women, but he preferred the company of his young wife when she was willing.

"You do not need Radburn Blakely and his sorcery, Highness," Hugh Neville, the third gambling companion urged.

All three men came from common stock and owed John loyalty and friendship for everything they possessed. John had learned from experience that once he ennobled his friends, his mercenaries, his creditors, they shifted their loyalty to their lands, titles, retainers, and peers. William de Briouze was a prime example of loyalty turned.

Radburn had worked hard to eliminate that particular parasite.

Brewer, Delisle, and Neville enjoyed a great deal of influence with their king as long as they kept their demands to money and positions at court and did not seek titles.

" 'Tis he who keeps you from finding a compromise with the Pope and the Archbishop," Neville continued.

John's eyes narrowed in deep thought.

Their influence had grown during the three days Blakely had absented himself from Worcester. As a matter of course, he allowed his eyes to cross slightly and concentrated on the layers of energy surrounding each man. Men might lie and cheat, but their auras never did.

King John's aura splashed widely about his dark head with streaks of purple and red, clear evidence that someone or something other than Blakely controlled his thoughts and actions.

"God's wounds!" Radburn swore under his breath. "He's managed to weaken the wards I set around him." He marched forward from the doorway toward King John and the three men who played dice with him. "This is what happens when you listen to bad advice, little brother," Radburn continued to mumble under his breath.

At least William de Briouze no longer whispered poison into John's ear. That man would never wield influence again.

"Two treys!" Brian Delisle chortled. The petulant whine in his voice disappeared. Apparently he had a good score in the complex rules of the game that occupied the king's attention. He ran a hand through his barely tamed black hair, then scratched his chin. The darkness on his chin was perpetual whether he had shaved or not.

Blakely shuddered slightly at the man's slovenly appearance. Delisle never looked or smelled clean.

Three nervous clerics in the back corner of the privy chamber fumbled with numerous scrolls that demanded the king's attention. But they dared not interrupt. Men had been exiled to the far reaches of Cornwall and Ireland for less.

"These dice must be loaded," King John complained as he studied them. "You could not have such uncommon good luck otherwise." His brown eyes nearly crossed during his examination. So unlike the rest of his big, blond, boisterous family, John's pointed chin and narrow forehead gave him the look of a weasel plotting mischief even when he was at peace. John was rarely at peace unless Blakely was near and kept strong wards about his younger half brother and king.

Delisle stilled, holding his breath. For any man to besmirch his honor with an accusation of cheating demanded a challenge to arms. His fingers wiggled near his belt where his dagger should rest. In the presence of the king, no man wore his weapons.

But no man dared challenge the man who ruled by divine right. Unless he had a death wish.

Blakely almost wished Delisle would issue the challenge. He'd gladly remove the bad influence for his king.

"We all know that Brian cheats," William Brewer scoffed. He lounged on his bench on the opposite side of the gaming table from Brian Delisle. From his half reclining position, he gestured to his companion to relax. Then he waved his hand boldly in dismissal. "How else could Brewer have won such a beautiful wife. How else could he entertain us so."

"Entertain?" The king lifted his mouth in a slight smile.

The entire company breathed easier.

"Yes. We do suppose the game of discovering his latest ploy is entertaining." The smile on King John's face spread to his entire mouth, but not up to his eyes. Only a woman could light John's eyes.

Radburn decided not to wait for privacy to reset the magical wards around John. Delisle, Brewer, and Neville could inflict untold damage to the careful protection he'd set in the king's mind and on his body. At least William Longsword, Earl of Salisbury, wasn't about. As John's illegitimate half brother, his words carried more weight with the King than Delisle's, Brewer's, Neville's, and Blakely's combined.

Such should not be the case. Blakely shared a father with Salisbury and the King. He shouldn't have to use magic to influence the king.

"Ah, Radburn, brother, come test these dice and determine if they are indeed loaded." John signaled his half brother forward with an imperious flick of his wrist.

Blakely ground his teeth together and ignored the ward against the evil eye that both Delisle and Brewer flashed in his direction. Neville had the grace to look away.

Blakely liked Neville. That man had few scruples and did not hide behind false ones.

"How can you trust a man who does not age, Highness?" Brewer whispered to John. A lesser man than Blakely would not have heard the words. "He tops you in age by a year and looks to be your son!"

"Aye, he is an uncommon man, fairer than even Our brother Richard. But not so tall or broad." John's attention never left Blakely. "But We think he might share Our brother's preference for boys over women. Have you ever seen him with a woman?"

"Certainly not my wife." Neville smirked at Blakely. He'd openly shared his wife with King John to gain influence and power. But he'd never offered his wife to Blakely.

"Pay no attention to Hugh, Radburn. We but tease because you have not pressed Us to send for your betrothed this week. We are loath to divide your attention, brother. Let the girl rusticate a while longer before introducing her to court." This time John's smile did reach his eyes as he turned them up to Blakely.

Good. All the easier to set the wards when he had John's total attention. Radburn took up his station to John's left—conveniently to the west, the side of the sunset and death. He needed John alive and planned his ward against death with care.

Deftly he took the dice from John's extended palm. He covered them with his right hand while holding them in his left. A quick flip of his thumb turned one of his rings upside down and dumped a volatile powder into his palm while he secreted the true dice up his sleeve. A thought brought cold flame to the illusion of bone dice on his palm.

While they burned, he recited an arcane phrase in a nearly forgotten language, setting the first ward and banishing death from the room. The illusory gambling cubes burned brightly for a moment, then dissolved to ash leaving two tiny balls of lead in their place.

The lead was real, the ash but another illusion.

"Delisle cheats," Blakely announced. He moved to John's south, pushing Delisle off his bench. He toppled onto the floor in a comic display of clumsiness.

The other men laughed. Blakely dropped another dose of powder onto the bench and set it alight. This time he gave the illusion of an unpleasant odor.

"Ah, Delisle's rotten digestion troubles him so greatly he cannot control his urge to win enough to pay for an exotic remedy." Blakely said. Another phrase set that ward in place, banning the ill humors borne on the air and in the water.

The men laughed again and held their noses.

Two points of the compass set. John's aura began to lose the false brightness that came with a weakening of the wards.

Blakely moved to John's east. What excuse could he use to set another bright flame? He usually did this about John's bed while the king slept and paid no attention to Blakely's actions.

Delisle crawled to his knees, frowning at Blakely balancing his hand on the edge of John's chair. His fingers curled against his palm, leaving the index and small finger extended in the ward against the evil eye.

" 'Tis not my eye that is evil, Brian Delisle." Blakely stared at the offending gesture. He outlined the hand in a small chain of illusory fire. Not as good as the real thing, but he dared not chance setting John's robes alight. If the king bolted from his chair before the warding spell was complete, Blakely would be left open, vulnerable, and weakened. Every spell needed completion and grounding, or it would backlash threefold.

Delisle jerked his hand away, sucking on the digits as if they had truly burned. This ward banned the touch of unwelcome influence.

Breathing deeply to replenish his energies, Blakely took up his stance behind John, hands resting lightly on the back of the ornately carved chair.

"A penalty for your offensive farts, Brian," John demanded around a giggle. "Send your wife to me tonight."

Had the king tired of Joan Neville? About time. Joan Neville's influence needed abrupt severing. Sybella Delisle was a rather vacant but pretty child with soft blonde curls and laughter as light as faery chimes.

She also had pert little breasts that she loved showing off. Radburn had sampled those delights once. She was too willing to offer him much sport.

Delisle shrugged compliance with John's demand while Brewer chortled and slapped his thighs. Neville heaved a huge sigh. Relief that he need no longer share his wife?

"Ah, Your Highness' passions burn tonight," Blakely said, joining in the fun. This time he set a chain of flames in a circle around John's head, level with the silver circlet that bound his hair out of his eyes. He needed only an instant of fire, extinguished before the others truly saw it. John wiped his brow from the momentary heat.

"Indeed, I burn for a woman even now," John said. His laughter sounded labored, heavy. Radburn needed to finish quickly before John became suspicious, or worse, left the room in one of his volatile mood shifts. His restless energy could take them to any part of the country at a moment's notice.

Blakely murmured the last incantation of obedience and completed his circuit of his brother's chair. A sudden weight in his gut and weakening of his limbs told him the spell had grounded. John would remain at Worcester until Radburn determined the time to depart and the destination.

John's aura showed a narrow dark band containing his natural colored layers of energy. Blakely smiled tiredly. No more would the gambling cronies seek to oust the king's brother as adviser and trusted companion. Luck and a repeat of the wards while John tupped with the lovely Sybella tonight would make him forget all that had been said against Blakely today. Tomorrow any complaint or negative innuendo would sound like gibberish in the King's ears.

Chapter 4

The ruins of Mendip Mor Castle

I BROKE free of my self-defeating loop of questions and panic when a blast of chill morning air struck my face. A thick cloak of wool and wolf fur protected the rest of me from the cold. I breathed deeply of the fresh moistness. Stale woodsmoke, male sweat, freshly turned earth, and the remnants of a hastily cooked meal permeated the dawn mists.

And still a lingering taste of the funeral pyre. I swallowed my tears and resolutely faced the future instead of my memories and regrets.

Tiny flying bits of color hovered in the air. I closed my eyes and willed them to be gone.

When I looked again, only one tiny red faery flew around me. A brief sense of control returned to my neck and the tips of my fingers. The wool rasped against my knuckles, making them itch. Gradually my body responded to my will again.

I knew I should thank the faery, but I could barely bring myself to acknowledge its existence. Where had it come from? Few outside my family could see them.

The faery winked and giggled, then disappeared with a tiny popping sound. I shuddered. I hadn't seen faeries since I had entered my first convent at the age of eight.

I hadn't needed them. The good sisters and the Holy Mother provided for my body and my soul.

My neck twitched and ached with the need to move.

I dared not shift my head and let Bellecôte know I was no longer frozen. When my chance came to escape, I must have the element of surprise.

"Rest easy, *ma petite*," The Traitor said as if innocent of all wrongdoing. "We buried the dead. And we said prayers for them all though we'll have to send priests back to do the job proper." His Norman-accented voice rumbled soothingly in my ear.

I hid behind my paralysis, not trusting him to be honest about anything.

Then I realized I wasn't still drifting in a dream cloud. Bellecôte carried me wrapped in his heavy cloak of wolf furs, lined with murrey-colored wool. The deep purple-red contrasted nicely with the pale greenish blue of my gown. A part of me longed to show off the lovely colors to Lady Hilary. . . .

She was dead.

Newynog yipped a happy greeting to me.

Newynog, I cried to my dog, my only remaining friend and companion. She had inherited me as much as I had inherited her, and we both had inherited duties, responsibilities, and secrets. *Protect me from him,* I pleaded with her. *We must get away and hide before he sells us and our secrets.*

My dog yipped again and pranced into my field of vision.

I could not escape the prison of my rigid body yet and I could not escape the tight embrace of Sir Hugh. Newynog did not seem inclined to assist me.

Sir Hugh's strides were long and confident. Around us, men with dark circles of fatigue around their eyes and ashen complexions of grief or shock went through the motions of striking camp.

But Bellecôte looked rested and fresh. He smelled clean, and he'd taken time to shave. He didn't need a beard to cover a weak chin and he must be wealthy enough to afford fine blades if he performed this task every day.

"Any more sign of those raiders stalking us?" Sir Hugh asked a soldier approaching us from the perimeter of camp. Gooseflesh rose on his neck and a slight tremor ran through his arms as he clutched me.

Didn't he lead the raiders? Why else would he be in command of the smoldering ruins of Mendip Mor?

"Aye, Sir Hugh." The soldier stood at sharp attention, his pike held across his chest in a kind of salute. "Every hour or so the shadows circle the camp—widdershins, always on the path away from the sun. We never see faces or bodies, just a sense of movement." His index and little fingers stuck out from his grip of the pike—the ward against the evil eye.

"Wolves?" Sir Hugh asked.

"Too regular a pattern, Sir Hugh. Too substantial to be ghosts or sprites."

"I'd say the raiders are still lurking. They want something, or someone they left behind."

"Raiders I can deal with." The soldier made a rapid sign of the cross.

The muscles in Sir Hugh's shoulders and chest eased. "I'll gladly leave these hills with their deceptive mists. I regret Sir Edmund's death, but I'm glad I will not be bringing my son here for fosterage."

I wondered if he feared wolves or ghosts. Sir Hugh didn't strike me as a man who feared much.

A shout behind us. The sound of breaking wood. Bellecôte swung around in an abrupt circle. A noble pavilion collapsed in on itself. Lumps of cloth bounced up and down as men trapped beneath the folds fought for freedom.

That must be Sir Hugh's tent. Where I had spent the night. I froze deep within myself at the impropriety. Who had undressed me? Who had bathed the sweat off my brow and back when I awoke from that nightmare?

Some memory darted in and out of my mind like the passage of an arrow. Something terrible. Something enticing in its frightfulness.

A man reaching for me, calling me Little One . . . Who used that phrase? Someone from long ago.

Bellecôte called me "ma petite," the same thing yet . . . different. A ridiculous sobriquet. I stood as tall as most men. And I belonged to no man. Why did men insist upon possessing me and calling me "little"?

"God's wounds, men, can't you hurry?" Bellecôte barked.

"My apologies, Sir Hugh," the sergeant spluttered and spat as he struggled free of the all-enveloping tent. His arms windmilled, shaking off the clinging folds.

Newynog, at least, appreciated it. She bounded forward and licked the man's face, then darted back to sit on Sir Hugh's foot. A look of innocent curiosity on her face masked the laughter I sensed in her thumping tail.

"Yeacht!" The sergeant spat again, wiping dog drool off his mouth with bits of the tent that still trapped his hands.

Bellecôte's chest rumbled and quivered with silent mirth. "Well, Archie, the dog likes your battle-scarred face. She might even trust you since you rubbed her belly and scratched her ears last night.

Newynog? My companion never let anyone scratch her belly except me.

I tried looking closer at my dog, but my neck wouldn't move. The faery blessing of control had evaporated.

Holy Mother, help me! I prayed. *I need to break free of these frozen muscles. And break free of these armed men who will surrender me to my enemies.*

"The ridgepole cracked, Sir Hugh. We bumped it trying to bring the chests out of the wagons. It collapsed," Sergeant Archie explained, still trying to rid himself of the taste of dog breath.

"We haven't time to wait for the wagons. Come with me, and bring ten men. Leave the rest with the baggage. I want them to sift through the rubble for any clue to the raiders' identity. They can catch up with us after we locate King John. I'm sure he said he'd be at Worcester this month."

The trembling began again, first in my hands, then my legs, and finally spreading into my shoulders and body. The luxurious cloak couldn't warm me. Sir Hugh clutched me tighter against his chest. His body warmth helped, but nothing would still the tremors that racked me.

"Trust me, *ma petite.* I've kept you safe so far," The Traitor whispered. "I will always keep you safe."

Newynog whined and paced a tight circle around his ankles. Her concern eased my distress more than the man did. She would protect me from my enemies with her life. I doubted a Bellecôte would.

No matter who stood between me and my enemies, I had to be prepared to flee on my own two feet. I had to break free of the chains that bound my body.

I struggled again to wrestle out of Sir Hugh's grasp. Nothing moved. If I blinked, I could not tell.

Start small, a faery whisper, faint as tiny bells, drifted across my mind.

So I concentrated on my fingers. I relived the brief sense of touch I'd had from the faery. Rough wool on my fingertips. Warmth. Comfort. Very slowly, carefully, I pictured my forefinger moving up and down. The trembling ceased, all except that one finger of my right hand. It twitched ever so slightly up and down.

I took a deep breath and tried again. A little easier this time. I could see the movement beneath the heavy cloak. Then I tried the thumb. With a thumb and forefinger I could grasp small objects or a horse's reins. The thumb defied me.

Exhaustion clouded my mind and my vision.

Still a small success. I would try again later.

"You'll have to ride pillion behind me, *ma petite,*" Sir Hugh said quietly. "I haven't a horse docile enough to take a leading rein. And I don't want to take a chance on you falling off. I've worked too hard to rescue you and keep you whole."

Why? So he could turn me over to my enemies for trial and execution.

With minimal jostling and with the help of Sergeant Archie, I found myself atop an enormous dun-colored war stallion. Why did Sir Hugh ride this beast rather than a common palfrey? A destrier couldn't be a comfortable mount on a long journey. Unless he expected a battle—like the raid on Mendip Mor—and needed the power and cunning of such an animal. I examined the equipage as best I could. A few jewels decorated the saddle, nothing anywhere near as gaudy as most noble men would use, as Bellecôte could afford. And Sir Hugh used only a plain brown *baudrè* draped over the saddle and horse's rump rather than a brocaded or embroidered one. This one barely hung to the horse's belly let alone the ground. Sir Hugh clearly needed his mount unencumbered.

He scrambled atop the tall horse and wrapped my arms around his chest. He tied them loosely together with a strip of soft cloth.

"Now, *ma petite,* we are bound together come what may." He tried to untangle the prayer beads from my hand. My fingers clenched tighter into my palm. A drop of blood oozed from beneath my ragged fingernails.

Sir Hugh gave up on the gold and ivory, though he did examine the intricate etching on the circled cross. "Very fine work," he mused. "Very old. How did you come by this?"

I couldn't answer him. That cross and the beads that decorated it was all I had left of my heritage, the only clue to my identity.

"You'll talk when you have something to say." He sighed again and settled the cloak around me. Then he kicked the horse into a jolting canter and pelted downhill from the remnants of his camp and the smoldering ruins of Mendip Mor Castle. The horse threw great clods of dirt from his hooves. The sound of his iron shoes striking stones embedded in the dirt track clanged ominously. He picked up speed at an alarming rate. Shrubs and boulders rushed past my limited vision, blurred by our speed.

Newynog raced beside us, tongue lolling, drool matting her beard, ears flopping. She glanced up at me, reveling in the chase.

My rump bounced against the steed's sharp spine and my feet thrashed haphazardly against his side. The cloak hood dropped over my eyes. I was virtually blind and helpless.

The only thing keeping me aboard the beast was the thin strip of cloth binding my hands in front of Sir Hugh's chest.

I couldn't help but think the immediate future looked more perilous than yesterday's raid.

Newynog, tell the horse to slow down!

The dog just laughed at me. And so did the horse.

Hugh kept up the breakneck pace for another hour. May flowers bloomed along the verge and in the fields, but the chill mists lingered in the air. He recognized the familiar wild endive and gorse. The other flowers, white and blue and pink passed in a blur of color.

No time to think of flowers, of the nosegays he had plucked for Ardyth while she lay dying. He had to put distance between himself and these mysterious raiders.

The girl clinging to him from behind the saddle upset his balance. He couldn't knee Orage into a faster gallop for fear of her falling off. She'd likely pull him out of the saddle at the same time. They would both end up hurt or dead. Her arms went limp around him, and she slid off center.

He let go the reins to clutch at her before they both fell beneath the horse's belly, between the huge, iron-shod hooves.

Miraculously, her grip tightened at the last moment. He smiled slightly to himself. Panic just might restore her when gentle persuasion couldn't. He'd have answers from her yet.

And then what would he do with her. "Have you family, *ma petite?*" he asked.

She remained rigid and silent.

"Surely someone cares for your welfare."

Still no answer.

Once he had answers to Edmund's death, he could not just cast the girl away, alone, unprotected. Surely she had family somewhere who would care for her. He did not think her related to either Edmund or Hilary Fitz Gyr.

Who was she and how would she complicate his life if he continued to protect her as the code of chivalry demanded?

Not many men of his acquaintance would honor the responsibility of a lone woman without dowry, family alliances, or a title.

Brightly colored insects flitted past his head. He thought he heard laughter on the wind, like delicate bells chiming in the distance. He batted at them with his gloved fist. The giggling came a little louder and more emphatic.

I do not see faeries. Faeries do not exist, he told himself over and over.

The laughter intensified.

Surreptitiously he touched his forehead, chest, and each shoulder. A true cross, made in faith, should frighten off any otherworldly spirits. But the girl's prayer beads and old-style cross hadn't affected them at all.

He bit back a sharp curse. He'd just admitted that the brightly colored insects were faeries. The ghost of Ardyth, his wife, mingled her taunting laughter with that of the faeries.

He could not ignore her in death as he had in life. She left her living legacy with her son. Every time Johnny took ill, he heard Ardyth's jeers at his incompetence, his inadequacy, his bastard beginnings.

Orage stretched his long legs a little to leap a boulder in the middle of the track that passed for a road in these parts.

The girl nearly fell off again. She gripped his ribs with her elbows, almost painfully in her desperation to stay on the horse's back. Her presence banished Ardyth back to the netherworld of his self-doubt.

"You are getting some response, *ma petite.*" Hugh patted her hands gently. "Even panic is better than frozen fear. We'll ease up when I know for certain no one pursues us."

She responded with a sharp exhalation of air that might have been a snort, or a sigh of agreement. He couldn't tell which.

"Pray tell me who led the raiders, *ma petite*. Give me answers, and I'll leave you with the good sisters at the convent. You want that, do you not, *ma petite*?"

Her arms remained rigid and her voice silent.

Archie moved his mount alongside. His horse frothed at the mouth, straining to keep up. The sergeant gripped his reins too fiercely. The horse fought the bit. He clamped his knees too tightly to the saddle, giving the animal conflicting signals. He'd never ridden until Hugh promoted him.

He wanted to knight the man, but Archie would have to learn to control a mount better first.

Archie shouted something about a path to the right.

Hugh couldn't catch all of the words over the thunder of the hooves. He nodded his head with a decisive jerk. Moments later he reined in. "Men, proceed ahead to the Gilbertine monastery at the end of this road. Archie and I will take a shortcut." He pointed to a narrow track half a dozen paces behind him. It looked more like a deer trail than a road. "Confuse the hoofprints as much as possible to misdirect anyone who follows. We'll meet you there."

Most of his men had begun their careers as mercenaries, just as Hugh did. They knew the stakes and would leave a trail so confused the keen nose of the wolfhound who raced at his heels would have difficulty following.

He grinned at the dog, almost challenging her to find the right path. The beast sniffed at the heels of every horse as the men eased their mounts past them. Then she lifted her head and barked once almost as if she signaled the column of troops into a wild gallop. They were over the next hill and around a bend before Hugh had a chance to draw three deep breaths.

Then the dog leaped off the road onto the deer trail and Hugh kneed Orage to follow. This time he clutched the girl's knees with his left hand while he controlled the horse with his right. She didn't slip. Archie followed more sedately onto the path through the rough grasses of these desolate hills. Hugh smelled nothing but mud and gorse and his own horse. The smoke clinging to their clothes and the girl's fresh, womanly scent didn't count in his assessment of the land. No men had passed this way recently. The gooseflesh on his arms and back eased.

Little shrubbery and no trees gave landmarks. Bare hills with irregular rock outcroppings stretched ever higher against the low horizon. Few places for him to hide. But so, too, for any who followed.

They wound around small hills, dropping into the occasional valley and then up and around again. Hugh's normally good sense of direction twisted and distorted soon after they left the main road. The dog strode ahead, nose to the ground, showing them the path rather than letting them stray onto the steep trails that intersected Hugh's planned route. Often, he couldn't tell the difference.

Maybe he should bring one of his own dogs on his next journey.

Suddenly the wolfhound stopped and lifted her nose. A deep rumble sounded low in her throat. Her tail bristled and the hackles on her neck stood up.

Hugh reined in, every sense alert. He swung his head back and forth, seeking signs of what had alarmed the dog. Even as he searched, he drew his sword. The blade fairly sang as he whipped it out of its plain leather scabbard. The keen edge reflected the weak sunlight.

Archie drew his weapons as well. He kneed his horse into a prancing circle so that he could look in all directions.

The hills rose sharply to the left and right, dotted with ragged outcroppings and tough shrubs that clung to the sparse soil with deep roots.

"Hide!" Hugh commanded as he ripped the cloth free from the girl's hands. It tangled in the prayer beads. With a jerk that must have wrenched her wrist bones, he pulled her right hand free and pushed her off the tall horse.

She landed on her back, winded. She gasped sharply twice, dragging in air. All the while she fought for breath her deep blue eyes, almost black in alarm, stared at him accusingly. Then she rolled to her side, breathing a little easier.

The movement saved her life. An arrow plunked into the ground, directly into the place where she had just lain. The broad arrowhead—large enough to bring down a boar—crumpled against the rock that she had rolled away from. The cloth yard came from a jumble of boulders above and to the left. Four black feathers fletched it. Crossbow.

"Hide!" Hugh ordered her again as he kneed his horse into a dangerous gallop up the slope. He hoped desperation would unfreeze her muscles. He could only do so much to protect her. She had to help herself as well.

A dozen or more men wearing black surcoats over black chain mail, full black helmets covering their entire heads, pelted down the hill, swords and pikes leveled at him.

The dog straddled the still immobile girl. Its fur stood on end. Slobber dripped from exposed teeth.

The raiders pressed Hugh and Archie closely. Metal weapons clanged. Horses neighed. Men shouted and screamed. Dust rose.

Hugh didn't think, reacting by instinct and training only. He'd fought dozens of minor skirmishes during his years as a mercenary on the continent. Never so badly outnumbered. Never against men more skilled than himself. His sword arm tired quickly. He parried a vicious blow. The clang of sword against sword numbed his ears. The force of the blow numbed his arm to the shoulder.

Orage reared, striking the attacker in the head. But Hugh couldn't hang on. His fingers fell away from his weapon.

And he was down.

Orage reared again, pawing huge hooves at the men who threatened his master. He bucked, felling two more raiders with his hind feet. They fell backward in silence, their chests caved in from the impact with the horse's heavily armored hooves.

Another dozen men erupted from the outcropping behind the girl. They swooped toward her, shouting insanely and brandishing more weapons.

She still didn't move.

Hugh tried desperately to rise. Three enemies held sword tips to his throat.

Archie tried to press his horse close, to defend his lord. Other black-clad men pulled him free of his mount and wrestled his weapons away from him.

Hugh recited a barely remembered prayer from his childhood.

A hot stillness replaced the spring breeze.

Lightning crackled. Thunder roared.

A strange tingling caressed every inch of Hugh's skin. His teeth ached, and he smelled the acid sharpness of lightning after a strike.

Then the bolt of light came. Metal weapons flew from the raiders' hands. Two dozen pikes and swords, daggers and axes hurtled through the air, arcing upward, tumbling and spinning, glinting in the weak sunshine. They fell a hundred yards away, shattering upon impact.

Blinding light flashed once more.

Hugh couldn't see anything but the afterimage of the boulders reaching up to snag the weapons out of the sky.

Chapter 5

BELLECÔTE'S face loomed in front of my eyes, worry lines radiating from his dark eyes. How dare this traitor appear so handsome! Perhaps that was why he evaded prosecution for his crimes. Kings and barons believed his innocence because legend claimed that crime would add ugliness to a person's visage.

I refused to be beguiled by him.

My eyes were dry and filled with grit. Splotches of black floated across my vision, as if I had stared directly at the sun. I realized then that I had been staring at nothing for a space of time.

"Who are you that these men pursue you so persistently? Who are you that my best friend died protecting you?" he asked, staring at me. He scowled. His dark eyebrows drew downward into a deep V with barely a break between them. His brown eyes looked cloudy with suppressed emotions I didn't want to understand.

My skin prickled, and my heart skittered under his intense gaze.

I didn't reply. Every muscle in my body protested my fall and the rough ride, but my control remained minimal.

"Do miracles follow you around like that dog of yours?" he asked as he clasped my hand, the left one that still clutched the rosary. "There must be a powerful vein of lodestone in that outcropping to yank those weapons away so abruptly. That breach in the bailey wall that so conveniently gave us exit from the undercroft seemed like a miracle, too. Probably just a weakening in the wall from the heat of the fire." He shook his head, dismissing the strange events as merely strange rather than true miracles or . . . or magic.

"Six dead. The rest flown," Archie said. "But they aren't common Welsh raiders, Sir Hugh."

"I guessed that the moment I saw their expensive armor and how they hid their faces."

Sir Hugh heaved me upright as he spoke. I swayed a moment until my feet got used to supporting my weight. He braced me with one hand on my shoulder, the other behind my waist.

The change in position felt good. My joints settled into position. I could almost move them of my own will. Almost.

Now I could see the dead bodies on the hillside above the path. Three of them had died from the horse's hooves. The others had gaping sword wounds in their torsos. Sir Hugh had killed four defending us. The pools of blood beside each of them were still liquid and bright. Why hadn't I felt them die? I should have. Guilt pressed down on my heart and my shoulders for not having the weight of their passing on my soul.

I wanted to gag at the stench of death. Avoiding the reflex took most of my concentration. I had none left over for control of my legs.

One dead man's eyes fixed on my face accusingly.

"Any idea who these men are?" Sir Hugh asked me.

I knew who sent them, but I wouldn't give him the satisfaction of a reply. One traitor deserves another.

"Let's look at their faces and see if that jogs your memory." He led me the few yards over the rough terrain. I stumbled. He kept a firm clasp of my hand and waist. My feet obeyed his direction while they refused mine.

Archie yanked the closed helm off one dead man's head and folded the chain mail away from his face.

I must have made some small sound, for Sir Hugh looked at me strangely. He shifted his gaze back and forth between the dead man and me.

"How do you know Walter Geoffrey de Chancell, chief knight of William de Briouze? De Chancell's patron is the king's confidant and gambling companion."

"Are you certain this is Walter Geoffrey de Chancell?" Archie asked. "He's supposed to be in Ireland. King John sent him there last month to keep an eye on the Marshall's family and holdings."

"I'm certain. I've fought alongside this man and de Briouze many times in King John's wars. He's a mercenary for hire, loyal to whoever pays the highest, like his brothers. Right now, de Briouze and John have the most money to spend on his like. Why would he turn outlaw and attack us? Or you?" Sir Hugh directed the last question to me.

"We don't know yet that he and his men raided Mendip Mor," Archie reminded him.

"I would bet a knight's equipage that he led the raid," Sir Hugh replied.

My conviction that Sir Hugh had led that raid himself wavered. His face and eyes held too many emotions for him to lie so convincingly. I wouldn't look into his mind or seek out his aura for the truth. The Sisters of the Blessed Virgin would never forgive me if I broke my vow to suppress my talents.

Would God forgive me?

If only I could suppress my dreams as easily. Were they a sign God wanted me to use my talent? Or just a curse visited upon my family for some past sin?

I stared back at Sir Hugh, daring him to make the connection between Walter Geoffrey de Chancell and his patron de Briouze and King John.

"King John believes in the law. He'd never resort to false raiders to eliminate a perceived enemy!" Hugh shook his head as if casting out unwanted thoughts. "He'd find a legal excuse and do it openly."

I continued to stare at him, daring him to continue the thought.

"The law is important to King John," he insisted. "We'll take the body and the problem to King John. He'll know what transpires," Sir Hugh said decisively.

I tried and tried to shout a denial. I couldn't go to Worcester, or anywhere near the royal court.

My body refused to obey my thoughts. But I meekly followed Sir Hugh Bellecôte, The Traitor, back to his horse.

Worcester Castle

Radburn Blakely sought a private place, any private place within the sprawling mass of Worcester Castle. Thick walls and tall towers offered fine defenses, but cut down on the number of rooms within the confines. The central keep was occupied by courtiers, servants, and the ladies—who generated more ladies and luggage than the rest of the entourage. Soldiers filled the bailey, the cellars, and the yards between curtain walls. Even the jakes in this place were communal and rarely vacant.

"I should have stayed at Nigel Burn," he muttered as he prowled the ramparts seeking an idea. His retainers knew better than to disturb their master when he required privacy. "But if I'd stayed home, I wouldn't have been able to renew the wards around John before his wastrel companions persuaded him into a dangerous course of action."

Radburn climbed the tall western watchtower stairs. Sometimes, the soldiers allowed their diligence to waiver in this chill and exposed station. All he needed was a few moments of looking into his scrying bowl. A few moments to check on his retainers and spies all over the country.

He paused a moment before mounting the last steps in the spiraling staircase up the interior of the tower. Three deep breaths restored his calm and assurance before he lifted the trapdoor above him onto the parapet. His next three breaths restored his energy enough to probe the watch platform above his head. The only life-form that responded to his quick mental touch thought in scattered images of seeking out the next meal of shellfish or garbage in the midden. The seagull cared not which as long as his belly was full.

Blakely pushed up the trapdoor and eased his narrow shoulders through. Bare heartbeats later he settled himself cross-legged on the wooden floor with his back to the low stone wall that defined this open perch. It kept out the wind. That was all he cared about now. No time to stand and survey the town and river below.

He settled his silver bowl before him and filled it with water from a wineskin attached to his belt. His trance engulfed his senses before the water had settled into a smooth surface. He had to finish this before anyone found him.

Having a reputation as a sorcerer added spice to the court gossip. Being caught working magic opened the way to church trials and probable execution. Radburn Blakely had no intention of sacrificing his life just yet. King John needed him. The scrying bowl gave him the information to maintain unity and peace or sow the seeds of chaos, whichever seemed most necessary at the time.

Images rose gradually to the surface of the water in his bowl. Fractured images, little more coherent than the thoughts of the bird perched on the parapet, flitted across his mind's eye.

He caught the impression of Robert Fitz Walter stalking through his castle near London, backhanding serfs for no reason but his own foul mood. That discontented lord muttered something about making demands upon King John, restitution for the exorbitant ransom he'd had to pay King Philip of France four years ago.

"Not bloody likely, Fitz Walter," Blakely muttered. "John and I need that money for another purpose." Through the water's surface, he sent a message to his spy to send Fitz Walter seeking John in York, the opposite end of the country from where Radburn directed his king.

The next image showed Eustace de Vesci of Northumberland. He ranted to a gathering of lesser nobles about King John's depredations, his lechery, and his crippling taxes. Mostly he preached against John's attempts to keep the barons under control. King Richard had allowed them to do as they pleased as long they paid for his foreign wars. De Vesci's tirade drifted from topic to topic and quickly bored his companions. He'd not raise a rebellion yet, but he kept the North uneasy. Time to send another agent there to keep the unrest at manageable levels.

Satisfied that John's most powerful enemies would not trouble him for the time being, Blakely checked on his own retainers.

"Fools!" he screamed. "Do not allow your quarry to flee! Follow them. Now. I need the secrets they harbor."

Loud footsteps and louder voices climbed the watchtower stairs. The wooden floor vibrated with their approach.

Radburn rose quickly and smoothly. He had just dumped the water over the edge of the wall and secreted the bowl inside his robe when the captain of the guard pushed up the trapdoor, grumbling about lazy soldiers more concerned with warming their bums than keeping watch.

"Do not trouble yourself over their lapse, Captain." Radburn flashed the man his most ingratiating smile. "I sent them below for a time. I needed some peace and quiet. This seemed the only place available. I have kept watch while I sorted through my troubled thoughts."

The captain grumbled something else before lowering the trapdoor and disappearing in search of his wayward troops. But without a reprimand. The troops would continue to leave this tower unguarded when Radburn wanted privacy because they thought they could get away with it.

The Mendip Hills, north and west of Wells

Sir Hugh picked me up and deposited me on the back of his horse.

"We'll need fresh horses, both of us riding double," Archie grumbled. He heaved Walter Geoffrey de Chancell's dead body over his horse's back behind the saddle with no more ceremony than Sir Hugh had given me. The beast shied at the smell of blood so close.

"We'll rest them at noon in Wells and take a bite ourselves. We've got to push on before those black-clad soldiers regain their wits and return for us," Sir Hugh replied.

Newynog entwined herself around the horse's ankles, whining and sniffing the air for the return of the raiders.

I tried to force my leg to move so that I could ride astride. Newynog reached up and nudged my foot in the proper direction, but to no avail.

Try again, I urged her with my mind. I couldn't move my foot, but I had felt the cold of Newynog's nose through the sole of my thin indoor slipper.

She moved away from me to sniff the ground and follow the trail of the fleeing raiders a few steps.

I tried again to lift my right leg across the horse's broad back. My head already pounded with the thought of jouncing uncontrolled on another pelting ride for hours on end.

Nothing moved but the hammer behind my eyes.

I had walked a few steps with Bellecôte's assistance. Why couldn't I swing one leg over a horse's back by myself?

I ground my teeth in frustration. Then I silently triumphed at that much control. With much concentration I managed to open my mouth. No sound rushed forth no matter how hard I tried.

"Go ahead and spit it out, *ma petite.* What do you want?" Bellecôte said.

A series of inarticulate grunts and gasps issued from my gaping mouth. He shook his head and prepared to mount. "Survivors usually have more courage than you, *ma petite.* True survivors speak up for themselves when necessary and remain silent when necessary. Your journey to court will be much easier and safer if you tell me what you desire."

Safety lay in silence. I closed my jaw, afraid that my secrets would spill out. He could make me walk. I prayed he'd not be able to make me speak.

"With this delay, the men will reach the convent long before us," Archie warned.

"Good. Since we aren't going there," Sir Hugh replied curtly.

Archie sighed in resignation and rolled his eyes upward as if asking help from heaven. "Do I dare presume to ask where we are going?"

"Since there is not enough cover to hide a coney, let alone a raider who can overhear our plans, you may presume." I sensed a low chuckle rippling in Sir Hugh's chest.

The sergeant sighed again. "Where are we going, Sir Hugh?"

"To the church in Wells. The engineer will know where King John holds court this week. He knows everything that transpires in this land."

"N . . . n . . . no." The word squeaked out.

"She has a voice after all!" Bellecôte lifted one eyebrow in ironic speculation. "If we aren't to go to Wells to find King John, then where do you want to go, *ma petite?*"

I didn't know. I knew of no place safe from my enemies. But once . . . long ago . . . I had been safe for a time. . . .

Chapter 6

Kirkenwood Grange, 1199, after the raid

The moment I saw Uncle Henry fall, I knew the promises of safety from the man dressed in white were false. I broke free of his compulsion and grabbed Mama's hand. Together we crept through the secret passages built into the curtain wall around Kirkenwood. One of the numerous exits led downward into a natural cave full of crystals and other marvels. I knew the cave and passageways better than anyone except maybe Uncle Henry. I knew them better than he suspected I did.

Familiar shadows embraced me. I took care to step into the center of several puddles before I lit fire with my thoughts.

Mama cringed away from my splashings, but she didn't let go of my hand.

"Hello," I whispered to the many wonders of the caves. I caressed one special crystal at the junction of two passages.

All Mama saw were rats and puddles and cobwebs.

The last door led into the crypt of the little church in the woods that gave our home its name—Kirkenwood, the kirk in the woods. I touched the special tomb of a king and his lady for luck as we passed it. Mama crossed herself over and over, muttering her prayers. I offered her the gold-and-ivory beads so she could keep track of her petitions. But she shook her head.

"Keep it, Resmiranda. You will need it more than I. You must forget all of the magic Great-uncle Henry has taught you. They will find you if you use the magic. God will lead them to you and punish you. Whatever happens to us, keep the cross with you always. Believe in the cross. That may be all that can save your soul." With that startling bit of courage from my meek mother, she took my hand and led me up a creaking wooden staircase into the sacristy.

Neither Father Truman nor his sprawling family was about. So we stole his only horse and rushed through the woods toward safety.

Behind us we heard shouts and horns and galloping hooves. As we rounded the forest pool beside the church, a flurry of brightly colored insects rose up from the ferns and grasses. My faery friends greeted me with laughter.

Come play, little friend, they pleaded as they darted in front of the horse's nose.

I may not linger with you, my friends. I am much afrighted and have to get away from the nasty men.

Do not fear, little friend, the faeries whispered conspiratorially. Then they shattered the illusion of seriousness with giggles. *We will lead them astray.*

We came to a crossroad, the faeries leading the way. I kneed the horse to the right. Mama and the horse protested. But I insisted, touching the beast's thoughts and directing it more firmly. Mama had no choice but to cling to the mane and go where I directed. Within a few hundred yards I pushed the horse onto a deer trail and concealed us in the dense forest.

Mounted men, led by the one dressed in white but shadowed by a black aura he could not hide, pelted past our hiding place. The faeries swarmed about their heads, tickling their noses with tiny tassels of grass. The man in white sneezed mightily. I giggled along with the faeries.

My friends pulled at the horses' manes and nipped at their hind-quarters. They confused the scent of the trail as they fluttered in front of both horses and tracking dogs. The beasts turned their heads to nip at their tormentors and ran into the mounts behind.

I closed my ears to the wild confusion. The man in white snarled and spurred his horse on.

When the sound of the pounding hooves died in the distance, I urged the horse back onto the road. We backtracked to the crossroad and took the opposite path.

Our pursuers did not catch us all that long night. We rode and rode until we nearly fell off the horse. The poor beast stumbled with exhaustion as Mama pushed him beyond his endurance. "There is only one thing to do. I must do all I can to save your soul, Resmiranda. In the years to come you will forgive me for this."

At the time I did not understand her words.

Fortunately the mid-April night remained mild. The earlier rain withdrew, leaving only a soft mist in the air. Tiny droplets beaded up on our clothes but did not penetrate for a long time. I stuck out my hand to gather a few precious drops of my element. It cleansed me of my fatigue, fears, and grief. For a time.

Finally, as dawn sent its first tentative rays of light above the horizon, we turned north on a narrow track. We were soaked, and the horse trudged wearily, barely lifting his feet off the turf before putting them down again. Less than half a league later the low wicker fence of a Benedictine cloister dedicated to Saint Dyfrig rose up directly in front of us.

The lovely lilt of nuns singing the hour of Prime ended just as we approached the gate. Mama heaved a sigh of relief.

She handed me down from the plain saddle. The two of us had fit snugly on it. Crying with uncertainty and exhaustion, I clung to her ankle.

"You must be brave, Resmiranda. Your soul is at stake," Mama said. I did not like the harshness in her tone. "We must say farewell for a time." Tears slid down her cheeks and she gulped back more of them. "Whatever happens, keep the cross. You may sell the beads if you have to, but keep the cross." She held my hand a moment, then gently pried my fingers away from her ankle.

"Be safe, my baby."

"Don't leave me! Where are you going, Mama," I wailed, clinging to the horse's mane, her skirt, any part of her I could grasp to keep close to the only familiar thing I could see.

"I don't know, Resmiranda. Somewhere safe. Our enemies will be looking for a mother and child. We must separate. Tell the sisters you are an orphan of no consequence. Tell them your name is Ana. You like that name, and it is almost a part of your real name."

"Benedicte, Lady. May we assist you?" A gentle woman of middle years, wearing the black habit and white veil of a Benedictine glided toward us on a pebbled path. Peace radiated from her eyes. She smiled invitingly, and I thought I saw the Holy Mother reflected there.

"Take care of the child, Sister. I ride to the king," Mama said, gathering the reins in her hands.

I didn't know this woman who sought to abandon me. My fingers slipped out of the tangle of her skirt.

"Don't leave me, Mama," I said quietly. Tears muffled my words and clogged my throat. I wasn't sure if I asked her to stay with me or to banish this strange, unforgiving personality that had overtaken her.

"Many rush to offer homage to King John, Lady," the nun offered. "You will find the roads heavily traveled and the inns crowded. Rest yourself and the horse. You may join us as we break our fast."

"Please, Mama, stay," I cried again.

"So it's true, Richard is dead," Mama said flatly, ignoring my pleas.

"Aye, God rest his soul. Killed in France by a stray arrow. The wound festered. He lingered for several days, and his suffering was great. The Good Lord took him at last not two weeks gone."

"Then my husband can return home from the wars. Thank you, Sister. Care for this orphaned child and keep her safe from those who do not know what they seek. Do what you can to wrest her soul away from the Devil." Without another glance at me, Mama dug her heels into the horse's lathered sides and retreated back the way she had come.

"Mama, come back!"

She didn't turn for one last look or a wave good-bye.

Sister Mary Ursula took my hand and led me into the convent.

I stayed there nearly two years. Longer than any other refuge I found during those troubled times before King John released Uncle Henry from prison with promises and treaties and spies. Only then was I allowed to return to Kirkenwood. Even then I stayed with Uncle Henry for only a few months. Two years of peace.

Would I find that again?

Not at the hands of King John. And certainly not with the traitor Bellecôte.

The Mendip Hills, 1208

"So, something in Wells frightens you more than roasting to death beneath Mendip Mor Hall," Sir Hugh stated as he twisted in the saddle to stare at me.

"No," I repeated with multiple meanings.

Stunned silence lay between us for three heartbeats. Then he cocked the right side of his mouth up in a half smile. The sun seemed to shine from his eyes.

"Say it again, *ma petite*," he urged. For that smile and the sense of safety that engulfed me, I would give my entire fortune. But could I speak again?

I hadn't really meant to say it. Rapidly I surveyed my body, noticing small sensations in scattered places. One toe on my right foot wiggled. An itch on my left thigh demanded scratching while the rest of that leg remained inert. My fingertips burned; my stomach felt queasily empty. My head and eyes still ached from the skirmish with Walter Geoffrey de Chancell's men and the rough ride. A ringing in my ears kept tempo with the too-rapid beat of my heart.

A small surge of power flushed my skin. Control was returning, but Bellecôte still believed me frozen. Surprise was on my side. Just a little longer. I had to pretend just a little longer. I could not trust the emotions this man evoked in me. Safety lay in silence and escape to a new hiding place.

Where?

Newynog circled the horses, sniffing up at me then racing forward on the path as if she knew that I needed to be gone from here.

"Not ready to talk yet, *ma petite?*" Bellecôte asked. "I know an inn near the old cathedral at Wells. We'll change horses there. And send someone back for the other bodies. De Chancell we take to King John."

Sir Hugh mounted and pulled my hands forward ready to tie them. Then he paused and twisted to stare at me. "Would you be more comfortable riding astride?"

Something in his eyes told me he needed a response or he'd leave me to bounce along on the horse's rear as if I were no more than a rag doll, or a piece of baggage.

I concentrated on moving my jaw, forming the single word I needed with my tongue. I didn't let anything else move. He needed to think me still paralyzed. I tried again. I blinked once, slowly.

"You can do better than that, *ma petite*. Tell me you want to ride astride. If you are very good, I'll hire a docile mare for you at the inn."

As if lifting a tremendous weight, I strained my neck until my head bobbed down and then up again, once.

"Not as good as talking, but better than nothing." Sir Hugh sighed as he released my hands. I kept my arms in place, still wrapped around him. Gently he pushed each hand down until he was free of my grasp. Then he swung his right leg in front of him and jumped down from the saddle. He landed nimbly, but I noticed he put most of his weight on his left leg. He must have practiced this maneuver often. Whatever hindered his right leg was not a new injury. He betrayed a weakness.

With one strong hand bracing my back, he shifted my legs until I nestled across the horse's spine. Every touch was gentle and strong, as if he cradled a helpless child. No wonder he called me *"ma petite"* if he thought me so young and vulnerable as he treated me. Let him go on thinking thus. My strength and resolve would surprise him.

When I was firmly in place, he paused to admire the length of leg my skirts revealed, but not so long as to be insulting. I wondered what his hands would feel like running from ankle to knee and above. . . .

Heat rose to the tips of my ears. I longed to look away, not acknowledge that moment of attraction. How could I be attracted to this traitor? Bellecôte and I locked eyes briefly.

The horse shifted and sidled at the change of my balance. My sense of control returned. I looked away. Some of the headache departed. The horse bent his head to snatch a little of the turf. He munched a moment then shook his head vigorously, spitting out the rough grass.

"So it's not sweet hay, Orage, You'll get a proper feed at the inn. You had oats last night." Sir Hugh coaxed the horse over to one of the rocks. Orage rolled his eyes and shook his head again. His skin rippled.

Instinctively, I grabbed the back of the saddle just before the animal tried to rear.

Sir Hugh didn't let him get his front feet more than a hand's breadth off the ground before he yanked the reins down hard.

"Enough!" he roared.

Orage bared his teeth and shook his head again but stood still.

Sir Hugh climbed atop the tallest rock and from there mounted Orage awkwardly, keeping his offside leg close to the pommel so as not to kick me off. When he was settled, he retied my hands around him. My arms shivered and stiffened at his touch. I told myself I was repulsed by this man. I loathed him and his family for the betrayal they had committed.

He had vowed to protect me. No one else had ever done that.

"Don't want you thrown, *ma petite*. This ride could get rough."

"Rougher," Archie grumbled a correction. "I don't like separating from the men and our baggage this way. We barely survived one ambush already."

"Easier to hide or disguise a small party of travelers on pilgrimage than an armed cavalcade on the king's business," Sir Hugh grunted as he dug his spurs into the horse. We took off cross-country at a gallop.

I spent the next hour contracting and releasing each muscle in my body. Starting with my toes, I worked upward until I was confident I could now run if I had to. With Newynog's help, I knew I could control almost any horse, perhaps even Orage. I could strand Sir Hugh Bellecôte with his weakened right leg on foot while I made my escape.

Where could I go?

In asking the question, I knew the answer. I had no safe refuge. I had no control over my life as long as my enemies pursued me.

How to stop the persecution?

Chapter 7

HUGH shielded his eyes from the warm sun. His back broke out in sweat beneath his gambeson, chain mail, and surcoat. The girl must be incredibly uncomfortable buried in his winter cloak of wolf furs. But she'd issued nary a whimper of protest.

He pulled Orage to a halt on the hills to the west of the city of Wells. The little community sat between the new Bath road and the ancient Roman road. Three wells flowed freely and cleanly through the church grounds and marketplace. The wells had made the place sacred and a natural gathering place from the beginning of time. A cathedral had stood here for two hundred years, atop a much older church which covered an even more ancient sanctuary. The buildings had fallen into ruins when the bishop moved his See to the much larger town of Bath. Now that Wells had grown into a major cross-roads town again, the Bishop of Bath had ordered construction of a new church, larger and more modern than his current headquarters. The new cathedral would have hundreds of stained glass windows, to give the place the ethereal airiness only the most modern architecture could achieve.

Hugh preferred simple chapels with no ornamentation to distract him from his perfunctory prayers. Better yet, no building at all. His relationship with God was based on simple needs, usually expressed on the battlefield or on behalf of an ailing friend—or Johnny.

His prayers hadn't saved Ardyth or his child. They'd both died in childbed. His prayers hadn't given him the son to inherit Bellecôte, but they had prolonged the life of Ardyth's sickly son by her first husband, Robért de Bellecôte, long beyond expectancy.

He didn't regret Johnny's life. Never that. The boy gave him reason and sanity when all else crumbled around him.

What other men called miracles, or the answers to prayers, he saw as the results of hard work and tactical expertise. He'd sat beside Johnny's bed many a night, nursing him through illness after illness when others gave up.

Luck could go either way, good or bad, depending upon which side received it. He'd seen too many battles won or lost by "luck" to consider either himself or his enemies lucky.

In the far distance, about twenty miles to the south, he spotted Glastonbury Tor rising majestically above the lush plains. The church of St. Michael perched atop the mound, its tower piercing the sky. Clerics said it was a symbolic prayer to heaven. More likely a last defense against the ills of this world.

A Benedictine community lived in the abbey on the lower slopes, guarding the recently discovered tomb of King Arthur Pendragon—or so they claimed and the world believed. Hugh doubted the legendary king had ever lived. His magical sword, Excalibur, was also a myth. Any sword could seem magical when wielded by a strong man skilled in the art of war.

From his vantage point, Hugh espied the quire, the center of the church where the monks chanted the offices of the day, and the first three bays of the church nave under construction. Scaffolding covered the walls of the new church, partially hiding the soaring beauty of the architecture. Hundreds of workmen should be scrambling around that network of wooden supports. The canons should be singing—the music of Wells was as legendary as its springs. The church lay quiet and undisturbed.

To the east of the quire, stood an octagonal Lady Chapel, separate from the main building. The Lady Chapel, the true heart of any large church, would be open for prayer at any time of day or night; the altar accessible to anyone needing sanctuary.

He suddenly knew a great temptation to dump his unwanted companion in the Lady Chapel and proceed with his own business. But that would not answer any of his questions, nor satisfy his vow to protect her. He needed to know why his dear friend Edmund had died. Only then could he know who had done the deed, and take his revenge. He hoped the girl wasn't responsible. She seemed too small and vulnerable, truly in need of his protection. He hated having to kill women.

He also needed to know why the town, especially the construction site looked so still and abandoned.

"We should have heard the bells calling us to Sext," he said quietly. He scanned the sky and had to close his eyes against the sun directly overhead. Noon. What had happened to the bells?

"What are those people doing gathered around the market cross and not at work or at their prayers?" Archie pointed to the center of town beyond the new church.

"Everything is too quiet." The lack of moving carts or horses bothered Hugh. He checked his weapons and scanned the area for signs of attack.

"I don't like mysteries. Let's ask at the inn. I know the landlord. He'll have the latest news." Hugh pointed to a prosperous looking place just to the north and uphill from the church. The inn fronted the Bath road with its stable behind, perched precariously on a hill that ran down to the lush spring-fed valley.

"I'll take Walter Geoffrey de Chancell to the priests. They will have news, too." Archie nodded in agreement.

"Have them send men back for the other bodies. Remember we take de Chancell to the king," Sir Hugh called after him.

Archie urged his mount down the hill.

Hugh kneed Orage toward the inn. He rode into the courtyard with a clatter and a shout for lads to tend his horse. Only a tall, skinny man wearing a pristinely white apron greeted him.

"Ah, Sir Hugh Fitz Chênenoir, my Lord of Bellecôte. Greetings. The lads have all run off to hear t' proclamation. You'll have to tend the beast yourself. I can't leave my kitchen." He paused a moment. "Where's your squire? A true knight never travels without a squire. Thought we taught you better than that, boy!"

"You and King Richard's men dragged me into maturity by the scruff of my neck. I learned proper knightly behavior from Lord Edmund, he was the only one among us who thought enough of manners to teach me any. I left my squire with my troops and baggage while Archie and I ran a different errand."

"You learned the rules of manhood kicking and screaming all the way, milord Bellecôte," the innkeeper chuckled. "You wanted to remain a reckless youth long after your beard came in." He ducked back into the dark interior without further pleasantries.

"I only hold the wardship for the true Baron of Bellecôte. The title will never be mine," Hugh whispered. He couldn't bite back the sadness at the loss of the honors promised him by King John. The promise had died with Ardyth and their child.

At the same time he did not begrudge young John Bellecôte his life. The boy had become as close to him as a son. So close and well loved he would only have trusted Lord Edmund Fitz Gyr to foster the boy into knighthood.

Fitz Chênenoir, from the house of Blackoak. Not Bellecôte.

Relief replaced the heaviness on my shoulders and chest. Sir Hugh Fitz Chênenoir had not led the raid against Mendip Mor. I should have known that when the men in black ambushed us. But the hated unicorn and boar blinded me to the truth.

Did I dare trust him? He still wore the despised crest of the Bellecôtes. One of that clan had sold Uncle Henry's son and heir to a Saracen warlord for the price of passage home. The Bellecôte heir had returned to a wife and rich inheritance.

The Griffin heir had died in a foreign prison. Tortured to death.

But who was Hugh Fitz Chênenoir? Norman by his name. Perhaps a longtime friend of Lord Edmund and Lady Hilary. I remembered conversations about Chênenoir now. He'd been a mercenary hired by Richard and then by John. He'd earned the king's trust and favor. In gratitude, King John had granted him the hand in marriage of a wealthy widow with lands and titles to bestow upon her children—Fitz Chênenoir's children.

His last words finally penetrated my spinning mind. He held the wardship for Bellecôte's true baron, a minor.

What had happened to the wealthy widow? Was she Robért Bellecôte's widow and her son the new baron? If so, what had happened to Robért Bellecôte The Traitor?

Too many questions and not enough time for answers. I still needed to find a refuge to plot the end of King John's persecution of me.

"I don't like mysteries," Sir Hugh muttered as he dismounted and lifted me down. "You are a mystery. Walter Geoffrey de Chancell is a mystery. This whole *bloody* town is a mystery. I'll be glad to turn you all over to King John. He delights in unraveling legal tangles. This puzzle should thrill him."

Sir Hugh grabbed my hand in one of his, Orage's reins in the other, and led us both into the stable.

Surreptitiously I tested my newfound control. Hands and shoulders worked independently. Did my feet? I couldn't tell until he dropped my hand.

Newynog slunk behind me, tail between her legs and ears drooping. Did she cringe away from my seeming dependence upon Sir Hugh, or against the unnatural quiet of this town?

Holy Mother, help me! I prayed, feeling the beads slide through my fingers. *I have to take control of my body and my life.*

Inside the stable, Sir Hugh pushed me gently. I sat upon a stool in the corner. Newynog plopped down upon my feet. She kept her head up, vigilant now that she had a job to do—protecting me. I didn't need Fitz Chênenoir to do that. I had my familiar.

I surveyed every horse in the stable seeking a likely mount for myself. A chestnut with a white splotch over his left eye and streaks of white in his mane poked his long nose over his loose box half door. The inquisitiveness in his eyes and the lively shuffle of his hooves told me almost as much as seeing him run.

Sir Hugh removed his equipage from Orage with meticulous care, inspecting the leather and brass for signs of wear or weakness. None of the trappings bore the unicorn and boar symbols of the Bellecôte household. Only the tabard over his gambeson and mail.

He hummed tunelessly as he groomed his mount.

I remembered hearing that same absent tone last night when I awoke from my nightmare. He'd soothed me as he soothed his horse. I was nothing more to him.

I should not have felt disappointment. But I did.

The humming broke into soothing phrases as he rubbed Orage down and brushed road dirt from the horse's hide. His skin rippled with each touch of the brush. He flicked his ears and sighed lustily. When his knight scratched his ears, he relaxed his knees, learning against Sir Hugh just as Newynog often rested her weight against me, begging for pats.

"Get off me, you great oaf!" Hugh slapped Orage's side. The horse heaved himself upright again, flipping his head back and forth. Newynog looked at him and the two animals seemed to share a laugh.

Sir Hugh's rough affection for his horse surprised me.

We can trust him.

*He is a Bellecôte by alliance if not by name. We can't trust anyone.
We can use him.*
We'll be better off on our own.

"Come," Sir Hugh held out his hand for me to grasp. I stared at it, unwilling to move closer to him.

"Why must you make this so hard?" Sir Hugh asked on a resigned sigh. Roughly he grabbed my hand and dragged me to my feet. I followed him into the inn, feigning meekness.

The landlord greeted us in the hall. "I'll serve you here. Can't leave the kitchen long enough to show you to a private room, milord," he grumbled. "Haven't had the pleasure of your company for too many years, Sir Hugh. What brings you away from your great estate and your young son?"

"I traveled to Mendip Mor to arrange fosterage for my boy. Where is everyone, John Howard?" he asked as he guided me to one of the settles before the hearth.

"Haven't you heard?" The landlord cocked his head to one side, curiously.

"No."

"They've all run to market to hear t' proclamation and to gossip and worry. Not me. I ain't leavin' me kitchen and lettin' the dogs steal my roast." He glared at Newynog as if daring her to try to steal from him. "Learned that back in King Richard's army. As long as there's a campfire, someone's got to mind it."

My dog stared back at him with wide innocent eyes.

"What proclamation, John?" Sir Hugh asked. His jaw worked and his fingers clenched to contain his impatience.

"Why, t' Pope's sent an Interdict. No more church in England until King John backs off his high horse and accepts Stephen Langdon as archbishop. 'Bout time. Three years they been arguin' about who's to be archbishop. Cain't none of them, brothers at Canterbury, king, or pope let t' other have the upper hand. Now King Richard wouldn't a' put up with all this nonsense. He'd a' marched in and banged heads together until he got what he wanted."

"And we would have followed him into hell and back. We did follow him into hell. Not all of us came back," Hugh muttered. "How will England survive without a church?"

"No church?" My words came out a croak of whispered despair. "The demons are loosed. Holy Mother save us all!"

Sir Hugh looked at me with that crooked half smile of his. "I knew you'd talk when you had something to say, *ma petite.*"

"You must take me to the Cistercians in Yorkshire, now, before they close their doors," I said, more firmly than I had said anything in many days. "Now."

"Impossible, my Lady," the landlord replied. "The proclamation has been on the road for three weeks now. It went to church officials first. We're far in the west, it came late to us. All the churches, convents, monasteries, cathedrals, and hospices are closed until Pope Innocent and King John reconcile."

"I know John. He'll not compromise," Sir Hugh added. "As long as the church is closed, all church revenue goes to him. He has no reason to reconcile."

"I don't even have the church to protect me now," I said.

Chapter 8

Worcester Castle

"WHAT think you of this case, Radburn?" King John leaned to his right, keeping his hand over his mouth.

Radburn Blakely smiled, also covering his mouth to keep the conversation as private as possible. Not an easy task considering the hordes of petitioners come to Worcester Castle for the king's justice. The smell of this many bodies packed into the hall on a warm day in May offended him.

He pulled a nosegay out of his sleeve and held it between his sensitive nose and the pressing crowd. An endless cup of wine would help, too. But John would not allow any of his judges and advisers to drink until he needed to. No befuddled senses marred the efficiency of the king's court.

Neville, Brewer, and Delisle had found occupations elsewhere on this fine spring day. Radburn had seen to that. John would listen to no one but him today.

"Highness, both men seem to be telling the truth. Martin the Blacksmith's son married Jerome the Carpenter's daughter. The young couple set up housekeeping on lands gifted by both fathers. Each gave half a hide. Now they have died in a tragic fire, leaving no children. Both fathers claim the land should revert to them. An easy case to divide the land along the original boundaries."

John wasn't usually this hesitant to pass judgment. In fact, he reveled in the intricacies of the law and justice. Most barons and many highly trained legal clerks had difficulty keeping up with the king's mental leaps and vast memory of tradition and law.

Petitioners waited months, even years for the king to travel near to them so they could have his learned and just decisions rather than the more arbitrary judgments of local lords or itinerant justiciars. Many came forth with extensive bribes of money and goods for the right to have their case heard by the king.

Perhaps the lengthy court session and the ripeness of the air had sapped John's mental energy as it had sapped Radburn's physical reserves. He suppressed a yawn but indulged in a slight stretch of his long legs clad in a distinctive shade of blue. Royal blue he called it. Bastard blue said his enemies.

He'd given up the affectation of white shoes, cotehardie, and braies. Too difficult to keep clean while traipsing behind the king, his restless half brother. But he didn't like the fashionable scarlet. It burned his eyes as this horde of populace burned his nose and John's need for order rubbed his nerves raw.

Oh, for a lovely little melee to brighten the day.

"I'm not certain both men tell all about that fire," mused John. "Was it truly an accident? If not, who set it? Who has most to gain by the death of two innocents?"

Radburn sat up a little straighter. John had seen something he had missed. Unusual. He must have drunk more than he intended last night while watching John sport with the vivacious little Sybella. Or he dwelled too much on the next step on his personal ladder of ambition.

"Are there younger brothers in either family?" Radburn whispered back. A laugh almost escaped him. He of all younger brothers should know to look for ambition and greed amongst the siblings. His and John's older brothers were prime examples of a family in discord. Radburn wanted no part of the constant struggle and warfare that had kept young Henry, Richard, Geoffrey, and John at each other's throats, as well as their father's, for most of their lives. Radburn would rather generate a war and sit back to reap the rewards than participate in one. He had worked long and hard to convince his half brother that the crown had no value to him—even if the barons would allow a bastard to rule. Radburn wanted a different sort of power. He was quite content having the king's ear at any time of day or night. That way, his enemies blamed John rather than himself.

He'd have to alter the wards around John so that Radburn remained less conspicuous as long as Neville, Brewer, and Delisle held the king's favor. Radburn hadn't been able to oust them from court. He'd tried often enough and failed.

John searched the crowd immediately behind the two petitioners. "Do you see the young man standing directly behind the carpenter?" John asked.

Radburn had noticed the young man's slim body and pretty face for another reason.

"The one in the gray tunic over red chausses," John continued. "This entire afternoon he has counseled his father. Every time we come close to a compromise, the boy whispers and the carpenter holds firm to his original plea that the land should be his as the return of dowry and the reversion of the bride price due to his daughter's death."

"Aye, I see him. Would you have me take him outside and— discuss—the matter?" Radburn smiled with genuine pleasure. At last he'd be able to remove himself from the stuffy hall and the damnably hard chair that bruised his backside.

"Yes, do that as soon as I pronounce judgment. Watch the boy's reactions."

"When I return, there is a matter I would discuss with you, Brother. The matter of claiming my bride," Radburn replied. The time had come to close that matter. He'd allowed it to drift too long and now he might lose her altogether.

"If you must," John dismissed the matter. Then he sat up straight again and adjusted his purple cotehardie. He scanned the room, commanding everyone's attention by the sheer force of his will. All of the Plantagenets had that ability. When the murmurs and shuffling feet had silenced under the weight of the monarch's gaze, John leveled his attention on the two petitioners. "Nothing more will be served by arguing this matter further. I decree that each of you shall reclaim one half of your original land grant. One quarter hide each. The remaining half hide and its rents shall be revert to Us as relief for the death of heirs."

"Highness! The death duties are too high for the son and daughter of tradesmen," the young man behind the carpenter protested.

"Quiet, or I shall exact an additional fine of a half hide apiece for your insubordination. There is no appeal. I have decided. Next case."

"Why such a huge fine?" the previously quiet blacksmith mumbled. "Take half a man's wealth for listening to a young man with a mouth that works faster than his brain?"

In the shuffle of removing the two petitioners and bringing the next case before the king, Radburn slid out of his chair and stepped off the dais. He rotated his shoulders to ease the tension out of them as he wormed through the crowd toward the main door.

He had no desire to hear the petitions of yet another widow who did not wish to be forced to remarry by her overlord and the king. Women did not belong alone. His bride had been missing too long. She needed to have her independent streak curbed now.

He stepped out onto the porch into bright sunshine, blinking hard until his eyes adjusted. Then he had to squint to see anything in the glare. *God's blood,* he should have worn a cap to pull down on his brow and shield his sensitive eyes.

The carpenter and his son had already descended to the bailey. They faced each other, gesticulating madly. Radburn couldn't make out their words, but from the intensity of the fists waving about, they argued hotly.

"I know that neither of you is willing to listen to reason at the moment," Radburn said, approaching them with silent footsteps. He loved the startled look on their faces when they realized their words were no longer private.

He'd spent many years developing the talent of creeping about more silently than a cat. Amazing how many secrets he learned that way. Secrets represented power. He needed to collect more secrets from these two as well as from his bride.

"I suggest you refrain from saying anything more until you reach the privacy of your own home," Radburn advised quietly. "Better yet, put this matter aside until you meet me outside the castle postern at one hour after moonrise." He smiled, baring his teeth in a feral gesture that always intimidated lesser beings.

"His Highness has a use for a talented arsonist." He threw out the last statement as bait. If the young man showed tonight, he'd know for certain who had set the fire. If no one showed, then he had intimidated them both into lawful behavior. If they both showed . . . ?

What an interesting possibility.

Back inside the Hall, John stood before his throne. "The hour of Nones is upon us, even though the church bells do not summon us to services. But since we no longer have the onerous obligation to listen to the bishop's platitudes about our sins of disobedience, let us ride along the river until dinner."

The case of the widow had been dealt with. Radburn spied her defiant stride exiting the Hall. Her intended—her overlord who had already seized a goodly amount of her marriage portion and her dower house as his due for death duties—strode beside her trying to take her arm. She slapped him away.

Radburn almost laughed. The groom would have a cold reception in his marriage bed. But his coffers would be warm with all of her inheritance instead of what he could steal in relief. And with the Interdict in place, the man could enjoy all the benefits of marriage by common law without giving the woman any of her rights under church law.

Radburn did laugh then, long and loud.

John clapped his hands for his servants and his dogs to attend him.

Radburn lengthened his stride to reach his brother's side before he involved himself with the logistics of getting himself and his entourage ahorse.

"Highness, about my bride . . ."

"Ah, yes, I can see you burn to consummate a marriage. Won't Lord Sinclair's wife suit you tonight? She's a wholesome, sturdy wench. Or better yet, our reluctant widow ought to provide interesting sport, especially if she thinks she can influence Us to change our mind."

"Brother, a marriage is more than easing an itch in bed." Radburn ground his teeth together in exasperation. He had to proceed carefully, lest he incite John's volatile temper. "The betrothal contract was signed over a year ago. I have waited a long time for this marriage." Since he'd first spied the girl at the age of eight.

"You have waited for the lady's titles and lands as well as her body. I've been told that she is lovely, if a bit skinny for my taste. And much too tall to dominate anywhere but in bed," John returned. The twinkle in his eyes betrayed his love of taunting his courtiers.

Radburn bit his lip, trying very hard not to let his impatience show. He knew how lovely she was. And how wealthy. And how her title could give him more power than John realized. Otherwise John would never have agreed to the betrothal.

"You have only to name the day, Highness. We can arrange a

marriage by proxy and you will have me, your most loyal servant owing you homage for a tactically sensitive area in the North."

"Ah, but you forget that we are under Interdict by the decree of Pope Innocent III. No marriages. No Mass. No Eucharist. And definitely no confession." John almost laughed. "If there is no church in England to collect their tithes, or waste funds on new buildings, then those tithes come to me, rightfully crowned king of England." An avaricious gleam entered John's eyes. "Perhaps I'll finally have the funds to win back my lands in France.

"About my bride . . ."

"If you can find Lady Resmiranda Griffin, heiress of Kirkenwood, you can have her and her lands, with or without the blessing of the church. Yes, find the girl and we'll have a public ceremony of your homage and your common law marriage. The court will attend the bedding to make certain you are—up to it," John laughed wholeheartedly as he headed for the stable.

John Howard's Inn, Wells

Hugh mulled over the implications of the Interdict. What would happen to all of the lands and serfs held in fief to the king by bishops and abbots? Would they remain in the hands of the church or revert to the king? If they remained with the church, did the Interdict nullify the obligations of the landlords to provide taxes and military service to the king? Did the Interdict nullify his own oath of loyalty to the king?

What a mess!

"If you will take me to the Convent of the Blessed Virgin in Yorkshire, I will pay you well," the girl said. She turned determined eyes up to Hugh. "I was one of them until a year ago. They will take me back."

"What will you pay me with?" He glared at her skeptically, arms folded in front of him. He towered over her where she sat on the bench. He intimidated hardened warriors with that stare.

"My family . . ." she almost choked on the words. "I have money."

"The only things you possess at this moment are your dog and those prayer beads. I wouldn't risk my life trying to take the dog away from you. For that cross I might sell my own mother." His mother had sold herself for less.

"No." The girl clutched the gold-and-ivory beads more tightly within her palm. "Not that. Anything but that."

Hugh turned his back on her and addressed the landlord, as if she were no longer of importance to him.

She reacted under provocation. He'd provoke her until he had answers.

"Talk to me, John Howard. Don't ask questions. Don't speculate, just talk to me of the neighborhood. Who visits whom. Outlaws in the region, suspicious strangers."

"Well, now, when you and I fought the French for King Richard and later for King John, you trusted me with your life." The landlord turned the spit for his roast and basted it with fat from a bucket beside the massive hearth.

"Many times. I do so again by being here. Talk to me." Hugh risked a glance back at the girl. She seemed as interested in the landlord's answers as Hugh.

"Strangers are the business of an inn. Most everyone who passes through here is a stranger." John Howard wiped his hands on his apron and fussed about his kitchen, never raising his eyes to Hugh.

What frightened him?

"Some strangers are different?"

"Some ask questions. Pointed questions. Who visits this person, who spends too much time confessing only to certain priests and not to others? Who rides a white palfrey north and west of here?" Howard rattled on as if the words meant nothing.

Hugh raised his eyebrows at the last statement. The girl sat a little more forward on her bench.

"And who does ride a white palfrey, traveling north and west into the Mendip Hills?" Hugh asked for both of them.

"Never given the lady's name. She kept the hood of her cloak shadowing her face for all the fine weather we had in the middle of March. Three men escorted her. They bore more weapons than either you or me on a patrol in enemy territory. I was never allowed to speak to the lady and she never said a word to me. But seems to me I caught a glimpse of golden hair beneath her hood."

Both Hugh and John Howard turned to look at the girl. Beneath her tattered and filthy veil, blonde curls escaped the coiled braids over her ears.

She stared back, daring them to challenge her silence.

"And where did this lady travel?" Hugh kept looking at her as he spoke, challenging her in turn.

"The road they took leads to the track that goes only to Mendip Mor Castle and then on north to the Welsh border," John Howard said. "Mendip Mor sits atop a hill that commands quite a view. A careful watcher can see most all the way to the Bristol Channel in good weather, can watch movement in the lower hills most any day but the foggiest. Good place for a castle. But 'tis out of the way, not many visitors wander close to it."

"A good place to hide someone who has enemies?" Hugh said more than asked. "Maps of the area are sketchy, the road narrow and often indistinct. I'd have lost it several times on my journey if I hadn't visited there many times and had detailed instructions from Lord Edmund."

He turned his back on the girl again. Let her stew on this information a while.

"And did the lady riding north and west on a white palfrey have a noble wolfhound pup, a little more than half grown, at her heels?" he asked.

"Like a shadow. The dog never left her," John Howard replied.

"And who asked after the lady? What manner of men?"

"Men who rode the finest horseflesh and dressed in fine surcoats that didn't quite cover their armor. Noble warriors I'd say, by the keenness of their swords and the fine saddles and bridles. No jewels or costly embroidery on saddles or hilts that might identify them."

"Black chain mail?"

"Aye."

"Whose device emblazoned their surcoats and their shields?"

"Solid black. No device. Same for the *baudrès* draped over their horses. Black. Short as if ready to go into battle."

Trained assassins. Hugh had heard of such men from Crusaders. Kings used them, few others could afford them.

Violence belonged only on the honorable field of battle where all participants understood the risks. These silent stalkers had no honor.

Hugh sensed the girl fidgeting on the bench. He half smiled at her unease. Soon she'd spill forth answers to his questions. Soon.

Then they could deal honestly together.

"Did you get a look at the faces of these armored men, John Howard?"

"One or two?"

"Would you recognize them again?"

"Maybe. Maybe not."

"Archie has taken a dead man to the church. I need you to go to the priests and look at this man. I need to know who attacked Mendip Mor Hall and killed every person within the castle except this lady who has lost her white palfrey."

"Can't leave my kitchen."

"I will watch your *bloody* kitchen, John. Go now. And hurry."

"The white palfrey?" the girl asked on a miserable squeak.

"All of the horses bolted from the stable, or were run off." Sir Hugh swallowed deeply. "Except your horse. Its throat was slit. It earned the same fate as Lord Edmund." Hugh nearly choked with grief again. His mind screamed 'Why?' and his fingers itched to wield a sword against the whoreson who murdered his friend. "Whoever hunts you, milady, will stop at nothing to bring down his prey."

"I liked and respected Lord Edmund and Lady Hilary very much. I grieve with you over their loss." She bowed her head, reciting prayers and fingering the beads in rhythm with her petitions. Then she spoke again, so quietly Hugh knew he wasn't supposed to hear. But he did.

"Too many have died already for the secrets I know and have recorded."

More questions rose in his mind.

"Why, milady? Why did they die rather than give you over to the hunters?"

She kept her head bowed and closed her eyes.

"Who are you, milady?"

She maintained her silence.

"You owe me a name at least."

"You may call me Ana. My title has died."

"Every lord in the land has a daughter named Anne and another called Elizabeth. Your given name tells me nothing."

She continued counting the beads.

He grabbed her hands, yanking her up to face him. "Tell me why my dearest friend in the world died the death of a traitor!" he nearly shouted. The knuckles of his hand turned white and his shoulders began to tremble with barely contained anger.

Thank Jesu he hadn't brought Johnny to fosterage at Mendip Mor before this. The boy would have died, too.

"If I could tell you I would."

"You can't or won't tell me?" He continued to hold her hands up around her chin. High enough to give her discomfort but not enough to truly hurt.

She returned his gaze levelly and unemotionally. Her dispassion chilled him as much as her tall strength attracted him.

"If you will not take me to the Convent of the Blessed Virgin in Yorkshire, will you take me to Sir Eustace de Vesci, Lord of Northumberland?"

"No." Hugh and the girl continued to stare at each other for several long moments. "We ride to King John and nowhere else. We need food, another cloak, fresh horses. We'll leave for Worcester as soon as Archie and John return," he said, releasing his grip on her. She recovered her balance with the quickness of a trained warrior and sat gracefully, smoothing her skirts.

"If you take me to the mound of St. Michael in Cornwall, I know they will grant me sanctuary. You won't need to bother with me anymore."

Perched on the last edge of land, the monastics of St. Michael drew their living from the sea. She could secretly take a boat to France or Spain from their shores. If he knew King John, no one of noble birth could obtain royal permission to leave the country until the Interdict was settled.

"We ride posthaste to Worcester or wherever King John holds court this month. We'll let him decide what to do with you."

Then you sign our death warrant.

He hadn't really heard that, had he?

Chapter 9

IN short order Archie and John Howard returned. They met us in the kitchen where Sir Hugh carved great slabs of mutton from the carcass roasting over the fire. I gave half of my portion to Newynog. She nibbled the meat from my fingers with better manners than Sir Hugh.

"Such rude fare for milady." John Howard clicked his tongue in disapproval. "Trenchers, milord, and bread and onions. I picked fresh greens this morning, too. We must feed the lady properly." He bustled about the kitchen, providing me with proper utensils and clearing a place for them at the cluttered worktable. With a flourish he drew up a stool for me and dusted it off as best he could.

My gown was so badly stained by smoke and the fall from the warhorse into the bracken—I'd never had clean hems so did not consider those damp mud stains worse than usual—the stool couldn't hurt it further.

"We haven't time for niceties. We're bound for Worcester and the king," Sir Hugh replied. He washed down a huge mouthful of meat and bread with half a tankard of ale.

I cringed at our destination but didn't protest. Now that I had broken free of the catatonia, I could watch for a better time to escape. Uncle Henry had had many friends scattered throughout England. For the sake of his memory, surely some of them would shelter me until I could find sanctuary or escape.

Perhaps some would help me plan countermeasures. Somehow I had to end this constant running. I had been chased from convent to convent for nearly seven years while Uncle Henry languished in King John's prison. Then, quite suddenly, the king had made peace with my great-uncle and returned him to his lands and honors. Only then had I been allowed to go home. I still did not know why that peaceful interlude had ended so abruptly. But Uncle Henry had roused me in the middle of the night and sent me to Mendip Mor by secretive routes and under heavy guard.

My pursuers had found me anyway. Why? How? Who?

"We need to be gone soon," Archie said, looking over his shoulder toward town.

Sir Hugh lifted an eyebrow in question.

"The castle guards have arrested a cleric for murder. The Bishop is raising a mob to free his man."

"The church has the right to try their own for any crimes!" I protested. "Just because an Interdict is in place, that does not give the king's men the right to arrest, try, or punish a cleric."

"This case is deeply tangled, milady," John Howard ceased his fussing over me for a moment. "A local man had beaten his son for not attending his chores, as is his right. The priest intervened. It seems the boy had neglected his duties at home to sing in the choir. We value our music here in Wells, we do. The boy has the voice of an angel. He wanted to take holy orders so he could sing to the glory of God." He paused a moment to revel in memory.

"His father prevented him for taking minor orders?" I presumed.

"Indeed. He beat the boy so badly his voice may be permanently damaged. Father Gerard intervened before he killed the boy. A fight ensued. The boy's father lies dead in the church mortuary. The priest walks free."

"The church won't do anything to one of their own, no matter the crime. Even murder goes unpunished!" Sir Hugh muttered.

"As I said, 'tis a tangled case. Some say the priest defended one of his own." John Howard shook his head and continued to lay out the rest of my meal for me. "Who has jurisdiction? The king who owns all of England, or the church which owns all the souls of the English?"

"Either way, the mood in the town is ugly," Archie insisted. "We must leave soon lest we be caught up in the riots."

"Archie and Lady Ana will need fresh horses," Sir Hugh said around another mouthful. His manners seemed to have reverted to his soldier days.

I planned to claim the chestnut gelding when we mounted.

"I'm glad you aren't leaving that great beast of yours behind to savage my stable lads," John Howard replied. "But he's carried double for many miles, with many more to go. He'll tire and slow you down. Best you take one of the other mounts and put Orage on a leading rein."

"Lead Orage?" Sir Hugh laughed, spraying ale out of his mouth.

His manners had definitely deteriorated. Or was I seeing the man as he truly was, his earlier rough but polite treatment of me merely a thin layer added recently.

I had to admit the easy camaraderie and humor among these men added depth to my understanding of my protector/warden.

"That horse will tear huge hunks out of the flanks of any animal that dares walk in front of it," Archie added on a chuckle. "I agree that you should ride a fresher beast than Orage, Sir Hugh, but perhaps you should allow Orage to lead the procession?"

All three of them chuckled and slapped each other's backs.

They left me out of their circle of affection. But then, I had been separated from all friendships and family since I had entered the quiet convent dedicated to St. Dyfrig when I was eight. No one had loved me since that day when my world shattered.

Witchchild!

Images of the man dressed in white trying to steal the prayer beads from Mama flashed before my vision. Once more I was a frightened child screaming my fear and confusion. The man in white both attracted and frightened me. How had the beads gotten from his hands to mine?

Had I worked the spell Uncle Henry and Aunt Lotta had only hinted was possible? Had I succumbed to Satan's temptation to use magic?

Witchchild!

Hide her!

I hid myself in silence once more.

"Come, Lady Ana." Sir Hugh beckoned me toward the back door and the stable.

I continued eating, ignoring him. Daintily carving up my meat, I speared small bites with the little eating knife the innkeeper had provided. I planned to hide it in my scrip when we departed.

Newynog continued to sit politely at my side. Her ears stood halfway up, hopeful but not blatantly begging. She'd had enough to sustain her for the next leg of our journey.

Sir Hugh marched back to stand before me. "Must I carry you

again?" he shouted. His mouth worked, fighting a smile. Not all of his humor had dissipated.

"I will finish my meal. I may not see another for a long time." If my plans came to fruition, I would certainly never eat another meal with him or any other Bellecôte.

When I had finished, I thanked John Howard and walked out to the yard without assistance. Archie led a packhorse with bulging panniers and the now shrouded body of de Chancell slung over the back. I hoped someone had thought to pack the body in herbs. Otherwise it would begin to smell soon and attract unwanted attention as well as flies.

I looked at the other mounts gathered in the courtyard. My spirited gelding stood impatiently beside the pack pony. Orage had been tethered on the opposite side of the enclosure. I started toward the chestnut.

Sir Hugh yanked me away and helped me mount a placid gray mare. His boost up suggested great haste but little grace. He then mounted the gelding I wanted. Once settled in the undecorated saddle, I tested the mare's mettle with a sharp heel to her flank. She turned her head to look at me inquiringly.

So much for any plans for a swift escape at a crossroad. This horse wouldn't go anywhere in a hurry.

Half a mile later Orage nipped at the flank of Sir Hugh's new mount. Sir Hugh slapped his war stallion on the nose for his impertinence. Orage sniffed and turned his head away. I caught a glimpse of his bared teeth in an expression resembling a sneer. Newynog opened her mouth and let her tongue loll in agreement.

I didn't want to believe the two animals conspired together, but I knew my dog too well. The rapport we shared sent ripples of good humor through me.

"Newynog," I said sharply.

Her ears drooped, and she looked back at me. Her tail hung low, guiltily. She edged closer to my horse and riveted her attention on me.

"Strange name for a dog," Archie said, eyeing my wolfhound. "The word means 'hungry' in Welsh, doesn't it?"

"She is always hungry," I replied. He didn't need to know that Newynog's ancestry followed mine in a straight line of descent. In each generation one member of the clan would claim a pup from the last litter of the previous favorite. All of the other pups became work-ing dogs sold to noble families for huge sums of money. None of those working dogs exhibited the intelligence or the extreme loyalty of a favorite. Familiar. I wondered if Uncle Henry had the same rap-port with his dogs as I shared with mine. He had claimed five special dogs in his lifetime before I inherited the right to choose my own companion and protector upon my brief return to Kirkenwood last year. No one else in the family was left to receive the honor of one of our dogs.

"Does that mean you hail from Wales?" Sir Hugh asked. He reined in to discipline Orage again.

"I no longer have a home," I replied.

"I'm taking you to King John." He set his jaw and dismounted. With a lusty sigh he prepared Orage's tack for riding. "You are more jealous than a woman, Orage, but if we are going to travel more than two miles, I'll have to give in and ride you," he addressed the bad-tempered beast.

Archie dismounted to adjust the girth on his horse. That beast had bloated his belly when first saddled, and now it slipped. Archie should have known that trick and circumvented it.

I jumped down as well. We all shifted about and when we re-sumed our journey, I was atop the more vivacious gelding Sir Hugh had forsaken. I turned the placid mare loose. She'd find her way home to her warm stall and bran mash with no trouble.

Sir Hugh raised an eyebrow when he noticed my change of mounts. I returned his stare as I kneed the gelding forward. Orage wouldn't stand for another horse getting in front of him and surged ahead.

The Roman road came into view, a straight line up the valley. Grass grew thick on the verge, but the paving stones remained solid and intact along this section. In other parts of England, those perfectly dressed stones had been pilfered for new construction projects, as had sections of Hadrian's Wall to the north. Much of the curtain wall at Kirkenwood had been quarried from the Roman barrier between En-gland and Scotland.

We made good time for a few more miles. The warmth of the noon sun disappeared beneath a bank of dark clouds that rolled in from the west. The sky took on a bizarre, yellowish tinge.

Goose bumps rose on my arms and the back of my neck. My tongue tingled.

"We have to find shelter. Now," I yelled over the rising wind.

A blinding flash of lightning set the horses rearing. Less than a heartbeat later, thunder crashed against the hills on all sides of us. It rolled around and around, echoing and amplifying.

My horse bucked and shied, dancing off the slight elevation of the Roman road. I concentrated on reins and stirrups to keep him from bolting. Archie barely controlled his own gelding. Orage sneered at the storm as if it were an enemy to attack on the field of battle.

The skies dumped their burden of moisture. Huge drops pelted us, stinging skin through several layers of clothing. In moments the deluge soaked us.

This was not the gentle caress of water at a spring, or from a puddle. I couldn't capture and use the essence of water in this relentless form.

Newynog yipped, signaling us to follow. I gave my horse his head. He fairly leaped across a swelling burn in the dog's wake. Together we plunged uphill to whatever shelter Newynog sought.

Before we crested the next foothill, I began to tremble all over. My teeth chattered from more than just the sudden chill of the storm. I yanked the reins back to halt the gelding. He ignored the bite of the bit and kept after the dog.

Sir Hugh galloped up beside me. He tried to grab the reins away from me. The gelding jerked his head at the last moment, dragging the wet leather out of Sir Hugh's hands.

And then I saw it. Newynog stood within the arched opening of an ancient cave barrow. Two huge slabs of upright stone supported a capstone of equally massive proportions around a natural cave opening.

"Shelter," Sir Hugh called and pointed.

"No!" I cried. "It's more than a burial chamber." My hands trembled so violently I couldn't hold the reins any longer.

"Nonsense." This time Sir Hugh succeeded in grabbing my reins and leading me into the disaster I knew awaited me. I had dreamed of this cave barrow many times and seen my death every time.

Chapter 10

A PERFECT circle of crudely shaped boulders lay directly in front of the barrow. We had to cross it to get to the dubious shelter of the capped standing stones.

I flinched and clenched my teeth even before the power contained within the circle struck me. My blood pounded through my body in a new rhythm. My ears rang and my eyes focused more acutely. I could see moisture pulsing through individual blades of grass in time with my heartbeat. My scalped tingled and my skin itched.

I drew the pelting rain around me, letting it cleanse my spirit and lend me strength to fight the otherworldly powers I knew dwelled in this ancient burial site.

A faint line of fiery energy hovered above the stones, enclosing them into a circle of power. To break the chain of power by entering the circle would make the power available to those who knew how to tap it; coming within the circle would also make us vulnerable to that power. I knew it. But I did not know how I knew it. Uncle Henry's lessons in magic those few months before I fled to Mendip Mor Castle had not been complete. I had engaged in the lessons reluctantly.

Witchchild! The echo of the long ago accusation made me close my eyes and duck my head.

"We'll be out of this wind in a moment. I can't promise you a fire, but we'll be drier and maybe a bit warmer," Sir Hugh said soothingly as he glanced back at me. Hopefully he took my defensive posture as abject misery rather than shrinking away from the supernatural forces that assaulted me from all sides.

He led the horses into the cursed circle.

Here was power begging for me to use it. I could tap a small fraction of it and bend Sir Hugh and Archie to my will.

But that would be an abuse of the gift. My enemies could follow my use of magic as if it were a well marked trail.

Whoever sought me so relentlessly wanted me to lose my soul by working magic.

I fought the need to gather that power within myself, to know the secrets of the universe and face God as an equal. I bit my lip until I drew blood.

By the time the capstone shadows surrounded us, I was shaking so badly I could not dismount on my own.

Sir Hugh held me close against his body, wrapping me in the thick wolf cloak. Newynog whined and draped herself across my feet. A little warmth penetrated my heart. The semidarkness of our shelter soothed my aching eyes. The barrow welcomed me like a mother's womb.

I feared that comfort most of all.

Witchchild! You've already lost your soul.

I cringed with the memory. Sir Hugh held me tighter.

"Easy now. We're out of the storm. There's room enough for all of us, including the horses," he whispered in my ear. His warm breath tickled my ear and sent a new tingle through me that had nothing to do with the ancient power of this place.

"The cave goes way back," Archie said. He inched his way deeper into the shadows, keeping one hand on the rough dirt walls that lay behind the portal stones—portal to what?

My death. But not yet. I did not live the dream of my death. In that dream I was alone except for one other. Not Sir Hugh. Someone else. Someone with a blacker than black aura.

"Don't go back there," I said through chattering teeth. The right person could stumble into another world back there. I would never dare be the right person. Archie would not know how to protect himself from the tricks and traps of demons or faeries.

I took one step after him. Immediately my skin crawled with the unseen touch of spirits and denizens of the underworld. A childish panicky voice in my head urged me to run deeper into the cave, no, out into the rain and wind, no, beat my head against the stones.

Try as I might, I could not straighten my thoughts or master the fears.

Clutching my temples with tense fingers, I stumbled backward.

The moment I stood beneath the capstone of the barrow my thoughts returned to their normal and logical pattern.

"Stay out of the cave, Archie. 'Tis too dangerous." I sought to detain him with a hand on his sleeve, but he moved away from me.

"The graves were robbed centuries ago. There's nothing back here to fear," Archie replied. "Hey, what's this?" A clatter of clicking wood followed his words.

I shuddered. Every nerve ending in my body cried for release from the tingling power trapped within the portal stones. Or did I need to release the power already within me but deeply hidden? I needed to lash out at something, anything, even myself.

Holy Mother, protect me. I fought the power with all of my concentration.

"Torches!" Archie cried. "Flint and iron. Tinder. We'll have light and fire in a moment."

"No!" I protested. "Do not invite the devil by lighting his way to us."

"I'll show you there are no devils. This is only an ancient burial site within a natural cave. The place was looted and abandoned long ago." Sir Hugh pushed me aside impatiently.

I stumbled against the upright stone at my back. The jolt of energy that flared through me freed my mind of gibbering fear.

"If this place was abandoned long ago, then why are there torches, firewood, and fresh tinder here?" I asked, clearheaded and determined none of us should venture deeper into the cave.

Sir Hugh paused a moment staring at a torch he held ready for Archie to light.

"I don't know. I won't know anything until I explore a little. For that I need light." He held the torch out for Archie to strike a spark onto the oily rags wound around a stout branch.

"The people who left these supplies are heathens. Witches who practice the ancient ways," I hissed.

Light flared against the walls to reveal the faint outline of a pentagram enclosing a demonic sigil.

"Witches," I repeated. Witches, like Uncle Henry and Aunt Lotta. And Me. But not like us. Where my relatives worshiped a benevolent goddess and revered the land, using their powers to heal and bring bounty to their community, other pagans worshiped darker forces, seeking power for power's sake, willing to do anything, commit any outrage, worship any demon, all for the glorious feeling of power granted them by magic. But any use of supernatural power opened the door to abuses.

Witchchild! Lose your soul in me.

"Well, no one will be coming to use this place until after the storm abates." Sir Hugh shrugged and lifted the now blazing brand. He cast a long shadow into the darkness beyond. "Light a fire and warm yourself. I don't want you getting sick from chill after I've worked so hard to rescue you. Rest, *ma petite*." He squeezed my shoulder affectionately, solicitously. As if he had the right to command my life.

I gulped back my fear, trying very hard to believe that if he disappeared into another world then I could take the chestnut gelding and ride for the nearest sanctuary without hindrance. My enemies need never know what happened to me.

But I would know what happened to an innocent man, an honest man who had vowed to protect me. I would regret his passing from this world.

Archie lit the fire already laid. It blinded me to all within the cavern except the flickering branch Sir Hugh carried.

Newynog stood, tail and ears high. She sniffed the air and took one step in Sir Hugh's wake. I grabbed the coarse fur of her ruff and held her tight.

"Newynog, sit," I ordered.

She obeyed, but her ears drooped and she looked at me in abject disappointment.

"Sometimes you are just too brave," I told my friend, petting her with long firm strokes. I needed contact with her to still my own fears as well as to appease her curiosity.

I stepped to the side of the fire, so it would not blind me to the interior.

Sir Hugh used the torch to burn away a thick cobweb that hung across his path. A dozen baby spiders and perhaps five trapped insects scurried away from his flame. He brushed them away from his face. The web caught fire in a shower of brightly colored sparks.

Suddenly the sparks took wing and flitted about our heads in a joyous dance. Not flame. Tiny winged creatures.

Newynog jumped up, nipping at them. Archie and Sir Hugh continued batting them out of their eyes, away from their ears and mouths with wildly flaying arms. The torchlight wavered with Sir Hugh's frantic movements. Wild shadows climbed the walls reaching for me, trapping me in the same shadow as the pentagram.

I crouched down, covering my head with my arms.

"Hey, watch it!" Archie bellowed.

"Watch yourself. Pesky mayflies. Where'd they come from?" Sir Hugh responded.

Something tugged my hair. I peeked to make sure the torch hadn't singed me.

A bright green-winged male, perfectly formed, totally nude, and about as big as my forefinger hovered before my eyes.

We have waited ages for you. Come play, an enticing voice sounded deep within my mind. The faint sound of tinkling bells followed the invitation.

Witchchild! The voice of my memory responded. *Only witches can see faeries.*

Only witches see faeries! The words took me back to another time, another place, but the same faeries . . .

"Pennyroyal banishes fleas and lice. You can also put it in vinegar and apply to the nose to keep ladies from swooning. It helps keep your teeth. And . . . and if you put it in your shoe, it guards against weariness. Aunt Lotta says it's a plant of peace and keeps people from arguing," I recited the litany of the herb to Sister Mary Ursula. Then I added the obvious conclusion to the lesson, "Your plants need compost. They're turning yellow."

Sister Mary Ursula frowned and inspected the tiny leaves growing close to the ground. "You are very observant, child." She straightened and smiled at me.

That smile made my loneliness easier to bear. Spring had flown and summer had grown hot. Yet still Mama did not come for me. Nor did I hear anything from Kirkenwood. I had no idea if Uncle Henry lived or died, though I was pretty sure Aunt Lotta had died during the confusion of my last night at home.

The accusation of *witchchild* continued to haunt me. Who had called me that with such loathing and contempt? Another voice had shouted the word in possessive triumph. Who?

"Now tell me about this plant, Ana," Sister Mary Ursula said, pointing to the common betony.

"Put it into wound dressings to help tissues grow back strong. Burn it for purification," I said, distracted by a flurry of colored flying things in the sunny corner of the convent's herb garden.

"And what else, Ana? I know you had a most thorough teacher. What else can betony do for you?"

Red, green, yellow, and blue beings flitted about the corner where the mullein grew.

"Ana!" Sister Mary Ursula said in the sharpest tone I had heard from her. She knew only the shortening of my name, not my true name. Mama had been most emphatic about telling no one my true name.

"A sachet of betony under the pillow prevents nightmares and visions," I added, keeping my eyes on the faeries. They kept to their corner, away from Sister Mary Ursula and me. I wore the family prayer beads and crucifix around my neck. Sister Mary Ursula wore a chain of plain wooden beads. Her cross kept the faeries away. They knew mine from ages long past and did not fear it.

Tell me news of home, please, I implored the faeries.

They giggled and hid among the leaves and tall yellow flower stalks of the mullein.

"What distracts you, Ana?" Sister Mary Ursula moved beside me. She clasped my hand and peered into the sunny corner of the garden.

"Can't you see the faeries? The willow green one is standing atop the tallest flower stalk. He thinks he leads this little flock and so he always stands taller than they. But they don't really have leaders. They just follow the winds." I tugged to break free of the elderly nun and run to my friends.

"You must forget these pagan beings, Ana." Sister Mary Ursula crossed herself as she spoke.

"But they are my friends," I protested.

"The Sisters of St. Dyfrig's are your friends now."

"But . . ." Willow and his friends waved at me sadly. Then they flew a slow spiral upward over the wall.

Good-bye, they whispered.

Sadness filled my chest, pressing hard against my heart.

"Good-bye," I whispered as I wiped a tear from my cheek.

Protect yourself, for we no longer can, the faeries chorused sadly.

"Good-bye," I whispered again. I swallowed the lump in my throat and dashed my sleeve across my face. "Mama didn't say good-bye. Neither did Papa or Aunt Lotta or Uncle Henry. The faeries are my only true friends." My lower lip stuck out and trembled.

Farewell, friend, the sad voices of the faeries chimed like slow tolling bells.

"You have new friends, Ana. A new family." Sister Mary Ursula crouched down, holding me close. "We will stand beside you forever. And when the time comes for us to separate, I promise we shall each say farewell."

"Promise?" I asked. Then I remembered an old tradition between Aunt Lotta and Uncle Henry. "Will you seal the promise in a circle?"

"I'll do better. I'll seal the promise in a circle of prayer beads. That way we make the promise to God as well as to each other."

Her smile lightened the heaviness in my chest. A little of the loneliness faded. Together we recited a chain of prayers, one for each bead on our chains.

I never saw the faeries again, until yesterday. But Sister Mary Ursula said good-bye when the time came for me to flee St. Dyfrig's.

The return of the faeries into my life disturbed me almost as much as my dreams.

"Why do you haunt me now?" I cried.

We offer you the sanctuary you crave. Follow us into the portal, and you will ever more be free of the fears that haunt you.

"I can't."

The faeries faded out of existence. *Remember the betony and the mullein,* they whispered on a last breath of wind and rain.

"Both herbs prevent visions and nightmares!"

"Who are you talking to?" Sir Hugh asked. He loomed over me, still holding the flaming torch.

"Didn't you see the faeries?" I looked up at him, heedless of the tears brought on by the lonely memories that streaked my face.

"Those mayflies? They aren't faeries. Faeries don't exist." He stomped back into the interior of the barrow.

"You'll learn," I threw back at him.

Chapter 11

"FAERIES? Bah! You've spent too many months engulfed in Welsh mists." Hugh denied Ana's statement as he stomped deeper into the cave, determined to investigate something, anything, rather than discuss pagan beings with the strange refugee he'd rescued. He fought the urge to cross himself. "Next you'll be telling me your dog talks to you."

He passed an empty chamber; not even the skeleton of the previous occupant remained. The tunnel should end here, but it continued on. More burial chambers?

"Sir Hugh," Archie called from around a bend in the tunnel.

Hugh lengthened his stride, heedless of the puddles, as much to put distance between himself and Ana as to answer the summons. "Find something interesting?" he asked.

"A door." Archie gulped. "This is no ordinary barrow, milord."

"A rich one, perhaps?" Visions of gold pulled Hugh forward now. He owed King John another year's revenue from Bellecôte as relief from the death of the last baron. The usual fee had been doubled as part of Hugh's bribe to gain wardship of the lands through marriage to Bellecôte's widow. Then John had doubled the relief again when Ardyth died in childbed. And still the honors of Bellecôte did not truly belong to him. "With an ancient treasure in my hands I could pay the death reliefs to John and buy lands and a title of my own. I'd have a heritage to pass on to my children." Something his own father had refused to give him.

The only thing Hugh retained of his so-called family—indeed his only possession that hadn't come from Ardyth's fortune—was his sword. And he'd had to win that from his half brother in a tournament.

His father had acknowledged him as a bastard son and educated him in the arts of war, but nothing else. Hugh's half brother, the legitimate heir had received everything. Shortly after Hugh's fourteenth birthday, he had entered a tournament hosted by his father. He had survived challenge after challenge. Heady with triumph and self-confidence he in turn challenged Alain de Chênenoir to individual combat.

He'd fought his brother long and hard. They were well matched in size and training. But Hugh was desperate to prove himself his brother's equal. To earn the respect of the other knights on the field, he had to be better than all of them—because he was a bastard and therefore inferior.

At last, bleeding from several shallow cuts and near exhaustion, Hugh had knocked Alain off-balance just long enough to disarm him. Alain fell to his knees, too tired to retrieve his weapon.

"My armor and horse are yours," Alain gasped. "How much more ransom will you demand from me, Brother?" He spat the last sentence. His lip curled in contempt.

Hugh had walked over to his brother's fallen sword and retrieved it. "This is all I claim, Brother. My father's sword and my father's name."

That night he had left Chateau Chênenoir and joined a band of mercenaries. He'd never looked back on his youth. Until now.

Now he faced the memory and nearly cried for the lost opportunity, lost family, lost innocence.

"With an ancient treasure, I could afford a horse of my own, and armor!" Archie's eyes grew wide with dreams.

"Gold will buy much, but it will not buy my brother's respect." Hugh heaved a sigh, knowing he'd never outgrow the sense of inadequacy his family had beaten into him. "Let's see what keeps this door sealed when all else has been stolen from the barrow." Hugh held his torch closer to the vague outline of the portal. Bronze hinges glinted back at him from the left side. He shifted his attention to the right. An iron lock caked in rust held together two hasps, one on the door, the other embedded in the stone.

"Bronze and iron in combination. This will be really old." Archie backed up three steps, taking his torch with him.

"It's so old it blends into the stonework surrounding it," Hugh mused. "Robbers bent on a rapid getaway probably missed it when they looted the other chambers."

A decorative iron ring in the exact center of the door caught his attention. A bronze dragon seemed to be spitting a ring of flames that encircled its snout. He reached to test it.

"Don't touch that!" Ana cried from two steps away. She'd crept up on him without his awareness. Her hair had come unbound and stood out in wild array, as if lightning had struck nearby.

She stood in the exact center of a puddle, unmindful of her soaked shoes, muddy hem, and the chill.

He dropped his hand back to his side in surprise.

"Why not?" he asked, watching her wide, staring eyes as closely as the torchlight allowed. She seemed to glow around the edges, green and otherworldly.

He had to bite his lip to avoid crossing himself.

"What do you know about the treasure behind this door?" he asked, forcing himself to look away from the eldritch glow that had spread to the walls and ceiling. The pulsing green halo around her spread to engulf the door. The sealed outline flared. Only the floor remained mundane and wet, safe to watch.

"I know only that the lock deep within the earth guards something that cannot stand the touch of iron. The burial chambers have been looted many times. Practitioners of ancient arts use this chamber regularly. But this portal remains undisturbed," she whispered. Even then her voice echoed about the tunnel as if she had shouted. Her words dug into his mind and remained there.

"An old legend with no basis." He tried to dismiss her words, but they would not go away. "See, the iron does not burn." He grasped the rusted mechanism with his free hand, keeping the torch high to illuminate as much as possible. Chills ran up his back as the cold, damp metal warmed under his touch. He thought he heard something rattle behind the door.

"Iron does not burn you or me, or even Archie or my dog. But there are otherworlds, other beings who are poisoned by it. I pray you, Sir Hugh Fitz Chênenoir, leave this one door a mystery. It is much more dangerous exposed than hidden."

"Perhaps you are right. The rain eases, and we must be on our way to King John."

The glow around her faded. The small fire at the entrance must have flared to give the eldritch glow. Now the fire burned down and so did the eerie light.

"I would rather face King John than what lies hidden behind that door," she said quietly. "Perhaps we'd best make haste for the Convent of the Blessed Virgin in Yorkshire. The good sisters will know how to negate this ancient evil or seal it for all time."

Hugh laughed at her single-mindedness. She'd be a great match for King John in stubbornness.

"The good sisters know no more of black magic than I do. We go to King John. If necessary, there is one who follows the court who might have knowledge to safely unseal this portal and retrieve the treasure."

"There is no treasure. Only grief. If you must have treasure, I can lead you to a true one. But only if you take me to the convent . . ."

"What treasure, milady? What wealth do you command?" Ancient treasure faded in importance if she could give him the dowry, lands, and titles he coveted.

"Will you take me . . ."

"What treasure?"

"My family is wealthy. I will see that you are suitably rewarded."

"With your hand in marriage? With your titles?"

"My title has died. My lands reverted to the king. I can give you only gold, hidden away."

"We go to King John and nowhere else."

The drumming of the rain on the capstones faded.

"We'd best leave now, before that door tempts you again," I said. Sir Hugh's resolve to go to King John firmed my own determination to escape to Yorkshire at the first chance. I needed time and the quiet offered by the convent to plan, to find some way to end my ceaseless running.

"It's still raining," Archie grumbled. But he snuffed the torch against the packed dirt beneath the stone portal.

"We'd best press on if we hope to reach Worcester tomorrow night," Sir Hugh said. "I called my messenger back. I want to be the first to give King John the news of the raid on Mendip Mor Castle and the death of my friends." He checked Orage's girth and bridle. Archie adjusted straps on the pack pony.

I clambered atop the gelding by myself, eager to be gone. Even before the men had finished fussing with their horses, I urged my mount out of the sheltering overhang. I couldn't get away from the barrow and that mysterious door fast enough.

The dragon fixture could refer to Arthur Pendragon, a heroic legend in Britain's history, beloved as well as respected. Or it could be symbolic of the demon the portal sealed in another world. I didn't dare investigate further. Arthur Pendragon I could find in other places with less danger to myself and Britain.

The power I had gathered from the stone circle remained in my blood. It sang with the wind in my hair as I urged the horse faster and faster away from the barrow and the demon portal. Newynog kept close to our heels, glorying in the run. We splashed through dozens of puddles, spraying water all over me and those who rode in my wake. I was halfway down the hill toward the road when Sir Hugh caught up with me. Orage nipped at my horse's flank until it slowed. Then the big war stallion surged forward, eager for the lead. Sir Hugh flashed me a grim smile as he passed me. His eyes had become hard and determined.

Newynog raced the stallion until Sir Hugh curbed his horse to stay closer to me.

"Don't even think about trying to run away from me, Lady Ana. Orage will catch you no matter how fast you run," he ground out.

I will find you no matter where you hide. His thoughts came to me clearly, without my trying to probe his mind.

"Why? Without me, you'd be able to go about your business in a timely manner." I reined my gelding to the right to avoid touching Sir Hugh. He edged close to me again—close enough to yank me out of the saddle if he chose.

"Until I know why my friend Edmund was murdered, you are my business, my only business. I want answers that only you can give me. Care to tell me why they died?"

"I can't."

"Can't or won't?"

I looked away from him, keeping my silence. He'd not live long once he knew my secrets.

"Very well. We stay together. For now, we ride hard to make up for all of these delays. King John won't stay in Worcester once he hears the news of Welsh raiders led by de Chancell murdering a royally appointed marcher lord. He'll head for Winchester or London to convene his barons and ask for troops to avenge this outrage."

"But they weren't Welsh raiders. We know that!" I protested.

"All the more reason to reach Worcester before the news comes to him by other means," Sir Hugh replied.

"I still can't figure why de Chancell turned traitor," Archie muttered, coming up on my other side. "He served the king's favorite. John gave him several small estates. Walter Geoffrey de Chancell should be riding high on influence and power."

"Philip of France may have bought de Chancell's loyalty. That makes him the worst kind of traitor." Hugh set his face in a grim mask of determination.

"Is de Chancell a traitor if his lord is no longer worthy of loyalty?" I asked. John would make a show of vengeance by burning and looting the border marches well into Wales. He'd take hostages and collect enormous fines. All without seeking the truth. He'd done it time and again throughout England, France, and Ireland.

He'd claimed the throne by similar means. Did winning make it legal?

"Nonsense. King John has his faults, but he's loyal to those who are loyal to him." Sir Hugh dismissed my argument with a wave of his hand.

"John owes you his life, and rewarded you amply for the favor," Archie snorted. "Good enough reason for loyalty."

"De Briouze owes the king huge sums of money. He dares not trespass on the king's favor lest he lose everything," I reminded him. "Walter Geoffrey de Chancell, as de Briouze's man, is also vulnerable to the whim of the king. Perhaps they serve a different lord as a way of ending that debt."

A brief memory flashed across my mind. Something concerning Uncle Henry and the night invaders at Kirkenwood who sent Mama and me running the first time.

"But John trusts de Briouze. They have been boon companions since the days of King Richard. De Briouze's son is Bishop of Hereford, appointed by King John. They both support Bishop de Grey, John's secretary, for Archbishop of Canterbury," Sir Hugh argued.

"But for all of the favors John has given de Briouze, he has withheld the title of earl," Archie muttered. I doubted Sir Hugh heard him.

Unlike his older brother, John kept a very tight rein on his barons. And they resented him for it. The era of King Richard's benign neglect of England and allowing his barons to do as they pleased had ended the day John grabbed the treasury and the crown. He'd used ancient traditions to assert his claim to the throne, throwing aside the law of primogeniture established by his father. He could as easily cast aside any other law or tradition.

A few words of the confrontation that long ago night between the armed intruders and Uncle Henry penetrated my memory like an arrow from the past. Richard had died in France, naming his nephew, Arthur of Brittany, as his heir. John had seized the crown and treasury in England before young Arthur and his followers could mobilize. The soldiers had said they came seeking Uncle Henry's oath of fidelity to John as well as his knights' service and money to subdue opposition.

What had they wanted with Mama and me?

The chain of prayer beads pressed deeply into my palm. Not Mama or me, but the circled cross. If John possessed this ancient artifact, he could claim his right to the throne through Arthur Pendragon, my royal ancestor. He hadn't needed the artifact to impose his authority over his barons. He might need it in the future to maintain control. Especially now that the Pope had placed Britain under Interdict.

One among them had discovered another treasure in me. Someone close to the king worked magic and recognized the talent in me; wanted to exploit it.

For the king or against? With John's knowledge? Or was he ignorant of this quest?

"And you trust King John?" I asked instead of dwelling on painful memories. I'd never believe him totally innocent.

"Yes. When I was nothing but a common mercenary who owned nothing but this sword," Sir Hugh patted the weapon lashed to his saddle, "King John knighted me and gave me all that I have. I owe him much."

Archie looked away at that statement, as if it were not the entire truth.

"And Archie says the king owes you his life. John does not like to be beholden to anyone," I added. I might have spent eight of the last nine years in various convents, but I had not been isolated from political gossip.

"I have no reason to betray my liege lord. I have sworn fealty to King John. I honor that oath above all else," Sir Hugh said adamantly.

"Above even your life?" I asked.

"Yes."

Then we must escape your vigilance before we reach Worcester, for we do not have the same faith in your king that you do.

I slipped the cross and prayer beads inside my bodice. John had no way of knowing I still possessed it. Now I had to make certain he never got his hands on it. My life was worth nothing to him without it.

Chapter 12

WE rode for hours without a break. The saddle chafed the inside of my thighs. The constant bouncing jarred my spine until I thought my neck must snap free from my back. I had ridden quite a bit in the last year with Uncle Henry, but not for this duration or at this speed. Prior to that, the convents that had sheltered me had not provided mounts for a mere postulant who needed education and reminders of obedience.

I longed to bathe my hands, face, and feet in any and all of the multitude of fresh springs we passed. Splashing through every puddle we encountered didn't suffice to renew my spirit and strength.

At the first major crossroad I held back, rubbing my neck and shifting my shoulders to indicate my discomfort. Sir Hugh glanced disgustedly at me. When he chose the road branching to the east, I eased my horse into the shadow behind the stone cross of the wayside shrine.

Patches of wild mullein attracted my attention. Even if Sir Hugh came back and discovered me, I had the excuse of gathering the herb to place the leaves under my pillow. My dreams were troubled enough without portents robbing me of sleep.

Most of these roadside holy markers consisted of a carved stone cross. Travelers placed offerings of food, wine, a coin, or some personal memento at the base as they recited prayers for a safe journey. Crossroads had always represented a powerful symbol of change and growth.

This shrine was more substantial than most, boasting a three-sided, roofed shelter behind the cross that stood taller than I while I sat atop the horse. The road probably forked at an ancient sacred place, a spring or well. That would account for the lush undergrowth and stand of tall willows behind it. The trees provided welcoming shadows to hide me.

I dismounted and held the gelding's reins while I let it browse. With my free hand I stashed two handfuls of mullein leaves into my belt scrip. Then I sat on a rock beside a bubbling spring that became a tiny rill that fed a larger creek. My shoes and hose nearly shredded as I stripped them off and sank my feet into the fresh water.

"Ah," I sighed as every muscle in my body relaxed. Magic tingled in my toes and coursed up my legs. I let the power contained within my element cleanse my spirit and renew my resolve to find a way to end John's persecution of me and my clan. With the magic filling my body, I willed myself to blend with the forest.

In short order, Sir Hugh pelted back down the road.

"Show yourself, Lady Ana!" he shouted.

I hushed the gelding before it could nicker a greeting to Orage.

"Lady Ana!" Sir Hugh called again. Then I heard him thunder up the northern branch of the road.

I counted to one hundred twice before peeking out.

"I told you I'd not let you go," Sir Hugh said calmly from the front of the shrine as soon as I showed my head.

"But you . . ."

"I sent Archie up the road just in case you had managed to elude me. But I thought you must be hiding nearby." He threw a coin into the offering box and remounted Orage. "Come. Archie will join us a little farther on where the two branches of this road meet. You'd not have gotten far, Ana."

Radburn Blakely waited within the shadows of the postern gate of Worcester Castle for his quarry. A flicker of movement drew his attention. The carpenter's son approached with inept stealth. If he had set fire to his sister's cottage with this degree of clumsiness, then why hadn't the woman and her husband awoken and escaped the blaze? The young man darted from shadow to shadow, but he chose the wrong moment to move. He did not wait for the guard patrolling the parapet to pass him, then dart to his chosen cover while the guard looked in another direction. Instead, he chose the moment of the

guard's turning back. The thought behind the young man's movements was obvious. Move while the guard was preoccupied with keeping his balance on the turn on the narrow walkway.

But the boy didn't know the guards and their catlike grace. Nor
did he know that Radburn himself had chosen the guards for their
keen night vision.

A half moon rose above the hills to the east. Radburn's quarry was
in full view on his next move. Radburn smiled and stepped out from
behind the bush the boy chose for cover.

"Tell me how you felt when you set fire to your sister's house," he
said as he raised a long dagger to the boy's throat. His quarry yelped
but froze in place. "Did your loins ignite along with the house as the
flames licked the thatch as a man licks a lover?"

The boy trembled all over. His skin radiated more heat. He licked
his lips. Then a brief movement of his head indicated a definite "Yes."

Radburn almost shouted with triumph. His own lust grew with
the boy's discomfort. He swallowed his joy at finding a kindred spirit,
a boy who loved fire more than sex. He could be taught to love death
more than life.

"Good." Radburn sheathed his blade and dragged the arsonist
toward the postern gate he'd left unlocked. "I have a job for you."
Together they would sow the seeds of disorder and chaos. The ancient
gods would reign once more.

"But . . ."

"No excuses. Either you work for me, or I have you executed for
murder. I need assassins, not sniveling boys too greedy for common
sense."

"My father—my clothes—"

"Does your father know you came here?"

"No. I need to send him a message, let him know I'm safe."

"You aren't exactly safe. A message will be sent." Later, after the
carpenter had simmered in worry for a while. The message would be
a flaming arrow to his cottage.

"My clothes?"

"You won't need them. As of this moment you are my retainer.
I'll feed and clothe you. And I'll train you. First you must come to
me and swear your loyalty to me."

"To you? Not the king?" The boy stopped. He attempted to hold
Radburn's gaze with his own.

"To me. You are mine and obey only me. My brother is far too weak of will to hold your loyalty for long."

"What about your loyalty, sir?"

Radburn laughed. "My loyalty is well placed, young man. Very well placed."

"I have a name, sir. I have rights."

"No, you don't. As of this moment you are invisible to all but me and the One I serve, Monsieur le Fantôme."

Sir Hugh skirted the towns whenever possible to avoid questions and confrontations. At every crossroad he urged speed. He kept looking anxiously behind us for signs of pursuit.

I rigorously clamped down on my need to extend my senses in the same quest. I could not risk leaving a trail of magic for my enemies to follow. Guilt tickled the edges of my conscience every time I used the talent. The sisters of the Blessed Virgin Convent believed my immortal soul was jeopardized every time I even thought about using powers beyond the norm.

The roads became more and more crowded with people pushing carts or carrying bundles to market in Bath. Some seemed to cling to odds and ends as if they protected all of their worldly goods. Had they been displaced by some catastrophe? I refused to believe that the monasteries would cast out their lay workers because of the Interdict.

A clever man could easily follow us, concealing himself in the masses that slowed our progress northward.

"We have to be the first with news of the raid," Sir Hugh said repeatedly, then dug in his spurs and pelted forward. Newynog relentlessly kept up with him, ignoring my commands to remain at my heels.

On the outskirts of Bath, the crowds thickened. People, carts, and other horsemen pushed between myself and Sir Hugh. Archie, too, dragged behind. I watched carefully for a chance to ease my horse to the side of the road, and then. . . .

Where would I go? I had no money. No luggage. Little knowledge of the world outside my convent or Kirkenwood.

A rough-looking man dressed in the stained and worn leathers of a mercenary—or a professional bully—riding a tired nag with too many bones showing through its dusty hide, nudged my horse's flank with his knee. I looked back at him, startled. He grinned, showing a mouth with only a few blackened teeth remaining. His breath smelled of rotten meat and garlic. I kneed the gelding forward.

Travelers who sought the hospitality of my convent frequently complained that too many out-of-work mercenaries wandered England these days. The professional soldiers flocked to King John's call to arms whenever he set off on campaign. When the war finished—or failed to launch—these professional soldiers had no income, and no prospects of employment until the next campaign season. Between wars they preyed upon innocent and vulnerable travelers.

The crowds pressed too close. The mercenary moved up alongside of me. He leaned over, bringing his foul mouth close to me.

I reared back, away from his rancid smell of stale sweat and dried blood.

"What's 'a matter, milady? Too good to share a bed with the loikes o' me?" he sneered in thick French that sounded almost German. Not Saxon. I guessed from his accent that he hailed from the Holy Roman Empire. A foreigner who earned his living by bullying the local population. He reached to pull me off my horse into his lap. I leaned away from him "Woman alone needs protection. You want the rabble turned loose on you?"

I became aware of how people watched me. Men and women alike eyed me with suspicion. Other men, the bolder ones, licked their lips and let their eyes linger on my breasts and the length of leg exposed by riding astride. A woman alone invited predators.

Revulsion welled up within me. "Sir Hugh?" I called into the crowd. Both he and Orage had moved ahead. The noise of the crowd separated us farther.

In desperation, I touched the mind of the mercenary's horse and made it shy and prance. He fought the reins to keep his seat. His horse yanked at the restraint.

My own horse plunged forward through a narrow gap in the mass of people. Sir Hugh's broad back came into view.

I sighed with relief as I sought the place beside him. Sometime in the last day I had learned to trust him to protect me. At least I trusted him more than the mercenary behind me.

Newynog yipped a brief greeting and concentrated on shouldering aside lesser humans to make a path for us.

The lines around Sir Hugh's eyes softened a little as he caught sight of me. "Where's Archie? We'll never get to King John in time. There has to be a better way around the city." He looked around hastily. The worry lines returned.

A great shout went up among the crowd. All forward movement stopped.

"Now what?" Sir Hugh rose up in his stirrups for a better view above the mass of people.

I caught a glimpse of flying fists and followed his example.

Ahead, not more than twenty yards away, a gang of plainly dressed merchants and craftsmen joined a few men at arms in menacing another figure. Their victim wore a cotehardie in a rich russet color, trimmed in fur with a jeweled clasp at the throat.

As I watched, a fist connected with his nose. Blood sprayed his attacker. The man at arms, wearing a gray tabard with a device I did not recognize, laughed and grasped the man by the throat to keep him from falling to the ground. Another soldier stepped in to plow his fist into the victim's belly. He doubled over with a painful "whoof" sound.

My own gut ached in sympathy.

"You have to stop them, Sir Hugh."

"We can't afford the delay," he protested.

"By the code of chivalry, you must. Your honor requires you to aid him. He is one man, set upon by a crowd of bullies. Even if he is guilty of some crime, he deserves a trial and just punishment. You must help him."

"Have at him, Bailiff!" someone in the crowd bellowed.

"Make him pay for robbing us of business!" another merchant, less richly dressed, screamed.

"Kill the foreigner."

"They're at fault. These foreign merchants made the Pope take away our church."

Sir Hugh sighed heavily. "You know of course that an appeal to a man's honor is the one thing he cannot resist."

I nodded briefly, then we pushed our horses into the melee without further consultation.

"What transpires?" Hugh shouted over the crowd noise. He drew his sword and pointed it at the bailiff.

The roughly dressed locals melted away, leaving the professional soldiers to deal with an authoritative voice issuing from a man riding a noble steed. Sir Hugh did not need the Bellecôte tabard to command men.

"I've a warrant for this man's arrest," the bailiff announced.

"Let me see it," Sir Hugh commanded. He held out his hand for the parchment.

The man made a show of searching his jerkin beneath the tabard and came up empty-handed. "Must o' lost it. Or this foreign scum stole it," he sneered. He pulled back his fist, ready to slam it into the merchant once more.

"Stop him, Sir Hugh," I pleaded with mind and voice. I did not know if my own belly would tolerate another empathic blow.

"Don't you dare," Hugh commanded in his most regal voice.

I sent a tendril of power to reinforce his words into the man's mind, too desperate to stop this outrage to care that I violated the laws of the church and endangered my soul. The bailiff froze in place, arm still prepared to pummel his victim.

"What charge do you claim against this man?" Sir Hugh asked, climbing down from Orage. All trace of the previous weakness in his right thigh had vanished.

"He charges too much for his goods!" a woman in the crowd yelled.

"His goods are exotic. People pay his prices, then don't have enough to buy from their neighbors," a man added. He wore faded and much patched robes. The emblem on his cap identified him as a member of the glassblowers' guild.

"These are not crimes," Sir Hugh protested. "Have you witnesses that he committed a crime?"

"Don't need witnesses. Only need a warrant," the bailiff returned.

"You don't have one of those either," Hugh reminded him.

"We don't need one of those either." The glass merchant shoved his way forward. "All we need is a rope to hang him."

Sir Hugh showed him the point of his sword.

I slipped off the gelding and passed Sir Hugh until I could shoulder the sagging weight of the foreign merchant. He stood nearly eye to eye with me. His slight weight advantage bore heavily on my arms, but I did not shy from him. The puddles in the rough road, and the mist in the air gave me more strength, both physical and magical. Newynog edged behind us, taking some of his weight on her massive shoulders. She bared her teeth at the bailiff until he released his victim. Once fully in my arms, I absorbed an awareness of the foreigner's internal hurts. The bailiff knew his business. The merchant would need many days of rest and strengthening broths to recover.

Unless . . . No, I could not touch him with healing. I had neither the extra strength—despite the water soaking my ragged shoes—or the quiet to prepare for such a spell. Performing it in public might very well brand me a witch. This crowd wanted blood. Mine would do as nicely as the foreigner's.

"We'll take this matter to the justiciar," Sir Hugh announced.

The bailiff laughed. "Sir Arundel don't know his ass from his dick. Only laws he ever learned were which fist makes a bigger dent in his enemy's nose."

My heart sank. Too often, the king's local representatives were appointed for every reason except their knowledge of law. Sir Arundel obviously bowed to the will of the townspeople when he had no opinion on fair play or justice.

The crowd pressed closer. Violence still colored the aura of the mass. No individual stood out among them. Their combined energies made the horses nervous. Newynog whined and pressed closer to the foreign merchant and myself. I'd never seen her back away from a challenge like this.

I noticed that Sir Hugh had not sheathed his sword. Archie finally came up beside us. He stayed ahorse and gathered our reins to keep our mounts from straying—not that they could in this crowd.

Frantically I searched for inspiration. A wooden cross poked above the roof of a building directly in front of me.

"There's a church, Sir Hugh," I said quietly. "We can take this man to sanctuary and let the local authorities sort it out."

"Church won't take the likes of him," the bailiff sneered.

"The Interdict," Sir Hugh said. His voice sounded heavy, almost defeated.

"He's a Jew!" another bully replied.

I sensed Sir Hugh withdraw within himself. He had no more liking for the Jews than most Englishmen. The first time I'd been punished for using magic, or seeing faeries, I figured out that people fear what they do not understand. Nuns and priests could not understand magic because they had no contact with it other than wildly distorted legends until they met me.

The general populace had little or no contact with Jews other than wildly distorted legends, and so they feared them.

I had never met a Jew before, though Uncle Henry had made me read some of their scholarly texts translated into Latin. Their racial characteristics remained a mystery to me. But I knew about three words in Hebrew. They should be enough.

"Boruch atah Adonai." Blessed art Thou, O Lord our God.

Words we should all know and hold in our hearts no matter what language we spoke.

As I said the beginning of the prayer, I stared into the man's bewildered eyes. Not a single spark of recognition lighted the dark brown iris.

Then I became aware of his swarthy skin and thick, black, curly hair. "Where do you call home?" I asked in Latin.

He replied in a liquid stream of syllables that resembled Latin a little. I caught only one word in three. *Venezia.* That was enough.

"You are a glass merchant from Venice?"

He nodded vigorously.

"And you are a Christian?"

He crossed himself repeatedly. In his eagerness he showed himself to be much younger than I first thought, and more handsome.

"How'd you know what them Jews say?" The bailiff peered at me closely. "You don't look like a Jew, but you speak like one. I'd as soon hang you as this foreign vermin."

Chapter 13

"KEEP your hands away from your dagger and back off," Hugh said. He waved his sword point beneath the bailiff's chin close enough to scratch at his stubble.

Black rage almost blinded him. How dare this filthy peasant threaten Ana?

He nicked the bailiff's throat for being too slow, for offering offense to Ana, for smelling like the unwashed peasant he was.

No one. *No one* must ever threaten Ana again. He'd kill any man who tried.

The man lifted his hands to shoulder level and took a step backward. He kept his eyes on the sword. Blood dotted his lip where he bit too deep.

"This woman and this merchant are under my protection. Does anyone here question that?" Hugh ground out between clenched teeth. He dared not shift his attention away from the bailiff, but he sensed the press of bodies about him lessening. He needed to see Ana, to make certain she faired well.

He did not care if she had a dowry, lands, titles. He had vowed to protect her. He needed to protect her.

"And who might you be, stranger? Just 'cause you ride a fine horse and keep a fancy lady don't make you right," the bailiff sneered as he retreated half a pace.

Hugh moved with him, keeping his sword just as close to the bailiff's vulnerable throat as before. This time, his nick drew a bright drop of blood.

"We will take this case to Sir Arundel. He might not listen to a foreign merchant you all hate because he is foreign, but he will listen to Sir Fitz Chênenoir, warden of Bellecôte, and King John's liege man.

A flare of recognition crossed the bailiff's face.

"Mount your horse, Lady Ana, and take the merchant up behind you," he ordered. "Archie, take this bailiff into custody. We go to Sir Arundel, right now."

"Gladly, Sir Hugh." Archie dismounted with a wide grin. He pulled a short length of rope from his belt along with his dagger. By the time Hugh settled into Orage's saddle, the bailiff had his hands tied behind his back. Archie almost gleefully kept his dagger edge close to the man's Adam's apple.

The crowd parted silently and sullenly as Hugh guided the horses forward.

He threaded through the narrow streets of Bath until they reached the old Roman buildings near the baths. The smell of sulfur from the hot springs made him long for a cleansing soak. His skin itched and he craved a shave. One of the few luxuries he took from Bellecôte as its warden were the fine blades for shaving. From the time his beard had begun to come in, he'd hated having itchy stubble.

The luxury of a bath would have to be postponed. Sir Arundel awaited them on the worn steps of an old building. A messenger stood panting beside the short knight, whose feet and sword seemed almost as long as he. His iron-gray coteheardie matched his hair and beard. His scarlet chainse looked too much like blood to please Hugh on this day of violence. He'd seen and smelled too much of it since yesterday at Mendip Mor Castle.

Was it only yesterday he'd hauled Lady Ana out of that undercroft?

Hugh dismounted in front of the justiciar. Ana remained mounted with the Venetian merchant behind her. From the way she handled her reins, he guessed she prepared to flee at the first sign of continued violence.

"Sir Hugh Fitz Chênenoir!" Sir Arundel greeted him. "What brings you to our fair city?" The justiciar clasped Hugh tightly by the shoulders. They exchanged a ritual kiss of peace on the cheek.

Hugh withdrew first. He had never taken the time to get to know the pompous little man who sought to make himself appear bigger with ostentatious weapons and gaudy clothing.

After a brief and hushed conversation, Sir Arundel waved his bailiff forward. With a showy flash of his jeweled dagger, he slit the man's bonds and cast aside the rope scraps.

"A fine of three shillings on the bailiff for arresting this man without proper warrant," Sir Arundel announced to the crowd in hesitant English. His accent spoke more of Normandy than the land he presided over.

The insolent sneer dropped from the bailiff's face abruptly.

Before Hugh could smile in relief, Sir Arundel looked past Ana's shoulder to the drooping merchant. "As for you, Monsieur Lorenz Casale, I fine you ten shillings for disturbing the peace."

"But he did nothing!" Ana protested. She looked as if she'd draw a weapon on the man if she had one.

Hugh admired her vehemence while he recognized his own frustration at further delay.

"This matter is settled. Let each of the parties depart peacefully with no prejudice from the town or from the law." Sir Arundel turned his attention back to Hugh, slapping him on the back.

"This is no court of law. The fine is unjust," Hugh muttered before Ana could.

"But who is to say what is justice?" The glass merchant from Venice said, resigned. He shrugged his shoulders and grimaced. "I am a foreigner. I must take my chances with foreign laws. I can afford the fine. Best I pay it directly to Sir Arundel to keep his goodwill . . . and his business." He dismounted awkwardly, clutching his side as he did so.

"You will see that he gets medical attention?" Hugh demanded of the justiciar more than asked.

"Of course." Sir Arundel dismissed the issue with a flamboyant wave of his hand. "Dine with me, Sir Hugh. I have a set of fine glass goblets purchased from this merchant. He carries only the most excellent wares." Sir Arundel slapped the merchant on the back with the same enthusiasm as he had Hugh. "In King Richard's time none of us could afford such luxuries, what with paying for his Crusade and then his ransom from Leopold of Austria. I intend to enjoy King John's prosperity to the fullest."

Monsieur Casale stumbled forward, groaning and clutching his sides.

Regretfully, we must decline," Hugh said, steadying the merchant. "I have urgent business with the King. This matter has delayed us too long. Now make sure this man is cared for." He reached Orage in three long strides and prepared to mount.

"You may come with us, Monsieur Casale. King John's court is open to all," Ana called.

Hugh frowned at her but did not dispute her offer.

"I find the judgment fair and will not appeal, milady," the man said and bowed carefully, taking in both Sir Arundel and Ana in the gesture.

"Good. We don't need any more delays." Hugh dug his spurs into Orage's flanks. At least Ana was safe from the crowd.

But how many of those black-clad raiders had had a chance to don civilized clothes and make their way to the king with their own version of the raid.

Every convent and monastery we passed on the road out of town had silenced its bells and barred its doors to all but its own members. None offered weary travelers a refuge for the night as was previous custom. An offering to the poor of the parish was all the payment they would have asked in normal times. Inns charged considerably more.

Sir Hugh reluctantly paid out the coins the innkeepers required for a private room for the three of us. I noticed how his purse seemed markedly lighter than at the inn in Wells. I considered asking for a separate room for myself. But the flatness of Sir Hugh's purse gave me pause. I had nothing of my own to pay for the extravagance of an extra room except the prayer beads. I wasn't sufficiently desperate to sell the beads yet. Perhaps to pay for passage to France from the local port. If I could get away from Sir Hugh long enough to find a ship willing to take a lone female without luggage. Suddenly that prospect seemed less safe than staying with Sir Hugh a while longer.

How I would escape King John when we arrived in Worcester remained to be seen. I prayed often and long for delivery from mine enemies.

For now, I must stay with my protector/warden for good or ill. I slept upon the single narrow bed. Sir Hugh and Archie slept on the floor. Both men kept their weapons close to hand.

That second night in Gloucester, the scent of the sea tantalized me and kept me awake for a long time after Archie began to snore and Sir Hugh grumbled in his sleep. Every time I turned over on the straw pallet, the men half-woke and settled again.

Fearful of waking them, I crept from my uncomfortable bed. The shutters of the tiny window fitted loosely and opened at a touch. The fresh air opened my senses and my longings for home. The window faced northeast. I imagined I could see the familiar sprawling buildings of Kirkenwood Grange clustered around the central Hall. The stars seemed incredibly close on this clear night. If I could just reach up and grab hold of one, I could swing over to Kirkenwood and land safely in the courtyard and find my way back to my childhood room. Safety. Warmth. Belonging . . .

I glimpsed reflected starlight in a puddle in the courtyard. My senses swirled. No. Not now. I couldn't fall into a dream of portent. Not now.

The slovenly rented room dissolved around me. The blackness of night enfolded me, isolating me from my senses, my problems, my need to continually run to a new sanctuary. A man's arms replaced the darkness. I pressed my back into his chest, resting my head against his shoulder in absolute contentment. He cherished me. A tingle of excitement filled my veins. This embrace should be more intimate. Too many layers of clothing and restraint separated us. I wanted nothing more than for him to hold me close for eternity.

With that emotion of longing came an accompanying niggle of guilt. By giving myself to this man, I betrayed another, one who truly loved me.

Then my lover—or would-be lover—separated himself from me. "You know I love you, *ma coeur.* I would keep you by my side always, if I could. But I have no choice. You are a threat to me and mine. I must follow the wish of one who is wiser than I."

"Don't leave me!" I implored him, turning at last to look at him. His face remained in shadow. I saw a slender man of my own height. My heart recognized him as a kindred spirit even when my conscious mind did not.

The shadows between us deepened.

"My adviser insists this is the only safe thing to do. I will never forget you, *ma coeur.* Remember that." He held my prayer beads up for me to see. "I have this to remember you by."

"But . . ."

I knew a sense of falling. I thrashed, seeking a grip, a foothold, something to anchor my life and my soul. Then I landed with a spine-jarring jolt. Total blackness disrupted my sense of up and down, right and left.

"I will never forget you, *ma couer*," he said. This time a great distance and deep darkness separated us.

Then I heard the ominous clang of a metal door closing firmly.

"Let me out!" I screamed and clawed at the stone walls of my prison until my fingers bled. I jumped, trying to reach the door above me. I touched only air and fell back to the ground with a snap of ankle bones and acute pain.

He'd thrown me into an oubliette, a dark hole in the ground where I would be forgotten until I starved to death.

"You don't love me at all," I whispered into the darkness. "No one does. I am forgotten already."

I came back into my senses in the dingy inn outside of Gloucester. A dull ache hammered at my temples. I shivered with cold and hunger. My knees gave way as I sank to the floor, still clutching the windowsill.

"Ana?" Sir Hugh reared up on one elbow to stare at me in the moonlight. "Ana, what ails you?" He crawled over to me, wrapping me in his blanket. I sank into the warmth and protection only he offered me.

"A dream. Only a dream," I whispered. But it was more than that. A vision.

"Highness." Radburn bowed low to his half brother. The top of his head felt as if it might fall off as he dipped it. He'd run too fast after expending much of his energy reserves. He used the moment his face was turned to the floor to breathe deeply and regain his equilibrium.

Fantôme, his trusted shadow, mimicked his actions precisely. Radburn smiled slightly, acknowledging the boy's progress. Already he was an accepted part of the court—Radburn's new body servant, always there, soon to be ignored, and then invisible.

"What causes you to interrupt Our ablutions?" John asked from the depths of the bathtub. He carted the huge wooden device from castle to castle, unwilling to make do with the smaller standing tubs used by most folk. As if to emphasize the importance of his bath over any news Radburn might bring, John signaled his bathman to pour another ewer of hot water over him.

William, a wiry man with overdeveloped shoulder muscles from carrying endless buckets of water from well to kitchen to royal chambers, complied, expertly aiming the water upon the king's soapy chest without dampening his beard.

"Ah," John sighed.

"I have received news from a private courier, Highness." Just how private, Radburn would never tell his half brother. The church condemned magic of all kinds, but did not actively pursue practitioners. As long as one did not get caught, one could work with arcane powers with impunity. "Welsh raiders have burned Mendip Mor Castle to the ground. All of the inhabitants are dead."

"Jesus, protect their souls!" John crossed himself. "Do We still have to make the sign of the cross, Radburn?" John asked, staring at his narrow, nearly hairless chest.

"I don't know, Brother. The Edict of Interdict did not forbid private prayers, only public rituals presided over by ordained priests, except baptism and last rites." Radburn wanted to giggle. He certainly didn't miss the daily observances of Mass and confession—not that he ever confessed *everything.*

"Well, We must teach these rebellious Welshmen a lesson. Send out a call for mercenaries—No. Fetch me a cleric with parchment and quill. I'll send word to the barons that we require their knights' service. This should give them an opportunity to prove their loyalty to Us in this troubled time." John rose from his bath. William rushed to drape him in a thick towel, but not before Radburn noticed his brother's partial arousal. John's nickname of "Softsword" referred to his tactics, not his penis.

If only John invited male lovers as his older brother had, Radburn and his shadow could teach the king much about true physical joy and trust. But John's inherent distrust of his barons was an essential factor in Radburn's plans.

John did love to plan a campaign. Too bad he couldn't follow through with one.

But then, order and peace might follow in the wake of a successful campaign, an unnatural order. That might have occurred in France back in 1203, but Radburn had bribed Robert Fitz Walter to surrender prematurely to Philip II of France the castle of Vaudreuil in Normandy. Because of that one act, John lost the entire campaign. He refused to ransom Fitz Walter. Fitz Walter blamed John for his near bankruptcy after paying the inflated ransom. The two might never fully reconcile.

"Highness, the Cygony brothers as well as the de Chancells and de Martins clan are at court now. You know these mercenaries will punish the Welsh border princes much more efficiently than your barons."

"Yes, of course." John grinned greedily. "Have them waiting and ready. When the barons have assembled, I shall offer them the opportunity to return home if they pay scutage. Make certain the payments are high enough to pay Our mercenary friends and leave a little profit for the crown."

"There is one other matter, Highness . . ." Radburn put on an expression of meek petition.

"Yes, yes, I know I promised to help you look for your elusive bride . . ."

"Yes, Highness. My—ah—courier thought perhaps Lady Resmiranda of Kirkenwood was at Mendip Mor these past two months since Lord Henry Griffin's death and her disappearance from her home. But she was not counted among the dead. It is possible she was rescued by the men who fought off the raiders."

The scrying bowl had shown him Resmiranda's location just before the ambush on the road. Then he'd lost her again. He thought he'd located her once more. The images in the bowl were vague enough to lead him astray as they had many times over the past nine years.

"And who might these valiant rescuers belong to?" John arched his left eyebrow in question. Their father's gesture, only old Henry had been able to quell his enemies with that expression. John merely looked like an inquisitive ferret.

"Sir Hugh Fitz Chênenoir." Radburn did his best not to spit the name in disgust.

"Ah, Sir Hugh. Loyal almost to a fault. And honest—I do not believe the man capable of telling a lie. He'll leave the lass untainted. You need not fear on that account. Where is he now?

"On his way to you, Highness." Radburn bit his cheeks to keep from showing his glee. He'd have Lady Resmiranda in his bed and her estates and title in his hands before John could think twice about his gift and rescind it.

"We ride to meet them at Sext tomorrow. After the day's session in court." John dismissed Radburn with a brief gesture.

"Very good, Highness." Radburn bowed himself out. He bit his lip in frustration. He should have anticipated the dismissal and left before John finished speaking. He'd lost a moment of emotional advantage because looking into the scrying bowl had sapped his reserves.

Bedding the lady tomorrow night would restore him—especially if she fought him.

As soon as he closed the door to the king's private apartment, he whistled a jaunty—and bawdy—ballad he'd heard in a tavern last night. An, yes. The lady would be his. *His,* before John could exercise his *droit du seigneur.* He'd share the girl after his common law marriage was recognized. Not before.

Chapter 14

THE next night, our third on the road and the fourth since the burning of Mendip Mor, we found shelter with a knight of Sir Hugh's acquaintance, half a day's hard ride from Worcester. Sir Nigel Marchand and Lady Sigrid greeted us warily at sunset.

The dogs met Newynog with greater enthusiasm. Nose to tail, tail to nose, they sniffed and bristled, nipped and growled until a pecking order had been established. Newynog would always be a dominant female, but she didn't have to challenge an alpha male on his own turf. Was this why my ancestors always chose a bitch puppy for their special bond?

As Lady Sigrid led me to the bedchamber behind the hall for a much needed bath, I overheard Sir Nigel speaking:

"You are the king's man, no one has ever doubted that, nor ever will, Hugh, but I owe land rent and knight's service to the bishop." He looked at the war banner hanging on the paneled wall, at the rushes, at the dogs greeting Newynog, everywhere but at Sir Hugh.

I slowed my steps to hear more.

"How is this Interdict going to affect your oath of fealty?" Sir Hugh asked. "As a secular knight, your service to the bishop is subject to the bishop's secular landlord duties to the king."

"I don't know!" Sir Nigel exploded. "The news is too new. None of this has been sorted out yet. All I know is that a number of the bishops are threatening to leave England until the matter is settled—even Walter of Worcester, my own patron!"

"Once they leave, then all of their lands and rents revert to the king," Sir Hugh added dispassionately.

"That's a part of the issue that got us into this mess with the

Pope. Three candidates to replace the last Archbishop of Canterbury because the canons of Canterbury, John, and the Pope all claim the right to select the successor. None of us knows who has rights to what when it comes to the king and the church. It's all tradition. Tradition that either party can alter on a whim." Sir Nigel began pacing his Hall.

Lady Sigrid beckoned me into the bedchamber up two steps and behind the Hall. Servants awaited us with steaming ewers of water and a standing tub—big enough to catch the water I poured over myself as I stood in it, not large enough to sit down in. I followed her, a plan forming in my head.

"You are on good terms with your bishop?" I asked as I disrobed. I clasped the prayer beads inside my chainse tightly.

"Aye." Lady Sigrid smiled and nodded. "He is a most generous landlord. We've had him as guest many times."

"Can you send a message to him?"

"Oh, aye. He may have closed the cathedral and parish churches, but his palace is still open to us."

"Then look at this cross closely. Study it until you can describe it in the minutest detail and tell Bishop Walter that the owner needs his help." I thrust the golden Celtic cross and chain of beads beneath her nose, dismayed that my hand visibly shook.

"Lady Ana, surely Sir Hugh does not threaten you. Mighty warrior though he is, he has always been most gentle to women and children. Why he dotes on his stepson, sickly though the boy is. He was always gracious to Ardyth, his late lady wife, though she did not want the marriage after Lord Bellecôte, her first husband, died. She had an heir and claimed she did not need a new husband. But King John insisted."

"Sir Hugh is but a minor player in this issue. Another, more powerful man threatens me and mine. The bishop will know of what I speak. He must let me join his household in exile."

"If we send the cross to him, 'twill be more convincing than a description."

"If I send him the cross, I'll never get it back. I cannot allow that to happen. It is my only proof of who I am."

"And who might you be, Lady Ana?" Lady Sigrid looked up at me with wide eyes, so light a blue they were almost colorless. As colorless as her pale skin and limp hair that was halfway between brown and blonde. Her round figure carried evidence of large bones. Her French had a decided Saxon edge to it. "We know only that you are under Sir Hugh's protection."

"The cross tells all. Do you see these words on the back of the cross?" She nodded, but her eyes didn't focus on them. "This is an A and this an R. Make certain Bishop Walter knows those letters."

"A and R. Does this spell your name, Lady Ana?"

I wondered briefly if she could read and cipher at all.

"In part," I replied. Arthur Rex was as much a part of me as Great-uncle Henry and Aunt Lotta. But in today's political climate, an uneducated person could mistake my ancestor, Arthur Pendragon, for Arthur of Brittany, the nephew King Richard had named as the next king of England rather than his brother John. John and one of his favorites knew the truth of what had become of his young nephew. I knew, too. And I had read the record of the truth. I had hidden it in the cache along with all of the other family archives before I left Kirkenwood.

"Now please, I beg of you, send to the bishop. But for your safety do not tell anyone but your most trusted messenger." One hint of the Griffin name would summon more than the bishop. This small manor house, built in the sprawling Saxon style and barely fortified, would never withstand the kind of assault Mendip Mor Castle had endured before it fell to de Chancell's men and the one who had paid them.

Lady Sigrid nodded her agreement and moved silently down the back stairs.

I stepped into the tub and let the steaming water relax tired muscles for the first time in many days.

I think I dozed on the bed for a time. When I came to my senses, my stained and torn peasant bliaud had been replaced by a rich purple outer garment woven of soft wool and decorated with silver braid and a fine white linen shift embroidered with purple flowers at neck, wrist, and hem. Lady Sigrid probably hadn't worn these garments since before her first pregnancy and probably would never be slender enough to wear them again. I donned the borrowed clothing, grateful for their cleanliness as well as their warmth.

May might have come to England, but rain and wind made the evenings cool. This Saxon grange was much more comfortable than a stone castle, but little warmth penetrated to the plaster walls painted with sprigs of delicate wildflowers.

When we all met in the Hall later for a light supper, I raised my eyes in question to Lady Sigrid as we ritually washed our hands in lavender-scented water. She nodded briefly as she took a soft linen towel from a page. The message had been sent. Breathing a sigh of relief, I took my place to Sir Nigel's left. We would share a trencher as a symbol of good faith as well as hospitality. Sir Hugh sat in the place of honor, to Sir Nigel's right next to Lady Sigrid. He shared her trencher. He, too, had bathed and changed to clean clothing. His three-day stubble had also disappeared. His tawny brocade cotehardie suited him, bringing out the blond highlights in his dark brown hair.

Archie sat at one of the long trestle tables beneath the dais. He was surrounded by the guards and warriors of the household—men of similar rank to his own. Though freshly bathed, none of them had shaved and probably wouldn't until Sunday morning before mass.

Except we would celebrate no more masses in England under the Interdict. Would the men still shave on Sunday mornings? How else would the Interdict interrupt our daily routines?

Newynog heaved herself away from the warmth of the fire and the other dogs. She ambled over to me and plunked herself down at my feet, where she belonged. I settled in to enjoy the food and wait. Help was on the way.

Rain on the thatched roof lulled me into a sleepy state where I could hear and understand the conversation around me but didn't much care if I responded or not.

A commotion in the courtyard startled me out of my drowsy contemplation of another half loaf of bread.

"Who travels after dark in this weather?" Sir Nigel half stood, gesturing for his men to arm themselves and investigate.

Sir Hugh shoved his bench back, hand automatically reaching for his sword. He crossed behind Sir Nigel to stand at my side. Archie followed his lead and deserted his drinking companions to stand directly in front of my place at the head table. Newynog stood up, ears cocked, tail and ruff bristling.

My heart beat faster in appreciation of their vigilance. Still, I shrank back, trying to make myself invisible. Every instinct in my body screamed for me to run away as far and as fast as possible. Every effort to move failed. The catatonic paralysis ruled me once more.

The doors burst open. A slender, bearded man of middle height wearing a rich blue-and-silver brocade cotehardie with silver fox trim marched in. A silver circlet on his brow glinted in the rushlight. Courtiers fluttered around him, bowing deeply.

King John.

My heart raced in half recognition. I knew this man, and yet I had never met him before. We shared much in spirit.

I took a deep breath to calm myself, amazed I still had that much control. My gaze swept past the king and lingered on the tall man standing behind John's left shoulder, in the position where death lingered. He wore light blue tonight instead of white. His silvery blond hair shone like a beacon in the torchlight. I could not help but see his aura, though I usually had to strain to find one. A black shadow hovered around his head and extended to John. They looked as if a dark rain cloud hung above their heads while all else stood in the brighter light cast by rushlights and candles.

An old legend placed Satan's daughter in a prominent position on the Plantagene family tree. Clearly that evil residue inhabited both of these men.

A servant mimicked every movement of the man in blue with the black aura, as if his own shadow. And yet—that phantom moved half a heartbeat out of rhythm with the blond man. The shadow would never totally belong to its master.

I had met this blond man before. Part of me wanted to rush to him and relinquish all of my problems into his capable hands.

That sense of security rang false. A compulsion. Just as he had tried to compel me to trust him nine years ago when he invaded Kirkenwood.

But I couldn't move to obey him or myself. My muscles remained frozen, my hand stopped halfway to my open mouth with a bite of stewed greens on my eating knife.

Everyone else in the room rose from their chairs to show their respect with bows and curtsies.

"Lady Ana, get up and make your curtsy to the king," Sir Hugh whispered as he urged me to my feet with a hand under my elbow.

Even his direction didn't propel me.

"Highness, you honor us with your presence," Sir Nigel said hastily.

Lady Sigrid added her welcome. Her eyes flitted from the nearly empty cauldron of mutton stew on the serving table to the pages. She jerked her head toward the kitchen exit. A bevy of wide-eyed and frightened boys scuttled out.

The newcomer flicked a disapproving glance toward me and proceeded to the dais. But he made no comment on my inability or refusal to stand.

"Ah, Sir Nigel, We apologize for not sending word ahead that We would join you for the evening meal. We did not know our route would bring Us here until the last moment," King John said. He slapped his host on the back then sat in the host's chair beside me. Too close. Sir Nigel took Sir High's bench.

John ignored the servant hovering behind him with a washbasin and towel as he nibbled at the remnants of the meal and gestured to his own gaggle of retainers to dish up more of the stew from the depleted cauldron. My half loaf disappeared into the king's mouth in three bites. At least he had enough teeth to chew it adequately before swallowing.

"I was on my way to meet you, Your Highness," Sir Hugh said. He dropped his hand from his sword hilt. I sensed him relaxing his stance behind me.

Newynog whined in confusion, looking from me to Sir Hugh and then to the king.

"We were on our way to Wells to investigate the raid on Mendip Mor Castle when we encountered a messenger who said you rested here with a firsthand account," King John replied. " 'Tis good to see you again, Hugh. You've been hiding yourself at Castle Bellecôte too long." He gestured for Sir Hugh to sit at his left hand—on my bench—as if I were not present.

"Thank you, Highness. My . . . son requires much attention." He perched on the edge of my seat, crowding me but not displacing my rigid body. He became a welcome barrier between me and the king. Nothing could stop the penetrating glare of the blond man with the black aura.

I supposed my absolute stillness attracted attention.

"Your boy is still alive?" King John asked with a mouth full of bread and meat. His manners weren't much better than Sir Hugh's. He hadn't even washed his hands before eating. The dog learns from his master.

"Yes, Highness," Sir Hugh said. "Young John has almost completely recovered from his childhood illness. Though still frail, I look forward to his living a normal life." A grimace crossed both men's faces briefly. So briefly I couldn't be sure of the meaning.

"So, tell Us why you left Castle Bellecôte and your son to venture into the wilds of the Mendip Hills?" King John continued to eat as he spoke.

"My son is of an age to require fosterage to a worthy knight," Sir Hugh explained. "Lord Edmund would have treated him greatly until he fully recovers his strength," Sir Hugh replied.

"And so you arrived just in time to witness the attack on Our castle and rescue the fair lady." John ceased eating long enough to stare at me.

My neck refused to turn to allow me to answer his gaze with word or gesture. My hand was still poised, ready to serve my mouth the dripping greens.

Did I recognize my lover in my dream when my heart raced to match the rhythm of his? Was that truly a vision of betrayal and pain in an oubliette or just a dream brought on by my fears?

Sir Hugh looked at me with mingled concern and distress. "Yes, Lady Ana was the only survivor of the attack," he said still looking at me.

"Lady Ana? I thought you used another name, milady," the king said to me. "A name worthy of the most ancient noble family in our land."

Alarm almost gave me enough momentum to say something, to move, to blink.

Sir Hugh nudged me when I didn't respond. Newynog nipped at his boot in warning to let me be.

"Ana was the only name she gave me." Sir Hugh narrowed his eyes in speculation.

"Is she ill?" King John asked, turning more fully to stare at me.

"When we found her, she suffered a catatonia," Sir Hugh explained. "I thought she had overcome it."

"Enough to give you a false name."

"Or a diminutive of her full name."

"Whatever." John flipped his hand in a flamboyant gesture of dismissal. "She has much to account for." He resumed eating. His retinue sorted themselves out and fell to the hastily prepared meal Lady Sigrid ordered for them.

The man with the black aura at John's right remained silent, observing all. His shadow, in turn, never left him. The lord and his servant even dressed alike. Except for the silvery blond hair of the one who sat and the darker locks of the servant, they could have been twins.

"Your Highness, there is another matter that requires your immediate attention," Sir Hugh said. "Perhaps when you have finished your meal, I could have a private interview?" Sir Hugh perched nervously on the edge of my bench beside the king. He kept one hand on my arm, as if to keep me from bolting away.

I could barely blink. How did he expect me to run?

"You know something about the raid on Mendip Mor Castle," King John stated rather than asked. His eyes narrowed in speculation; eyes that saw too much and not enough at the same time.

"Yes, Highness. I have information that is—ah—sensitive."

"Sir Nigel, direct us to a place of privacy." The king's eyes didn't leave me.

"The chapel, Sire, no one will disturb you there," Sir Nigel offered.

"Perfect!" King John laughed. "We appreciate your sense of irony, Sir Nigel. It is my understanding even God can't disturb us in the chapel until the Interdict is lifted. We will remember your inventiveness when we formally take your oath of allegiance to regrant you tenure of these lands. Do you fancy adding that water meadow on the other side of the river to our demesne? Bishop Walter of Worcester no longer has need of it. He's packing to flee to the continent as we speak."

The king's retainers, led by the man at his right, laughed in response to his mirth. The others kept silent, biting their lips in apprehension. Some, at least, did not view the Interdict as a laughing matter.

"Come, Hugh. You shall have your interview now." King John rose.

The rest of the room hastened to stand until he left the room. The scraping of benches against the stone floor, despite the new layer of rushes, grated against my ears. Still I remained fixed in my seat, staring at the rapidly cooling lump of greens as if it were the crown jewels.

"Oh, and bring her, too," the king directed. "She's part and parcel of this situation."

"But, Sire, she can't move!" Lady Sigrid protested.

"Then Hugh will have to carry her." His words held the impact of an order.

John's right-hand man rose to assist Sir Hugh.

"Finish your meal, Radburn." John gestured the man and his shadow servant to remain in place.

"Forgive me, milady. I have to obey," Sir Hugh said as he bent to lift me into his arms.

I wanted to run away. I tried to kick. Nothing worked. Finally I let my mind scream: *Ask John how he knew of the destruction of Mendip Mor Castle before we told him. Which messenger could have reached him before us, other than one of the raiders? Their story will be false.*

Chapter 15

HUGH shook his head slightly to clear it. He hadn't really heard Ana whisper questions into his mind. He'd been hearing strange things ever since Mendip Mor. Welsh dieflyn—fire imps—faeries, the dog . . . What next?

Thinking too hard made him forget to walk straight. His thigh ached abominably, he limped in John's wake. A weakness he hated in himself, and he hated to show it in front of the abbreviated court. So abbreviated not even the queen accompanied King John.

He thought about slinging Ana over his shoulder like a sack of grain rather than listen to his imagination. As long as he didn't look into her eyes, he could convince himself he hadn't really heard her question King John's early knowledge of the raid. For the sake of propriety he carried her gently. He just didn't look into her eyes.

The simple chapel had been added onto the manor with entrances from the Hall and from the forecourt. Sir Nigel lit an oil lamp near the entrance and waved them in, then he drew the painted linen curtain across the doorway, giving the illusion of privacy. Perhaps ten or twelve people could stand comfortably in the nave at one time. The altar rail was wide enough to accommodate four kneelers. Two tiny stained glass windows up near the ceiling reflected the vigil light. The simple sanctuary was unadorned except for a polished pewter cross on the altar and a bowl filled with delicate wildflowers.

The shrouded body of Walter Geoffrey de Chancell lay on a bier before the altar within the rail.

Hugh set Ana on the single step separating the altar rail from the nave. She remained upright with her back resting against the rail. He had to push her hands back into her lap. She looked at him pleadingly. Her big, midnight blue eyes seemed to bore clear through to his heart. What did she want?

He ached for her. The old injury to his right thigh throbbed in sympathy, reminding him of the day he'd received the wound in battle. He'd lain on the battlefield, alone, helpless, in deep pain, for hours. His throat had ached with thirst. As his blood fed the earth, he'd grown weaker, drifting in and out of consciousness. Several times he was certain that God and Saint Maurice, the patron of soldiers, called him home. He hadn't the strength to fight for life. No mortal shared the vigil with him.

Then, just as he was ready to give his soul back to God, King Richard's medics had found him and carted him back to the hospital. Someone had washed the wound with wine and he'd screamed with the pain. But the treatment had saved the leg and his life.

He knew how helpless Ana must feel. No control. No ability to help herself. Dependent upon strangers for the simplest necessities and protection.

"I won't desert you, Ana. But you've got to try to help yourself. You did it once before," he whispered as he adjusted her hands into an attitude of prayer.

He thought he felt a slight flicker of pressure from her fingers pressing against his. But he wasn't certain, so he turned back to his king.

John paced the tiny chapel while Hugh related the details of his journey to Mendip Mor to negotiate terms of fosterage for his stepson. He told of seeing smoke before he spotted the castle. "The black-clad raiders melted into the shadows at first sight of us. We were left to deal with the fire, the dead, and the rescue of the sole survivor," he said in a rigid monotone. If he gave his words any inflection, all of his anger and grief for Lord Edmund and Lady Hilary and all of their household would come pouring out. He couldn't allow that. Not yet. He needed to be a soldier, reporting facts, not a friend in sorrow.

John nodded his acceptance of the details. He, too, had been a solider and knew the procedures for dealing with the aftermath of a siege.

Hugh launched into recounting the ambush in the hills as he, Archie, and Ana had ridden away from Mendip Mor Castle. "Walter Geoffrey de Chancel died in the fray. I slew him, not knowing his identity until afterward. From his armor and equipage, I must presume he and his men invaded Mendip Mor." Hugh ground his teeth against disclosure of just how he had won that little skirmish. The miracle of shattered weapons and fleeing raiders bothered his logic and his pride. He hadn't won the battle. The miracle had handed him survival only.

With that thought he finally asked himself the question that had been bothering him ever since. *If a lodestone had separated the raiders from their weapons and shattered them, then why did I still have my sword? It should have flown into the rocks as well.* Archie had retained his weapons as well.

"Walter Geoffrey de Chancell," King John said, almost spitting the name. "We have withdrawn our goodwill from his patron, de Briouze. De Chancell should have returned to his brother's mercenary ranks, or to me, as my liege man rather than risk our wrath. Obviously this raid was some form of revenge against me. De Briouze will pay for this as well as his other crimes against me." King John's composure slipped along with his use of the royal "we."

"What did de Briouze do to earn your displeasure, Sire?" Hugh asked rather than speculate on miracles.

"He owes us a great deal of money. We called in the loan to help pay for our newest campaign. De Briouze refused to pay even a part of the £10,000. He is not welcome at court until the loan is paid in full."

De Briouze had to have trespassed more than that. He'd owed the money for years. Suddenly Hugh realized that John liked having his barons in debt to him, that he controlled their loyalty more fully as long as they owed him. Hugh certainly owed John his wealth, his position, and the wardship of young John. The promise of a title of his own had died with Ardyth and their son.

Hugh swallowed. His throat worked as if a heavy lump impeded his speaking. He owed John a goodly sum of money as well as his loyalty. At least he had repaid part of the debt each year. Would he be safer borrowing the balance from the Jews to stay in John's good favor?

Not likely. The Jews could cripple him financially with their usurious rates. They could not repossess his land, only his chattels and leave him in need of larger and larger loans each year just to maintain Bellecôte. If he died in battle tomorrow, the debt would continue as Johnny's responsibility. He'd never see Bellecôte financially free.

Would the church still impose their curbs on Jewish usury during the Interdict? If not, he'd be much safer with the whims of King John.

"Where is my mother, King John?" Ana asked, startling them both. "Do you keep her alive as hostage or did you have her killed?"

Both men turned their attention back to her. Hugh's eyes opened wide in alarm at her impolite and incautious words. The king's eyes narrowed, glittering in the faint light of the oil lamp. Hugh couldn't read his emotions beneath the shadows.

"The lady has a voice after all?" King John asked Hugh instead of replying. "A voice with the sting of a viper."

"Nine years ago, your men invaded my family home and took my mother hostage in return for my Great-uncle's support of your claim to the throne. My uncle ordered us to flee to safety. We became separated. She went on to your court. I know not why. What happened to her?" Ana leveled her gaze on the king's face.

Hugh ground his teeth. She accused the king without regard for her own safety.

"Your mother came to me willingly rather than remain under your uncle's ungodly influence," John replied, returning her steadfast stare. They both ignored Hugh, locked in their private battle with the past. "She disappeared again after a few months at court. I presume she joined your father in Normandy. She is outlawed, of course, since she left the court and England without our permission. She did not bring the symbol of your family's importance with her."

Ana clutched at something in her pocket. Then she nonchalantly returned her hands to her lap, as if she hadn't truly betrayed the location of something important.

She kept the golden Celtic cross with its chain of gold-and-ivory prayer beads close about her at all times. Hugh would willingly bet possession of Orage that she checked on the safety of the beads. He'd almost be willing to bet his father's sword on that.

"The artifact was not hers to give," she replied calmly.

"Perhaps the symbol passed to you, milady. No one has seen it in all these nine years, not even after your uncle died and the castle reverted to us. We searched high and low for that cross and for you." John grabbed the cloth of her purple bliaud at the location of the hidden pocket.

She returned his gaze, steadily, courageously. Foolishly? Silence grew around them like a malevolent being. Hugh was reminded of the dragon portal in the cave barrow and was suddenly afraid of the girl and the green glow that had poured out of her.

"I claim trial of Mort d'Ancestre for the death of my Great-aunt Lotta and Lord Henry Griffin at the hands of your men," she glared at him.

"The old lady was breathing her last anyway, according to the reports of my men. You have no claim. We refuse the trial. Where is the cross, milady?"

"And the wrongful imprisonment and later murder of Lord Henry Griffin, Baron of Kirkenwood?"

"You are not Griffin's widow or daughter, you have no right to claim trial." John set his face in a stubborn grimace.

Griffin! Ana couldn't belong to that notorious clan. Rumors of magic had followed them for generations. He immediately thought of the dragon head on the portal in the cave barrow. A griffin was a form of a dragon. What association had she with that doorway? What treasure had her family hidden behind it?

"A Celtic cross of gold with ivory beads," Hugh said. He had to break the impasse of wills between these two. He owed John the truth. He owed Ana his protection. He could not protect her if she remained defiant of the king's will. "The golden decade beads are filigree. The cross is etched with ancient knot work. A very old relic."

"Is the cross inscribed with the words Arturo Rex on the back?" John asked, not lifting his gaze from Ana's face.

"I do not know," Hugh replied. He'd never learned to read. His father had granted him the right to train with other warriors but not any other form of education. Bastard sons did not deserve more.

John dipped his nimble fingers into Ana's pocket and drew out the long chain of beads. Ana tangled her fingers around the cross, retaining possession of the artifact.

"The messenger we intercepted was on his way to Bishop Walter in Worcester. He was to describe this cross and declare its owner here and in need of help. He said the inscription carried the initials 'A' and 'R'. Arturo Rex." John left the beads entwined around her hand as he examined the cross.

Hugh took one step forward, ready to protest the king's violation of her privacy. Caution overrode his first instinct.

"Did the messenger continue on his way?" Ana asked.

"Unfortunately, no. His knees gave out and we carried him back here on one of the packhorses." John smiled, showing his teeth in a feral grimace. His pointed beard almost quivered with his expression.

"You hamstrung him so that he couldn't carry his message to its intended destination," Ana accused. She yanked the cross away from John's avaricious grasp.

Shut up! Hugh wanted to shout at her. Didn't she know how dangerous John could be to his enemies? Hugh couldn't protect her once John got his hands on her.

He suddenly knew he needed to protect her, cherish her, keep her safe from the cruel fates—as he hadn't bothered keeping Ardyth safe.

He'd merely assumed she and their child would survive the hazards of childbirth. He'd assumed that Ardyth's son by her first marriage would succumb to his various illnesses.

He'd assumed that John would honor his promise of a title and estate for Hugh to pass to his children.

Ana reached up and touched his hand. His guilt and self-doubt faded before his need to protect her.

"Now, now, dear lady, you attribute us with far too much ingenuity," John said on a chuckle. "We assure you, the messenger is quite hale if a little groggy from a knock on the head. Out of common decency we returned him to his lord for safekeeping."

The messenger's fate told Hugh he'd best tread warily. King John Plantagenet held their lives in his anxious hands that still twitched as if in need to hold the prayer beads and cross once more.

Ana shivered. The chapel suddenly felt too cold and Hugh's skin grew too hot.

He shifted his weight restlessly until his thigh protested sharply. His mind began to spin with plans of escape, words of placation, anything to end the strain between his king and the young woman.

"Recent events have left me greatly fatigued, Sire. May I retire?" Ana asked as demurely as any of John's usual courtiers.

"Don't you wish to know the fate of your father and your mother, milady?" John stopped reaching for the cross and folded his hands before him. "I know Sir Brian de Griffin has not communicated with you since you disappeared into the night nine years ago."

"If you have that information to give, Sire," Ana replied. She appeared sweet and docile. But Hugh knew she planned something— like her attempted escape at the crossroad shrine. Like the green glow that surrounded her in front of the dragon portal.

"Sir Brian de Griffin was the second son of a second son," John recounted. "He had few if any hopes of inheriting anything but his family's good name. However, your family had extensive estates in France. When we . . . withdrew from France and our barons had to choose either us or our royal brother Philip of France as their overlord but not both, your father chose to pay homage to Philip for your family lands on the continent. The family estates here in England should have passed to a cousin or older brother, but alas they have all died."

John narrowed his eyes. His feral smile betrayed his involvement in some of those deaths.

Hugh shuddered with chill this time. Had he signed his own death warrant by involving himself with Ana?

"I am the last of my line," Ana sighed heavily. Then she seemed to shake herself out of her sad reverie. "You—withdrew—from France five years ago, Highness. I have spent most of the last year under my Great-uncle Henry's tutelage. Neither of us had official word from my father about those lands since news of King Richard's death nine years ago."

Hugh sought frantically through his memory of Richard's last days for Sir Brian de Griffin. He had a vague image of a tall man with Ana's golden blond hair. The man had hovered around the edges of Richard's general staff on that last siege. Respected but not truly part of the inner circle. Had Ana's father obeyed Richard's dying wish to aid the royal nephew Arthur of Brittany in gaining the throne of England?

If so, he might very well have shared Arthur's mysterious fate. Only King John and his boon companion, William de Briouze, knew for certain what had happened to Arthur and Brian de Griffin.

And now de Briouze was in disfavor and not likely to live long if John caught him in England.

"I am happy for my father's good fortune," Ana said. "I shall have to record that information in the family annals, as we record all of our history—official and private. Now I would like to retire if I may." She rose unsteadily to drop a polite curtsy to the king of England.

"Your family records everything?" King John blanched.

"Aye, Sire. Everything." Her expression remained sweet and her eyes open in a guise of innocence. She knew something about John that the king did not want made public. Hugh thought again of the dragon door. Was that where the Griffin family hid all of those dangerous records?

Hugh took two shaky steps forward to clasp her elbow, supporting her wobbly knees as best he could before they both collapsed under the strain of this interview. She swayed slightly, leaning her weight against his shoulder. He wanted to relish her touch, the closeness they shared. Instead, a battlefield wariness kept his senses alert to every shift in John's posture and expression.

"We will graciously share the warmth of our bed with you, milady." John traced her cheek with a surprisingly gentle finger. "We are certain Sir Hugh can spare you for one evening."

She remained unmoved by his touch. But Hugh saw the strain in her as she bit her cheeks.

"Something tells me, we are bound together by more than shared responsibilities for titles and lands," John said, barely above a whisper.

"She's a virgin, Sire!" Sir Hugh protested.

Ana and John both seemed startled by his harsh tone. King John had frequently exercised royal privilege with the wives of his courtiers, but never before the lady had borne a son and heir for her husband. Except for his very young queen, Isabelle, he'd not shown a preference for young, untouched women.

"Do you know her to be untouched for certain, Hugh?" John asked with a half smile that didn't reach his eyes. "She is well beyond the usual age of marriage."

"Unmarried at least. Young and sheltered by convents until recently," Hugh replied. He didn't quite have the courage to state he'd left her alone these past three nights. Not every man saw honorable behavior as anything but cowardice.

"I can defend my own honor, Sir Hugh," Ana interjected. "Thank you for the gracious offer, Highness. But I would be a poor companion this night." Without waiting for permission to leave the royal presence, she dipped a hasty curtsy, made a proper obeisance to the altar, and fled the chapel.

"Lady . . . Ana," King John called after her when she had opened the linen curtain to the hall and revealed several avid listeners. "Since the death of your great-uncle and guardian, you are a royal ward. Now that we have found you, we must make a place for you at court."

She stopped dead in her tracks.

Hugh swallowed back a thick lump in his throat, wondering which imp he'd offended that he'd gotten embroiled in this mess.

"Surely, Highness, you will appoint a suitable guardian for me." She looked to Hugh with imploring eyes.

He had no idea what he could do. Royal wards had their own protections as well as perils. He suddenly doubted his position at court was sufficient to claim her wardship—or her hand in marriage.

He hadn't realize how much he wanted her hand in marriage until the threat of losing her left a huge hole in his gut.

"No," John said. "We think we shall retain your wardship, Lady Resmiranda, until we allow your betrothed to claim you. You shall remain close by our side. You will sleep in our chamber tonight, if not in our bed. Your intended groom has the means to make our life miserable if we take you before he does. You will not escape us again." The king chuckled.

Chapter 16

I CONTINUED walking out of the chapel woodenly. A numbness crept up from my toes to my knees. If I didn't keep walking, the catatonia would possess my body again.

King John's black aura had faded and intensified during that hateful interview. I wondered briefly if the black One's control over him could be broken.

King John's parting words kept echoing through my mind. "You will not escape Us again."

Trouble, like death would hover over my left shoulder as long as I dealt with King John.

Ahead of me, the blond man with the black aura lounged on Lady Sigrid's bench at the high table. A satisfied smirk crossed his thin face.

Lady Sigrid touched my elbow almost as soon as I stepped through the curtain into the Hall.

"I heard," she whispered as she clamped a firm hand on my upper arm. "I'll set up a separate pallet near the fire for you. With that dog to guard you, you should sleep unmolested." She glanced back at the chapel anxiously.

"If necessary, I'll warm the king's bed," she continued. "God's wounds, most of the ladies of the court expect to be called by him. I've heard Lady Neville actually offered His Highness two hundred chickens for the privilege of sleeping with her own husband!"

One of the reasons I had thought to run to Eustace de Vesci of Northumberland was that King John had called Lady de Vesci to his bed frequently. Lord Eustace had taken his wife back to the remote fastness of his northern lands and never forgiven his liege lord.

"I heard the same tale about Lady Neville, but presumed it to be merely rumor spread by those who dislike His Highness' ways," I replied, not daring to remove my gaze from the blond man.

I knew a compulsion to run to him and throw myself on my knees before him and beg him for protection. Almost as soon as I thought it, I realized the falseness of his illusion of sanctuary. I had to protect myself. No one, not even the king's beloved half brother, could truly help me.

John had unknowingly given me two weapons. Knowledge that my mother had run to my father in Normandy. I had a place to run to if I could get to the continent. The king had also let me know that the location of the cache of family secrets was still secret, which insured that John would keep me alive until he had possession of those records. I had to make certain he never found the cache.

Newynog wandered away from me to sniff at the dogs by the fire. I called her to my heels with a hand signal. She came back in two long strides, ears and nose up. My hand found the long fur of her ruff almost by instinct. I tangled my fingers there as I had done during those long hours in the cellar beneath Mendip Mor. Instantly Newynog's tail shot straight out behind her, fully fluffed. She moved her nose in small circles tasting the air for signs of danger.

In a manor this small most of the household bedded down on pallets in the Hall. Only the lord and lady had the privacy of a separate chamber. On the rare occasion important guests honored the manor, Lady Sigrid would expect to give over the bed and the privacy to her guests. Sir Hugh and I weren't important enough for that privilege. King John was.

I settled into the cot Lady Sigrid prepared for me before the hearth in the bedchamber. I kept my chainse on rather than discarding it as was custom. One more layer of protection between me and the king, more symbolic than actual.

My mind spun with all the events of the past week. I needed quiet and prayer to sort them out, settle them into some kind of pattern I could deal with, one issue at a time. I craved sleep as much for the oblivion as the need to restore my mind and body. The more I tried to push away the turmoil, the faster it whirled. The muscles in my back and neck knotted.

Every creak and moan, rustle and clatter within the manor house made me jump or twitch. I listened more closely for the indications that King John retired for the evening. His retinue was much reduced by his haste and the impromptu nature of his visit. But dozens of servants and courtiers still dogged his every movement. His valet, Petit, would surely precede him into the chamber to place hot bricks in the bed for warmth and set out a washbasin, night lamp, and whatever else the king required as part of his nightly ritual.

The noise in the hall continued for hours. Drunken songs, shouting, and much male laughter.

I must have slept a little. When I awoke, I heard the snores of several men. A quick glance confirmed that the bed-curtains were closed around King John. Petit, the king's valet, Blakely, and a few other highly placed courtiers stretched out on pallets scattered about the room.

The Black One did not behave as an ordinary man. I did not want to trust him with my welfare. I had trusted no one since that night nine years ago when King John's men invaded Kirkenwood.

A man dressed in white with silver-blond hair . . . Blakely had led the invasion of Kirkenwood.

After several moments of watching me—and I knew he knew I watched him—he heaved himself over on his pallet, turning his back to me. I knew he did not sleep. He waited. For what?

Silently I gathered my clothing and slipped out into the Hall. No one followed me. I crept toward the kitchen, hoping to make a bed in the pantry. Did I dare steal a horse and ride posthaste to join Bishop Walter's household in exile?

A hard, callused hand pressed against my mouth. My heart stuttered and raced. I heard it pounding in my ears.

But Newynog didn't growl.

"What are you doing out here, milady?" Sir Hugh whispered into my ear from behind.

"Running away again, as I have spent my life running. I am so tired of this running, Hugh. But I do not know how I can stay here and be safe." I sighed heavily, leaning into his warmth and strength. Part of me wanted to cry, to trust him as I dared trust no one.

"Come with me," Sir Hugh said. His mouth lay next to my ear. With each quiet word his breath tickled my nape. Delicious shivers raced down my spine, replacing my fears.

Sir Hugh clasped my hand and tugged me toward the back doorway, the one that led to the kitchen building. Newynog followed without protest. So did I.

We circuited the many outbuildings that had become attached to the Hall. A chill, covered passageway led to the armory. Sir Hugh pushed the heavy wooden door open. It creaked on worn leather hinges. Inside the large room—almost as large as the Hall and bed-chamber combined—a dozen men and women stretched out on pallets snoring. Lady Sigrid must have sent the overflow of retainers here. A small oil lamp gave off a soft glow from a niche near the door. Pikes, lances, axes, swords, and suits of mail hung from pegs set into the stone walls. No plaster, tile or wainscoting blocked the drafts.

I shivered in the sudden draft.

"Don't be afraid. You're safe here," Sir Hugh whispered in my ear. His breath stirred the fine hair of my face, renewing the tremors snaking through my body.

"So, you finally recognize John's threat," I replied.

"Not John. It's Radburn Blakely I don't trust. He's been known to put a knife in a man's back with less provocation than you gave our king tonight. He claims he does it to protect John, but I've seen how he enjoys taking a life, almost seems to renew his strength from death and pain." His face took on a wooden look that I knew meant he hid painful memories.

"Tell me about him."

"Not now. We both need sleep. I've put a pallet against the inside wall for myself. You may sleep there, I'll prop up a wall beside you Then tomorrow we must talk. You must tell me everything if I am to protect you."

"We'll share the pallet, Hugh. As we have shared rooms and pallets these past three nights. You need your sleep."

He grunted his assent and led me to the right a few paces. Shuttered windows lined the room except on one short wall near the passageway. A little warmth penetrated that wall from the adjacent kitchen.

Sir William's home was only a grange, barely fortified, but he kept knights and trained them in defense of his home as part of the service he owed his liege lord.

But how did we defend ourselves from treachery within?

With knowledge, Uncle Henry had said. *Knowledge is the strongest weapon of all.*

Some of the knowledge I needed was secreted at Kirkenwood. Even if I could get home, King John, through Radburn Blakely, would watch my every move. I dared not access the cache lest I be observed and the secrets hidden there fall into the wrong hands.

I had another course of action if only I would use it. My enemies had already found me.

God forgive me, I do this for the safety of many—not to blaspheme You!

I waited. Gradually the restless shifting, snoring and small sounds of a dozen people sleeping settled into the deep rhythm normal for the hours between Matins and Lauds.

Sir Hugh was one of the last to drift off. I'd slept in the same room with him three times, yet never had I had the courage to watch him as the masks and armor of daily living fell away. He looked younger as he slept, more vulnerable, and decidedly handsome.

I squelched that thought. When I finished what I had to do, I would have no right to expect anything from him but contempt—and maybe fear.

After a brief period of light sleep, his eyelids fluttered as he viewed his dreams with closed eyes. He heaved himself over on his back with a heavy sigh, flinging his arms outward. His left first nearly connected with my jaw.

Then he dropped deeper, beyond the realm of dreams into true sleep.

I touched Newynog with a gentle hand. She awoke instantly, alert and ready to leap to my command. I needed nothing more from her than watchfulness. She dropped her head back onto her forepaws, eyes open, ears half-cocked.

We have not done this for many months, friend. Help us remember how to do it quickly. Guide us directly to the place in his mind where he hides the memory of Radburn Blakely.

With my right hand on Newynog's head, I lifted my left hand over Sir Hugh's face. I swallowed deeply as I gathered my courage. As Uncle Henry had taught me, I placed my forefinger in the center of Hugh's forehead, thumb on one temple, little finger on the other temple.

He stirred slightly under my gentle touch but did not awaken.

In full contact with my victim and my familiar, I took three deep breaths to steady and prepare myself. With the third breath I felt myself rising above my body. The shadowed room jumped into sharp focus. Impossibly bright colors haloed sleeping heads. I watched a moment as the auras fluctuated with dreams, sometimes flaring upward with emotion or darkening with fear.

Then, before my courage failed, I sent my astral self plunging into Hugh's mind.

A wall of memories struck me an almost physical blow. Always before I had retreated rather than violate a person's privacy. Uncle Henry, a willing partner in the exercise, was the only person I had been able to penetrate deeper than the surface.

I concentrated on sorting through the jumble of thoughts about Hugh's most recent experiences. I lived with him again the conversation with King John, the feel of my body in his arms as he carried me to the chapel, his distrust of Radburn Blakely's too pretty smile, his fierce sense of protectiveness and possessiveness toward me.

In his mind I saw myself as a beautiful and fragile woman who puzzled, intrigued, and attracted him more than even his late wife and her riches.

The knowledge that her wealth had been his motivation for marrying her and not love gave me a sense of satisfaction.

His overwhelming love for his wife's sickly son surprised me. Oh, to know that depth of love for anyone! From anyone! My own loneliness brought tears to my eyes.

That sense of caring deep within him almost sent me back into my own body and mind. How could I violate the trust of this honest, incredibly loyal man?

But Radburn Blakely haunted us both.

I plunged deeper, past memories of Hugh's wife, a cold and unemotional woman who had borne her first husband a single child after many years of marriage. Hugh had liked her intelligence and determination, but had never loved her. Guilt and inadequacy clouded most of his memories of her. We relived her belittling arguments against him time and time again. Then we plunged deeper to the night she had died bearing Hugh the son he craved. The child had outlived his mother by a few hours only.

Regret and bitterness flowed past me. I couldn't let it touch me. If I melted into empathy with him, I'd never ferret out the memory I sought.

Radburn Blakely, I whispered into his mind.

Images of the fair-haired man fractured and Hugh dragged up instead the memory of the day King Richard had knighted him for valor on the battlefield. Pride, joy, and validation filled him. He'd proved to one and all that he was worthy of the sword he carried, the only possession he truly owned.

I lived with him again the day he'd won the sword in a tournament from his half brother, their father's legitimate heir. His excitement, the smell of sweat and fear and dust rose up around us. Horses stamped and snorted. The crowd roared.

Hugh fought long and hard against Alain. Both gave and received many painful blows. Cursing and spitting blood and a tooth, the heir faltered. Six more blows and Hugh disarmed his opponent. Two more thrusts against a battered shield and he held his brother's life in his hands.

All he wanted was his father's sword.

Everything else Hugh now held in his possession belonged to his seven-year-old stepson John de Bellecôte.

Blakely, I pushed him to remember.

The king's pet assassin, Sir Hugh replied almost as if we carried on a conversation.

"Shall I kill young John for you?" I heard Radburn Blakely ask Hugh as he knelt in prayer for his newly dead wife. "With the boy dead, John will give you the title. For a consideration of course. My brother is always short of cash. . . ." Blakely licked his lips almost in sexual excitement.

Sir Hugh and I shuddered away from that memory.

I gulped and pressed deeper. Certainly the offer of murdering an innocent child was reason enough to fear Blakely. But Sir Hugh's memories were darker, more primeval. I had to push deeper to find them, know precisely who and what I must face.

You saw him murder someone in cold blood. Who? John de Bellecôte still lives.

Immediately his mind shifted to another scene. A memory he had buried deeply. I felt as if we smothered in uncarded wool as we reviewed snatches of conversations, hints, and suggestions.

I knew the sensation of tiptoeing down a long tunnel beneath a castle. Water seeped through cracks in moldy mortar, but I could not touch my element through Hugh's dream. We must be deep underground. Rushlight flickered ahead and behind. We stepped slowly around puddles and broken paving stones, careful to remain quiet and shrouded by shadows between the torches. The corridor curved left and sloped down. We lost the hint of light behind us. We hurried a few steps to keep our quarry within view.

After a long and twisting trek beneath a . . . a foreign city . . . the tunnel opened. We felt the passage of cold fresh air. A natural cave spread before us.

France, his memory told me.

Paris? I asked.

He did not reply, but I felt his affirmation.

The tunnel had been improved by Romans, but the cave was much older. Old cold, fear, and awe penetrated us both when we touched the stones of the wall.

The little rushlight dissipated to nothing in the vastness of the chamber we entered. We heard more water, rushing rather than dripping. A stream. A free-flowing river, primal, elemental. I longed to renew myself and my powers in it.

Ahead of us, Radburn snapped his fingers and more light flooded the cave. We shivered as we realized he held a ball of cold flame in the palm of his hand.

Like the caves beneath Kirkenwood, long white stalactites hung from the ceiling. Water dripped from their ends. Columns rose from the floor to meet some of the limestone growths. Blakely's light reflected off the white stone augmenting itself a hundred times.

With the added illumination, Blakely picked his way across a natural bridge arching across the underground stream. His steps took him up a series of steps, perhaps carved by men's hands long ago, perhaps eroded by the gradual change in water level.

On the thirteenth level above the stream lay a large slab of black stone—an alien altar in this white cave.

Atop the stone lay the inert form of a naked woman, arms and legs stretched outward and held in place by heavy shackles.

From our hiding place by the tunnel entrance we watched the woman's eyes flutter open. We smelled her fear. I clung to Hugh's memory lest I invade this image and share the woman's aching cold and terror.

Blakely ignored her. He reached behind the altar and retrieved a copper vessel. First he poured a thin stream of water along the woman from forehead to toe as he chanted strange words. I think the cadence fell into the pattern of a language from the Far East, but Hugh's memory didn't retain enough of the individual syllables to know for sure.

The woman gasped at the touch of the cold liquid. Goose bumps rose on her flesh.

Blakely repeated the dousing of the woman with wine and oil, all the while chanting strange words and moving his hands in arcane gestures. The blue/blackness I had seen hovering around his head and shoulders intensified. Sparks of red crackled within the dark aura.

The woman moaned and shook her head repeatedly, murmuring one word over and over. "No, no, no, no!"

The chill in me grew.

As the chant drew to a climax, Blakely stretched both hands flat above the woman's shaking body.

She screamed. The sound echoed and amplified, bouncing off the walls, spreading and engulfing.

Hugh in his memory covered his ears and closed his eyes to blank out the hideous scene. But he had to see, had to know who and what he dealt with. He opened his eyes and bit his tongue on an exclamation.

Flame shot from Blakely's fingertips. Fire, his element. Tamed Fire, a cleansing element like water. Wild Fire, an agent of chaos. Ten lines of fire found fuel in the wine and oil on the woman's body. The flames invaded her vagina and she arched and writhed, desperately trying to escape the pain. She screamed again and again, her cries echoing around the chamber.

Hugh and I cringed, afraid to rush out to help the woman. Deep-seated self-doubt kept us frozen in place. We beat at our temples, trying desperately to rush out, sword drawn, and murder the sorcerer.

We were too late. Killing Blakely would not save the woman. We had failed again to live up to our expectations of ourself.

Blakely smiled. The black aura grew. The red sparks lengthened into lightning bolts.

"Thank you, mistress whore. You have given me much power tonight," Blakely announced. Then he plunged a long vorpal-bladed athame—his ritual knife—into her heart, silencing her screams forever.

Chapter 17

I DROPPED out of Hugh's mind and back into my own with stomach-jarring abruptness. I swallowed my revulsion but couldn't stop the shaking in my arms. Cold sweat poured down my face and back, between my breasts and under my arms.

Hugh had not the talent to share death with the woman, so I did not have to. But the insanity, the senselessness of her death plagued me.

Hugh thrashed back and forth, moaning. His arms flailed about, fighting the memory.

"Wake up, Hugh," I whispered. I clung to his shoulders shaking him slightly. " 'Tis only a dream. Wake up, please."

His eyes flew open. He stilled his body as he searched the shadows with a minimum of movement. The sheen of his perspiration gleamed in the faint light from the oil lamp.

Sensing his need for physical contact, I left my hand on his shoulder.

"You've had a bad dream. A dream only," I whispered, soothing him with words as well as an extra push from my mind. The intimacy of our previous contact allowed me easy access to the vulnerable portions of his thoughts. "Sleep now. Sleep easy and dream free."

He heaved over onto his side, back turned to me. "I'll not sleep again. I've had this dream before," he muttered.

My mind hit a wall of resistance. I couldn't penetrate his thoughts to force him into restful sleep.

When I closed my eyes, the scene of torture and ritual murder played itself over and over in vivid detail. When I stared into the shadows of the armory I saw Blakely's aura and the crackling red demon faces hiding within it.

Withchild! The accusation of that night of invasion and death at Kirkenwood nine years ago rang again in my head. He had been my accuser then. Like seeking like.

I shuddered again.

Never. I had used magic of a sort. But I would never succumb to the temptation of following Blakely's example.

He had made a pact with Satan's dark forces, that much was obvious. What could he do with the magical power he gained from the pact?

I needed more information.

As much as I wanted to go home, hide myself in the healing peace at Kirkenwood, I needed to stay close to King John and observe his pet assassin. No, Blakely was Satan's pet, not John's. But did John allow Blakely to manipulate him? Did he know the forces Blakely tapped?

For England's sake, I prayed John had become another innocent victim of Radburn Blakely. He needed my help to separate himself from the dark aura that extended to him and threatened to smother whatever goodness and wisdom were left.

I would need control over my own powers to even hope to counteract Blakely's evil.

I shivered with a new chill. To defeat Blakely I would have to resort to magic, to condemn myself in God's eyes by using Satan's own methods.

The light guides me.
I work for the light.
I work with the light.
Darkness has no power over the light.
Let God's light shine through the ages.

I murmured Uncle Henry's litany for reassurance.

"Rest easy, Lady Ana Griffin. 'Twas my dream, not yours," Hugh murmured. "You have no need to fear the darkness. I won't let anyone throw you into an oubliette." He rolled onto his back. His hand crept across the pallet to touch mine.

I entwined my fingers with his. *Holy Mother! He read my dreams and innermost fears while I read his.*

We lay awake, for a long time, connected by our joined hands, his terrible memories, and my dream of portent.

With the clarity that follows a long sleepless night, I knew what I had to do. I must spend long hours alone practicing my magic, relearning skills Uncle Henry had tried to teach me but which I had resisted. Only with my magic intact and under full control could I ever hope to negate Radburn Blakely's evil influence upon King John and England.

My first step was to re-create Uncle Henry's morning ritual, without Uncle Henry's guiding hand.

At the first lightening in the sky, I crawled out of my bed. As silently as possible I rummaged through the tangle of blankets to find my bliaud, stockings, and shoes.

"What?" Hugh whispered, rising upon one elbow. He looked at me suspiciously through narrowed eyes.

"No one must find me here," I hissed back at him. I padded out of the armory with Newynog at my heels.

No one seemed to be stirring in the Hall. I tiptoed down two steps and through another short passage to the kitchen. Like all kitchens it smelled wonderfully of fresh bread, spices, and roasted meat. I inhaled deeply of the rich scents. My stomach growled in response, reminding me that I had eaten lightly the night before.

Newynog looked at me expectantly.

"Not yet, but soon," I reassured her. She followed me to the postern door, looking back toward the hearth as if to find her breakfast there.

"Who's there?" a querulous voice sounded from the pantry. Probably the cook getting ready to put the bread into the oven.

I closed the outside door quietly before he could shuffle out to investigate.

Predawn chill slithered into my bones the moment I stepped out of the kitchen hut. Instead of shivering and wrapping my arms around myself to ward off the cold, I opened myself, embracing the discomfort as the first herald of the new day.

Uncle Henry had greeted each dawn barefoot, bareheaded, and wearing only his underdrawers. I think he'd have gone nude except to appease my convent-reared sensibilities.

I wasn't about to shed my clothing out here in the open, but I stooped to remove my shoes and stockings. Barefoot, I ran lightly toward the herb garden behind the manor. The surrounding walls here were low, more ornamental than protective. Barely taller than I, they offered only a slight protection from the wind and concentrated some sunshine within the space. But they gave a semblance of privacy.

Magic grounded in the light relied on contact with the earth and a true balance among all the elements. I sank my toes into the rich loam of the vegetable plots, feeling it squish and mold to my feet; a comforting cradle of moisture. Instinctively, I shifted until my feet found a puddle left over from last night's rain. Gently I opened myself to the sensation of connection to the root crops growing within the dirt.

The paganism of my actions made me heavy with guilt.

"God created Adam from clay. Then he created Eve from Adam's rib. Humanity began within the earth and to the earth we return. Water nurtures the earth as it nurtures my soul. Air supports the light of God's love as it fills us with the fire of faith and hope. We are part of the whole. One with God." I created my own litany, blending the old ways with the faith I had relied upon all my life. I couldn't run back to the familiar comfort of the chapel yet. I had to complete this.

A bird chirped from the pear tree in the corner. I chirped back at it. The bird returned my call with a question. Warm joy spread from my smile down toward my heart.

I wiggled my toes again, seeking . . . I didn't know what I sought, only that Uncle Henry thought it important to greet the dawn every morning with joy and thanksgiving. I could do that. Every day God gave me was a gift to be treasured. With all of the uncertainty, peril, and confusion I had endured of late, this dawn was special. Filled with light to banish the darkness of bad dreams and memories. I lived for a while longer at least.

Gradually the light increased around me. I looked east and waited.

More birds joined the one in the pear tree, singing their morning ritual. I longed to lift my voice in song, one of the songs Uncle Henry used each morning. But he sang in Gaelic, the old language. I didn't know enough of it to be certain the words remained true to my faith. I had to fully believe in this ritual, this connection to God, the earth, and every living thing for it to help me.

A prayer Father Truman had taught me when I was very young to say each morning at Prime wiggled into my memory. I let the words flow quietly through me and out my mouth. A tune followed the words and swelled within me.

Blessed Mary, Holy Mother of God,
Give me strength to live this day
With love in my heart
With joy in my mind
With Praise on my lips.

Sweet Jesu, Son of God
Receive my thanks for another day.
Receive my prayers for another chance
To praise you in every deed.

Guiding Spirit most Holy,
Fill me with faith unshakable,
Show me the path of truth,
Let me not go astray
Along roads of darkness and peril to my soul.

Hollowed Father of all
Creator most wise,
Bless me this day that I may be a daughter true,
That I may walk in this world holding
Reverence for the earth,
Respect for your people,
Obedience to your Church

Just as I finished, the first ray of sunshine poked above the horizon. I stared at the red-gold shaft of light with new appreciation. It looked so close, so tangible I could almost touch it. I reached a hand toward the brightness and grasped empty air.

My lungs deflated. My joy fled.

The birds took flight.

"So, Lady Resmiranda, you too practice the old ways. I had hoped to make you an ally, to enlighten you to true power. It seems you already embrace the truth," Radburn Blakely said as he leaned indolently against the gate.

"Truth has many faces, is seen from many eyes. I embrace the truth as revealed to me by God." I faced him unflinching. The glory of the morning still filled me with resolution despite the black shadow that encircled his head.

"I have the time and patience as well as the authority to teach you differently, Lady Resmiranda."

"I recognize only the authority of the church."

"And of your king?" A chuckle filled with satire began deep in his chest and bubbled outward. He continued to lean against the gate.

That sense of safety I had felt so many years ago when he invaded Kirkenwood repulsed me now. The haven he offered reeked of evil and black sorcery. "King John is now my guardian. I must acknowledge his authority over me."

"Ah, so you will also accept the betrothal agreement signed by your late guardian, Lord Henry Griffin."

A chill began in my belly and threatened to freeze my muscles again. I fought it with a deep breath and flexing fingers.

"I did not know that agreement still existed. Uncle Henry died before any vows or bride gifts could be exchanged. As far as I know, no one has attempted to see it through."

"Oh, but vows were recited—yours by proxy before King John, mine by proxy before Henry Griffin—when the agreement was signed and witnessed by the church as well as the king's representative. The betrothal was the price he paid for his release from King John's prison. Did your great-uncle even tell you the name of your betrothed—your husband in all but ritual consummation?"

I shook my head, unable to say the words. My heart stuttered and began to pound furiously.

"Your uncle and your king arranged for you to marry me. The decree is signed. You are mine, Lady Resmiranda, you and all of the secrets hidden within Kirkenwood. We have only to consummate the relationship to complete the transaction.

Chapter 18

WHAT happened last night? Hugh shook his head. The images of his dream persisted, as vivid and tangible as if he lived them again. He could even smell the damp earth, burning sulfur, and the blood within the cave.

He thought he'd buried that memory so deeply even God couldn't find it.

Groggily he made his way into the courtyard and the corner well house. A few splashes of very cold water raised goose bumps on his arms and banished the memories from the realm of reality back to nebulous dream quality.

Ever since he'd confronted the burning ruin of Mendip Mor, he'd been seeing things, hearing things, now remembering things best left alone.

What was happening to him? None of this had anything to do with the practical business of everyday life.

The only difference in his life was Ana. Beautiful, vulnerable Ana, who needed protection and guidance, and probably a severe reminder of court etiquette.

Rumors surrounded the Griffin clan with witchcraft. Never anything truly sinister, like his memory of Radburn Blakely in the cave—he quickly banished those images—but things like their strange affinity with animals.

That dog, Newynog, seemed almost human. Ana communicated with it on a level more intimate than normal mistress and pet. And the high-strung gelding she'd commandeered outside of Wells. That beast had needed a tight rein and steady balance. Hugh didn't think she had the physical strength to manage the beast, but it obeyed her slightest whim easily. She'd even scratched Orage's ears without losing a hand.

His emotions as well as his sensibilities had been in upheaval ever since he carried her out of the fiery cellar. He had no doubt that Ana could manipulate him as easily as she did her dog. He cringed at the possibilities.

Enough dithering. He had never retreated from a fight before. He wouldn't start now. Blakely was the enemy, not Ana, not his Ana. He needed to talk with her, now before the crowded manor came to life and King John made demands upon them both.

A single female voice chanted a morning hymn in the garden. Who else but Ana would be up and singing at this hour. Though he thought her exhausted by the late night disruptions and restless dreaming.

He wended his way around the outbuildings and the dawn bustle toward the voice.

Dew caressed the spring flowers bursting from their buds. Sunlight glistened on the drops of moisture, bathing the walled square in misty rainbows and shimmering otherworldly colors.

Hugh paused at the gate, drinking in the sense of peace here. A few brightly colored insects flitted from flower stalk to tree branch.

Ana knelt in the exact center of a circle of silvery herb plants. Her purple gown spread around her like an uncut amethyst. Radburn Blakely stood before her. Gently the sorcerer cradled Ana's face in his hands and kissed her forehead.

The insects disappeared with an audible pop.

Heat and pressure shifted in Hugh's ears.

"How dare you?" He raised his fist to Blakely and charged forward.

"You question my attention to my betrothed?" Blakely raised one blond eyebrow in amused query.

"Betrothed? Ana, you never said anything about a betrothal. . . ."

"You never asked."

What else could I say? I was trapped. Trapped by promises made by men who thought only of their own political gain and nothing of my welfare. Marriage to Radburn Blakely?

How could Uncle Henry have agreed to such a match? He must have known that the king's half brother was the Back One of legend. He must have known!

Or did he? Blakely had said the vows were said by proxy. Perhaps he had never met Radburn Blakely to know him for the man who had invaded Kirkenwood all those years ago.

I clung to that possibility rather than dwell on the thought that Uncle Henry had deliberately bound me to this evil man.

My betrothal in return for his release form prison. Why had Blakely and King John waited eight years for the agreement. Young girls were often betrothed shortly after birth. They need not have waited for me to grow to marriageable age and beyond.

Why did they wait?

Because I had eluded their pursuit. Time and again I had fled from one convent to another, mere steps ahead of my black-clad pursuers. Blakely had sought another way to gain possession of me and Kirkenwood. He needed my cooperation to find the cache of secrets.

I could not allow him to take possession of me or my secrets. I had to defeat him with magic or not at all.

How? Uncle Henry had barely had time to train me before he sent me fleeing once more. Had he discovered the truth about my betrothed?

I could learn magic from Blakely, glean all of his secrets from his mind, ferret out his weakness and then destroy him with his own weapons.

No. That would mean feigning belief in the rightness of his methods. I was not certain I could do that. I knew I would never willingly participate in his rituals of death and humiliation, of torture and depravity.

But to counter him, I needed knowledge. I had to get to Kirkenwood. Soon.

"I'm sorry, Hugh. The betrothal was made years ago, without my knowledge or approval. I only just now learned the name of my groom." Shakily, I stood up. Blakely offered me his hand. I ignored it, keeping my eyes on Sir Hugh, putting all of my bleak emotions into my eyes.

Please understand. Please accept this role of complacence I must play, I pleaded with him with every bit of magical gift in me.

His mind remained closed to me.

Suddenly I missed the incredible intimacy of those quiet moments in the dark as we held hands and fought his nightmare memories and my dreams of portent together.

"With an Interdict in place and King John not likely to compromise with Rome, you must wait for both the marriage and consummation." Hugh's voice sounded absolutely flat. He turned on his heel to exit the garden.

He didn't retreat.

He exited.

"We English do have the ancient and honorable custom of a common law marriage," Blakely countered.

I detected a hint of defensiveness in his tone. He needed this marriage now. Why?

"Doubtless many couples will follow that custom if King John and the Pope Innocent III do not compromise soon," I said. *Trust me, Hugh,* I pleaded with my mind. *I do not go into this union willingly.*

Hugh stopped abruptly, as if he'd heard me. He turned back to face Blakely. The two men continued to glare at each other with the kind of assessment I attributed to warriors preparing for battle.

"But among nobles, when titles and lands and fealty are in question, I doubt the barony, or the king will uphold such a union," I continued.

A measure of hope brightened Hugh's closed expression. Blakely's eyes narrowed.

I wished I dared probe his thoughts. I'd never manage it without his knowledge.

"Then we will merely gain King John's permission to cross the border into Scotland," Blakely announced. He shifted his shoulders as if the matter were settled.

To get to Scotland we would have to travel close to Kirkenwood. Surely I could divert my path to my home. Once there I'd have access to the knowledge I needed.

I'd have allies, and if necessary, places to hide.

"We will hold court this morning," King John said as Blakely, Sir Hugh, and I entered the Hall. He lolled in the large chair in the center of the dais, the only true chair in the household. His rich cotehardie looked crisp and clean. The silver circlet on his brow glinted in the morning sunlight streaming through the high windows. His eyes shone with vigor and enthusiasm.

"Your Highness," Sir Nigel bowed low before the king, biting his lip. "We have no cases pending. All disputes go to the bishop. I hold these lands in fief to him." The lord of the manor looked weary and slightly rumpled in comparison to his king. He and Lady Sigrid must have worked long into the night to accommodate the royal entourage.

"The bishop holds the honors of this land no longer!" King John bellowed. He leaped to his feet, dropping the scroll that had rested in his lap. The parchment bounced down the one step and rolled to my feet. I picked it up and held it idly at my side.

"You will make your obeisance to me. Now. This moment." John's face blotched red. Spittle foamed at the corner of his mouth. The blackness of his aura deepened.

Beside me, Radburn Blakely barely contained his laughter. His shoulders shook and his mouth worked to contain his mirth.

Hugh glared at him with disdain.

"Your reaction is inappropriate," he said quietly from between clenched teeth.

"Oh, but it is appropriate," Radburn whispered. "My brother is showing his temper. One of these days it will get the better of him. You'll see. And when it does, we—you, me, all the rest of the barons— will be rid of him for once and all."

Hugh stepped back, gasping his surprise.

Sir Nigel looked about him in indecision. I don't think he'd heard the quiet conversation by the door. "My oath, Highness . . . ?" he asked, bewildered.

"We have recovered these honors from the bishop. Your oath to us, now, this moment, or forfeit everything!" John rested his hand on his hip where a sword might reside if he strode the field of battle instead of paced the dais of a small manor. He looked angry enough to execute Sir Nigel on the spot.

I remembered the rippled and twisted athame Radburn Blakely had used to murder a nameless woman in a cave many years before. Did he still carry it, still use it on John's behalf? Or did he save it only for ritual slaughter?

The lord of the manor sank to his knees before King John, holding up his hands.

"I wish we had a priest here to interpret the ramifications of this Interdict," I whispered, as much to myself as anyone. The scroll I had retrieved for John almost burned my fingers. I itched to read it.

"You'll never get a straight answer from any priest. I spent ten years training to be one of them. Circuitous rhetoric is their favorite topic," Radburn said. Chuckles still sparkled in his voice.

If I didn't know the evil he was capable of, I might think him handsome and charming. But the black shadow surrounding him marred my perceptions. Only then did I notice that his other shadow, his servant, was missing.

Frantically I searched the gathering crowd for the nearly invisible man. He wasn't here. Cautiously I reeled out my other senses, the ones I hoped to fully waken and hone, and sought Blakely's servant.

Nothing. He seemed to have vanished. I nearly panicked, not knowing why the man's presence was important.

"Gather 'round, all of you," King John called loudly. He smiled brightly, his humor restored.

His chaotic mood shifts frightened me almost as much as his anger. Anger to bonhomie. Cold and calculating ruthlessness to blind destruction. What next? How quickly?

"All of you shall witness Sir Nigel's oath of fealty and rejoice that he has joined our company," John shouted.

Courtiers, and servants arranged themselves in a semicircle below the dais. Blakely dragged Hugh and me forward to stand slightly behind the king. Lady Sigrid knelt beside her husband.

John folded his hands over Sir Nigel's.

"By the Lord before whom this sanctuary is holy," Sir Nigel looked around as he recited the ritual words, momentarily at a loss because we did not observe this ceremony in the chapel, where we should. Then he sighed and continued, "I will to John be true and faithful, and love all which he loves and shun all which he shuns, according to the laws of God and the order of the world. Nor will I ever with will or action, through word or deed, do anything which is unpleasing to him, on condition that he will hold to me as I shall deserve it, and that he will perform everything as it was in our agreement when I submitted myself to him and chose his will," Sir Nigel recited in a clear voice the ancient oath, beloved of barons in this land for centuries before the Normans came.

John replied less distinctly. I heard only that he promised to give aid to Sir Nigel, protect his widow and heirs should he die, and honor Sir Nigel's rights as baron and landlord.

Hugh breathed a sigh of relief. Tension left my chest along with a long exhalation of air.

"Now what?" I whispered.

"Now we inform my brother of our intent to wed posthaste." Radburn grabbed my hand and pulled me forward.

Hugh followed closely upon my heels. I sensed him fidgeting with his dagger.

"Not now," I hissed to him, staring at the weapon on his hip.

"But . . ."

"I'll think of something!"

"Think fast." Hugh paused a moment. "Where's Newynog?"

I searched for her, knowing that from the moment of her birth she and I would never be truly separated.

"Running," I replied. For an instant we shared the wild freedom, the tongue-lolling joy of dashing across open fields in pursuit. Something tasted dark on the tip of our tongue. The phantom servant of Radburn Blakely. He rode away from the manor, pelting toward his goal. A mission drove him.

Suspicion sent me back into my single body and mind. Blakely had sent his servant on a mission. *Stay with him, Newynog. We need to know.*

"Sire, I have found my bride. I would marry her today," Blakely stated without preface.

John smiled, showing his teeth. His pupils grew wide and his beard twitched around his mouth. Something about his half brother's statement gave him joy.

"We are under Interdict," Hugh reminded us all. "There can be no marriage."

My heart swelled a little that he would continue to fight for me. He kept his promises.

"With your permission, Highness, I would take my bride to Scotland and marry her there. 'Tis my right. You promised me this marriage." Blakely persisted with his arguments.

King John searched the floor. A puzzled frown crossed his face. The scroll weighed heavily in my sleeve. I retrieved it and offered it to the king.

He smiled at me. For the first time I felt the warmth of his genuine pleasure. No plots. No deceptions. A glimmer of his true self, intelligent, charming, humor lightening his visage and his aura.

I had a chance to break Blakely's control of him. A small chance if I could return home long enough to retrain myself.

Then the moment disappeared and my heart returned to its normal state of anxiety.

He unrolled the scroll.

"Unfortunately, Brother, we were in error in our promise." That feral smile opened his mouth and showed his teeth. He still had most of them.

"What do you mean?" Blakely's eyes narrowed. I felt his body grow chill beside me. The blackness in his aura that I could never totally ignore reached out to engulf both me and the king.

"When first you broached this matter to us in Worcester, we sent for this decree from the Chancery. It arrived not ten minutes ago." John paused to read the lengthy missive. "Quite handy having all of our records in one building in London with a staff to search out what we need," he added idly.

Tension among those of us on the dais thickened. Hugh edged closer to me. Blakely's fingers hovered around his belt scrip—not his dagger. He must keep his magical equipment there, and he instinctively trusted his magic more than his mundane weapons. I saw no evidence of the vorpal blade he had used in his murder rituals. He must reserve that as an athame.

I crept closer to Hugh, despite Blakely's crushing grip on my wrist. The heat of Hugh's body welcomed me. He would keep me safe, not this black sorcerer.

"What does this antique scroll have to do with a lawful betrothal signed by you and the girl's guardian?" Blakely asked.

"Our esteemed great grandfather, Henry I, bestowed upon the then Baron of Kirkenwood the right of succession to his honors. In this decree he made Kirkenwood independent of the monarchy. The honor was confirmed by our father, Henry II, and our brother Richard." John allowed the scroll to roll closed with a snap.

"That has nothing to do with my betrothal!" Blakely's voice rose in pitch and volume. The tips of his silver-blond hair quivered as his neck trembled in agitation. His grip on me tightened. I yelped, but no one paid me any attention. All eyes remained fixed upon the king.

"It has everything to do with your betrothal," John replied. "Because Lady Resmiranda is now the fully independent Baroness of Kirkenwood. She has the right to decide her own future—with our permission, of course."

Chapter 19

"YOU promised!" Rage flared through Radburn Blakely. Rage at his unfaithful brother. "You have never broken a promise to me."

John's aura flared orange, bursting through the black layer that encased him.

" 'Tis the law." John shrugged his shoulders. "Of course, we may withhold permission for Lady Resmiranda to marry any man but you. We shall see." His smile did not reach his eyes.

"Or you might give her to another! Sir Hugh, for example."

"Not yet. We think we will allow the lady a chance to enjoy her freedom for a time."

Radburn fought for control of his emotions. He needed rationality. Now, before he unleashed a spell that would strike his brother down and ensure his own doom.

The court suspected him of witchcraft and accepted it as long as they saw no overt evidence of his dabbling in otherworldly powers. Besides that, Sir Hugh Fitz Chênenoir commanded the respect of enough of these warriors to subdue him and burn him at the stake without benefit of trial. That might solve Britain's problems with the church, but it would not serve Radburn at all. He needed to live to control John's infant son upon John's death.

He needed to sow more seeds of chaos before John dissolved into a grain-counting perfectionist. He'd have to reestablish the wards again. This time he'd make them unbreakable.

Radburn clenched and released his fists again and again, letting his fingernails gouge his palm until he drew blood. The pain centered his energies. He settled his shoulders and faced his brother squarely.

"We have an investiture to celebrate," John rubbed his hands together gleefully. "We shall proceed to Kirkenwood by way of Durham. Only fitting that the new baroness should host the court for the ceremony."

Radburn sensed the girl flinching at the cost of hosting the court. Then he saw Fitz Chênenoir reaching to squeeze her hand. Jealousy flared almost as hot as his previous rage. He had no doubt that given a choice, the lady would take Sir Hugh to her bed.

"Kirkenwood is mine!" Radburn whispered to himself. "Kirkenwood and all of its arcane secretes—and its lady." Then he smiled. John planned to lead them all to Kirkenwood, dangerously close to the Scottish border. Easy enough to kidnap the girl across the border and force the marriage. Presented with a *fait accompli,* John would have to bless the union.

"The road to Durham passes Bellecôte. We shall rest there and visit with our namesake, young John," the king continued. "You say, Sir Hugh, that your stepson is healthy enough for fosterage. We will consider taking the boy into our household."

Sir Hugh bowed low, accepting the king's decision without question or protest.

Radburn couldn't help smiling. A great surprise awaited them all at Bellecôte.

Resmiranda shook her head and closed her eyes. Then her mental voice blasted his inner ear with urgency. *Newynog! Stop him, stop the shadowy servant.*

Merde, Radburn cursed. His anticipation of watching his rival's castle and stepson burn to the ground must have alerted the girl. She possessed great power to read him so well without his awareness. But she had little or no training if she could not keep her commands to her familiar private.

Very well. He knew her talents and her greatest weakness now. So much easier to guide and corrupt her when he knew what he was dealing with.

She needed to learn to depend upon him as she did her familiar. The blasted wolfhound would not survive the day.

Newynog! I continued to call my familiar. My seeking lost focus and wandered without a recipient. My last image had been of thick underbrush offering her a cool resting place while her prey watered his horse at a free-flowing creek.

My rapport with her ended abruptly. The emptiness in my belly nearly doubled me over.

Newynog! Why didn't she respond?

"Are you ill, Lady?" Blakely cradled my elbow solicitously. His fingertips burned through the thick layers of clothing to my sensitized skin.

Hugh took my other arm. The tension between the two men threatened to tear me apart. I almost welcomed the pain to replace the emptiness of losing Newynog.

The images of flame and smoke engulfing an unknown castle haunted me. Where?

Had the shadowy servant discovered my wolfhound and hurt her? *Newynog, where are you?*

Logic forced me to believe Radburn chose to strike someplace that would inflict a lot of damage upon King John. Which castle and what had his servant done to my dog?

"The court will join us on the road," King John said. "Since Sir Nigel had no disputes pending for us to judge, We will be on our way as soon as we break our fast. We trust, Lady Resmiranda, you have suitable mounts and need not ride with the baggage?"

"She will ride pillion with me," Blakely asserted.

"Sir Hugh hired a mount for me. I am perfectly capable of riding on my own." Though I'd borrow a pair of braies and chausses to cover my legs while I rode astride. No sense in providing a view to entice Blakely further.

I also needed the freedom to leave the road in search of my familiar.

The gathered retainers and courtiers dispersed to make journey preparations. Others servants brought bread and ale and meat to break our fast. Thankfully, Blakely followed King John into the bedchamber.

I remained on the dais, still seeking Newynog with my mind.

"What is the matter, Ana?" Hugh hissed at me, still clasping my elbow.

"Something has happened to Newynog," I whispered back. "She was chasing Blakely's servant. Then my contact with her vanished." I trusted Hugh with the knowledge that my rapport with the dog went beyond normal bounds. I no longer cared if he knew me for a witch.

I cared, but I trusted him to accept my gift.

"Blakely doesn't have a servant," Hugh stated.

"Yes, he does. A man who mimics his steps so precisely he seems no more than a shadow. A man so ordinary he becomes invisible among the bevy of other servants. Now he is gone and there are images of flames and destruction in Blakely's mind."

Hugh drew in a sharp breath through his teeth.

"We must talk, Lady Ana."

"In private," I replied.

"Very private. We'll be at Bellecôte tonight. I know a place where even Blakely won't be able to find us."

"I have to find Newynog."

Hugh raised his hand and signaled Archie over to us. In a few terse words he sent his sergeant at arms running out of the Hall. "If anyone asks, he rides ahead to alert Bellecôte of our coming. On the way, he will keep alert for signs of your dog."

"Thank you, but I'd rather search myself." His hand drifted from my elbow down to my hand. Our fingers entwined again, as they had last night in those dark hours after a nightmare.

The moment of sharing stretched and grew. We looked at each other, silently acknowledging that we belonged together. We trusted each other.

"You must draw no more attention to yourself than necessary," Hugh said quietly, never taking his eyes off me. "Blakely and John look for reasons to bring you down."

"I am the last of my line." As was Newynog. The implications suddenly dawned on me. "If I die without heirs or naming a successor, Kirkenwood reverts to royal control along with all of the records my family has kept since Arthur Pendragon ruled all of Britain." I let Hugh draw his own conclusions about the damaging information my great-uncle and my father had written into those records.

Like me, Newynog had to live long enough to whelp her successor to help my heir. We Griffins always worked in pairs.

"John cannot take a chance anyone will find those records. As long as they remain hidden, I am safe." If John did ransack Kirkenwood and found the secret room within the foundations of the curtain wall, neither I nor any child or heir of mine would long survive me.

Through the long exhausting day on horseback, Hugh kept careful watch over Ana, Blakely, and the king. He saw how courtiers moved forward and back in the line of procession. He noted who John allowed to linger and who he dismissed quickly. Blakely was the only one he allowed to ride to his right in the trusted position of adviser. That place used to belong to William, Earl Marshall. But that formidable knight had retreated to his estates in Ireland rather than forsake his oath of fealty to Philip of France for estates he held there.

All of the barons who held lands under both kings had been required to relinquish one or the other. Some traded holdings with lords who wished to serve the other king. Others sent younger sons to claim lands and titles in the other country. The Marshall had built his reputation and his fortune on the strength of his word. He refused to break it now even under threat of royal displeasure.

Hugh had tried to follow the Marshall's example, but at the age of thirty he owned nothing but his sword. If Bellecôte earned a little profit after tithes to the king and church, repayment of death relief and repairing neglected lands and castles, he gleaned a few coins for himself. Nothing more.

For the first time in nine years of service, Hugh questioned if John was as truly loyal to him as Hugh was to his king.

He shook away that thought. Ana had planted the seeds of discord in his mind. Her boldness worried Hugh. Didn't she know the danger she courted?

She must if she controlled the kinds of power she had hinted at.

She searched for the dog even now, sniffing the air first this way and then that, as if she shared the animal's senses. Hugh had seen nothing of Archie or dog on this long trek to Bellecôte.

Then Ana reined in her gelding. The animal shied at the bit, prancing in place. She placed her left hand on the horse's neck, whispering softly to it. It calmed immediately and stepped onto the verge so the rest of the procession could pass.

Hugh worked his way over to her. "What are you doing?" he asked quietly.

"Newynog left the road here," she said, equally quietly. She dismounted and lifted the horse's offside foreleg, inspecting the hoof.

"You can't leave the royal entourage in search of a dog. Look, even now Blakely misses you and alerts John to your absence." Hugh's own horse shifted his hooves restlessly, not liking being left behind. Hugh had had a hard time keeping the beast in line when they both wanted to charge forward and lead the procession.

"I think we've picked up a stone," Ana said loud enough for the passing knights and their ladies to hear.

Hugh jumped down to join her. He dug a pick out of his scrip and began clearing debris from the frog of the hoof. He inspected the now clean hoof and shoe for any sign of cracks or bits of gravel.

"That hoof appears sound." He prodded the frog seeking signs of tenderness. "Can't tell if it's bruised or not."

"Do you need assistance, Lady Resmiranda?" Blakely rode back from the head of the procession. He remained mounted, looking down upon Hugh as if examining an ant he wished to squash.

"We have the situation well in hand, milord," Ana answered with a bright smile.

"Climb up behind me, milady. The horse needs to rest until the swelling eases," Blakely commanded.

"I will walk the horse for a time. The procession moves no faster than a walk. I won't lag behind," she said, drawing herself up to her most regal pose. Somehow, standing on the ground twisting her neck up to the tall man ahorse, her authoritative bearing gave the impression of looking down her nose at an inferior being.

Hugh wanted to laugh at the look of consternation on Blakely's face.

"You!" Blakely pointed at a minor knight behind them. "Give the lady your horse." The retainer eased his mount over to them and dismounted with easy grace. He cupped his hands to assist Lady Ana in mounting his own placid palfrey.

Blakely hopped down and shouldered the man aside. He offered Ana his own assistance.

Hugh suddenly felt inadequate next to Blakely's elegance and regal bearing. His right thigh began to throb from the old wound.

"Go with him," Hugh whispered. "I will seek your bloody hound."

"But . . ."

"I don't believe in witches and familiars, but I know you cherish

Newynog. I'll find her and catch up to you." He pushed her back toward the waiting horse.

Ana bit her lip in indecision.

"Don't antagonize him or the king," Hugh ordered.

She mounted easily without the gallant help of either the knight or Blakely. With a conspiratorial wink, she eased back into the line of march.

Hugh turned his attention to his task. A narrow game trail wound off through the underbrush into a stand of trees. In the distance he heard a creek cascade over a small tumble of rocks. He knew the place. Years ago he had brought Ardyth here, when their marriage was new and he still wooed her affection. He had won her acceptance in bed but not in daily life. They had never met before the day the Bishop of Bath had presided at their wedding. All had been arranged by King John.

Hugh took no pains to trod quietly through the tangle of new greenery. He thrashed at bracken and vines with a vengeance, wishing the stems were Blakely's neck and this a battlefield.

Gradually, the sounds of King John's entourage marching through the countryside faded into the distance. The rush of the creek grew louder. He stopped a moment and breathed deeply. No sense in letting his anger and jealousy get the better of his good sense. He still held King John's trust. He still had the profitable wardship of his stepson. He could still prevent Blakely from marrying Ana so that he . . .

Did he really wish to complicate his life with Lady Resmiranda Griffin?

Before he could decide if the lady's lands and honors were worth the battle with Blakely and King John for her hand, a new sound intruded upon his senses. A soft whine, the whine of a dog in distress.

He increased his pace. The trail wound down to the creekbed just above the little cascade—barely two feet high. Not much had changed since he had come here last autumn with young John; except the signs of a horse recently grazing beside the alder trees and the impression of a man's booted feet in the soft mud beside the water.

The prints blurred two paces upstream. A scuffle. Something landed heavily in the mud. The man got up and walked away. Did he drag something heavy from the water? Something that left a trail of blood, crushed grass, and bracken in a new direction. The boot prints went back toward the alders and the horse.

The soft whimper of a beast in pain drew Hugh along the blood trail back into the thick bracken. Cautiously he parted the drooping fronds. He spotted the slight twitch of a brindle-brown tail first. "Newynog?" he whispered?

The fur rippled and the whine turned into a low growl.

"What's wrong, Newynog?" He squatted down, not touching the dog until she acknowledged his presence as friendly.

Another whine and the wolfhound twisted enough to stick her nose out of the underbrush. A smear of blood crusted across the top of her muzzle.

"Ah, Newynog, what has he done to you?" He held out his hand, palm up for her to sniff. "I won't hurt you, Pup, but you have to let me look at you.

The very tip of Newynog's tongue caressed his fingertips. Taking that as permission to investigate, he edged closer yet so that he could see the entire dog beneath the ferns.

Hugh drew in a deep breath sharply. "I've seen less vicious wounds on the battlefield, Pup," he gasped at the gaping wound in her side. "A wicked blade, short and sharp, possibly vorpal, I'd guess."

Newynog moaned again and tried to lick the sluggish blood caking her fur.

Hugh resisted the instinct to end the dog's suffering here and now.

Ana would never forgive him. He wanted her goodwill. He wanted a lot of things from her, but he'd start with her goodwill.

"Pup, I don't have a lot to work with, but I'll do the best I can," Hugh said as he started tearing strips off the hem of his chainse. He kept up a soft, reassuring patter as he gathered some basic emergency field dressings. Moss, willow bark, water, bandages. A chirurgeon or a nun would probably find miracles in other plants along the creekbed.

"Let's get you bound up for travel, Pup. I'm sure Lady Ana will know more of how to help you heal." He dribbled water from a clean bandage along the wound, cooling it, removing some of the caked blood from her fur. "If I had some potion to make you sleep, I'd shave the fur around the wound, but I don't think you'd tolerate that."

Newynog agreed with him, licking the water and blood free of the wound site.

Trying to shift her gently, Hugh wrapped the bandages around her middle, covering his packing of moss and bark. She didn't try to bite him, but she did protest being lifted.

"Now what, Pup?" he asked as he tied off the last binding. "I don't have a sling to carry you between two horses. I don't even have a second horse. Do you trust me?"

Newynog opened wary eyes to glare at him.

"Trust me or not, I'm going to put you across Orage's back, before the saddle. We will carry you to my home. I know a shortcut. We'll be there about the same time as Ana."

At the sound of her mistress' name, Newynog lifted her ears and whined again.

After much repositioning, Hugh finally lifted the dog into his arms and hiked the few paces back to Orage. Thankfully, Newynog was young and hadn't reached her full adult size and weight. He'd never have been able to hoist her onto the horse's tall back if she had.

"If Blakely's servant did this to you, Newynog, the king's pet assassin has one more crime to answer for." Hugh caressed the dog as he dug his heels into Orage. His affection for the dog grew, almost as deeply as his feelings for Ana.

Merde! He didn't need a beautiful witch with secrets and a grudge against the king.

But he did need a title and land of his own. Could Ana give him that—or should he wait on King John?

They trotted easily along forgotten trails over the ridge and across a sheep meadow to the first village that served Bellecôte.

The familiar scents of woodsmoke, and stews cooking on the crisp evening air made him urge Orage to move faster.

The smoke odor grew stronger, more sour.

"Holy Mother! Not again." As he crested the line of hills to the south of Bellecôte, he spied the thick cloud of smoke rising above the walls of his home.

"Johnny!" he screamed, pelting forward. "Holy Mother, let my boy be safe."

Chapter 20

"FASTER! Move those buckets faster," King John commanded. The line of peasants, courtiers, servants, and knights increased the pace of passing buckets and bowls full of water from the well to the blazing kitchen at Bellecôte Castle. I dropped my bucket into the water and withdrew it, passing it on to the next person in line. Seconds later Petit, the king's valet, ran back from the head of line and dipped his bucket into the spring-fed well.

I'd heard so much about King John's failures on the battlefield, I had forgotten that he had won many more battles by exercising the Plantagenet genius for lightning strikes against crucial targets. Showing his gift for organization, the king had his entire entourage plus the bewildered inhabitants of the castle fighting the spreading blaze efficiently and successfully.

Blakely's shadowy servant, now very much in evidence, threw his bucket of water carelessly. The stream arced out and landed three yards to the right of the kitchen building. Given a momentary rest from the onslaught of moisture, the fire blazed up, sending a spray of sparks toward the next building, the stable.

A little boy, not more than six or seven, sat his pony next to the king. At a word from John, young John Bellecôte kneed his pony into a gallop. He reined in beside the stable, shouting orders to the grooms. Immediately the horsemen began escorting the precious beasts outside the curtain wall.

The king had masterfully included the boy in the battle to save his heritage, not only making a child feel useful instead of thrust aside, but earning the boy's trust and loyalty. Probably for a lifetime.

Some of my antagonism toward John dissolved. I knew him ruthless and dangerous. Now I knew him to be thoughtful, a leader, and—I suspected—a good father. My emotions got lost in the hard work of fighting the fire before it spread to the old-fashioned thatched roof of the great tower.

Then into the smoke and organized chaos pelted Sir Hugh Fitz Chênenoir. He reined Orage so tightly, the warhorse reared, pawing the air with massive hooves. Newynog and Hugh nearly fell from the saddle. Hugh scanned the bailey anxiously. When his eyes rested on his young stepson and found the boy whole and hale, he relaxed a little.

"Newynog!" I screamed and ran from my place in the fire line. Other bodies carrying buckets and vessels filled my place immediately. "What have you done to my Newynog?" I screamed, ducking under Orage's thrashing hooves.

"Quit showing off, Orage," Hugh commanded. The horse snorted but settled down enough for me to brush Newynog's flopping ears away from her eyes. "She's hurt badly, Ana. I bound the wound as best I could, but she needs a true healer." He dismounted clumsily, as if his right leg truly pained him.

Together we eased Newynog off the saddle. Hugh carried her to a quiet corner beneath the gatehouse tower. "Stay here, out of harm's way," he ordered and stalked back to the fire line. A few words with the king, and he gathered four men from the well. They each grabbed a pitchfork, ax, or shovel and began demolishing the kitchen, separating the wooden building from the stone keep.

I turned my full attention to my dog. Newynog panted heavily where she lay in the sun-warmed corner. The jolting ride draped over Orage's saddle had not helped her. I had to act fast to save her.

"Thank you, Newynog. Thank you for delaying *Monsieur le Fantôme*. If he had arrived here any sooner, the fire would be too far gone for us to fight it," I spoke in a lulling singsong, the beginning of a trance for both of us. I hadn't done this since the night I tried to heal Great-aunt Lotta and failed.

"I can show you an easy way to do it," Radburn Blakely said. He stood over me, blocking the sunlight.

"You should be helping with the fire," I replied. Carefully I cut away Hugh's improvised bandages. I owed him a chainse by the looks of it. I'd embroider the new one with much gratitude and . . . and love.

"The fire is almost under control. You must act quickly before curiosity brings observers who will condemn witchcraft before acknowledging the benefits." He sounded almost sincere in his concern.

"I can do it. But I need privacy." I stared at him, willing him to return to the line of firefighters.

"I won't reveal your secrets."

"I said 'I need privacy.' Even from you. Turn your back, at least," I insisted.

Grudgingly he turned around. "It helps if you use the same phrase to trigger your trance each time," he added.

"I know that!" Would the man never leave me alone?

"Frankly, I'd end the dog's suffering. Familiars are easy enough to procure."

"Shut up!" I had to fight to keep my voice from carrying to the stable hands who still guided panicky horses through the nearby gate.

"But then, the Griffin wolfhounds are legendary. I look forward to claiming one of Newynog's pups after we are married," Blakely said casually over his shoulder.

I ignored his taunting tone and hummed an ancient tune Uncle Henry had taught me when I first returned to Kirkenwood after eight years in the convents. The words eluded me, but the simple tune repeated itself endlessly in five catchy phrases. After two repeats I was able to shut out the noise and press of bodies in the bailey. Nothing existed except Newynog and me. My dog's breathing eased and she looked at me with grateful eyes.

Two more repeats of the tune took me deeper into myself. Under my gaze, Newynog took on a green aura. I touched the gaping slash in her side. The green light extended to my hand. Still I continued the tune, letting the hum grow within my throat into full-fledged song. In my mind I saw flesh knitting together, severed blood vessels rejoining, illness and fever abating.

"Not so loud!" Blakely hissed. "Sir Hugh is looking at you most strangely. The church may not pursue magicians, but when confronted with an accusation of witchcraft, they will prosecute and condemn."

His words jolted me back to the bailey of Bellecôte Castle. I coughed out smoke, too tired to fight the noisome invasion of my body.

"Have you finished?" Blakely asked. "The fire is under control and people are returning to their chores."

"For now." I think I passed out momentarily with exhaustion. The wound beneath my fingers still oozed surface blood. The outer layers of skin still gaped, raw and jagged, but the deeper injuries no longer threatened my Newynog.

"A fine piece of work. I'll make a disciple of you yet." Blakely stooped to examine the wound. Newynog nipped at his questing fingers. He yanked his hand out of reach. "You could have completely healed the wound, though. Removed even the scar. Why leave her with lingering pain?" he sneered.

"If she has a scar to remind her, maybe next time she will be more cautious. Besides, Hugh saw the depth of the wound. Several others noticed as well. They will raise . . . difficult questions if she has no trace of hurt so soon after the injury. If I healed a person, they would call me a saint. Since I used my powers on a beast, they will call me witch."

We continued to eye each other, challenging the other's authority. Newynog's whimpers turned to low growls.

"And I will never be your disciple, Radburn Blakely. If I choose to continue to grow into my powers, I will do so on my own terms."

Racking coughs choked off my words and brought me to the point of gagging. The sour smell of smoke permeated everything, as it did at Mendip Mor. All thoughts gave way to the need to keep breathing through the coughs.

When the spasm passed, leaving me weaker than the previous one, I looked up to find Blakely smiling at me. He unclenched his fist, spreading his fingers wide.

Newynog nipped at him again. He slapped her nose. She bared her teeth in a menacing growl.

Blakely backed off and withdrew his hand from proximity to Newynog's strong jaws.

Somehow, his slight retreat released the tension in my chest. Then he closed his fingers again and the pressure built within me, needing to break out with another round of coughing. I resisted.

His smile turned into a grimace. Fatigue lines creased at the corners of his eyes. He released his fingers again.

My chest eased accordingly.

"You will come to me willingly, Little One, if for no other reason than to keep your lungs clear of rot. When you fight for every breath, you will crawl to me on any terms." He closed his fist again. "You will perform the next spell my way and completely."

I doubled over, unable to hold back the barking expulsion of air from my lungs. Desperate for a clean breath of air, I reached an imploring hand to him. He leaned back on his haunches out of my reach. His clenched fist remained directly before my eyes. The choice to breathe or not remained with me. Follow him or die from a painful wasting disease.

Archie threw one last bucket of water on the smoldering embers of the kitchen remains. Hugh breathed a sigh of relief. Warily he looked around the entire bailey as if seeking out any signs that a stray spark had spread to one of the other outbuildings. All looked fine. His people milled about, slowly returning to their usual tasks or cleaning up the soggy mess. Already four of his serfs prepared a new fire pit for the evening meal.

"Papa, did you see me?" Young John slid awkwardly down from the back of his pony and hurled himself against Hugh.

"Yes, I saw you delivering messages for the king," Hugh replied, returning the boy's hug, kissing the top of his head. He crouched down to his son's level and brushed his light brown hair out of his eyes. "You did a fine job of protecting your manor, John de Bellecôte."

"I wasn't scared a bit, Papa," he lisped a little around a gap in his mouth. His first adult tooth poked through his gums, but didn't yet fill the hole. Johnny had been late getting his milk teeth. Later yet in losing them. All part of the many illnesses that had nearly killed him.

Hugh hugged him again, grateful for every moment he had with his son. Perhaps fosterage was not the answer to raising the boy properly.

"You behaved so well, Johnny, that I have decided to make you my own page. I will train you to be a proper knight."

"Really?" Johnny's face glowed beneath the soot smudges.

"Yes, really. You will come with me when I have to travel or attend the king. At first you will merely tend to my clothes and armor and your pony, but soon we'll start teaching you feats of arms and how to care for a warhorse."

"You'll let me groom Orage?" Johnny's eyes widened to the size of a trencher.

"If Orage will let you." They laughed together at the thought of the temperamental warhorse standing still while Johnny curried him.

"Orage likes me. I give him apples."

"You do? No wonder he's getting fat and lazy." This time while Hugh held his son tight against his chest, he scanned the bailey once more. King John was mounting the steps to the tower entrance, a full story aboveground. Petit danced about him, William, the bathman, hauled a huge tub in the king's wake, and courtiers stood in tight gossipy clusters. Archie signaled him with waving arms. Time for him to become the gracious host.

His eyes slid over Ana and Blakely in the gatehouse corner. He frowned at the difficulty Ana seemed to have in catching her breath. The smoke was thick enough to disturb anyone, but it dissipated rapidly. Why was she still coughing?

Then Newynog growled and snapped at Blakely. He yelped and stood. His curses filled the bailey. He aimed his foot to kick the dog.

Hugh lunged to intervene, dragging Johnny with him. "The animal is wounded. You must have hurt her more," he said as he knocked Blakely off-balance. The taller, but slighter man had to drop his foot back to the ground to retain his equilibrium.

"King John requires your presence, Lord Blakely," Hugh stated.

Blakely composed himself, settled his posture, and straightened his cotehardie. With a last furious glare at Ana marring the perfect proportions of his face, he stalked off to join his half brother in the great tower.

Ana stared after him, coughing weakly.

"I'll reserve a bath for you, Ana. But there is a long waiting line. Everyone is covered in smoke and grit, including the queen." He brushed ash from his sleeve.

"I can't move Newynog yet." She looked up at him. A weird vacancy filled her eyes, reminiscent of the catatonia she'd recently mastered.

"Do you wish me to assist the lady, Sir Hugh?" Johnny asked in a very good imitation of a squire well aware of his duties.

Hugh couldn't help smiling at his son. "Yes, Johnny. Please do the lady's bidding until I need you at the evening meal." He stood and ruffled the boy's hair again. "You will make a fine squire, Son."

Young John beamed. He also fidgeted from foot to foot in his excitement. A bad habit Hugh would have to break—in time. Johnny had only recently celebrated his seventh natal day.

Somehow, the entire court managed to bathe and change while Hugh's cooks improvised a meal of sorts—though the larder was severely depleted afterward. Tomorrow's ale would be green and almost undrinkable. Hugh kept a wary eye on the seating within his very crowded hall. Young John solemnly provided towels to all as they washed their hands at the sideboard. He wasn't quite big enough to handle the water ewer yet. That chore fell to an older page, Robert, almost ready to advance to squire duties.

Ana did not appear for the meal, and King John did not seem to miss her. Blakely's attention wandered frequently from his half brother to the postern door.

As soon as everyone was seated and food brought to the tables, Hugh signaled Johnny to his side. "Where is Lady Ana?" he whispered.

Johnny shrugged his shoulders. Fatigue deepened the shadows around his eyes. He'd had a long and exhausting day. As had they all. Hugh knew from experience the boy would sicken if not sent to his bed now. "Send Archie to tend to the lady, then you eat something and hasten to your bed." His son nodded agreement without protest. A bad sign.

He had made the correct decision to train the boy himself. Any other lord would have insisted young John continue his table duties until the last remove had been cleared and the tables stored for the night.

"I've fought too many of your illnesses to lose you now, Son," he murmured to himself. "You'll stay with me even if the king wants to foster you."

At dawn, Hugh still had not seen Ana, or Archie. He missed having her at his side, both at the meal and as he slept. But he had duties as lord of the castle and had made his bed upon a stack of grain sacks in the storeroom, too tired to dream. Thank sweet *Jesu* he hadn't dreamed of Blakely again. Those memories would have robbed him of what little sleep he had managed to snatch.

Around him, the castle awakened. Sleepy-eyed servitors and knights stacked their pallets in a corner of the Hall and stumbled outside to the privy. As space on the floor cleared of sleeping forms, men in simple tunics and braies set up the trestle tables for breakfast.

Hugh drank in the familiar smells of too many bodies packed into the confines of the stout castle. He welcomed the sounds of *his* people preparing for the coming day.

"I thought we would hunt today, Your Highness," Hugh said as King John joined him at the high table.

John's face brightened. No trace of early morning puffiness or befuddlement marred his features. "An admirable idea," he replied. The only thing John preferred to sitting in judgment over disputes was a day ahorse chasing game through forest and field.

Radburn Blakely descended from the upper level looking altogether too handsome, too graceful, and too wide awake. Behind him, a servant followed, more a shadow than a solid man. Hugh peered at the ghostly shadow, seeking a face, a name, anything substantial about the man. He echoed Blakely in height and posture. Young judging by his large hands and feet in comparison to spindly arms and legs. He wore clothes cut by the same tailor as Blakely's but in muted hues of grays and browns rather than the brighter blues and purples favored by the king's half brother.

Fantôme. Ana had named him correctly. Was he responsible for the fire as she suspected?

Hugh stepped over a still sleeping, and snoring, younger son of a lord, for a better view of both men. Blakely rubbed his left wrist absently where Newynog had bitten him yesterday. Fantôme favored his right hand, sporting a thick bandage around his palm and fingers. A bulge in his shirtsleeve suggested the bandage wound higher up his arm. A small smear of blood blotched the whiteness of his shirt at the neck.

Newynog had given wounds almost as severe as she had received.

Ana shuffled into the Hall. Newynog limped stiffly beside her. The dust on Ana's borrowed purple gown blended almost perfectly with her wolfhound's brindled coat. Echoes of each other, as Blakely and his Fantôme were.

The only thing that appeared normal about Ana was the muddy hem of her gown. She never managed to avoid puddles, bogs, and streams. He couldn't count the number of times she had delayed their progress from Wells because she had to stop to bathe her hands and face, and sometimes her feet as well. He despaired that she'd catch a chill, just as easily as Johnny.

"Ah, Lady Resmiranda," John called to her from the dais. "You must join us today on the hunt."

Ana coughed in reply. A deep, soul-racking cough.

Hugh felt the blood drain from his head. He'd heard Johnny cough like that too many times, just before a fever nearly killed him.

Chapter 21

"MILADY?" John poked his head into my alcove. The curtain hid most of him. A shy grin spread across his face. The black encasement to his aura was hardly visible.

I returned his smile weakly.

"You are awake." With that pronouncement he thrust aside the curtain and stepped within my cramped space. Then he closed the slight privacy barrier behind him, blocking out some of the sounds of people in the Hall preparing for the evening meal.

Groggily, I struggled to sit up. I'd slept a little, free of the dreadful pressure in my chest for a time while the men hunted. Even though my breathing eased, a terrible weakness assailed me. I feared the on-slaught of a fever.

"You needn't rise, Ana. I know how ill you have been." John perched on the edge of the bed, holding his hands behind his back. The conspiratorial grin on his face banished years of worry lines around his eyes and mouth. "I brought you a gift. To make you feel better. So you won't feel so left out."

He thrust a nosegay of spring flowers into my hands.

"Thank you, Highness," I mumbled, burying my face in the cluster of bluebottles, woodbine, verg d'or, and elf leaf, nestled artistically in a bed of ferns. The wild combination of symbols almost sent me giggling. He wished me lust, protection, money, and chastity. A complicated message from a complicated man.

"We want you to know that we intend to care for you as a full member of our household, Ana. We will not mistreat you or thrust you into a marriage you detest, *ma coeur*. Nor will we plunder your estates." The regal mask settled over his features once more.

"Thank you again, Highness. I had wondered at my status as your ward and also as an independent baroness." We grinned together.

"Please understand, that as an unmarried lass, you are vulnerable. We protect you as a one of our own children." All of John's older children—bastards born before his marriage to Isabelle d'Angoulême—had been well fostered and well married.

"I would return to Kirkenwood, Highness. I have no wish to remain at court. I am well past the age of marriage. I should take up the responsibilities as chatelaine."

"We will take you there, Ana. Just as soon as you are well. In the meantime, rest and get over this dreadful cough." He caressed my cheek with a delicate finger. "We would see the bloom return to your face, Ana."

I could not help blushing a little as I sighed and leaned into his gentle touch. His hand cupped my face a moment longer.

"Kirkenwood is my home, Highness. I will heal quicker there than anywhere," I argued.

"We are not yet ready to quit Bellecôte, and we have business in Durham. We are not willing to send you out on the road alone, Ana. You will be home soon enough, *ma coeur*. We will take you home and help you settle in as chatelaine of Kirkenwood, as is our duty."

In other words he would not allow me the opportunity to hide my evidence against him before he arrived.

But he did not know Kirkenwood as I did. My ancestors had built many secret passages and hiding places into the walls and foundations. He'd not find the evidence readily.

He squeezed my hand in reassurance.

"Highness, you can trust me. You can trust yourself. I trust you not to lash out at me in betrayal to keep me from betraying you first. Do not give in to your fears, fears that are pressed upon you by . . . by others. Trust in me as I trust in you, and all will be well."

Where did those thoughts come from? I could not suppress them.

For a moment he burst completely free of his aura. He believed me. At least until Blakely reasserted his influence.

"Highness, the time is long past when we should have moved to Kirkenwood," Radburn Blakely said in his most conciliatory tone. They had been riding all day without sight of a deer or boar, and barely a fox or coney. Doves and songbirds made their nests elsewhere. Nor had they brought home enough to feed the court this entire week. After three weeks of extensive kills, the game had disappeared from Sir Hugh's lands. "This forest is hunted dry. Even the birds refuse to fly here. Sir Hugh's larder is empty beyond reprovisioning."

"We have not finished hearing claims and disputes," John returned. More and more he refused to listen to anything he did not want to hear. And Castle Bellecôte was too crowded for the privacy Radburn needed to put stronger wards in place.

"Besides, we like Bellecôte. The queen and our son like Bellecôte. Send bailiffs to Feckenham for provisions. We will tarry a while longer." John dismissed the subject.

Sir Hugh flinched.

"Why send all the way to your royal residence, Highness. We can confiscate goods from a dozen manors between here and there," Blakely argued. He needed John to heed his advice on at least one issue—any issue.

"We will not confiscate without compensation. We do not wish to deplete the treasury for foodstuffs when Feckenham has surplus. Make certain they use full London measures for food and wine. We will not be cheated because each shire demands the independence to set their own standard of measures," John continued his discourse.

"At least allow your bailiffs to collect carts and horses from other manors. Feckenham has not the means to transport what the court requires." Blakely continued to push for actions that would alienate the barony. John had been all too agreeable and reasonable these last weeks. Unnatural order and peace prevailed.

"Compensate the lords for those horses and carts. And make certain they send several ells of cloth. Lady Resmiranda requires more clothing. As our ward, she must appear presentable at court. Better find some truly elegant silk for the queen as well. London yards and of a proper London width, not provincial yards. We will not skimp on clothing our ladies."

Sir Hugh flinched again. "Highness," he interrupted the monologue. "Would you consider the cost of housing the court for this extended period part of the repayment of my debt to you for the death reliefs of Bellecôte?"

Radburn gripped his reins too tightly. His horse shied and

pranced. He thought he'd managed to intimidate Sir Hugh into keeping silent on this issue. He wanted John at odds with his barons and the matter of debt was a key issue for his plans.

"Of course, Sir Hugh. Our clerics will remove half the debt." John waved blithely toward the cowled man who was always in attendance, even on the hunt.

Sir Hugh almost sagged in his saddle in relief. Half the debt represented a huge sum of money.

How could Radburn reimpose that kind of debt upon his chief rival for Lady Resmiranda? More death reliefs for the loss of young John? Radburn's groin tightened with pleasure at the thought.

A pleasantly chaotic gibbering awakened in his brain. Someone else would be pleased at the sacrifice of an innocent child.

Remaining at Bellecôte would only tighten the bonds of loyalty and trust between Sir Hugh and King John.

"Are you certain lingering here is wise, Highness? Eustace de Vesci in Northumberland is protesting the call to arms to defend the Welsh border. He needs to be reminded of his oath of loyalty to you," Radburn protested. He didn't care a twit about de Vesci's problems. Robert Fitz Walter was also raising discontent.

But Radburn needed old Henry Griffin's spell book, his athame—a ritual knife of great antiquity and power—and if possible his staff and the records the old man had maintained for three generations. Those treasures remained at Kirkenwood north and west of de Vesci.

Radburn also needed Resmiranda, the last of the Griffins, under his control, legally, morally, and spiritually. A quick marriage in Scotland—with or without the lady's consent—seemed the only way to achieve his goals. He might even allow her to live long enough to bear him an heir, reinforcing his blood with the blood of King Arthur Pendragon and The Merlin of old that flowed in her veins.

Such an heir would have as great a claim to the throne as John's infant son, Henry. Perhaps the recalcitrant barons could be persuaded to elevate Blakely's heir to the throne rather than John's. With Blakely as regent, of course.

"De Vesci protests everything that takes him, his knights, or his money outside Northumberland. We will not dignify his complaints with a royal visit," John dismissed his half brother's arguments.

Grinding his teeth in frustration, Radburn chanted a long phrase in Arabic under his breath. A light trance settled about him almost immediately. He wove his fingers in a complicated gesture. When the power tingled in his fingertips, begging for him to release it, he turned his attention on John.

"Lady Resmiranda's cough has become bothersome. Perhaps she will fare better in her own home," the king chanted half a syllable behind Radburn's quiet mouthing of the same words.

"No, Highness." Sir Hugh's horse jostled John's. The king shook his head slightly and refocused his eyes on his favorite knight.

Radburn felt his control over his brother slip. He had to make time tonight to renew the wards. No more delays despite the risk of discovery.

"I have seen these lingering coughs turn to murderous fevers overnight. Lady Ana should not be forced to move," Sir Hugh insisted. His close proximity kept John from looking back to Radburn.

Without eye contact, Radburn's compulsion over the king weakened. The Griffin witch must have cast her own spell over John.

"We will move to our royal demesne of Geddington and then on to Durham at dawn," John announced. "Lady Resmiranda must remain at Bellecôte. We will not risk the life of our son and queen should the cough turn virulent." His eyes darted back and forth in panic. He allowed his mouth to gape slightly and his nostrils flared. His horse absorbed John's emotions and pranced, wild-eyed, ready to bolt.

"Surely the lady must accompany you, Highness. She is your ward, under your protection." Radburn nearly panicked along with the horse. He needed to be within a few yards of the lady to maintain his control of her breathing. The wolfhound had bitten him at the crucial moment of the spell, before he could complete it. Surely she must have noticed by now, that her breathing returned to normal while he chased after the king on these endless hunting trips. Only the debilitating weakness remained during his absence. He had not planned on that. Before long she'd succumb to any number of normal diseases because she no longer had the strength to fight them off. He'd have no control of her strength if that were the case. He didn't know if he could repeat the spell to increase his control over distance without killing her. He didn't want her dead. Yet.

"We have decided. We leave at dawn." John set his spurs into his horse's sides and galloped off on a new track.

"Highness, may I remain at Bellecôte to secure my lands and ensure the lady's health?" Sir Hugh hastened after him.

"Not without me, you don't," Radburn muttered, setting his own spurs.

"Ana?" Hugh crept into the curtained alcove carved into the west wall of the great tower. A dozen such narrow spaces, large enough for a narrow bed and not much else, had originally been intended for his five knights and their ladies to have some privacy as well as for storage of arms close at hand to the Hall.

He hated to disturb her rest. But King John had already risen and begun the long process of getting the court on the road. The court and all of its retainers outnumbered the normal household two to one. All of those extra bodies needed extra time to complete the morning routine.

"Hmm?" she replied sleepily ending on a hacking cough.

He let the spasm pass before speaking again, hoping she wouldn't awaken anyone else in this dark hour before Matins.

"John insists I accompany him to Durham with the court. I can't stay and protect you, *ma petite*." He caressed her hair and face, wishing he could hold her in a loving embrace and never let her go. Her pale beauty touched his heart and soul more than he thought any woman could. She lifted a hand to smooth his hair off his brow. The gentle caress soothed sore places in his mind and healed them with her smile.

As she roused, Newynog lifted her head from her paws at Ana's feet.

Worry tied knots in Hugh's neck. Newynog should have been alert to his first approach and growled or nudged Ana awake. The dog ailed as much as her mistress. He hoped the knife wound in the hound's side hadn't poisoned. He'd seen that happen often enough after a battle.

A man might be well on the way to recovery, walking, eating, laughing with his comrades. Then overnight the wound would turn angry red, fever would fell the man, and in days he died.

Newynog had hung on for nearly three weeks. She should be past the sickness. But she limped still and followed her mistress listlessly.

"I want to send you and Archie to Huntington, Ana. Earl Robin Locksley is the only man I know who will resist John to the death. And John ignores him rather than recognize the outlaw Robin Hood as one of his barony. You will be safe with Huntington." Hugh shifted a lock of limp hair off her brow. His fingers lingered, tracing the shape of her face. A deep ache of loneliness moistened his eyes and made his shoulders droop.

"No," Ana said quietly. "I have to go to Kirkenwood. I can't get well until I go home."

"The journey is too long, *ma petite*. Too perilous. Newynog isn't much healthier than you are," he pleaded with her for understanding. He had to know she was safe. "Please, Ana, go to Huntington."

"I can't. I have to go to Kirkenwood. Newynog and I will both heal there. I can heal us once we are home." She turned her face to look at him with imploring eyes. The deep blue orbs opened wide enough for him to fall into.

Her hand on his cheek was as tender as a butterfly. Her sweet breath brushed his lips as she rose up the few inches to meet him. He needed to press his mouth closer to hers, deepen her faery-gentle kiss.

"You know who I am, Hugh. You know *what* I am." She lay back on her bolster, seemingly exhausted. But her eyes hardened with determination and her hand lingered in his. He ran his thumb over the back of her fingers, wishing for greater intimacy and ease with her.

"My uncle hid special books and tools for me at Kirkenwood," she continued. "I have to have the knowledge secreted there in order to break Blakely's hold on me and his hold upon the king. 'Tis no normal infection that brings me low, but his need to control me."

"How?" Anger firmed his resolve to protect her from Blakely and the king. He tightened his grip on her hand and felt her tremble. He had no doubt that King John's bastard half brother did not act on his own. Like a knife to his heart, he suddenly realized his unfailing loyalty to the king was not reciprocated. John had made promises. Promises of honors—land and title of his own—of positions at court, of monetary rewards. John had broken every one of those promises. The only one he had kept was marriage to Ardyth, a wealthy widow with an ailing son. The son thrived to inherit his father's honors, while the widow lay in her grave with Hugh's infant son these past four years.

"I will defy John and take you to Huntington myself." While he held her hand he had the strength of will to fight for her, fight for himself.

"Rebellion will only bring you grief. Send me to Kirkenwood. Only there will I gain the strength and the knowledge I need to bring Blakely low. Once free of his brother's evil influence, John will be a good king. He has the talent and the skills. But Blakely warps him." Ana clutched his hand with desperation. Her fingernails dug into his wrist, nearly drawing blood.

"Ana . . ."

"Hugh, 'tis the only way. I promise. Now help me into the garden. I need to greet the dawn. I need to stand in the morning rain and cleanse my spirit. I've allowed Blakely's spell to divert me for too long." She sat up, clutching his arm. For a moment her pale face blanched whiter and her eyes rolled. But the dizziness must have passed, for she swung her legs off the bed.

"Send Archie to Kirkenwood with me. I trust him. When I am well and strong, I will return him to you. Please do not allow John and Blakely to come to Kirkenwood until I send Archie to you. He will carry a message only you will understand. Until then, trust no one but yourself."

He hung his head. Ana reached up to lift his face. Gently she kissed his lips. They lingered together a long moment, cherishing the sweetness of that caress.

"You can trust yourself, Hugh. You have no reason to doubt your judgment of your abilities." She lay back against the bolster, exhausted by her slight movements. "And please, try to soften Blakely's influence on the king. You can do that, Hugh. I know you can."

"Ana . . ."

"Please, Hugh. I know what I ask of you. I know what I ask of myself."

"I ask only that you give your heart to no one else until we see each other again, *ma petite.*"

"That I can promise you."

Chapter 22

ARCHIE insisted I regain strength before leaving for Kirkenwood. He fed me nourishing broths and fortified wines until I thought my stomach near to bursting. But with Blakely's leaving and the withdrawal of the cough, my body healed. Newynog lapped up more of the broth than I did. She, too, seemed to gain strength as the distance between us and Blakely increased.

I had no way of knowing if Fantôme's knife had poisoned Newynog or if her strength waxed and waned with mine.

We waited four full days before beginning the long trek across the northern moors to Kirkenwood. Each day my natural strength worked at banishing the lingering effects of the cough. The Black One passed beyond his range of control of me.

How could I separate him from King John to bring about a similar effect there?

We trekked across country by slow stages, staying at inns every night. The fat purse Hugh had given Archie grew thinner by the day. Gradually the terrain took on familiar silhouettes. The hills grew taller, their slopes steeper. Rivulets became dark brown, filled with peat. The sheep became woolier and wilder.

At long last I spotted a circle of tall stones with a village clustered among them. Above the small plateau of stones and huts hovered an ancient hill crowned by the sprawling mass of Kirkenwood.

Tall ramparts, made of stone stolen from Hadrian's Wall twenty miles to the north, encircled a squat tower and a dozen connected outbuildings. Kirkenwood had begun life as a timbered grange. As my ancestors gradually replaced wood with stone, the shape of a long hall with scattered and attached outbuildings had remained much the same.

A long road wound its way up the steep slopes of the hill past many ditches filled with spikes and thick brambles. Before siege warfare had become an art form during the early Crusades, the citadel had been impervious to attack. Before the days of the Norman invasion, my family had held off Saxon invaders from here. Romans had dismantled one fortress. Generations before that, the lords of the hill had been the invaders and had stolen the battlements from Picts and Gaels.

Through invasion and treachery, intermarriage and periods of abandonment, and a dozen different names, Kirkenwood had remained.

My heart opened with a song of joyful greeting upon first sight of my home.

But with the joy came sorrow. Every member of my family that I knew had died—too many had fallen victim to murderers, war, and outlawry. I was the last of my kind. Perhaps my parents lived, but they lived out of my reach, on the continent, and they could not communicate with me readily. Neither Brian de Griffin nor his wife had ever exhibited the slightest trace of magical talent that would allow communication that transcended the mundane barriers of distance and oceans.

Memories crowded 'round me. Mama and Papa arguing as he rode out the gate to yet another war or tournament. Uncle Henry breaking a pike over his knee when word of his son's death in a Saracen prison reached us. Aunt Lotta clutching her chest in pain. Mama never looking back as she rode away, leaving me at the Convent of St. Dyfrig.

Tears pricked my eyes. So many good-byes. So few welcomes.

As I rode the twisted path among the standing stones, I reached out with my senses to feel their power singing in my blood. Only sad loneliness came to me. Not a single glimmer of fire connected the stones' crests, giving them life. The stones, huge sentinels of time, seemed to sag with weariness and loss. No one had nurtured them for the many years Uncle Henry spent in prison. And now he had died, too. Two stones had fallen onto their sides and not been righted since I'd seen them last. One of the stones that had fallen many years ago lay in pieces—many of them missing.

I hurried on. Archie crossed himself repeatedly as we passed the stones. "Who would live in such a place?" he muttered. "Pagans. The stones are pagan and should have been pulled down centuries ago."

"You did not fear the stones outside the barrow as we fled Wells." I turned in my saddle to watch his expression.

"Little ones. And no one lived among them. No one had to face them day after day, have their thoughts ripped from their mind by them." He pushed his horse closer to mine, trying to pass the stones as quickly as possible.

I touched his hand. His panic threatened to invade me. Only panic, not a true menace from the stones.

"We have lived among the stones so long we have come to accept them—even cherish them. They have protected us for longer than anyone cares to remember."

"If they are so much bloody protection, why build a castle with stout walls?" He looked over his shoulder as if expecting the stones to come to life and chase him.

"They offer protection of a different sort than from mundane armies." As long as the stones stood, I could learn from them, ally myself with them against enemies such as Blakely.

"Where's the church? I was told there was a church in the wood here, that's why it's called Kirkenwood." He rode ahead of me now, as I lingered closer to the stones.

"On the other side of the hill, inside that little copse just visible from the first turn in the processional way." At that moment, I knew I could do nothing until I'd visited the little church.

The guards on the wall above the gate tower challenged us. I threw back my hood and without a word they let me pass. Hard to believe I had ridden out of this very portal less than four months ago. As I looked around the large bailey with its circular outbuildings spreading out from the great tower like a hen's chicks, nothing seemed changed, and yet . . . nothing could ever be the same again.

The old raven who perched on the well as if it were a throne croaked a greeting. Whispering among the echoes of his raucous call, I heard my name, "Resmiranda. You are home."

My three knights dropped their practice weapons and called their wives to greet me.

"Lady!" Daffyd, the fat steward, bustled out of the hall, out of breath and smelling of garlic. A memory flitted across my mind, of pages and scullery maids lazing in the kitchen until they smelled garlic on the wind. Then they hopped to their chores as if they had been hard at work all along. Within moments, Daffyd would enter the kitchen, pleased with his industrious crew.

I could not help smiling.

"You have come home at last, Lady Ana." Brigid, Daffyd's wife and my maid, hustled after him. She was as slender as he was fat, dark as he was fair, tall as he was short. An oddly matched couple who loved each other intensely.

I dismounted by myself and embraced Brigid heartily. Each of the ladies had to embrace me as well, perfunctory and short, a duty only. The three knights bowed and each took my hand, kissing the back of my wrist. Their greetings were more genuine and enthusiastic than their wives'. At least they made me feel I belonged here.

As soon as I could, I took Daffyd aside and asked, "Where is he?" We both knew I would ask after only one man.

"We buried your uncle in the old church. 'Twas his dying wish." Daffyd crossed himself as he imparted the sad news. The only other place he would want to be buried would be among the stones. The villagers would not permit that. Nor would the church.

I could only nod. Tears choked me. I hadn't cried when I first knew Uncle Henry was dead. Now I had no choice. Every step through the postern, down the steep path into the woods brought more and more memories of my great-uncle and his loving care of me during the last year of his life. The castle was permeated with his presence. I knew for certain Daffyd and Brigid managed the entire demesne as he would have wished. Nothing would be changed in the way of doing things until I ordered it.

Archie respected my pilgrimage to the church. The kirk in the woods.

The small stone building had stood at the base of an escarpment beside a cascade and pool since . . . I forgot how long it had been here. I knew only that Uncle Henry and Aunt Lotta had revered it as a most holy site with or without the church. Too many generations of my family had been buried here to count. I only hoped my people would remember to put my body in the crypt with them when the time came.

The foundations backed up against a cliff face on solid ground that the spring and pool would not erode. The crypt, instead of being beneath the church, was actually part of the cave system that led back to the secret exit beneath the kitchen of Kirkenwood on the hill.

I barely held back my tears for Uncle Henry. I didn't need more tears for that last harrowing escape Mama and I had made through the same tunnel nine years ago.

A low ridge connected the castle hill to this cliff. Too many steep ravines and unscalable crags severed the ridge to make it a bridge to the castle. One had to walk beneath the hill or around it. Today I took the long path around, fingering my beads and reciting prayers for Uncle Henry with every step.

At last I ducked beneath the low lintel of the church. Instinctively bowing to the altar, I crossed myself while my eyes adjusted to the dim light. After a few moments I saw the granite slab covered in fine linen drawnwork and clumps of wildflowers. A waft of fresh incense and the glow of the vigil light told me that someone had said mass recently.

Had Father Truman celebrated for himself? Perhaps fifty people could stand comfortably within the nave. I couldn't imagine it empty at Mass. The overwhelming sadness of celebrating Mass alone opened a cavity deep in my chest that quickly filled with tears.

Blessed Virgin Mary, please let this estrangement between Holy Mother Church and our king end soon, I prayed and crossed myself again. No comforting presence caressed my mind. I had no idea if my prayers were heard anymore or not.

Against church law, I had worked magic. As long as the Interdict lasted, I could not confess my sins and receive absolution.

Biting my lip to choke back the onslaught of emotions, I made my way to the sacristy. More evidence of Father Truman's presence littered the tiny alcove. His alb and stoles hung on pegs rammed into the walls. His missal lay open on the *prie-dieu*. Two chests lined one wall, filled with candles, incense, and sacramental wine. Long, narrow horizontal windows in the eastern wall allowed some of the afternoon light in.

I pushed aside the prie-dieu. Behind it, I could see the faint outline of a low door. My fingers found the latch by memory, and the stones swung inward. I had to crouch and crawl through the space that my eight-year-old body had found comfortable. Three steps cut into the natural rock led downward into the crypt.

Another entrance to the crypt opened through a grate at the foot of the altar dais. But I didn't have the key nor did I have Uncle Henry's talent for opening locks with my mind. Not yet anyway. I intended to have that talent by the time I met Radburn Blakely again.

If I could yank metal weapons from ambushing men in black armor and blast a passage through a stone wall when fire and smoke chased me, then surely I could learn to manipulate little locks.

The door led directly into the cave filled with crystal formations. I closed my eyes tightly and concentrated on light. When I opened them again, a tiny flicker of cold flame rested in my left palm. Not much bigger than a faery, the witchlight kept me from tripping over the uneven floor. One by one I picked out the tombs of my family. King Arthur Pendragon and his lady lay in the center. A short distance lay between them. I always thought they should have been buried together. No name graced the plaque set in the side of her tomb, only a small carving of a wren. His huge stone enclosure and her lesser one dominated the room, as his personality had dominated an age and her quiet influence had guided him. Everyone else seemed pale in comparison and their last resting places remained smaller, plainer.

Not much room left in here for recent additions. I threaded my way toward the cave entrance and the tunnel. Great-aunt Lotta lay up against the wall beside the archway. I couldn't see where another stone casket had been added.

"Where is he, Aunt Lotta?" I asked the air. My hand rested atop her casket, reading the inscription with my fingertips. I caught my fingernail on a roughness that should not be there. Surprised, I peered at the crudely formed letters. The light was so dim I had to put my nose almost on top of the carving.

Together with God
Henry Talbot Griffin, Baron of Bellecôte,
Knight of the Cross
And
Carlotta, his beloved wife, Lady of lake and forest,
Princess of Swansea.

Someone had scratched an amendment to the end. To those who knew how to read it, the epitaph now read: "May they rest in their love and share in the peace of the Goddess."

"He's here, with you where he belongs, Aunt Lotta. Where he belongs. He loved you to the end. Now you are together." Choked with tears I slid to the ground beside them, letting my memories take me. . . .

Chapter 23

I REMEMBERED another homecoming a little more than a year ago. Early April.

Rain had followed me and my two-knight escort all the way from the Convent of the Blessed Virgin in Yorkshire to Kirkenwood. We approached the village and its sentinel standing stones at sunset. A single ray of light poked beneath the low clouds as the sun hit the horizon. For a moment the reflection of that single ray made a halo of fire along the tops of the stones. When my eyes cleared of the dazzle-blindness, I saw faces within the stones, smiling faces in the whirling grain of the rock. One of them Aunt Lotta, another Arylwren of ancient memory—King Arthur's mistress, daughter of The Merlin. 'Twas her wren emblem that graced the tomb beside Arthur Pendragon, not his queen's motif, whatever that had been. Arthur's face, too, revealed itself in the stone beside his beloved. And could that be The Merlin himself, or was it Uncle Henry?

I dismounted, despite the drizzling rain. Standing there in the midst of the stones I turned in a tight circle, arms outstretched as if embracing stones, village, my heritage, all of me.

The senses I had fought for eight years, while hidden in convent after convent, opened. I saw brighter colors, sharper details, and layers of energy surrounding every living thing including the stones. The continuous halo of fire along the top of the stone ring leaped into the growing darkness of night. In that moment I knew the stones were alive. Alive with the spirit of my clan, alive with a spirituality I had experienced only a few times before and only at the height of the Sacrament of Eucharist.

Grateful for the moment, for my life, and the chance to come home, I dropped to my knees in prayer. As if participating in the most holy of sacraments, I lifted my face to the heavens seeking a psalm to express my joy.

I welcomed the rain upon my face.

Uncle Henry limped down the hill from the castle before I could think of the appropriate words. He leaned heavily upon a curious staff affixed with a dragon's head. Vaguely I remembered him carrying the long pole—half again as long as he was tall—a few times in years gone by. He knelt beside me, in the mud, and embraced me.

"You came, child. You came home. I didn't know if you would trust my missive." Tears mingled with the thickening rain to run down his cheeks and drip onto his broad chest.

I hugged him back. "The letter could only have been written by you. Half in French with sprinklings of Greek, Latin, and Welsh." The letter had come when I needed it most. I'd lived at the Convent of the Blessed Virgin for over a year. I thought I might stay there. Many of the sisters had become friends. Mother Superior took me under her wing, training me to assist her in running the vast estates owned by the convent.

A week before the missive arrived, Mother Superior died quite suddenly. Her replacement did not want my help, did not trust my education. I could read several languages and cipher rapidly and accurately—talents my new superior did not have. Another sister became her assistant. Both of them deplored the constant state of mud and damp upon the hem of my habit.

"Did you note the tiny paw print by my signature representing my Diddosrwydd?" Uncle Henry asked.

"Yes, I saw it and knew that if coerced to write the letter by our enemies, you would not have included that precious reassurance. You always name your wolfhounds 'shelter.' Kirkenwood is now my safe shelter. How many dogs of that name have you had in your lifetime?" We laughed and hugged again.

"Six now. But this one is the last." As if called by our conversation a huge wolfhound lumbered down the hill in the wake of her master. Her teats hung heavy, filled with milk for a new litter. She skidded to a halt, head lodged between us. Her weight nearly knocked me flat. Standing, her head would reach my shoulder.

Uncle Henry wrapped one arm around the dog, including us in her joy.

"This is not the same dog you had eight years ago." I inspected the hound for distinctive markings, noting a white patch on her nose and another on her left rear paw. The old Diddosrwydd had had black spots on front paws and over one eye. At the dog's prompting, I added my own caresses to Uncle Henry's.

"Heavens, yes. This pup was born only a few months after you left. Born in my prison cell and nearly murdered by King John's men along with her mother and the other eleven pups. I managed to save this one. Barely. Now she has a new litter born last week. One of the pups will be yours."

There was a long stretch of silence as we both pondered the importance of that statement.

"But . . ." I swallowed back the lump that suddenly formed in my throat. "But the family only bonds with one pup from the last litter from an aged hound. The rest of the litters become hunting dogs or are sold. The current holder of the Pendragon seal always has first choice. Unless . . ."

"Do not question me, Resmiranda. Some things about the future I can see, and I know that one of these pups is meant to be yours."

If Uncle Henry relinquished his rights to the pup, then he must foresee that he would not need to replace Diddosrwydd. Suddenly saddened, I rose to my feet unsteadily. Eight years as King John's prisoner had taken its toll on him. He'd lost weight and muscle tone. His eyes looked dim and milky. His hands shook. And there was the limp.

What had they done to him?

"It's getting dark and you are getting wet, Uncle Henry. I can't allow my affinity with water to risk you getting chilled. We should retire to the castle with a cup of mulled wine before the hearth."

"Aye, child." Uncle Henry levered himself up on stiff knees, using his dog and the staff as a brace. Diddosrwydd stood still and firm until he removed his hand from her shoulders. She knew how difficult this maneuver was for him.

The fire took the chill out of our bones and dried our clothing as we sat close to the hearth, a semicircle dug into the dirt floor and covered with stone paving against the long outside wall of the Hall. An opening in the twelve-foot-thick wall drew the smoke up to the roof. The floor above had a similar arrangement. Better than the central hearth with a hole in the roof when this was still a timbered Saxon grange instead of a stone castle.

Uncle Henry sipped his second mug of warm spiced wine after gulping the first. I peered more closely at his swollen knuckles and twisted fingers, sure signs of the joint disease. His pain must be deep and constant. Wine wouldn't ease it. I knew some herbs that might, but not for long. He'd need increasing doses of them to keep the pain at bay.

"Don't trouble yourself with me, child," he said gently, as if he had read my mind. "I am old. My time on this earth is drawing to an end. I hope I have had enough time to atone for my sins." He stared into his cup as if seeking answers within the deep ruby color.

I touched his arm, not knowing what to say.

"I have made my peace with King John, not that I ever defied him. He wanted something from me, but never asked directly—in fact I never saw him, only his minions. They were not ungentle. I had the freedom of the castle where he held me, but few luxuries and almost no contact with the outside world."

He fell silent a moment staring into the dregs of his wine.

I did not know what to say in reply.

Then he roused from his reverie. "Kirkenwood is in order. I have done everything I can to insure your inheritance is peaceful."

"You mentioned a marriage for me. . . ." The words caught in my throat. I had never thought of marriage until the letter arrived. Until then, I expected to continue a celibate life within the cloister. I expected to take final vows before long. Most women of sixteen had their lives settled—married to a man or to the church by the time they reached their fourteenth or fifteenth natal day.

"Your betrothal is part of my pact with King John. Advantageous to us both, politically. And I understand the man is fair to look at. But we need not concern ourselves with wedding details yet. I have not even met the groom, but his pedigree is strong. You have much to learn before I pass you to another's care and allow myself the freedom of death."

"Who am I to marry?"

"Someone special. Someone powerful and wealthy to help maintain our heritage." His eyes twinkled with merriment, and I knew I'd get no more information from him on the subject tonight.

"What truly happened that night eight years ago, Uncle Henry? Where is my mother?"

"I don't know about Mathilde. She disappeared into the night with you. But I always knew where you were. I do not have the same blood connection to my nephew's wife."

"And King John's men?"

"They truly came here seeking money and troops to aid John in securing the throne. I'd have given it willingly. Unfortunately, the Black One found something else he wanted more, wanted so badly he risked using foul magic to get it."

"The Black One?" I shivered at my memories of that awful night.

"A sorcerer of great power. I hope that you need never deal with him. Your husband will protect you from his machinations."

"I do not need a husband. Especially one you will not name."

"Later, child. We will discuss the marriage later."

I knew I'd get no more information from him. "What of King John and your pact with him?"

"After that night—when you and your mother ran away—when I regained consciousness, alone, lying beside Lotta . . ." He gulped and closed his eyes. Then he sought comfort from the wine before continuing. "They took me away from Kirkenwood and Lotta's grave. They did allow me to bury her and attend the funeral Mass. I stayed in an isolated castle near the Welsh border for eight years with only my wolfhound for company. No books, no visitors, no family." He grasped my hand and held it tightly.

"The Black One?" I pressed him again. All of the men had been dressed in black except one, and he wore pristine white. He stood out in my memory as a shining beacon in the chaos. He had compelled me to trust him. I had broken the compulsion because it tasted false. He had underestimated me.

"His aura is black, without light or color of any kind."

"How is that?" I did not easily see auras, so I did not look for them, and did not depend upon them for insight into a person's character and motives. I relied upon other clues to know if a person lied to me.

"Many times over the centuries, demons and faeries have tried to mate with humans, to give them a bridge into this world." Uncle Henry spoke as if reciting a ballad of old in a lilting cadence. "Rarely is the mating fruitful. When a child is born to that union, it is always sterile. Except once. One time in all the centuries of records, have The Pendragons heard of a demon child being fertile."

I gasped. Part of me thrilled at the danger and adventure, turning my blood to hot honey. Part of me chilled. I took a deep swallow of wine.

"When, Uncle Henry? And who?"

"Over fifty-five years ago, on Samhain. All Hallows Eve. The night when the barriers between worlds thin. Demons and faeries can cross over to this world on that night between sunset and dawn with little trouble and no need to transform into a corporeal being. A demon invaded the body of a man and raped a girl in our village. He must have been an incredibly strong demon. Lotta and I could not contain him, no matter what we tried. When the demon spirit departed at dawn, the man was broken in mind and body. He stared at the world through vacant eyes, incapable of speech or work. He had to be fed and diapered like a newborn. We all breathed a sigh of relief when he drowned in the pool as his daughter came into the world." He stared into the fire. Deep furrows of pain creased his brow. I reached out to soothe him, but he cast off my hand.

"The rape victim bore a demon child," I said, drawing him back into his recital.

"A beautiful baby girl. Probably the most beautiful child I have ever seen. Pale blonde hair, clear, delicate skin, perfectly proportioned features. We hoped that the stone circle and special tutoring would negate the demonic influence of her father.

"But then she left the village one day. The stones could no longer contain the demon within her. She seduced a—a powerful man and bore him a child. She died at the birthing. I'd never seen so much blood except on the battlefield. The baby tore her insides to shreds as he entered the world. His aura was as black as a sealed oubliette."

"What happened to him."

"Hen—his father claimed him and raised him as a noble, giving him education and privilege way beyond his mother's station in life. I heard he trained for the priesthood and hoped he had overcome the blackness in his soul."

"Until that night eight years ago," I added.

"Until that night eight years ago. I knew him instantly though he appeared still a youth and not a middle-aged man. I was afraid."

That would explain why the men who sought me so relentlessly never respected the sanctuary of a church. Demons did not recognize the authority of God.

A man who had demon blood running in his veins would not

need mundane spies to find me. He needed only a scrying bowl and clear water. My own natural need to remain hidden would keep him at bay for a while. But always he found me again.

"Who was his father?"

"I am not certain. A priest and wet nurse arrived on the day of the boy's birth and took him away. The soldiers who accompanied them bore the device of the Archbishop of Canterbury. Many powerful lords could have commanded such a retinue for a baby. I will name no man lest he be innocent and tainted by my accusation."

"You have called me home. You must not fear the Black One anymore."

"I have called you home so that I can train you to fight him should he ever threaten you or Kirkenwood. I forced myself to live this long only to see you again and give you as much training as I can in the brief time allowed us. Then I can die in peace. At last I will be able to join my Lotta. I miss her with every breath I take. I am incomplete without her."

He joined her in death less than a year later. But before he had succeeded in fully training me. I knew literally nothing about the powers I would need to fight the Black One.

The witchlight in my palm faded to nothing. I sat alone in the black tomb beside my great-uncle and his wife. I sobbed with loneliness and rekindled the witchlight.

I could put a name to the Black One now. Radburn Blakely. His mother had seduced none other than King Henry II who took pride in acknowledging and providing for his bastards. Blakely threatened me and my heritage. I was not ready to fight him.

And Blakely had murdered Uncle Henry as well as his faithful familiar Diddosrwydd. But they had both lived long enough to give me Newynog. I petted her with long, firm strokes, reasserting our precious bond.

"Oh, Hugh, I miss your solid strength and logic," I whispered into the familiar darkness of the crypt. "You stand in the background, faithful, quiet, strong. Help me figure out where to begin."

I conjured Hugh's face in my imagination. All I saw were King John's eyes, gentle and caring as he handed me the bouquet of spring posies. He could be redeemed. If only I knew how to break Radburn Blakely's hold on him before he became so used to evil and chaos that it became a part of him.

Chapter 24

UNCLE Henry's library seemed the best place to start my quest for knowledge. But first I took the opportunity to pray in the kirk. The old dampness of the place bathed me in cool reassurance. I drank in the smells of incense and beeswax until the chill embedded in the stone flooring numbed my knees and feet.

"Holy Mother, forgive me for tampering with arcane powers," I implored over and over again. With each prayer I slipped a bead through my fingers. "Sweet Jesu, keep me safe from the powers of darkness as I begin this journey in the cause of light."

When I had completed the chain of ivory-and-gold beads and held the circled cross in my palm, I sank back onto my heels and stared at the crucifix on the altar. "Holy Mother, I cannot believe your son gave me and my family these powers only to forbid us to use them when the family, indeed all of England, needs them."

The vigil light continued to burn low and steady, a mere glimmer in the gloom of the interior. Suddenly the old incense and candle wax cloyed at my senses. I needed to be outdoors in God's sunshine and fresh air. I needed to open myself to the wonders of His creation and make them more a part of me.

I stumbled to the porch and down the few steps only to fall to my knees again in the grass beside the pool. My knees and bliaud landed in the water, soaking through immediately. I yanked off my boots and shifted so that I sat with my feet in the water. Cleanliness and lightness washed over me.

Weak sunlight filtered through the scattering cloud cover. Patches of blue broke the continuity. I closed my eyes against the sudden glare. A soft giggle like the chiming of tiny bells came to me on the wind. I opened my eyes to find a faery hovering in front of my face. The pale blue female with shimmering pink wings winked at me and flew upward in a delighted spiral to join the rest of the troop.

Welcome home! they shouted in a single voice that sounded like a full chorus of finely tuned bells. *Come play with us.*

I looked at the dozen faeries flying a tight circle around my head, like a crown of bright flowers. "I have much to learn," I said hesitantly.

We will teach you. We are creatures of magic. Make us a part of your lessons. That statement brought another chorus of giggles that dissolved the tight formation. The faeries scattered, flitting to the pool, to the trees, hiding among the foxglove and ferns at the verge.

I couldn't help but smile. With one swift movement, I rose and waded into the pool, oblivious to the damage I did to my borrowed purple bliaud. Cool mud squished between my toes. Water plants tickled my ankles. I stood and spread my arms, circling as I embraced the day, the pool, the kirk, and my life.

Joy sang in my veins, and the earth thrummed as an echo of my heartbeat.

A psalm of thanksgiving rose in my heart. I fitted a tune to the harmony of the earth.

Then the vibrations of the earth against my feet took on a new intensity. Instantly the psalm died. I stilled, listening. The scents of the forest told me that I was alone. And yet . . .

I looked to the pool, knowing the source of whatever disrupted my song came from there. And yet I did not flee to dry ground. The water vibrated, sending ripples out from the center. Fear sent my heart beating faster, louder, drowning out the small sounds of the forest. I rose up on my toes, ready to flee whatever monster rose from the unknown depths of the pool.

But first I had to see it, know it before I let it drive me away from this special place.

The blue faery flew a bright circle around me. She giggled and landed upon my shoulder. *Watch. This miracle happens rarely.*

The faery's confidence kept me in place but did not still my fears. As much as I wanted to trust the otherworldly beings, I dared not. I dared not trust anyone. . . .

I had learned to trust Sir Hugh Fitz Chênenoir.

The disturbance in the water floated closer to the shore. An alluring song in an ancient tongue I almost understood drew me closer. Step by step I fought the compulsion to draw near to see and believe the miracle the faery promised.

I bit my lip, fearing some ancient monster would rear out of the water and devour me in one gulp. Water lapped at my knees. The rippling waves grew larger. I stepped into deeper water. Lady Sigrid's purple gown floated out around me like a vast flower, hiding the depth of water that now came to my waist. I gathered the folds of wet wool close and watched the water.

The ripples died. A glimmering white vision beneath the water drew my eyes and eased my trepidation. A pale lady with silvery blonde hair drifting in the water current rose up from the depths of the water. She lay just beneath the surface, clad in white samite. Diamonds glittered on her fingers and bespangled her gown. She clutched a magnificent sword to her breast; the gold-and-silver hilt rested just beneath her heart. Ancient runes ran the length of the magnificent blade.

In one graceful movement she thrust the sword upward. Only her hand and forearm cleared the water. Sunlight struck the blood-red jewel in the pommel of the sword.

"I gift to you Excalibur!" Her words echoed around the glade.

EXCALIBUR! The trees and shrubs and faeries took up the cry.

"Excalibur," I breathed. "Why? How? Who?" I didn't know how to use this formidable weapon, the sword of King Arthur Pendragon.

"You are The Pendragon. The sword is yours. When the time is right, you will know how. The sword will recognize your enemy." The Lady had not moved her lips, yet her words sang in my mind.

Her arm began to sink beneath the water, still clasping the sword.

Take it! The blue faery whispered into my ear. *Take it before she withdraws the gift.*

Breaking out of my awestruck stupor, I reached down and clasped the hilt just above the lady's hand. Her fingers brushed my hand in a loving caress. And then she was gone, sinking back into the depths of her watery home.

Chapter 25

"THE balance is tipped! And not for the good." Radburn Blakely whispered to himself. The fine hairs on his forearms and on the back of his neck stood on end as if lightning hovered over his left shoulder like death.

"Did you have something to add to the debate?" His brother John looked at him strangely, as if he had heard the comment.

"The . . . um . . . raiders from Wales must be punished for their destruction of Mendip Mor Castle," he stammered. They had been discussing the fate of the border castle, hadn't they? He couldn't remember. The shift in the balance of powers, light and dark, Earth, Air, Fire, and Water in harmony, the portals into other worlds opened and closed as they had not for centuries, sent his thoughts skittering about like a mouse with a cat on its tail. He should be the one to make changes. In the opposite direction, away from harmony. But not yet. He wasn't ready. He did not control Kirkenwood, its secrets, or its heiress.

This shift was in the wrong direction.

What had happened? He needed to retreat to his scrying bowl. John continued to stare at him as if he were insane.

For the moment he was.

"We decided against that action half an hour ago," Hugh Fitz Chênenoir reminded him.

Had he been entranced by the shift in natural powers for so long? Radburn shook his head to clear it of the lingering fuzziness. It didn't work. The room threatened to spin about him in ever quickening circles. He grabbed the edge of his bench seat to anchor himself.

"The men at arms might have retreated to sanctuary in Wales, but

they were led by Englishmen." Sir Hugh ardently pounded the council table at the head of Durham Castle's Hall. "Traitors to the crown.
Their leader must be sought. I will have vengeance for the hideous
death of my friend and his gentle wife."

Several of the other lords in attendance echoed his sentiments
loudly.

Radburn smiled slightly. They'd found the leader but didn't know
it. He'd never tell. Not if it threatened to put a noose around his own
neck. "An admirable path, Sir Hugh. How do you propose to go
about this formidable investigation?"

Let the self-righteous fool preach a few moments while Radburn
sought equilibrium once more.

He needed to see what had caused the psychic disturbance. John
wasn't likely to excuse him even for a supposed trip to the privy. John
had an iron bladder while enthralled in the business of running the
kingdom. His courtiers and councillors were required to have the
same.

More so since that witch Resmiranda had done something to
John. She'd broken through years of carefully planted seeds of fear
and distrust and banished them.

Every time Radburn tried to implement new wards, they appeared
weak shadows of his former control.

The room continued to spin, and his skin tingled all over. An
incredible itch developed on his palms. Whatever had happened did
not portend well for Radburn's plans for himself and England.

Lacking his silver bowl and clear water from a free-running
stream, he could use any other clear liquid, any other vessel. With less
clear results. What?

The wine in his cup was too dark. The rough ale typical of this
town was like drinking bread—too thick. What could he use?

Nothing came to mind.

He had to see. Now.

His stomach twisted from the disturbance. The magic within him,
ever ready at his fingertips, retreated to a huge knot in the back of his
neck. His eyes lost focus, further upsetting his digestion. If John
didn't give him leave to retreat to his bed immediately, he'd embarrass
himself right here and now.

"You do not look well, Brother," John said, reaching a solicitous
hand to touch Radburn's moist brow. The king had to twist awk-

wardly to his left. Sir Hugh sat to his right—Radburn's formerly honored position.

Would John push him to the end of the table next? And then out
of the council chamber altogether?

Not while he still lived. The future was not written in stone. He'd
regain his trusted position and control of Kirkenwood, too.

Kirkenwood. His senses told him the disturbance centered there.

Deliberately Radburn knocked his wine cup over. The dark red
liquid pooled onto the scrubbed boards of the table. He bent closer,
seemingly in a faint, but his eyes remained open slightly.

"Help him!" John shouted, pushing his demi-throne as far away
from his stricken brother as possible. Benches crashed against the
rush-strewn floor. Men's boots scraped and shuffled.

Radburn murmured spell after spell, in Latin, Arabic, and an obscure eastern dialect that depended upon inflection and pitch to determine meaning. He avoided Greek as the language of logic and alien
to his purposes. He peered intently at the wood grain visible through
the puddle of wine.

All he could see was a lightning-kissed sword. The sword of his
doom.

"I'm not dead yet," he said. He sat up straight, new resolve anchoring his spinning senses. "I am not dead yet, and I will not die
quietly. Please excuse me, Brother, before I distress you further."

Slowly Radburn pushed back his bench and rose to his feet. Unsteadily he made his way to the chamber behind the Hall where he
promptly vomited.

The sword grew heavy in my hands. My shoulders and forearms trembled from the weight of it. I balanced the blade with my left hand,
fearing to drop it in the suddenly chill pool.

I gritted my teeth in concentration as I eased the weapon to rest
on my shoulder lest I drop it and cut myself. How did men swing
these monsters hour after hour in practice and battle? I was no weakling, nor slightly built. I had spent most of my life in heavy physical
labor on the land as prescribed by the Cistercians. Still the weight of
the sword on my shoulder pressed me severely. Carefully balancing
each step, I withdrew from the pool.

"Thank you, Lady," I called as I found dry land once more. A brief ripple in the water's surface was all the acknowledgment I received.

"Now what do I do with it?" I asked myself, the faeries, and any other entity who might be listening.

"You learn to use the power within and without the blade," a male voice replied.

Startled, I looked about as I extended the sword into what I thought was a defensive posture. The blade dipped much lower than I wanted.

"I'll not harm you, lass. Welcome back to Kirkenwood." Father Truman stepped from the shadows of the church portal.

I let the sword dip until the tip touched the ground, grateful for the release of the weight on my upper body. Seven pounds? Ten? Surely not more than that or a mortal man could not wield it for long in battle. Yet it seemed to weigh more. Because I did not know how to use it?

"How long have you been here?" I asked the priest as I took several very deep breaths. He hadn't changed much from my childhood memories. Had he aged at all?

"Long enough to know you are bewildered and exhausted. Come inside, milady. We must discuss this miracle."

If the priest of this demesne called the event a miracle—as did the faeries—I need not fear the gift of Excalibur. But I did. Surely the appearance of the sword after so many centuries portended tremendous change and challenge. I was so tired, I didn't think myself up to anything more challenging than sinking onto the step at the front of the church. I had to drag the heavy sword in the dirt in order to walk the fifty paces to the building. *Forgive me for treating Excalibur with less than reverence. I just can't lift it anymore,* I apologized over and over to the Lady and to my distant ancestor and to the power within the weapon.

"Have you kept up your training at all, lass?" Father Truman asked, cocking one eyebrow. The setting sun cast a long shadow from his tall, slender body into the church nave from the doorway. Prematurely gray, with smile lines around his eyes and mouth, he looked as ancient as the church itself. I had never known another priest at Kirkenwood. I had never heard of another priest at Kirkenwood.

The thought of another, less gentle and understanding man guiding the people of my village unnerved me.

A raven flew down to the rooftree of the building and settled on the peak overlooking Father Truman and myself. It croaked a greeting and cocked its head as if it understood every word we said.

"I have avoided all forms of magic during the years of my absence," I replied quietly. "Mama warned me that my enemies could follow me by tracing any use of power. That seemed doubly important after . . . after Uncle Henry was murdered." I swallowed deeply, blinking back hot tears that pricked my eyes.

"Correct." Father Truman inclined his head in a brief acknowledgment. "But talented people quickly learn to avoid notice." He sat beside me, pointedly inspecting the sword without touching it. When I offered him the hilt, he shook his head and buried his hands within the deep folds of his robe. "The sword was given to you, milady. No other may touch it and live."

"But what am I going to do with it? I can barely lift it!"

"Metaphorically as well as physically." His pale blue eyes met my own. The twinkle in them told me to look deeper within his words.

"I need practice and learning in both magic and swordplay before I can safely wield it against my enemies."

"And until then . . . ?" The priest lifted his left eyebrow again in that maddening gesture that made him look so wise. 'Twas his face I had seen in the stones earlier today—not The Merlin or Uncle Henry. Or was he The Merlin?

"I think I must hide the sword as I never learned to hide myself."

"I will leave you to it, lass. This kind of work is best done alone." He stood and withdrew into the woods. One moment he stepped between two fern fronds and the next he disappeared. I knew of no path at that place.

The faeries vanished from their dance above the water at the same moment.

"Is that my first lesson?" I asked the air.

A brief chuckle on the wind was my only reply.

"All I truly know of magic is the properties within herbs," I said aloud, as much to relieve the sudden quiet of the clearing as to sort my thoughts. "Love-lies-bleeding is supposed to grant invisibility."

How many times during my youth had I braided a crown of the flowers and worn it while I slept? Always when I was newly come to a convent. But then I would grow complacent or one of the sisters would discover the garland and confiscate it. Nuns did not need false adornment. As brides of Christ, the beauty of our souls was all we needed.

Within a few days of losing the flowers, one sister or another would bundle me up in the middle of the night and flee into the darkness. Sometimes a donkey carried me to the next sanctuary. More often we walked.

One time we had to hide in a rushing creek, sheltered by tangled willow roots and drooping branches as the men in black armor beat the bushes about with swords. They had not found us. How had I sent them looking elsewhere?

I'd had a few of the love-lies-bleeding in my scrip.

Where would I find love-lies-bleeding flowers? They did not grow wild in this harsh northern climate. But I thought I remembered seeing a few in the herb garden. I'd have to trudge back up to the grange. Certainly not carrying the sword. Not only could I not lift it above the ground—dragging it would certainly dull the blade and possibly negate some of the power that throbbed within it—it would no longer be a secret from anyone.

"Well, I guess you might rest comfortably beside your original master," I addressed the sword. It fit neatly beneath the crossed hands on the effigy of King Arthur Pendragon as if the stone image had been carved with that in mind.

Something fluttered in the back of my mind like a sigh of relief. The shining blade took on a dull cast, merging with the tomb as if carved of the same stone.

"You don't see me," I whispered. "Look over there, I'm not here." I murmured the words that had worked for me as I secreted myself in the underbrush while black-armored men rode hither and thither in search of me.

At Mendip Mor Castle, the black-armored men had found me because I had trusted in the mundane defenses of the place to hide me.

I hoped this spell worked for one and all. It had to. I sensed that if I lost the sword before the coming trials, I would lose everything. And so would England.

Chapter 26

AS quickly as the disturbance had come upon Radburn, it disappeared, as if the source had retreated into the netherworld. No. Not quite a full disappearance. A—resonance—remained, subtle but *there,* all the same.

Radburn breathed more easily as he took stock of his mental and physical condition. His muscles moved at his command. His stomach steadied. His head had stopped spinning, but a curious vacancy remained at the back of his neck.

"I can function," he said, drawing a deep breath.

"I should hope so," Sir Hugh said from the archway of the alcove. "His Highness is most concerned for your well-being."

"Is he really?" Radburn raised his eyebrows in query. Part of him—the childish part that needed love and security and the approval of his legitimate brother—desperately wanted John's concern. The older, more cynical and realistic part of him knew better than to expect or want anything from John. John was a tool, nothing more. Radburn couldn't spare the emotion to care what his younger half brother thought.

"Concerned enough to dismiss the council for a few hours while you recover." Sir Hugh continued to lean indolently against the wall, watching, waiting for a sign of weakness.

Radburn wasn't about to give it to him.

"Recover or die?" he asked. "I assure you, last night's fish might have taxed my system, but it is not about to kill me. I am made of sterner stuff."

"Then why are your hands shaking and your face the color of newly milled flour? I think you had best retire, Lord Blakely." Sir

Hugh finally heaved himself away from the wall. But he didn't go away.

"I think I shall do that. I shall retire from court for a few days until I know for certain His Highness is safe from whatever ails me." Radburn smiled to himself at the double entendre. Fitz Chênenoir would never appreciate it.

"You are going to Kirkenwood!" Sir Hugh said through clenched teeth.

More perceptive than he thought. "Why would I do that?" Radburn stalled.

"Because what ails you is the same thing that ails me. John is dangling lands and titles in front of both of us. As long as we dance to his tune, he will continue to hold out that promise. But once we stray, the offers will evaporate as mist in sunshine. You plan to grab Lady Resmiranda and Kirkenwood without waiting for permission."

Radburn laughed. He didn't know how else to reply. This man was much too perceptive. He'd have to be eliminated. Soon. But first he had to neutralize whatever force of light had surged forward.

"Forget this conversation," he said quietly, holding his palm before Sir Hugh's eyes. With delicate fingertips he closed the other man's lids. "You did not find me. You know nothing of my whereabouts or my plans." Satisfied that the knight had accepted his statement, he withdrew his hand.

Hugh stood a moment, eyes closed, then promptly turned on his heel and left the alcove.

How long would the suggestion last in the man's mind? Sometimes Sir Hugh Fitz Chênenoir saw just a little too much. That quality made him an admirable warrior and landholder, but Radburn didn't need a warrior or a landholder. He needed a dupe to lie to the king.

That could be arranged, too.

Radburn smiled. With a snap of his fingers he summoned Fantôme. "Pack two horses lightly. We ride within the hour."

His shadow nodded and slipped away, as silent and forgettable as a ghost.

Radburn needed to go to Kirkenwood and confront Lady Resmiranda and whatever aid she had managed to conjure. Her training was scattered. Her actions merely instinctive reactions. She was no match for him. For the time being.

But first he had a demon to visit; a demon who lived beneath a barrow with a dragon guarding its portal.

Hugh stopped walking in the midst of the bustle of court life. He had been about to do something . . . What? Something tasted foul in his mouth and his mind. Everything looked a little hazy and unfocused. He fought to clear the miasma from his mind.

Something strange had occurred in the last few moments. What?

He scanned the Hall for inspiration. The queen and her infant son had replaced the grim-faced lords who attended the king at council. John caressed the boy's head in a loving gesture. Hugh remembered touching young John the same way. For a moment the king's expression softened, shedding years of care from his face.

Queen Isabelle smiled, displaying a fine set of pointed teeth to go with her sharp features. Her long chin and nose were offset by fine dark eyes—slightly almond in shape. When she had come to court eight years ago, barely twelve at the time to John's thirty-three, she'd been a sallow, shy child who hid behind her nurse and dull clothing. Now at twenty, she had blossomed into an exotic beauty who favored bright colors and fine jewels. She shifted the burden of young Henry to his father's arms. They made a fine picture of familial bliss.

Hugh ached for the time he might share a similar moment with Ana. At least he still had Johnny.

The king had sent Hugh on an errand. He remembered that much. He shook his head to clear the fuzziness of his thoughts. His ears continued to buzz.

He needed a cup of wine to remove the acrid taste in his mouth. Like sulfur?

Blakely often smelled of sulfur and blood. Hugh shook his head trying to remember if he had encountered the king's sorcerer half brother.

Ana would know how to retrieve the memory.

He missed her every hour they were separated. But for her own safety he needed to keep the king and Blakely away from Kirkenwood. Blakely wasn't likely to step more than two paces away from his half brother. So where was he now?

Political power lay in having the king's ear. Blakely made certain no one else got close enough to the king to countermand his influential whispers. Strange that the entire council—most John's aging contemporaries, two score and more in years, heeded the words of one so young and untried in battle as Blakely. Blakely couldn't be more than twenty-one or two.

"Will you sit at court this evening, Your Highness?" Hugh asked to cover his memory lapse. Something to do with Blakely.

"We have been here two weeks." John yawned hugely. His son, Henry, did likewise. The momentary likeness between father and son touched Hugh's heart. "We expected more disputes and finer hunting. Perhaps we should resume our intended progress toward Kirkenwood. Did you find Lord Blakely? What ails him?"

"I did not find Lord Blakely," Hugh replied. That did not sound right, but he couldn't remember seeing the king's brother. Or had he? Where else would the taste of sulfur come from?

He started searching every shadow for evidence of the king's half brother or the shadowy servant.

"I should like to visit Kirkenwood, John," Isabelle said. Her soft syllables spoke of her origins in southern France. "I have heard many of the legends surrounding the Griffins. Are they truly a clan of giants with magical powers?"

John laughed, bouncing his son on his knee. The boy joined his father in delighted peals. "Lady Resmiranda is tall, nearly as tall as us, but hardly a giant. All of the Griffins are merely men and women, our dear Isabelle." He kissed her cheek in reassurance, then continued. "The fact that they honor their genealogy more than most—inventing most of it, we are sure—makes the Griffins appear more formidable and important than they are. Everyone knows that King Arthur Pendragon is my ancestor, not hers."

Hugh almost laughed at that bald-faced lie. Henry II had planted the legendary King Arthur of ancient times in the vague nether ends of his family tree when the Abbot at Glastonbury had discovered a tomb beneath the ruins of his church that might or might not have belonged to Arthur and Guinevere. Hugh suspected the tomb had been created to attract pilgrims, and therefore money to rebuild his fire-ruined buildings.

John narrowed his eyes. "Yes, we do believe the time has come to invest the Baroness of Kirkenwood into her honors. She has had ample time to heal from the menacing cough. Send word for her to meet us there, Sir Hugh. We leave at dawn."

What if Hugh could not find Blakely before then? Did the sulfur on his tongue mean that Blakely had used a spell to hide himself. Possibly to travel to Kirkenwood ahead of the king and kidnap Ana?

Hugh sent a bevy of servants in search of the errant lord.

Life settled in at Kirkenwood as if I had never left, as if Uncle Henry and Aunt Lotta still ruled there. Except for the garden. The herbs had always been the private preserve of the family. No one entered the walled enclosure without permission from one of the family.

I found the weeds a formidable barrier in my quest for an herb that would help keep the sword hidden. A native of warmer climes, the love-lies-bleeding plant should be in a protected corner, probably near the wall that faced south where it would trap the most sunlight and heat. The paths between the once orderly rows still existed. Barely.

Early on the morning after I returned to Kirkenwood, I took my basket and my sharpened athame—Uncle Henry's ritual knife actually—and ventured into the garden. I longed to begin at the entrance, pulling weeds and clearing the delicate plants before they choked. But if I did that, the sword could be found a dozen times before I found the purple-red flowers of the love-lies-bleeding.

Even though dew still clung to the greenery and chilled the earth, I slipped off my clogs and slippers. I must focus and maintain contact with the earth for each part of the preparation for the magical spell of invisibility. I considered stripping off my gown, but too many people wandered the courtyard and the garden walls stood only shoulder high for me to be comfortable in such dishabille.

"How did you move over here?" I asked the wild endive that grew thick all along the north-facing side of the garden. I checked the other walls where the pernicious plants should be confined within their own bed. Sure enough, it grew thicker and more lush over there. "Well, I guess we will have fresh greens for supper."

I should really dig out the entire plant, saving the flowers for dye and roots for roasting, but I hadn't thought to bring a trowel, and I couldn't blunt and defile my knife with vigorous digging.

"Thank you, God, for the gift of these leaves and flowers. They shall provide me and mine with nourishment and delight. No part of you will be wasted," I promised. The concept of thanking the plant itself still felt alien. Everything came from God. So if I thanked Him, wasn't I also thanking the plants?

My mouth started watering at the thought of a large bowl of fresh greens dressed with hot vinegar, bacon fat, and spices. Yes, indeed, the entire harvest would be put to good use. I could have a new gown and dye it the same shade of yellow as my hair with the blossoms.

Gradually I worked my way through the copious wild endive toward the protected bed where Aunt Lotta had placed the most delicate plants. They had come from the Holy Land and other Mediterranean countries, brought back by Crusaders. Many of my family had taken the cross. Some had come back with treasures and knowledge. Most, like Uncle Henry's son and heir, had not returned at all.

The epitaph on Uncle Henry's tomb suggested he had followed one of the Crusades in his youth. I could not image that most gentle and nonviolent man wielding weapons in battle. Bits and pieces of stories I'd heard as a child suggested he had returned broken in faith as well as body. He had hinted of Aunt Lotta's healing of him. He referred to her as his salvation. I truly wanted to hear the rest of that story. Another time, when I could immerse myself in the numerous scrolls and books in the hidden library.

At last I spotted the drooping purple-red flowers of love-lies-bleeding. Was the name symbolic of the broken dreams and promises of so many of my family? I swallowed back the portents and omens and cleared the last of the overgrowth around the plants. One solitary stalk of love-lies-bleeding remained with a pitiful cluster of blossoms. All of the others had died.

No matter how I stretched my imagination, I could not harvest enough flowers to hide an entire sword. I didn't dare harvest more than two or three flowers. The rest must remain to propagate new plants. My spell would fail with this pitiful harvest.

Chapter 27

THREE quick slices of my athame gave me the few flowers I could safely harvest. Depressed and uncertain, I made my way back to the kitchen with the greens.

Already I could sense the sword emerging from the temporary look-the-other-way-you-don't-notice-me spell. The hairs on my arms and the back of my neck stood up and tingled. With the awareness that Excalibur reemerged into this reality, I imagined every person with magical talent suddenly began a journey to Kirkenwood to claim the artifact of power.

Perhaps I was the only one who could handle the sword safely. But until I knew how to use it, magically and physically, those who would claim Excalibur would want me dead.

Radburn Blakely would lead the charge. I hadn't much time to devise something, anything, that would conceal it again.

I remembered Uncle Henry saying something about harmonies and sympathies. If I could bury something akin to the sword with a miniature crown of love-lies-bleeding flowers, would the real sword then become as invisible?

No one paid me much attention as I scavenged Kirkenwood Grange for two identical eating knives—the smallest blades I could think of. Every person on the demesne possessed their own unique tool and wouldn't relinquish it willingly. I finally found a dull blade identical to my own stashed among the kitchen tools.

By that time, Cook had rung the bell to summon us to a midafternoon light refreshment. Supper wouldn't be served until sunset, very late in the day as May progressed toward June and the Solstice. I presided at the high table, achingly aware of the empty places on either side of me. Uncle Henry and Aunt Lotta should be here. Mama, too. Instead, my steward and Archie shared a trencher to my left. Three knights and their ladies sat to my right. I knew none of them intimately. Conversation revolved around planting and spring tournaments. None of it interested me at the moment, though I knew I must pay heed eventually.

As I left the table, I realized I'd given permission for all three of my knights to enter tournaments this season. They'd be gone for months, leaving me and Kirkenwood without mundane protection.

"Uh, Sir Simon," I called the senior of my military aides. "If King John requires my knights' service, you will have to leave the tournaments."

"Certainly, milady. 'Tis understood. Tournaments merely keep us in training for military campaigns." He bowed and kept a straight face at my naivete. His wife, Lady Hilda, twittered behind her hand. Horse-faced Hilda had acted as chatelaine of Kirkenwood in my absence. She belittled every word I spoke. Her yellow bliaud made her sallow skin look like old parchment. The fashionable wimple and chin band did nothing to enhance her narrow face and overly long jaw.

I had forsaken the required headgear for a simple but old-fashioned veil and circlet that matched an old woad-blue bliaud.

"And if King John demands scutage in lieu of your service?" Sir Simon asked.

"I pay and you come home." I had no idea if Uncle Henry's coffers contained enough silver pennies to pay the king for my three knights' service.

I'd best find out. But first I had to hide the sword.

Hidden inside the curtain wall, accessible only through the secret exit in the large bedchamber behind the Hall, was a room filled with the records of my family going back nearly seven hundred years. Along with the records, Uncle Henry had kept a grimoire, a book of spells compiled by himself and Aunt Lotta over their lifetimes. As I made my way through the dark tunnel to the room, I prayed the little book would contain a hint of the ritual I must follow.

It did. The words were written in an ancient dialect of Welsh, not my best language; Latin, French, and Saxon (and therefore German) I managed quite fluently. Welsh and Greek came to me in snatches and phrases that I had to think about. Of Arabic, Hebrew, and Persian I knew almost nothing. Uncle Henry had a complete command of them all. I puzzled over the words, trying to glean some meaning from the nonsensical syllables.

By the time I had memorized the incantation, my little oil lamp had burned low and my stomach growled, reminding me that the bell for Vespers should be ringing. But the church bells would not ring today, or any day until John reconciled with the church.

I suddenly felt lonely and empty at the prospect of missing mass every day for a long time to come.

Heaving a sigh of regret, I pushed back my chair and extinguished the oil lamp. Perhaps I should allow the spell to penetrate my mind during sleep. I'd start again at dawn.

As I exited the musty, familiar room, using only a tiny dot of witchlight, I tripped. A number of arcane tools, books, and cast-off furniture tumbled to the floor with a loud clatter. I cursed under my breath in Welsh, a language rich in nuance and filled with imaginative epithets.

Something long and thin rolled to my feet. I bent to move it out of my path, determined to set the room to rights tomorrow. My hand closed over the smooth wood of Uncle Henry's staff.

An image of the standing stones brightening with a ring of fire around the crowns flashed across my mind followed by a low chuckle. "Uncle Henry?" I asked the air, crossing myself in atavistic fear of a ghost.

Silence.

I thrust the staff out of my path. It rolled back on top of my feet, threatening to trip me. The chuckle sounded again.

"I get the message, Uncle Henry. I need to reanimate the stones before I try anything else."

The chuckle brightened to a laugh.

The last sliver of moonlight broke through the scattered cloud cover, highlighting the Midlands plains in cold streaks of silver light. Radburn reigned in his horse. The foul-tempered animal had run cross-country for nearly twelve hours. His own horse had foundered after nearly a full day of all-out running. Now his hired mount stood head drooping, breath heaving, hide sweating, legs splayed. It might not recover from the grueling journey. They had left Fantôme behind at midnight. Both the servant and his lowborn mount had collapsed after fording a stream only a fraction lower than full spate. Blakely had left royal orders for the peasants to build a bridge there. He could use the toll collection to add to his treasury.

If he were closer to his destination, Radburn would go ahead and slit his horse's throat. His demon would appreciate the blood.

Still several hours from Wells and the barrow northwest of the town, the blood would benefit no one.

"Come, you need to walk it off a bit before you catch pneumonia," he said, dismounting. The horse was too exhausted to snap at him, resist his tug on the reins, or move faster than a snail.

Radburn did not relish the prospect of walking the rest of the way to Wells. He wished his demon dwelled farther north—much farther north. But Henry Griffin and his wife Carlotta had banished the demon to this remote portal many years ago. They did not want it anywhere near their home and its previous hunting ground.

If they'd found a closer portal for the demon, then Radburn wouldn't have to waste so much time on this desperate dash nearly the length of England. But he needed the demon's help in negating whatever power Lady Resmiranda had unearthed. Even now the presence of that power made his skin itch unpleasantly. He had no doubt that his intended bride had brought the power forth. Only she, in all of England, possessed the raw talent to match his own. Other sorcerers lived throughout the land. Some of them could even rouse true power, but only after lengthy preparation, bloody sacrifice, and total exhaustion so they had no strength left to wield the power. Radburn knew them all, knew the taste of their magic, and could trace it from great distances.

This new menace had a different signature. He did not know the lady well enough to recognize her magic by taste alone. But no one else lived who could draw forth something this ancient and deadly to him. He had to negate it before she learned how to use it. For that he needed help.

Every hour he delayed on the road to his personal demon gave Resmiranda another hour to learn more about her powers and how to wield them. Radburn pressed on.

When moonlight made a narrow arrow of light in the big bedchamber behind the Hall at Kirkenwood Grange, I grabbed my shift and escaped to the courtyard. Tiptoeing through the assortment of sleeping bodies required every sense I possessed and too much witchlight. The staff with the dragon head was clutched tightly in my left hand. It seemed empty and vacant. As I emerged into the courtyard, I placed the small ball of cold flame atop the dragon.

The thing still looked and felt strange in my hand, but it lighted my path more efficiently. I needed the better light to find my way down the processional way to the village and the standing stones. The village slept, but not for long. I felt the chill moisture of dew hovering around the edges of my senses.

Before I could lose my courage at the pagan nature of what I must do, I touched the staff to the center stone. It rang slightly, the sound tingling at the base of my skull more than in my ears. The staff vibrated its full length, through my hand, and up my arm to my teeth.

Not a totally unpleasant sensation. I moved east to the stone that marked the sunrise on the summer solstice. This is where I thought I'd seen the face of King Arthur Pendragon. Fitting that he chose the east, the place of new beginnings and hope. His stone sounded a little dull, almost hollow when I rapped it with the fire-crowned staff.

From there I moved deasil around the outside circumference of the village. Some of the stones had become walls for various huts. These I struck lightly with the staff, afraid of awakening the inhabitants. Other stones still stood free and received as hard a blow as I could give them and not damage the staff. When I encountered a damaged stone, I chose the largest chunk that stood closest to its original position. For the missing stones, I could only stand the staff upright in the partially filled depressions where the stone had stood and recite a little prayer of grief for the breaking of the circle.

The trek seemed to take hours. In that time I learned a bit about each of the standing stones. Every one of them was slightly different, as if suited to one personality only. No wonder the ghosts of my ancestors had found homes within. As I worked my way around the circle, I looked for the one that would be mine when the time came. I found it, just west of south, a transitional place that needed filling. The chiming sound that rippled across the moors when I struck it reminded me of faery laughter. Legend claimed that when the faeries left England, they moved west, far, far to the west. I smiled and moved on.

At last I returned to my starting position at due east. Fatigue left a hollow feeling in my middle, and the staff seemed too heavy to lift anymore. But my mind lightened and brightened.

Dragging my feet and breathing heavily, I stumbled back to the center stone, the largest of the lot. Weakly, I touched it again with the staff. I just did not have the strength left to give it the mighty blow the magic needed.

My eyes closed on their own while I breathed deeply.

A great weight suddenly lifted from my body. I seemed to be floating up along the crown of the stones.

As I opened my eyes, a chain of living flame leaped from the dragon head of the staff to the top of the center stone. From there it raced out to each of the cardinal directions and around the circle of stones, bringing them to life.

Laughter and joy filled my tired body as the stones and the ghosts within came to life. I had awakened the protection they offered the village, the grange, and all who dwelled within.

The fire faded from my physical sight, becoming one more of my heightened senses.

At that moment the dragon head broke free of the staff and dropped to my feet. Alarmed, I bent to retrieve it. The staff was important to working magic. I'd need it to hide Excalibur as well as to build up my psychic muscles while I learned to use the sword.

The ancient wood carving crumbled to dust when I touched it.

Only then did I realize that someone, many generations ago, had cut the sigil of birth and fertility into the turf where I stood barefoot. Nearby, I detected similar symbols for male, female, death, and infinity.

"I thought you would be the one to awaken the stones," Father Truman said, stepping out of the morning mist into the circle of stones. He seemed to step out of some distant time and place as well. "They do not respond to me even though I sense their resonance in my blood."

"I broke the staff," I sobbed, running my fingers through the fragments and dust of the dragon head.

"No. You made it your own. The dragon head belonged to Lady Carlotta Griffin. You need to find your own symbol." He half smiled and drew his hands from the deep sleeves of his priestly robe. In his left hand he clutched a pewter-circled cross. "I believe this might suit your purposes and ease your sensibilities."

"I can't take it. It belongs in the church," I protested. My knees cramped from staying in my crouch too long. I stood and faced Father Truman, feeling almost his equal in this decision.

"The church is closed while the Interdict rests heavily in this land. The cross will do more good on your staff, following you as you bring healing back to your people, and to England."

"I have no such great ambitions."

"Perhaps the stones and your ancestors know better." He glided over to me, seemingly heedless of the rough turf, the sheep droppings, and the ancient, pagan sigils. He grasped the staff and levered the crown down to his eye level. My hand never let go of the oak. I didn't know if I could allow another to take possession of it at that moment. Magic still sang in my blood and the fire atop the stones still brightened all of my senses.

"I unscrewed the cross from its flat base. Let's see if it fits." He affixed the cross to the old wood. "Almost as if made for it," he chuckled. "A little magic glue wouldn't hurt, though. You'll figure out how to do that on your own. Now I think you should go back to bed and rest before you begin a new day with a new destiny."

The moment he released the staff, I pulled it upright again. A sense of completeness, of rightness, flowed down the length of wood.

The fire flared again atop the stones and along the lines of the sigils in the turf.

Birds sang as the sun rose, clearing the mist. Bright drops of moisture sparkled like the clear crystals in the cave.

Chapter 28

THE horse did not recover enough for Radburn to mount it. He climbed up onto the slight elevation of a Roman road, the horse dragging and stumbling after him. Both he and the horse found the footing easier despite the missing paving stones and the tall growth between the remaining quarried rock.

As false drawn brought the birds awake, traffic on the ancient byway increased. Radburn hadn't seen many traveling on his mad dash across the country. Most people kept to the roads, new and old, that he had disdained as too indirect. Now he welcomed the presence of people. For them to be out and about this early meant some form of civilization must be nearby. An inn, castle, or manor would serve him with the opportunity to change horses and continue his journey.

The innkeeper at the next ford only haggled a little for a new mount. He recognized the worth of the animal Radburn led. A few days of rest and good feed would restore him. Radburn wasn't sure the horse he took in exchange would ever match the one he gave up. It plodded at a steady rate, little faster than Radburn could have walked.

By sunset, the rooftops of Wells came into view. The town looked curiously empty without the horde of craftsmen scrambling over the half-built walls of the cathedral. The air seemed strangely silent without the canons singing Vespers. Beautiful music soared from Wells at every service and through much of the day between.

As long as Innocent III maintained the Interdict, no money flowed into church coffers for maintenance, let alone new construction. No Masses inspired men to sing to the glory of God.

Good, he thought. *More money for the king's treasury. Money I can access with or without John's permission.* Of course, sometimes, the king gave a signed writ to pay his half brother without realizing what he signed. John's mind should be easily clouded by suggestion, but lately Radburn had to whisper directly into the king's ear, not from any distance. More often than not, the suggestion worked better when inserted into the king's right ear. Was he going deaf in the left?

Nothing to worry about. Once he'd tapped the demon's power again, he'd easily oust Sir Hugh from the favored place to the king's right and reestablish the wards that had crumbled whenever Lady Resmiranda Griffin neared the king.

He'd been on the road for a day and a half, without sleep and barely anything to eat. The sustained fast sharpened his perceptions and allowed him to focus his energies toward a conclusion.

Lady Ana had had the same day and a half to study her new power, learn how to use it, and hone her skills for the coming confrontation.

He skirted the city, using his demon-enhanced sight to pick his way up the broken Mendip Hills. Steep ravines didn't bother the newest horse. It neither slowed nor sped, no matter the terrain or Radburn's spurring. A sharp jab to its sides produced merely a disdainful glance.

With the loss of daylight came an influx of clouds and mist. Demons could hide in the mist, wraiths and barrow wights did the same. But not his demon. His demon needed specific words spoken at the dragon door along with a specific ritual before it could come forth.

Pieces of the spell and ritual had eluded Radburn for most of his forty-two years. He'd never confronted the demon face-to-face, only gleaned some of its power through a tiny crack in the partially opened door. That power kept him young and vigorous while his younger half brother aged daily.

Radburn opened his senses, welcoming whatever kindred spirits lurked in the mist. The night seemed unusually quiet and empty. He missed the tiny *shushing* noises made by night creatures of this world and the others. Atavistic fear and loneliness chilled his spine and sent his heart racing; it was the kind of fear mundanes felt in the presence of the Otherworld. He searched the landscape high and low with all of his senses for a hint of some other life-form.

Nothing.

You are alone, he thought he heard his demon whisper. *Utterly alone as you have never been alone before.*

He shuddered and pressed the horse forward. It continued uphill at the same slow pace it had maintained for hours without sign of fatigue or stress.

At last Radburn caught a glimpse of the upright stones marking the barrow entrance. He breathed deeply and easily for the first time since leaving the city behind. The small circle of stones before the barrow greeted him with their usual waves of barely contained energy. He stood in the exact center, letting the power bathe him, renew him, prepare him for the ordeal of opening the dragon door. Maybe this time he would get it right.

The moment he stepped beneath the lintel stone he reached for the torches. No sense wasting his energy on extrasensory sight. He closed his hand around empty air. The lights he'd left here, ready for ignition, had been disturbed.

Someone has been here. Someone dangerous!

He knew of only one person with the audacity to disturb a barrow. Lady Resmiranda Griffin. When had she been here? Before or after his men had put Mendip Mor to the torch?

"Curse you, milady," he muttered as he wasted a little energy seeking the torches. One of the three he'd left here lay on the wrong side of the opening with flint and iron stacked neatly beside it. She'd left a clear reminder of her presence. Or was it a warning?

Stumbling in his haste, Radburn made his way along the familiar path to the dragon door. He pressed his left palm flat on the wooden panels.

"Grandsire, I am here," he announced himself with thoughts as well as words.

He sensed a gentle stirring behind the door. It should have been stronger, more anxious for escape.

"Grandsire, is something wrong?" he called.

The portal is sealed, the demon replied so weakly Radburn had to strain to hear it.

"Of course the portal is sealed. I sealed it last time I left you."

The portal is sealed. Had he truly heard the echo of the previous statement or merely imagined it? The sounds were so faint, barely as loud as worms moving through the earth.

With trembling fingers and anxious thoughts, Radburn examined the perimeter of the doorway. He jerked his hand away from the burning green glow he encountered. When he touched the dragon's head handle, the entire portal blazed with the same eldritch green.

In the back of his mind he heard faeries giggle.

"Damn you, Lady Resmiranda! You have double-sealed the portal so that I cannot open it. I'll kill you. I'll torture you until you beg for death. I'll send you back through this very demon door as food for my grandsire and his kin!"

"Please reconsider, Your Highness," Hugh said as he walked down the steps of Durham Castle toward their waiting horses.

The sun had risen several hours ago and continued its relentless march toward noon. Still the queen and her ladies dallied over their trunks and preparations.

He had to stall. Ana had not contacted him yet. She wasn't ready to face Blakely.

"Lady Resmiranda has had only two weeks to recover from her cough. Even if she is stronger, the journey to Kirkenwood could bring on a relapse. Do you want to expose yourself, your wife, and your infant son to this pernicious ailment?"

John stopped short. Hugh nearly overran his heels. "You have a point, Sir Hugh. Tell the queen she may join us at Kirkenwood in a few days, or perhaps another week, when we send word that Lady Resmiranda presents no health risk to our heir." The king continued his march toward his horse, pointing to various courtiers, lords, and soldiers to remain behind with the ladies. The party was reduced by two thirds before he finished.

"Highness, shouldn't you wait to hear from Lord Blakely?" Hugh tried to stall him one more time.

"The devil take Radburn. If he fled our court without permission, he can get himself out of whatever trouble he's stumbled into. We will not pay his creditors this time." John slapped his thigh with his riding gloves. White patches emphasized the downturn of his mouth and the pinch of his nostrils.

Hugh decided he'd best keep quiet for a while rather than anger his king further.

"And you, Fitz Chênenoir." John whirled and pointed angrily at

Hugh. "You will lead our troops into Wales and capture the sons of every prince you can lay your hands on. We will hold them hostage against their fathers' good behavior. They'll not burn another of our castles."

"Me? Why me, Your Highness?" Hugh fumed. He couldn't allow John to proceed to Kirkenwood without him. Ana relied upon him for protection from this man and from Blakely, wherever he'd gotten to.

"You demanded revenge for the death of your friend, Sir Edmund and his lady wife. Take it." John mounted and dug his spurs into his horse. He rode through the gates before Hugh had a chance to gather his thoughts for another argument. The abbreviated court clattered after their king.

"He and the queen had words last night," Lord Silvester of Lincoln said from directly behind Hugh. "He's off to soothe his dick without her."

Hugh did not want to hear that.

"Frankly, I'm surprised John hasn't put Isabelle aside, as he did his first wife. She causes him more trouble than she's worth. Her continental lands and allies turned to dust since her first betrothed betrayed John out of jealousy," Lord Silvester continued. "She is strong willed and does not bow to any man's wishes—even her husband's."

"I am certain John loves his wife, especially now that she has presented him with an heir," Hugh retorted.

"And she's pregnant again. She doesn't care where he sleeps, as long as it's not with her. For all our sakes, I hope he finds a willing lady at his next stopping place."

"And I pray he doesn't," Hugh whispered. The image of Ana sleeping beside him in the armory, holding his hand, soothing away his nightmares lightened his heart a little. Don't give your heart to him, Ana. Please don't succumb to his charms.

"Silvester, follow the king. Be my friend and look out for my interests at Kirkenwood."

"I'd rather bash heads in Wales. You follow the king, and I'll take your command."

"I cannot disobey my king. No matter what my heart tells me. Please, Silvester, honor your vow of friendship from the time I stopped that German knight from running you through."

"Very well." Silvester heaved a sigh. "But you know, I have little influence with John. He has less use for me since I preferred to stand castle guard in Lincoln to paying him to find another to take my place."

"Saddle up, Silvester. I need you to protect Lady Resmiranda when I cannot."

I woke late after the exhausting ritual with the standing stones. The sun rested two hands' breadths above the horizon. My belly felt bloated and tender. *Merde!* The monthly flux had stricken me at the most inopportune time. Three days early. My mind shouted, *Unclean!* How could I work the invisibility spell while my body betrayed my purity?

I pounded my fist into the straw mattress of the great bed that had belonged to Aunt Lotta and Uncle Henry. Well, if I couldn't work the magic, I could spend the next four or five days reading through the massive annals collected by the family. I needed to find a particular document that King John feared. I needed to copy it and entrust it to several hiding places, each with a different keeper. If anything happened to me, those keepers must publish the letter far and wide.

I might also find a more effective invisibility spell for Excalibur in Uncle Henry's grimoire.

The household went about their daily routine. They had done this without supervision for months. My presence as lady of the manor seemed redundant. I could see many changes I wanted to make, things I had learned in helping run a convent. But for now, my people knew their traditional work better than I did. After snatching some bread, cheese, and ale, I made an appearance in the Hall and listened to Daffyd report on the planting. Feeling absolutely useless, I glanced about the Hall looking for something, anything, to justify my existence among these people.

Newynog paced beside the length and breadth of the Hall, ears perked at an odd angle. She worried at the closed doorway to the kitchen, then at the door to my chamber. Nose up and then down again she worked her way back to the main doors opening into the courtyard. Something about the angle of her tail and the thickness of her drool warned me that all was not as it seemed.

"Daffyd, see to it that Newynog is kept away from the other dogs. I believe she is coming into her first heat—much too young to bear a healthy litter." After her injuries on the road to Bellecôte Castle, I wasn't sure she had the stamina to bear a litter. And if she did mate with one of the hunting dogs, she would become too cumbersome and self-absorbed with her young to adequately protect me in an emergency. I'd not be comfortable fleeing again without her.

Why did I know that soon I must leave Kirkenwood again? I'd had no dreams of portent. Yet . . .

We had no oubliette at Kirkenwood.

Just then Archie opened the main doors and stalked toward me. Newynog dashed out the moment the opening grew large enough to admit her sleek body.

"Catch her!" I yelled. Daffyd and Archie dove after my dog. They lunged for her together, colliding in a heap. Archie held a handful of tail fur.

Newynog, the little hussy, turned and grinned at them. I could almost hear her doggy laughter at their clumsiness. She pranced side-ways as she descended the steps to the courtyard, full of her cleverness and her need to attract a mate.

"Newynog," I called to her with mind and voice in the tone I reserved for my familiar. *"Newynog, come to me. Now."* I made each step toward her deliberate, nonthreatening, while packing as much authority into the words as possible.

She ignored me, prancing about the courtyard ever closer to the kennels beside the stable.

"Catch my dog," I ordered in the same tones I used to communicate with Newynog. *"Do not let her near the other dogs."*

Every person within physical and mental hearing distance turned to look at me for the space of two heartbeats, then each dove to intercept my errant dog.

"How . . ." I shook my head in bewilderment. How had I done such a thing? How could I do such a thing? I'd violated the privacy of all of my people at once. I'd commanded their actions and they obeyed. How? I should never have done such a vile thing. I should never . . .

Only then did I realize that I held the staff and had firmly grounded the butt in the earth at my feet.

Off in the corner of the courtyard, the cranky old raven cawed from his perch on the well. Father Truman stood beside the nasty bird. In his black robe with the hood pushed back just enough to reveal his prominent nose, he looked akin to the bird that had haunted the well for as long as I could remember. He nodded toward me and smiled.

You are learning, Little One. Learning the extent of your talent. But you have much more to learn. A man's voice—Father Truman's or Radburn Blakely's, I couldn't tell which—came into my head unbidden.

Instinctively I shut out the voice and the thought that I might be required to use this invasive—and vile—talent of mine again. When I encountered Radburn Blakely, I'd have to resort to tricks and ploys that made me feel more unclean than the flow of blood the nuns had taught me to despise.

A round of wild barking and desperate howls rose from the kennels.

"Newynog!" I had more important things to worry about.

Chapter 29

We cornered Newynog eventually. I wasn't sure if we were in time to keep her away from the male dogs or not. Hoping we had, I collared and leashed her and took her with me to the secret room. She settled happily on the floor beside me. Not a good sign.

Uncle Henry and Aunt Lotta had shared the grimoire. Aunt Lotta's tight and tiny handwriting challenged my eyes, but her neat and precise instructions gave me easy rituals for every conceivable need—from warding the entire demesne against intruders, to attracting bees, to specific plants for cross-pollinating. Uncle Henry's large and florid handwriting was easier to read, but his instructions tended to be symbolic and oblique.

I settled upon Aunt Lotta's spell for hiding within the pantry toxic plants needed to purge illnesses so that Cook and his helpers would never mistake them for something more tasty to season the meat. As I read the ingredients, I ticked them off mentally, knowing I could find all of them readily—including a feather from the cranky old raven who perched on the well.

But what was this? She had used her own menstrual blood in the formula. I cringed and turned the page quickly. My own prejudices kept me from asking why or investigating the spell further. I checked three others, one for warding the four corners of a room so that no word escaped it to unwanted listening ears, another for preventing sticky fingers from dipping into a treasure trove, and one more specific than my own clumsy spell for wishing others to look anywhere but at the spell-caster and never notice her presence so that she could eavesdrop. All of them required the spell-caster's own menstrual blood.

My nose wrinkled in disgust at my own smell. How could I use such a tainted and unholy ingredient? Why would I want to?

The challenge to my preconceived thinking gave me a headache. I turned the page again, seeking a spell I was more comfortable with. Folded many times, a piece of parchment fluttered loose from the grimoire.

Slowly, I retrieved the parchment. Did I dare read anything meant to be kept secret from the rest of the world?

I had no choice. Uncle Henry had wanted me to become the next Pendragon. He had begun my training to use this little book in whatever way seemed necessary.

Castle Libellule, On the Feast of Raphael the
Archangel, Anno Dommine 1204
To my beloved Uncle, Lord Henry, Baron of Kirkenwood,
Knight of the Cross, now residing as guest of King John in
Carlisle Castle,
Greetings.
How fares my daughter? Since the disappearance and
presumed death of her mother, I have longed daily for you
to send the child to me. But I know the journey is too
dangerous; the chances of our enemies discovering her while on
the road and vulnerable are too great. I also know that
she must remain in England to take up the staff and ring of
our family when you can no longer wield them. Cherish her,
dear Uncle. Love her as if she were your own daughter and
not just your distant relative who must inherit your
responsibilities by default.
After much reflection, I cannot perform the heinous
deed required of me by my king, Uncle Henry. For the
safety of John's reign, I know I must arrange the murder of
a man innocent of all wrongdoing except to be born son of
a prince and grandson of a king. Yet the rules of
chivalry, the ties of blood to this man, and my own
conscience will not allow me to murder Arthur of Brittany.
The young prince I have come to know could follow King
Richard as a leader on the battlefield, but has not the
skills to rule a country through law as John does. Arthur
has not the education nor the familiarity with the English
people John does. If he had managed to engage John in
battle, I could have slain him with honor. But as my

prisoner, I hold his safety uppermost.
Please know, Uncle Henry, that I will abide by your
decision in this matter. Until then, I hold Arthur captive
in the family stronghold. Should he outlive me, I entrust
his safekeeping to you or your designated heir as Pendragon
of Britain and head of the Griffin Clan. I pray that my
daughter will grow in wisdom to continue our proud
tradition of peace, justice and rule by law. I trust you
to teach her that honor, loyalty, and promises are
important.
Your loving nephew,
Sir Brian Griffin

I stared at the letter from my father. He loved me and missed me. Tears of joy and loneliness burned my eyes.

My father loved me!

Arthur of Brittany lived. Or he had in October four years ago.

John would give much to ensure the man's death. King Philip of France would give more to use Arthur as a means of defeating and humiliating John once and for all.

This was the piece of evidence John sought and must never find. As long as its existence threatened his crown, I could manipulate him, keep him from abusing his powers.

But if he ever found and destroyed it, then my life and many others were likely forfeit.

I emerged from my subterranean lair blinking at the brightness of the courtyard. The thick cloud cover should not have forced me to squint and look away from the light. I perceived an unusual clarity to each image around me, while the edges seemed just fuzzy enough to begin a blending of one into the other.

I drew a dipper of water from the well. A bright reflection on the water's surface stabbed my eyes with pain. The raven clacked his beak. He sounded almost concerned.

I knew I would dream, soon, possibly while still awake. A quick glance at the sky confirmed the approach of an unusual storm. This far north storms came more frequently than fair weather. But this one . . . a storm of visions?

A chill wind wrapped around me, raising goose bumps on my arms and the back of my neck. I hurried into the Hall, dragging Newynog with me, eager for the roaring warmth of the fire.

Serfs arranged the trestle tables down the length of the room in preparation for the evening meal. I had closeted myself in the dark room of scrolls for longer than I thought. The knowledge I carried with me weighed heavily on my heart and my mind.

"Mulled wine, please," I called to the scullery maid who wiped the tabletop with a damp cloth. "And hurry."

Darkness crowded my sight. I hoped to hold off the vision as long as possible. Wine sometimes worked. It dulled all of my senses, natural and otherworldly.

"Hurry, please," I whispered as I sank onto a low stool before the hearth. The flames eased the chill in my back, but I still wrapped my arms tightly around myself, rocking forward and back. Newynog was no help. She took herself off to a corner to groom herself and dream her own dreams.

I couldn't succumb to the visions yet. I needed time to decide who would honor the trust of copies of that dangerous letter. I had to figure out how I, as The Pendragon, fit into the complicated puzzle of dynastic intrigue.

Someone thrust a tall cup of warmed wine into my hands. I sipped gratefully. But I mustn't look into the wine. I mustn't look into the fire or someone's eyes. Any one of these glances would trigger the dream.

"Holy Mother, why? Why must I be the one to endure these terrible portents?" I prayed. The strand of beads with Arthur Pendragon's cross slid through my fingers. I sipped and prayed, unaware of anything that went on around me.

"Forgive me, Holy Mother. I was born into an unclean clan. I never wanted this talent. I want only to live a godly life as a wife and mother. Help me, Sweet Jesu. Help fight the demons that plague my senses."

"Are you ill, milady?" Archie asked. He stood between me and the rest of the room, guarding me.

"I . . . ah . . . I . . ." I looked up to answer his steadfast concern. Firelight glinted on the metal studs in his leather armor. The image of flames bounced back into my eyes and I fell. . . .

Riders. Many riders coming to Kirkenwood. From the southeast.

From the west. From the south. All were dangerous. All brought fire and death with them.

"Post double guards!" I said. Though the words echoed loudly in my ears, the dozens of people assembling in the Hall for dinner went about their business without looking at me. Only Archie bent lower to listen more closely.

"Turn the dogs loose, assign one to each of the guards on the wall. But bring Newynog to me first. Sound the alarm at the first sign of movement on the moors." The words fell from my mouth without thinking.

"Aye, Lady. I'll see to it. Are the black raiders from Mendip Mor headed this way?"

"Yes. No. I'm not certain. All I know is that men come from three directions. All of them seek my destruction."

Excalibur called to me. I sensed it humming in the crypt, could almost see it glowing with the need to defend me. To defend England.

But I did not know how to use it. I could barely lift it with my magical strength. My enemies would find it before I could wield it with impunity. I could stall no longer. I must work the invisibility spell tonight, at the dark of the moon, with my own menstrual blood.

I shivered again with repugnance and fear. Working the spell with unclean ingredients would drive me farther away from the Holy Mother.

"Archie," I called to Hugh's most trusted companion. "Tomorrow at dawn, will you begin to teach me how to use a sword?

Radburn reined in the plodding stallion. His awareness of other people pressed on his temples. He needed to observe before proceeding.

The stupid horse took six steps before he realized something was different about the pressure of the bit in his mouth. Then he looked back at his rider in inquiry before slowing until he stomped in place, still walking but not moving.

The view from the top of this hillock spread out over miles of new growth in the freshly tilled fields, fat sheep and their bouncing lambs grazing on the hillsides, and clear running streams. The land seemed to glow with benevolent power. Absolutely lovely and totally disgusting. Not a bit of strife or anger to disrupt John's reign.

The moving mass of men and horses that disturbed Radburn's senses were not yet within view.

Whatever artifact Lady Resmiranda had unearthed had to be destroyed. Now, before its mere presence uprooted all of Radburn's seeds of chaos. The next king might not be as malleable as John. Philip of France had rooted out Radburn's followers in Normandy and either executed or converted them back into the bosom of Holy Mother Church.

For the last four years, since John had retreated from the continent for the last time, Radburn had worked patiently, diligently to rebuild his supporters among the disgruntled. A few more years of pushing John into stupidly betraying his barons before they could betray him would have them all so angry, they'd do anything to be rid of John Plantagenet. John's only legitimate heir was an infant. Who better to rule as Henry's regent than his doting uncle, Radburn Blakely.

Then all of England would fall before the ravenous demon horde now hiding behind sealed portals.

He could afford to be patient. Time moved differently for Radburn Blakely than for other men. His demon blood kept him young and vigorous.

If only he weren't so fatigued. This journey had taken a greater toll on his reserves than he liked.

God's wounds, he was tired. He rubbed his face, easing the sagging muscles. Beneath his beard stubble, his skin felt loose enough to generate wrinkles.

He just hoped his youthful appearance would not crumble because he had not been able to free the demon enough to renew his vigor. Dryness rasped on his hands as he rubbed his face again.

Perhaps if he killed someone and bathed in their blood?

But first Radburn had to stop Lady Resmiranda Griffin and her artifact of power.

He watched the bucolic landscape a moment more. A small cloud of dust near the horizon signaled the approach of men and horses. Soon, Sir Hugh Fitz Chênenoir's banner of the boar and unicorn rampant floated above the horde. Twenty—no—thirty knights and nearly two hundred men at arms followed the banner, heading for the Welsh border.

So, John had followed through with Radburn's plan to seize hostages among the Welsh princes. An ill-advised move that would sow the seeds of discord and weaken John's position as a war leader.

Radburn grinned. Sir Hugh would work diligently to achieve John's orders—so diligently that the Welsh would be up in arms within a month. *And* Fitz Chênenoir was far away from Kirkenwood. He'd not interfere with Radburn's plans for a hasty marriage across the border in Scotland.

He waited for the cavalcade to pass into the distance. Then he dug his spurs into the stallion. The horse lifted each of his feet in turn without moving and returned to munching the sweet grass beneath the low bushes.

"Move, damn you!" Radburn yelled at the horse.

It turned to look at him and sighed as a tired mother reacted to a two-year-old throwing a temper tantrum. And, like a mother, the horse returned to his meal, ignoring Radburn's demands.

"I'll feed you to the Griffin's pack of wolfhounds—my pack of wolfhounds—if you don't get moving!" Radburn threatened, digging in his spurs once more.

The horse reached for another tuft of grass two steps along the path they had been following.

"Well, that's progress."

Suddenly the sky brightened as if the sun had burned through a light haze—but there had been no haze. The auras around every plant, tree, creature of field and forest, and person tending the fields flared and intensified.

Images of a flaming sword burned Radburn's eyelids.

He screamed and covered his eyes with both hands, trying to blot out the instrument of his doom.

"Excalibur!" he gasped. "She's unearthed Excalibur, and she's using it. Demons help me, I've got to destroy it before she learns all of its secrets." If he got to the sword in time, before Resmiranda bonded with it and made it her own, he could break it and the magic embedded into the blade. But every time Resmiranda worked magic with or was even close to the sword she strengthened both herself and the blade.

"Hurry, horse. We have to stop her."

This time the horse obeyed his prodding and trotted north toward Kirkenwood of his own volition.

Too nervous to eat, I made my way back to the lair—as I had begun to call Uncle Henry's sanctuary—for the recorded ritual and many of the ingredients. Swallowing my disgust, I added the rag soiled with my own bodily fluids to the herbs that would burn on the brazier.

Before that, I had to set candles at North, East, South, and West and light them in a sun path beginning with east, the position of sunrise. Aunt Lotta had said that I must light the candles and the brazier from my mind and not with flint and tinder. True fire was different from a ball of witchlight. Many years ago, Uncle Henry had helped me summon the element of fire. Bringing forth one tiny spark had required intense concentration. A headache and exhaustion had laid me low for hours afterward. I had never repeated the feat on my own.

Actually I had tried it only once, convinced that if I used any portion of my talent I would burn in hell for all eternity. That one time I tried, the vigil light by the altar had sputtered and died in the middle of singing Lauds. At such an early hour, between midnight and dawn, I thought relighting the oil lamp with my mind might be easier than refilling the oil chamber and borrowing a flame from the altar, with proper prayers repeated at each stage of the ritual.

I had been very young and hadn't realized that all fire—especially the kind I ignited with my mind—needed fuel. The flame had flared briefly and then died before anyone but me noticed. I had ended up going through the elaborate process of renewing the lamp on my own, while half asleep and nearly blind with a headache.

My only consolation as an adult was that I had brought a cold light to my hand with ease when I entered the tomb.

Taking several deep breaths, I stared at the wick of a small working candle. "Holy Mother, bring light into this world of darkness," I whispered while I fingered the gold-and-ivory beads on the prayer chain. My foot touched the staff that I had leaned against the desk.

The candlewick glowed red, then hot yellow, and burst into flame before I could mutter a second prayer. Carefully, I lit each candle in turn, invoking the spirit of each direction and each element. Then I used my working candle to ignite the tinder in the brazier. It, too, flared hungrily. I fed the tiny flames more fuel. When the fire crackled cheerfully, I dropped the first herb into it, reciting the Welsh words I barely understood. Aromatic smoke filled the room. My eyes focused more sharply at the center of my field of vision while it became fuzzy around the edges.

The walls of the room seemed to dissolve, replaced by shimmering light that wavered as if silver cloth caught in a light breeze.

I took a deep breath, filling my being with the smoke. Then I dropped the next herb into the fire and the next. At each addition I recited the words of Aunt Lotta's spell followed by my own prayer. Power tingled in my fingertips. My hair crackled with energy. I could almost see through the thick stone walls of my lair.

Finally, I dropped the bloody rag into the fire. A new odor rose pungently, but not unpleasantly. Each component of the rag and bloody fluid, the herbs and the twigs separated in my senses. My head spun, and I lost track of time.

When I opened my eyes again, the brazier had burned nearly to ash and the candles looked several finger-lengths shorter. I hadn't much time. I had to finish before the fire burned out.

I held the two matching eating knives over the flames, letting the fire warm the blades. Reciting more Welsh and Latin prayers, I placed a love-lies-bleeding flower upon each blade, and dribbled wine over them. My hands trembled with the magic I had invoked. My eyes lost focus. I could no longer clearly see the knives.

Now, my senses screamed. *Bury them now!* I placed one of the blades behind a loose stone in the lair. Then taking my working candle, the staff, and the second blade I traced a doorway through the magic circle described by the directional candles. Only then did I step through the wall of power into a mundane and rather shabby room.

I made my way through the curtain wall tunnel, down the trapdoor, and into the cave system. Shadows of fluttering silver followed me, cloaking me from sight. The imperfections and puddles along the path receded, replaced by the same shimmering silver as my cloak of invisibility.

Excalibur awaited me. It seemed to gather light and power as I approached it. I touched the hilt reverently. A soft hum sounded in the back of my head. The little eating knife with its tiny crown of love-lies-bleeding nestled neatly upon the blade, mimicking the sword in position and shape. Just before I withdrew my hand from the knife, I reached into my pocket and brought out the letter from my father to Great-uncle Henry. I tucked it beneath the blade.

Then I stepped back and watched as the two weapons faded from sight, taking the dangerous letter with them into whatever nether-world hid them.

Would I have the strength and resolve to retrieve them when I knew how to use them?

Only time and my own pursuit of knowledge could determine that. "Sweet Jesu, grant me the time and peace to learn what I must to counter the evil that abounds in this world and corrupts those in power."

I don't know if anyone heard my prayers.

Chapter 30

THWACK! My wooden sword landed solidly against a canvas mannequin. It swayed and spun from its suspension rope. The fixed sword in its "hand" waved wildly. I followed my sword's momentum in a circle and struck again. This blow skimmed the mannequin's midriff and continued, pulling me off-balance.

I struggled to remain upright and in place. Sweat poured from my brow, blinding me with the salty sting. My shoulders ached and burned. My knees trembled. But still I swung the sword, determined to learn the balance, the swing, how to use the momentum.

Archie and I had been at this every day for nearly a week. My men watched with half smirks at the sight of their lady wearing boy's braies and chausses, leather tunic, and boots. Barbaric clothing. They also nodded approval each time I did something right—not very often.

They kept constant vigil on the curtain wall and atop the watchtower. The dogs prowled with them, sniffing the air for the enemy we all knew must come.

My teacher stood to one side, arms crossed in front of him, a deep frown on his face. "Interesting follow-through," he muttered, heaving himself off the horse trough that supported his broad frame. "But if our friend here had been alive, he had the chance to hamstring you as you turned."

"What if I'd knocked him off-balance with the first blow?" I asked, trying to salvage something from my lesson with the mannequin.

"Possibly, you'd have time to recover and reengage him on the upswing. That's lesson number one: keep your opponent off-balance and on the defensive as much as possible. Here, let me show you.

Take it slow and count the steps." He grabbed the fixed sword from the mannequin and proceeded to demonstrate precisely where I had gone wrong. But this time I had a mind open to me. He revealed every movement to me before he flexed a muscle.

I countered each, feeling the rhythm and flowing with the motion. As we danced about the courtyard, I became aware of him as a man, more than just a sparring partner. His musky sweat tantalized my senses, as did the warmth of his body and the burning touch of his skin. With my senses open, I knew the desire of every man within sight. My own needs flared. I might be the lady and they my hired guards, but for a few moments we all knew each other as men and one strong, desirable woman.

I clamped down on those senses. I needed to practice swordplay, not flirting. Then I began noticing Archie's subtle shifts in posture, glance, and balance. These clues provided almost as much information as his gullible mind. Blakely had mental shields I could not hope to break. But he had a body with muscles and skin and eyes he must use. My confidence grew, and I stepped into Archie's next swing to block it.

He shifted his grip in mid swing and knocked me down on my bottom with the flat of his sword.

I heard a little chuckle run around the walls of watching men.

"Lesson number two: watch every move your opponent does and does not make until you know his rhythm. But you still need to remember I'm as tricky as you—maybe trickier. I've had more experience outfoxing men who wanted to kill me." Archie offered his hand to help me up.

I glared at it a moment, nursing my hurt bum and my sore pride. After several long heartbeats I clasped his fingers, but instead of scrambling to my feet, I used his arm as a lever and hauled him off his feet and into the dust. In seconds I was atop him with my belt knife at his throat.

A flush of gloating sent power—magical and mundane—through every fiber of my body. I was in control. A heady sensation.

"Very good, milady. Lesson number three: never trust anyone on the field of battle. I yield. But you should have made me land flat on my back rather than my shoulder so that landing knocked the wind from me."

"Show me," I ordered, standing up and offering Archie my hand. He scrambled up himself, keeping his eyes on my hands.

"Very well, milady. Stand thus." He demonstrated his earlier stance. Seconds later I found myself flying through the air over his head. Instead of landing on my back, winded and helpless, he jerked his arm at the last minute, so that I got my feet under me.

"Show me again."

I found myself on the ground five times before I found my own balance and leverage points—different from his because of his greater height and body mass. Three more times and I knew my body would remember the right posture to throw an opponent.

When I'd mastered the flip, we returned to more swordplay. By the time we finished, I could barely raise my wooden sword—a tenth the weight of Excalibur—as high as my waist.

"How do men do this? Day after day, hour after hour," I gasped, grabbing my knees and pulling great draughts of air into my laboring lungs. But even with aching lungs and drooping shoulders I knew an exultation. My blood fairly glowed as it pounded through my body. The feel of the sword in my hand, the rhythm of blows, an awareness of my sparring partner was all coming together. I could foresee a time when I could use Excalibur.

"Freemen begin practicing with weapons almost as soon as we learn to walk. By the time we engage in our first tournament, we have the muscles and skills to wield almost every weapon in the arsenal. Have you considered a bow, milady? You have a keen eye and sense of distance. It might be a better weapon for you." Archie leaned indolently on his sword, as if it were a convenient walking stick. His breathing was as easy and slow as if he hadn't just engaged in hours of practice.

"No. I must learn to use a sword. I must develop the strength and skill to handle one," I affirmed. Just as I must develop the magical strength and skill to combat Radburn Blakely.

"Riders!" came the sudden call from the watchtower.

"How many?" I called up to the guard. A surge of excitement and dread banished my fatigue.

"Twenty, no more. Moving at a walk. Lots of banners," a second guard added his information.

"Baggage?" I asked, hastening to the wooden ladder that led to the tower. Why had I let my knights ride off to tournament? I needed them here, now, to defend Kirkenwood. At least I had remembered to accept their oaths of fealty before they departed. Instead of half an army, I had a handful of men at arms and a pack of wolfhounds. Not enough.

"Sound the bell, bring the villagers within the walls!" I had more than just my home to defend.

"No need, milady," the guard said as I mounted the parapet beside him. "They carry the red lion rampant. King John approaches. He has not the baggage or siege engines to mount an assault."

"Hugh?" I breathed, searching the approaching cavalcade for a sign of his banner, his broad shoulders, Orage's proud gait, anything that would identify him.

Search as I might, Sir Hugh Fitz Chênenoir did not ride with his king.

My shoulders felt heavier than when I'd first put aside my sword.

"Merde!" I muttered. Playing at men's work with the sword, exposing me to their rough world, had broadened my vocabulary. "I won't be able to practice while I entertain him. Why didn't he send messengers ahead to warn me?"

"Because he likes keeping his barons off-balance. It's a duel of politics instead of swords. A few days' rest might help your sore muscles, milady," the guard offered.

"Unless John is the one I have to use my sword against." I doubted John himself would ever engage me in battle—mundane or magical. But the man who always rode with him, whispering into his ear, would most certainly fight me and Excalibur with every strength and skill he possessed.

I searched the mass of riders for traces of a black aura or a silvery blond head. I could not see him either. But I'd know Blakely's black shroud anywhere—almost as readily as I could pick out Hugh Fitz Chênenoir in any crowd as my heart sought to match his in rhythm and tempo. I could find neither man in the crowd. I sought again, using my newly awakened magical senses.

John rode alone—with only traces of Blakely's black aura clinging to him—or as alone as a king could be with his servants, retainers, and clerics, plus a handful of knights, their servants, retainers, and clerics.

I don't know if my relief at not having to face Blakely outweighed my disappointment that Hugh had not come. "I miss you, Hugh," I whispered into the afternoon breeze. An intense lonely ache opened within me, a hollowness that could not be filled.

"Open the gates," I ordered. "We must welcome the king. Daffyd, we will have to feed these people. What's in the pantry?"

My people scampered about making rudimentary preparations. They knew what to do better than I.

"Hadn't you better change, milady?" Archie asked, mounting the ladder.

"Thank you for reminding me." I had become too comfortable in my borrowed braies and leather jerkin.

I was still brushing my hair when I heard the pounding of many hooves and the voices of many people in the courtyard. Hastily, I crammed my feet into blue slippers that matched my gown while I slapped a white veil onto my head and secured it with a braided blue cord. Not necessarily elegant or even modest for court fashion, but serviceable for the little notice I'd had. My sense of camaraderie with my men vanished the moment I assumed the attire of a lady of the manor. "Don't create loneliness, Ana," I ordered myself. "You are the same person garbed in blue silk as you were wearing coarse wool and leather."

Then I ran to greet my king. Not a single restorative puddle lay between me and the cavalcade in the bailey.

I skidded to a halt before him, breathless and flushed. I felt strong in my magic and my body, ready to meet whatever challenge the king brought me.

"So eager to greet us, my dear?" John chuckled, deep and throaty. He flashed his charming smile at me. Bits and pieces of the black aura seemed to flake away from him.

I had something to learn from that. What?

I dipped a curtsy to him, using the moment of lowered eyes to assess my dress for wrinkles or stains. The gown had been new when I returned to Kirkenwood last year. I hadn't had time to mire the hem permanently.

"Enough formality for now, Lady Resmiranda." John raised me from my curtsy by pulling my right hand to his lips. His mouth lingered on my fingertips, warm and inviting.

A small thrill coursed through my veins. When he smiled like that, years of care and mistrust fell away from his face, and his aura flashed bright red, almost devoid of black. For a moment he was just an attractive man who wanted to flirt with me.

I'd had precious few chances to enjoy the company of men in my life. He wasn't Hugh, but he was here.

"Sire," Petit, the valet interrupted.

John kept his eyes on me, merely cocking his head toward his servant to indicate he listened.

"Sire, forgive us, your bathtub seems to have been left behind with the queen's baggage.

A frown marred John's handsome face. The charming smile vanished. Black patches crept into his aura.

"Send for it!" the king snapped at his valet.

A niggling voice in the back of my mind reminded me that I could use flirtation to win influence over John, possibly negate Blakely's evil manipulation.

Somewhere my people found three geese. Brigid stuffed each with a duck, and then a game hen, inside the hen came a songbird and finally an egg. A different spice rubbed into the skin of each bird gave subtle flavors to each layer. King John, Bishop de Grey, and I each received the little brown eggs and the songbirds as the best delicacy of the entire feast. The rest of my people made do with the outer, more common bird flesh for their meal.

Fresh greens made a pretty frame for each portion of fowl. The people sitting below the salt ate turnips and onions. I would have loved to share the hearty vegetables with them, and did most nights, but court etiquette had proclaimed any root crops to be barbaric—as barbaric as the rough clothing I found so comfortable while practicing swordplay. Tonight I had to appear the gracious Norman lady.

John tore a morsel of dove off a bone and offered the delicate meat to me. He held it before my mouth so that reaching for my eating knife or silver spoon was awkward. Hesitantly I opened my mouth. Suddenly the heat of his body so close to mine, his smile, the longing in his eye swamped my senses. The noise and bustle of the crowded Hall, the love ballad sung by Widsyth, the itinerant minstrel, faded from my awareness. As I took the offering into my mouth, John's fingers lingered on my lips, tracing them with the gentle touch of a lover.

His aura appeared calm and pale.

My heart beat a little faster. I knew a moment of great power. Power over this powerful man. If I could bind him to me, I might be able to break the chains of evil forged by Blakely.

Hugh had never touched me like this. I pulled away from John in confusion. I searched his brown eyes for his true emotions and found a smile reserved only for me.

"We are most happy to find you hale and fit, milady. We feared for you after the intensity of your ailment at Bellecôte," he said. The implied intimacy of his tone sent shivers up my spine.

"I needed the fresh air and peace that only Kirkenwood offers me, Highness," I replied, lowering my eyes demurely.

"You need help maintaining this beautiful grange, Lady Resmiranda. You should consider taking a husband." He held my gaze with his own.

I did not need to read his mind to know that he thought me more likely to warm his bed if I had given my maidenhead to a husband.

"The choice is mine, Highness, as you have reaffirmed my independence. I have not yet found my husband of choice." I had, but I was not about to throw another man's name at him while he flirted so outrageously. John, warm and inviting, was a much nicer man to deal with than John as the arrogant king. Or John as Blakely's puppet.

"I have several candidates in mind. My half brother . . ."

"I have no liking for Lord Blakely, Highness." I stiffened my spine and cooled my tone. "I know he killed my great-uncle. If you press this marriage upon me, I will claim a Writ of Mort d'Ancestre. I will have him tried and judged. If necessary, I shall find a champion for a trial by combat." Hugh had made it clear that he would welcome the challenge. But could he withstand Blakely's magical attacks?

"Trial by combat is an archaic and barbaric tradition that has not been invoked since our father's time."

I held his gaze steadily, letting him know my determination.

"And if I allow you to choose a husband elsewhere, will you dismiss those charges?"

I considered a long moment before nodding.

"Very well. We shall assist you in looking elsewhere for a husband." John sighed and returned to dismembering his dinner. "I can see that the walls of Kirkenwood will resist all but the most ardent sieges," he continued.

I smiled at his double entendre. The tension between us broke.

He chucked my chin, returning my grin.

We both laughed and resumed eating.

Soon he smacked his lips and proclaimed the feast of birds to his liking. Daffyd immediately clapped his hands, and the kitchen people came forth carrying a fawn on a litter. I knew the subtlety was made of spun sugar, colored with cinnamon most cunningly, leaving a few spots of white. The life-sized sculpture delighted the court. King John clapped his hands in approval.

The fawn had required all of the sugar in our storerooms. Wild honey would have to serve the grange for the rest of the year.

I sat back surveying my people and the court, making certain no one was slighted of their due, nor imbibed too much. A few royal men at arms shouted at each other. Fists clenched. Arms raised.

Archie stepped between them.

I nodded my pleasure at his quick action. Some lords might look the other way at nightly brawls in their Hall. I did not.

The distraction masked a disturbance at the entrance. One of my guards hurried to my side. He bent at the waist whispering to me. I doubted John, engrossed in the division of the sugar fawn, heard his quiet words.

"Earl Eustace de Vesci requests admittance, milady,"

"De Vesci?" I asked a little louder than I intended. He had left the court without permission several years ago. Court gossip claimed he would no longer abide John's affair with Lady de Vesci.

"De Vesci?" John echoed me. "What does the Earl of Northumberland wish with us? Did he bring his lady wife?"

"I do not know, Highness. His cleric merely requested admittance. The earl has not dismounted."

"Fetch him in, lad. Fetch him in," John said airily.

Eustace de Vesci took his time dismounting and entering my Hall. Broad at shoulder and hip, long of leg and arm, the grizzled, middle-aged man stalked into my grange, curling his lip in disdain.

The hair on the back of my neck bristled in defense of my home, just like my wolfhound at my feet.

"King John, I need you to remove the kidells from the River Tyne. Ye're agents have nae collectit the fish in the traps and they rot. My own people starve for lack of fish, but ye're people say they can nae have ye're fish," he blurted out without preamble or courtesies of greeting.

"Join us for a portion of this excellent subtlety," John said.

De Vesci glared at the remnants of the spun sugar. Such frivolity obviously had no place in his mission to the king. The issue must weigh heavily on his mind to pry him out of his home. He never left Northumberland. He had never visited Kirkenwood even though my lands abutted his.

"No one can navigate the River Tyne because of your kidells. Ye'll remove them promptly." His thick northern burr only made his demands harsher.

"No, Lord Eustace. We will not accede to your wishes merely because you demand it. Prepare your case and present it tomorrow when we sit at court. You may withdraw," John ordered.

"I'll not be treated like some common lackey, man. I have rights. I demand a trial of this issue. I am an earl, I deserve your judgment *now*."

"Every man, lord and freeman alike, must present evidence in court. We will hear your case tomorrow. Unless, of course, you are willing to part with some of your legendary stash of gold to pay the costs of an immediate trial?"

"I'll not pay ye're bribes to ensure my rights. I helped put you on the throne, John Softsword. I can pull you down just as easily." He turned sharply and stalked out of my Hall as abruptly as he'd entered.

Silence hung around the room like an unwelcome ghost. Someone coughed. Another giggled nervously. Daffyd shuffled his feet. His people began clearing the tables.

At last Widsyth struck a slightly sour chord on his lute. He followed with a jaunty song about a goose girl who raised her eyes too high to a mighty lord and lost her virtue as well as her geese.

The assembly relaxed, slapping the tables in rhythm with the almost discordant song. They began drinking in earnest.

John joined them, singing the chorus at the top of his lungs. His rather pleasant tenor broke through the raucous voices to dominate the room.

Eustace de Vesci was seemingly forgotten.

His final words made me think. If John offended enough barons, could they unite and bring him down? Who would replace John as king?

Would I join the rebellion?

Or would I try to keep him from offending one and all?

Chapter 31

THE next day I rode to the hunt with John shortly after we broke our fast at Prime. If Eustace de Vesci returned, he'd have to cool his heels until John decided to hear his case.

The Earl of Northumberland did not return.

At the evening meal, yawns overcame me. Entertaining the king was more exhausting than working magic.

"You must rest, *cherie*. We do not wish you to become ill again," John said, gently patting my hand. "We will retire early," he announced to the assembly. As he took my hand and kissed my fingertips, his thumb caressed my palm in sensuous invitation.

I retrieved my hand, half reluctantly. When the household bedded down shortly thereafter, I fixed a pallet in the lair. John slept in the lord's solar behind the Hall. Alone.

Before dawn I arose and searched for a spell that would break Blakely's magical influence over John once and for all.

I did not like what I found.

That day, we hunted again with moderate success. We'd feast on venison and duck this night. I entered the Hall flushed and full of high spirits. I had never seen John so carefree, so personable. He displayed a fine sense of humor. His deep laughter tickled me all the way to my toes. For a time, my fear of him dissolved.

Perhaps I would not need to work the ancient spell in the grimoire that Aunt Lotta had copied from someone else much older than herself. I wished I had the staff with me. Answers to unanswerable questions seemed easier when I touched the smooth oak.

We passed another dinner in accord.

Until some careless tongue mentioned sending to the disgruntled Earl of Northumberland for some fish to supplement the feast.

The courtier—I don't even know which one—must have meant it as a joke.

John did not find it funny. "We will have de Vesci's honors within the month. We are no longer pleased with him as one of our barons," the king muttered into his wine cup. His aura sprouted new patches of black that grew almost as I watched.

Blakely still had a great deal of influence on the king, especially when anger governed his temper.

My belly went chill.

If John deposed de Vesci, imprisoned or executed him for no other reason than his own displeasure, many of the barons would rise up in rebellion to avenge a very powerful and wealthy man. They would make him a martyr.

Images of battle, blood, chaos, and death flickered around the edges of my vision.

In the back of my mind Blakely's voice chortled with glee.

With one hand on Newynog for strength I recited a few words of the spell I was reluctant to try. Without the ritual they would be weak, but they might help.

John continued to frown. He summoned a cleric to his side and asked him to draft a letter informing de Vesci of his extreme displeasure

For *no* reason!

I could not break Blakely's black chains without creating new ones that tied John to me. The new chains had to be forged with love and tender caring to be strong enough to negate darker and more evil influences. I could not release John to act on his own as long as Blakely lived.

A new rumor replaced the dark mutterings against de Vesci. It spread through the court rapidly in excited whispers. Someone in the village had spotted a rare and magical twelve-point white stag deep in the forest.

Merlin of legend was supposed to ride such a beast. Sighting it portended great and good fortune to all.

"We must seek this beast on the morrow," John proclaimed with a sly grin, de Vesci seemingly forgotten. I wondered who had begun the rumor and why.

Again I slept alone in the lair with the staff at my side, very much aware of what I must do on the morrow.

Perhaps the spell outlined by one of my long forgotten ancestors would work to everyone's benefit. But would I betray someone who trusted me?

Hugh had asked only that I not give my heart to anyone else. He'd said nothing about my body.

Was the fate of England worth this?

At dawn, we chased through the forest on horseback seeking the elusive twelve-point white stag. John quickly tired and suggested he and I sit by the forest pool while the others crashed through the dense forest. I had expected John to lead the charge. He loved hunting above all other pursuits. Except perhaps one.

He spread a blanket on the mossy turf near a sheltered inlet on the far bank of the pool. The church at the base of the cliff remained out of sight on the far side of the deep water. Anyone who did not know the forest as I did, who had approached from this path, might presume this a different lake.

A giggle like the tinkling of tiny bells stopped my words and gestures. The faeries had joined us.

"Why did you come to Kirkenwood without your court, Highness?" I asked John as we lazed over a meal spread upon the blanket.

Even Petit, his valet, and Brigid, my maid, seemed to have disappeared. Only the faeries kept us company and they flew wide paths around us, never truly visible. John did not seem to notice their presence.

"I came to invest you as Baroness of Kirkenwood and receive your oath of fealty," he replied, sipping wine. "That does not require the entire court. I would not bankrupt my new baroness by asking her to feed and entertain the entire court during the celebrations. Public and private." His sparkling eyes met mine above the rim of his cup.

I held his glance in direct challenge. Heat blossomed in my breast and radiated outward. The lazy drone of bees in the warm sunshine seemed loud enough to totally block out the rest of the world. I smelled wildflowers and new green plants pushing up through the earth. A budding fern felt like velvet to my fingertips.

The spell could work. I'd make it work no matter the cost.

"Tonight?" I asked, licking my lips. The hunger inside me suggested more than the investiture. Tonight I would end Blakely's influence, hopefully for all time.

"Tonight," John confirmed. He sealed the promise with a kiss. His mouth upon mine tasted of wine and desire.

After several long moments we drew back and took deep breaths. He had kissed my cheek or hand often these past two days, almost as often as he dropped the royal "we" when we spoke privately.

"Then I must prepare a ceremony," I replied, breaking the eye contact at last. "My knights are following a circuit of tournaments, they should be here. Perhaps we can hold a larger festival at midsummer for them to repeat their allegiance to me and you. We will have a great feast indeed tonight if they find the white stag."

"I need only for you to say the words, Lady Resmiranda. 'Tis between us."

Silence strung out between us. The double meaning inherent in his words banished coherent thoughts.

"You could have commanded me into your bed, Highness. Many times." Would that make the spell easier?

No, I had to invite him into my body in order to bring him into my magic.

"I want you to come to me willingly, free of guilt, sure of yourself and of your love for me."

Hugh should have said those words to me, not King John.

"You can be certain that once we are joined in body and spirit, I will not willingly share you with my half brother," he added as further persuasion. "I shall burn the betrothal agreement before all witnesses."

"If I . . ."

John stopped any objection I might have offered with a searing kiss. As his tongue probed mine, we fell back against the blanket. His weight on my chest sent new thrills of desire coursing through my body. Without thinking I draped my arms around his neck, pulling him closer.

I drew a sigil on his back with my finger.

He groaned as if enticed by a gentle caress.

A fresh breeze touched my shoulder where my gown should have been. I bit back my protest.

How could I refuse my king? I had to do this to save all of England.

A renewed sense of power tingled in my fingers. I drew the second sigil on his brow.

The faeries vanished with a popping sound that left a vacancy in my ears.

What was wrong?

Holy Mother, forgive me! I prayed as John's hands found my breast. His gentle fingers kneaded and caressed, rolling my nipple into a tight bud. Then his mouth replaced his hands.

I drew in a sharp breath of astounded pleasure as I drew the third sigil on the backs of his hands. Bright flecks of colored light danced before my eyes; my own emotions, not the faeries.

All my doubts and misgivings faded before John's easy manipulations of my body. I succumbed to his ministrations, exploring his body willingly as he touched mine. Sigil followed sigil as our pleasure grew.

And then our clothing fell away from us. I gazed hungrily at him, memorizing the texture of his skin, the gradations of body hair, and the features that intrigued me most. His fingertips followed his gaze as he traced delicate circles on my neck, around my breasts, down to my navel and lower. He worked magic of his own. I arched to meet his hands as they opened and prepared me.

At last he thrust deep inside me.

I shouted at the knife-sharp pain that ripped up my spine. He stopped my protest with another deep kiss, his tongue dancing with mine. I closed my eyes and gave myself to the increasing rhythm of our dance.

At last I recited the words of the spell, making each Welsh word a verbal caress against his ears.

The pace of his thrusts slowed, then increased, and slowed again, tantalizing me with promises of more to come. Every sensation grew and expanded until I knew I must explode.

The weight of the blackness surrounding him fell away.

We reached new heights of pleasure together.

Now your magic is complete! the faeries whispered, finally returning.

At the same moment I felt the standing stones flare with renewed fire and strength. The fire that lit my blood connected the stones with a ring of otherworldly flame and reached out with beneficence to all of the land that John ruled.

I awoke two mornings later warm and contented in my own bed. While Kirkenwood Grange slept, I called a ball of witchfire to my palm easily. The faeries had been right. My magic seemed fuller, easier, since indulging myself with John. I did not even need Newynog or the staff to focus my talents.

No trace of darkness, anger, or mistrust that would drive him to insane acts of revenge before betrayal marred John's aura.

I set the ball of cold light above the bolster to better look at my lover.

John's arm rested heavily across me, claiming me as his own. I kissed his fingers gently. They tightened around my middle convulsively. He slept on. His tousled dark hair flopped youthfully across his brow. I brushed it away, allowing my fingers to linger and trace the line of his jaw.

In sleep he did not look his forty-one years. In sleep his cares passed away. I thought I had come to know the true man beneath the crown and I liked him.

But I loved Hugh. I knew that now. Guilt flashed through me briefly. But only briefly. John had taught me a lot about love, about my own body and how to enjoy it.

Small bonuses in my campaign to break my betrothal to Blakely and smash his evil influence over John.

But I had not given him my heart. That I reserved for Hugh.

Coarse sheets and blankets scraped erotically against my sensitized skin. Our usual sleeping nudity took on new meaning with a man nestled with me. I wondered if we had time to share one more quick joining before I must rise.

I had discretely waited until Kirkenwood slept before creeping in to join my lover last night. I planned to be gone before the first bird chirp heralded the dawn.

Still I had few doubts that everyone within Kirkenwood knew what had transpired between the king and me. Privacy was a mere illusion within the confines of a castle, where one room gave on to another and that room into the next. The grange, built in the old Saxon style, had multiple guest rooms sprawling out from the Hall. Generations of building had incorporated the circular rooms into the timber and stone central tower. More people had beds of their own here than in places like Mendip Mor where everyone crowded into the Hall and the single bedchamber.

Still, my largest bedchamber was littered with pallets for a dozen knights and more servants.

I doused the witchfire and gingerly lifted John's arm to escape to the *garderobe* and go about my duties. I needed to spend some time in the lair renewing my reading, checking the wards I had set about the castle. That chore was long overdue, neglected while I awakened the stones, set the spell of invisibility around Excalibur, and then trained with the men. The dark of the moon had passed. We entered a new phase; the best time to renew wards. I needed preparations and privacy to work tonight. Would John allow me that time?

"I want you," he whispered as he tightened his grip.

His soft breath wafting across my ear sent waves of heat flashing from my belly outward. A sense of power washed through me, akin to but not magic. I kissed John's mouth, long and deep. We needed no more words between us.

He took little nipping kisses across my breasts, down my belly to the thatch of hair between my legs. Hot moisture met his questing tongue. He lifted his head, dark hair tousled and appealingly young. A sly grin spread from his mouth to his eyes.

"Ready for me so soon?" he whispered. He shifted his weight onto his knees.

I reached for him, needing to feel the full length of him heavy in my hand.

"Not yet, my dear. I have more interesting things in mind." He guided my hips with his sure hands until I turned over. One finger traced the soft folds of my femininity.

Then without warning he lifted my hips and thrust sharply into me.

A jolt of sensation, not painful, more like a pleasure so intense I could not understand it, ripped through me and weakened any resistance I might have offered.

With each of his thrusts, new ripples of wild magical talent coursed through my veins. I closed my eyes against the colored star bursts exploding before my vision. The power built within me, demanding release.

He rammed deeper into me. My magic forced his mind open to me. Primal. Hot. Greedy. Out of control.

Now I knew the meaning of some of Aunt Lotta's cryptic remarks in her grimoire. Sex was both the most intimate form of communication and a powerful tool in magic, not to be feared, but to be gloried in. It had certainly worked in negating Blakely.

Exultation choked us both at the same time.

John collapsed on top of me still inside me. Both of us spent, sated, joined in body and soul.

The bed-curtains opened with a furious thrust of wind, seemingly by themselves. I gasped, clutching the discarded counterpane around me. I tried to protest this rude intrusion of the king's privacy, but all that came out of my mouth was a squeaky gasp. John stirred a little and opened one eye in query. He remained where he was, firmly clutching my breast.

Radburn Blakely poked his disheveled head through the opening in the curtains, a sly grin creased his face, making a light slash in the furrows of road dust and nearly a week's worth of beard. His silvery blond hair had taken on the dull cast of iron with grease and dirt. He looked a decade older than the last time I'd seen him.

Where had he been that he'd neglected his person? What mischief had he worked? How dared he push himself into the king's private bed?

"Well, Brother, I see you have exercised *droit du seigneur* with my wife. I hope I don't have to share her with you for the rest of my marriage." Blakely placed one knee on the high bed as if he did indeed intend to join us.

Horror chilled my spine and dulled my thoughts. A new darkness seemed to hover over John's left shoulder.

"Wife?" John levered himself awkwardly off me, dragging the counterpane over us both. Sleep and sex still tugged at his eyelids, while a lazy smile at me and the pressure of his hand on my hip revealed his possessiveness.

I remembered the tales of how John had commanded Hugh Neville's wife to sleep with him so often she had to ask permission and offer a bribe to share her husband's bed.

"Yes, Brother," Blakely said. He ran a possessive hand down my shoulder and arm. I jerked away from him. He grabbed my hand and started playing with my fingers as if deciding where to place a ring.

"I have just returned from Scotland. The church there agreed with me that my betrothal to the lady, signed by her great uncle and legal guardian, is still valid. The bishop married us by proxy two days ago."

He held up the writ, the Bishop of Edinburgh's seal dangled from the bottom, bold, unquestionable.

"No. I do not agree. This marriage is not valid. I will not allow it." I thought I screamed, but the words came out barely louder than a breath. I did manage to reclaim my hand and hide it beneath the counterpane. "Tell him, Highness. Tell him that you plan to burn the betrothal agreement at the time of my investiture."

Around us men began to stir on their pallets. I saw two knights raise up on their elbows, clearly interested, lascivious grins on their faces.

"Burn it? That I do not accept since you entrusted the only copy to me before I left Durham Castle some weeks ago," Blakely said. His mouth smiled, but his eyes narrowed, and I sensed magic pouring out of him.

I didn't know how to counter him except with logic.

"Highness, tell me you knew nothing of this," I turned back to John, pleading with my eyes for him to deny this nightmare; to give me time to plan a counteroffensive.

He stared blankly into Blakely's gaze. I could almost see the magic compulsion pass between them.

"Sorry, *ma coeur*. While we did not discuss this possibility with Radburn directly, we suspected he might try this. we are not pleased at his audacious act without royal permission, but the end accomplishes what we had intended all along." He yawned hugely and rolled over, removing his arm, and his claim on my body.

Chapter 32

OH, Hugh, where are you when I need you most? What am I to do now? I hadn't thought about Fitz Chênenoir in days. Now I ached for his solid and comforting presence. Even though I had betrayed him.

"You intended to honor the betrothal all along," I said aghast. "You promised me that if I shared your bed, you would withdraw Blakely's claim." Any good I had accomplished in breaking Blakely's control of John had ben negated by one sharp stare from the sorcerer.

"No, *cherie*. We said that we would not willingly share you." He shrugged, but his voice sounded flat, as if another spoke the words for him. "Now we give you over completely to our brother's care."

"You told me and him," I sneered and pointed derisively at Blakely. "Before the entire court you announced that Kirkenwood and its baroness are independent. You wooed me as if you wanted me, for myself, and not some petty rivalry between brothers!"

He betrayed me as he betrayed everyone.

As I had betrayed Hugh. As I had betrayed the church by willingly giving myself to my king and working magic. Was Blakely my punishment?

"Oh, we did woo you for our own pleasure. But now, we must relinquish your delightful charms to your lawful husband."

The royal "we" grated on my ears as false pride, false loyalty, false everything. I ripped the counterpane off of him and draped it tightly around me as I scrambled from the bed. John was left naked and exposed to the chill morning air. His erection shriveled before our eyes.

Blakely grinned in genuine mirth. His handsome face relaxed. For half a heartbeat I almost felt the same allure emanating from him that

I had known long ago in this very room when he and his men had invaded Kirkenwood.

Then the illusion of trustworthiness and compulsion to obey him passed, and his true, black aura reasserted itself. I saw the same black tainted shadow creep over to envelop John's life energy. But it merely shrouded; it did not engulf.

Perhaps . . .

I needed time and privacy to find a new spell . . . if I could convince myself King John was worth it.

Perhaps the only true answer lay in rebellion; starting over with a new king and a new set of councillors.

"This marriage will never be consummated, Blakely. I do not acknowledge the marriage. I will have it annulled if I have to journey to Rome by myself." I stalked out of the chamber trailing the counterpane behind me.

"We forbid you to leave England, Lady Resmiranda. We forbid you to leave court," John said lazily.

I ignored him. I heard light footsteps behind me. Booted footsteps. Only Blakely was dressed at this early hour.

"I will have you now, before witnesses, to ensure that I have a stake in any child you might bear in the next year," Blakely said. His laughing face took on the cast of a gloating demon.

A knot of ice formed in my belly as he fumbled with his braies beneath his grimy cotehardie.

He grasped the counterpane and yanked its protective covering away from my body.

"Take a good look, Blakely, for it will be your last!"

Power still sang through my blood. I grasped his wrist firmly and flipped him onto his back. He hit the stone-covered rushes with a whoosh of air from his lungs. Magic gave me more strength and balance than I had used on Archie in the training yard. As he landed, I relieved Blakely of his belt knife with just a hint of levitation. Straddling him with the blade nicking his throat, I placed one foot firmly on his chest. "Rise at your own risk, Blakely. Before these witnesses I declare this marriage false."

For weeks I had doubted that I could ever take a life with a blade or with magic. I knew how my soul fought to follow the dead. At this moment, I would willingly rid the earth of Radburn Blakely by any means possible.

"Release him, Lady Resmiranda," John ordered. Authority seemed to ring around the room. He stalked over to me, now clad in a loose silk robe.

The royal hand that clasped my wrist and pulled me away from Blakely's throat seemed to belong to another man than the playful lover of a few moments ago.

"Magnificent," Blakely breathed. "The embodiment of a warrior queen of old. I look forward to tonight, my dear. We will be magnificent together."

The knife clattered to the ground as John pressed his thumb against a vulnerable pressure point on my wrist. I glared at him.

Blakely scrambled to his feet. "By your control of her, I presume you found what we came for," he said, straightening his clothes.

"Found what?" I knew, though.

John smiled slyly. He held my gaze with his own, almost willing me to betray the location of precious information. "Unfortunately, no. But the lady has shown such willing cooperation, I do not believe the evidence of treason necessary now."

"Fool," Blakely muttered.

I wasn't sure anyone but me with my magic sensitized hearing heard his slur against the king.

"We have to find it," Blakely insisted.

"No, We don't. We need only receive both your oaths of fealty for Kirkenwood and then we will return to court. We weary of the north. Winchester seems the place to go next." John dropped my hand and returned to his valet. Petit stood at the foot of the bed wringing his hands. The knights on the floor shifted restlessly, recognizing the king's signal to rise, but not certain they should reveal their nude bodies while I still stood watching.

"I will gladly swear fealty to my king as Baroness of Kirkenwood," I announced. "But I will never share that oath with your half brother."

"You will both swear or you will both hang." John turned his back on me and began dressing for the day.

"We must say the oath together!" Radburn insisted. Anxiety clawed at his gut, as it had ever since he'd crossed the threshold of the standing stones. "You said so, Highness. You said we must say it together. As husband and wife." He hated the petulant whine that came into his voice. Almost as much as he hated the woman who defied him at every turn.

What magic had she worked that weakened his control of John?

He had no idea where she had slept the last three nights, certainly not with him or the king. He'd even entered the solar above the Hall and lord's chamber where the women slept—a place forbidden to all men during the hours of sleep. She hadn't slept on any of the pallets laid out there. He'd checked with both his magic and mundane senses. She couldn't hide from him. She didn't have enough magic for that.

But she'd broken his control. She no longer coughed at his command. John had moments of clear logic and trustworthiness. She had double-sealed the demon door. Radburn had aged visibly—though he still looked fifteen years younger than his actual age instead of his normal ageless two decades beneath his forty and two years.

"I will give my oath, by myself, before *he* does." Resmiranda almost spat the pronoun. "Afterward, you may do as you wish. I will not remain in the same room with *him* any longer than I have to." She whirled to pace the dais. The gold silk of her bliaud swirled about her feet revealing the pattern of embroidery. First one of the elemental symbols and then another showed clearly. They flashed golden eldritch fire with every step she took. The gown itself was antique in cut, probably inherited from some sorceress in a family noted for producing at least one per generation.

The miserable wolfhound paced with her. Every time Radburn thought about kidnapping Resmiranda, the dog growled at him—as if it could read his thoughts and emotions. It never left her side for more than two minutes to answer the call of nature.

"You do not dictate to me, madam!" John sneered.

She merely raised one eyebrow archly. A slight movement of her hand made a signet ring on her right thumb flash in concert with the symbols on her skirt. A red dragon rampant set in gold. The Pendragon of Britain. Legend claimed no one but one of Arthur's blood could wear the ring and not be burned to a crisp. She flaunted it today.

She flaunted that as if Arthur Pendragon of ancient legend lived in her.

Arthur Pendragon's cross hung enticingly between her breasts, suspended from the gold-and-ivory prayer beads. It dominated the bodice of her gown, bounced with her movements, drew the eye of every man in the Hall to her lush charms—which he as her husband had never sampled. He ground his teeth in frustration.

John and his men had not been able to find evidence that Arthur of Brittany, John's nephew and a contender for the throne, still lived no matter how minutely they searched Kirkenwood Grange. Radburn hadn't been able to find it either, by magical or mundane means. He had discovered that four messengers had left Kirkenwood between the lady's return and the king's arrival. None of those messengers had returned, and no one knew their destinations.

Had one of them taken the evidence to a trusted recipient? A bishop perhaps? A bishop who would gladly betray John with the Interdict in place.

"Very well, my dear. You will swear separately. The lady of the manor first." John cowered before her natural authority.

Even Radburn took one step backward.

"You are my wife, I will take the oath as Baron of Kirkenwood," Radburn insisted.

"Are you? Has the marriage been consummated, witnessed, ac-knowledged by the church in *England?*"

"She has you there, Brother." John slapped Radburn heartily on the back. His camaraderie seemed forced. Induced by the lady? Rad-burn detected no trace of magic. Still anxiety gnawed at him.

"Let us get this over with." Resmiranda raised her hand to signal her steward—Radburn's steward by rights. He rang the bell for the people of Kirkenwood to assemble. Slowly they trooped in. They all bowed or curtsied to Resmiranda and totally ignored Radburn. They, too, wore ancient elemental symbols painted or embroidered upon their clothing. The last of them was a tall thin man in a clerical robe with the hood pulled over his head, shadowing his face. Something about the man, his posture, the surety of his step, was familiar.

He looked as if he'd just stepped out of one of the standing stones in the village; eerie stones that repelled Radburn. A raven croaked in the courtyard. Its grating cry echoed off stone walls in stern disap-proval of something.

Filthy peasants. Radburn spat into the rushes. He should yank the hood off the tall cleric's face, teach him to respect his king and his lawful master. Every time he tried to take a step toward the man, he met a wall of resistance.

What had happened to his magic? He should be able to enter the mind of every person in the Hall. He should be able to force them all to do his bidding with a thought.

The stones, Resmiranda's voice whispered into his mind. *The standing stones protect us from you. As long as they stand, you must work for your magic against us.*

You won't always have the stones to protect you, Radburn replied. He'd had to force himself to enter the circle of stones. Once inside them, he'd automatically erected all of his magical shields to ease the growing sense of dread. A lesser magician would have turned around and fled the region. He took a deep breath to steady himself and renew his mental barriers. Then slowly, carefully, he extended the control to his half brother along familiar pathways of his mind. *I will force you to leave the stones. I will separate you from them before sundown.*

She sucked in her cheeks and gave him a tiny superior smile as she knelt before John and offered her two hands to his while she said the words that bound her honor, her life, and her lands to the king.

John raised her to her feet and kissed her cheek in peace. The embrace lingered.

Radburn flushed with jealousy.

"And now, Brother, your turn." John finally released Resmiranda. Reluctantly? "We want to leave immediately for Winchester. We will have the good bishop bless the marriage—we don't believe the Interdict prohibits a simple blessing, only the marriage sacrament itself—and you will consummate the alliance at last," John said, half giggling.

"I cannot leave my lands, Highness. They have been neglected too long. For your own benefit, I must remain here," Resmiranda protested.

"You will accompany us, milady. We command it upon pain of our extreme displeasure."

Radburn grinned at her in triumph. *By sundown you will be mine!*

Perhaps, but Kirkenwood will always be mine. And I belong to the stones. Lady Resmiranda gathered her golden silk skirts and swept out of the room. Every one of her tenants and retainers followed her.

Radburn was left alone to swear fealty for Kirkenwood alone. Without the people, the land and keep were worthless.

"Outfoxed you again, Radburn. Your marriage looks to be very entertaining to us." John smiled, on the point of more annoying giggles.

Chapter 33

HUGH thrust up his shield to cover his head. Three arrows rained down upon him. The metal heads plunked against the metal boss. A rock landed at his horse's feet, sending the massive destrier prancing in an uneven gait.

"Easy, Orage!" Hugh shouted to the beast, taking a deep breath. Orage settled. Hugh took another deep breath and directed his men into the next position of assault.

A wooden hill fort in the Welsh foothills shouldn't present too great a challenge to his hardened warriors. But it had. The defenders had held out for three days.

Every delay grated on Hugh's nerves. Another day away from Ana. Another day for Radburn Blakely to gain power both political and magical.

Had Silvester managed to help Ana?

"They must be nearly out of ammunition," Sir Andrew, Hugh's senior knight from Bellecôte, said beside him. "The children are reduced to throwing rocks at us. I don't see any men on the walls." The knight looked disgusted.

This chore of collecting small boys as hostages sat no easier on his shoulders than on Hugh's. But their king had commanded. The church had withdrawn from England. No one in England dared challenge John's decisions now. No one else held authority over them.

"Stones can kill as easily as arrows and swords," Hugh muttered back. But his fellow knight had assessed the situation correctly. This Welsh hill fort couldn't hold out much longer. They had defied King John's orders to release their sons as hostages against good behavior.

And Gyron of Yvain Fell had closed his gates and defended his walls before Hugh's herald had arrived to read the orders.

They had been warned. By one of their own traveling fast cross-country, or by the Englishman who had organized the raid on Mendip Mor Castle?

Hugh sympathized secretly with the prince. He'd fight, too, before he gave Johnny up to the king.

Ten Welsh boys and Johnny waited for him back at his camp. Ten very small children who cried for their mothers every night. The three youngest fell asleep with their thumbs in their mouths. Johnny reacted to them with pale skin and frightened eyes. Perhaps Hugh should have left the boy at home rather than throwing him into the life of a knight's page with so little preparation.

Hugh's heart ached at the necessity of John's harsh measures—necessary but cruel. Suddenly Hugh felt very grateful John had not claimed Johnny Bellecôte hostage, though he masked the demand under the name of fosterage and knightly training. So far Hugh had made certain John had no complaint to warrant such action. But if the time came, could he give up his boy, knowing he'd be educated and cared for under John's supervision?

Gyron didn't trust John to keep his sons safe.

Would John honor his vows to protect the boys as long as their fathers remained loyal and obedient? The question nagged at him.

Hugh didn't dare take that chance.

Years ago, when he'd first run away from his father's castle to join a troop of mercenaries, a siege like this followed by open battle would have excited him almost to the point of sexual pleasure. Eighteen years later he found no joy in this mission.

"Let us finish this quickly. Use the battering ram!" he called to his small force. The fortress seemed to sag atop its small plateau, as broken as its inhabitants.

Another shower of rocks greeted the men carrying the tree trunk with its sharpened and metal-encased tip. Three men fell under the onslaught.

"Get those shields up!" He kneed Orage up the slope and closer to the ram, extending his own shield to cover the nearest man. Five other knights followed his example.

Kathunk! The ram hit the fortress gates. The wood shuddered but held.

Again and again the men swung the ram in its harness with increasing momentum. One gate plank splintered. A woman inside the walls screamed.

Kathunk. The ram struck again. Two more planks split. Slivers the size of arrows sprayed the attackers. One man howled and clutched his head. Then he dropped in his tracks. A chunk of wood as thick as Hugh's three fingers protruded from his skull. The stench of violent death, loosened bowels, and the sweat of fear broke out.

The smell of battle. Hugh nearly gagged with revulsion. Why now? He'd never shied away from war before. He thrived on it, drew his livelihood from it.

But he'd lived in peace since the majority of barons had refused John's call to arms to invade Poitou in 1204. For these past four years he had concentrated on life, the life of his son and Bellecôte.

"Swing it again!" Hugh called, motioning another man to replace his fallen comrade.

An unnatural silence settled on the hill fort. The only sounds Hugh detected came from the battering ram. The gate crumbled and broke from its hinges with the next blow. Hugh led his mounted men into the breach. Three women, two girls, and five peasants stood in the doorway to the Hall sobbing, heads bowed, shoulders slumped.

"Where are your men?" Hugh called.

The tallest of the women, the one who stood in the center with her arms around the shoulders of two of the children, looked up and met his eyes.

"Where are your men and sons?" Hugh repeated his question.

The woman continued to stare at him without responding.

"Perhaps they do not speak French," Sir Andrew said quietly.

"Do you speak Saxon?" Hugh asked. He knew he'd never put together enough Welsh to make his demands known.

Sir Andrew uttered a string of guttural sounds. The woman replied in similar words, hesitantly, as if she had to piece them together from a faulty memory.

"She says the men have fled, taking the boys with them. The women alone have held out for three days." Sir Andrew slapped his thigh in frustration—or was it sympathy?

"They've gone to ground so deep in these hills we'll never ferret them out," Sir Andrew added.

"I feared as much as soon as John gave me orders to come here.

These people melt into the mists like ghosts." Like the men who had attacked Mendip Mor.

Again he wondered where the warning had come from.

The woman spoke again. Hugh looked to Andrew for a translation.

"She says that women are of no use to King John. She begs mercy for herself and her daughters." Sir Andrew's face flushed a deep red.

"She offered something more," Hugh guessed.

Sir Andrew looked away.

"Tell her we are men of honor. Her virtue is safe with us, but I must take the oldest daughter hostage until her men return with a son," Hugh replied. He'd heard that Welsh women freely offered themselves to any man. He suspected this woman and others like her offered their bodies in return for the safety of their homes and dependents. Not an honorable trait, but frequently an effective one.

His mother had done the same more than once. But Hugh's father hadn't been honorable about the results.

"I give you my word, madam, that you and your daughters will be treated honorably." Hugh wheeled his horse around to depart.

"Is that wise, to stake your honor, and possibly your life on the whim of King John?" Sir Andrew asked with a smirk.

"Perhaps not wise, but the only action I can take and still live with myself." The Welsh princes did not trust John. And it seemed neither did his own knights.

Ana certainly had no reason to trust John. But was John the true menace, or was it the sorcerer who whispered in his ear?

None of them were safe from Radburn Blakely. Certainly not Ana. *Please, God, let Silvester find her and protect her.* But she was the only person Hugh knew who could counter the king's half brother at all.

"Sir Andrew." Hugh summoned his comrade forward with a raised hand. "Take the ten hostages we have, and one of those girls and ride posthaste for Bellecôte. Take Johnny with you, too. Ride as if demons themselves pursue you. Leave the baggage carts behind. Let each knight take a child upon his saddle. But you must be safely within the walls of my castle in two days. No more."

He proposed a grueling, almost impossible ride for the men, let alone for the more fragile children.

"And what are we to do once we arrive there, milord?" Sir Andrew's eyes opened wide in shock, giving him the look of a frightened frog.

"Keep all of the children, including my son, safe from any and all who come for them."

"Including the king?"

"I do not believe John will menace them right now. He has other quarry in mind. I ride to join him and prevent mischief to him and by him." A need to hold Ana safe in his arms, make certain she was safe, ached deep within him.

"God speed, milord. You'll need it."

The magic that sex with John had generated in me faded rapidly as we rode away from the standing stones and crossed the burn. I seemed to leave the magic behind with the villagers and Kirkenwood. I huddled into my winter cloak, chilled from the loss of magic while the rest of the party laughed and sang in the summer sunshine. Bright insects fluttered about. None of them my faery friends. Even they had deserted me.

A gentle hum in the back of my mind reassured me that not all of my magic had disappeared. I carried the staff as a knight would carry a lance while ahorse. Excalibur resided deep in my leather traveling chest, wrapped in wads of underclothing. I had buried the little eating knife with its crown of love-lies-bleeding with Excalibur. The original, damning letter from my father remained in Arthur Pendragon's hands. Literally. I'd placed it inside the tomb with his skeleton. Four copies resided in the hands of four close friends of Uncle Henry, two of them bishops headed into exile on the continent.

The letter was safe. As for the sword? Hopefully, no one would rifle my belongings, including my so-called husband. I wasn't certain how well the spell would hold up since I'd moved the sword from its original hiding place.

For this ride, I wore proper court dress, a tight chainse of finest linen, a bliaud of deep murrey color with matching veil over a modest wimple and chin strap. I did not feel comfortable in the trappings of a courtier nor riding sidesaddle on the placid mare John provided for me.

But I carried the staff despite Blakely's stern disapproval.

I looked into the polished metal disk suspended from my neck on a silken cord. Reflected in its surface, the party behind me was a blur of colors. I couldn't distinguish my people from the king's. My magic slid off the mirror, refusing to enhance my vision.

More of my powers dribbled away as we climbed up onto the road. The same road I had taken mere weeks ago when I fled Radburn Blakely in Durham.

Now I rode beside him. Once more he seemed to have the upper hand magically. He leered at me and clenched his fist. My chest tightened in memory of the cough he had induced in me.

I mastered the urge to expel the tightness. One deep breath gave me control. A second breath flowed freely through my lungs and slowed their laboring. A third breath gave me the strength to build a shield between us.

Blakely reared back as if stung.

"Do not close me out, Resmiranda. I own you. You, your magic, your secrets, and the artifact you have so skillfully hidden from me. Where is it?"

I stared at him blankly. "Where is what?"

"If you do not open your mind to me, I will force it open, very painfully." He rode closer to me. His knee brushed mine.

My skin seemed to burn at his touch, a precursor to the burning in my mind, or my body, should he force it open. I remembered the vision of the unknown woman he had ritually slaughtered with fire and knife and shuddered. But I hid my fear from him, ignoring his gibes with stony silence. I thrust the staff between us. Then I touched my stallion's thoughts and it shied away from Radburn's fractious gelding. Carefully, I reerected the shield around me.

John and sex awakened a new source of magic within me, and the stones amplified it. But it came from me. *I* controlled it, not Radburn Blakely.

"Later, Little One. I'll settle this later." Blakely urged his mount forward until he reined in next to John.

I resumed my place in the line of march, grateful for the plodding pace of the royal entourage rather than the breakneck speed I had traveled at before.

John had ordered Kirkenwood Grange stripped of all but the barest of staff and replaced most of my guards with his own. I knew he left men who would search diligently throughout the buildings. He didn't want interference from people who owed their loyalty first to me and then begrudgingly to their king.

We passed through a section of woodland. The tall canopy of intertwined branches allowed little light to penetrate to the open forest floor. The accumulation of half-rotted leaves from the previous autumn muffled the sounds of our passage. The guards turned their attention to the trees and away from my retainers. Many of them crossed themselves as protection from whatever might hide within the shadows. John and Blakely bent their heads together in earnest conference. I raised the staff a little, waving it right and left ever so slightly. Then I looked into the polished metal disk that hung about my neck. Behind me, one of my men peeled off from the line of march and into the woods. He'd seen my signal.

In a few moments another man slipped away. They carried messages to my knights. I needed them back home protecting Kirkenwood. John's men wouldn't find their evidence that Arthur of Brittany lived—a threat to John's crown—nor would they find Excalibur. In their frustration they might turn aggressive against my people. They might burn Kirkenwood, content to destroy the ancient hill fort and its contents if they couldn't find what they sought.

My people knew how to fade into the moors to evade danger to themselves. Buildings could be rebuilt.

We approached a deep burn, swollen beyond its normal banks and running wildly down from the hills toward the north fork of the River Tyne. Everyone came to a halt while the advance riders negotiated the ford. We waited for the signal that the king could safely cross.

"Lady Resmiranda, you will build a bridge here," John commanded while we waited. "You will build the bridge and charge a toll. Send half the revenues to the Exchequer in London."

"Before or after the tolls repay the cost of building the bridge?" I asked. "Or will you pay the cost of lumber and workmen. Will the toll keeper be one of my people or one of yours?"

"You will build the bloody bridge. We will post the men to enforce the toll. Erect a lodge for them. One on each side of the bridge." He almost sneered. His good humor had vanished. Then he urged his horse into the wild stream.

Three more of my men melted into the woods. Half an hour later when the last of the royal entourage splashed out of the water on the far side of the burn, another half dozen of my men had left on their mission. Some of them should get through to my knights. I had only to wait.

I had wanted to send a message to Hugh as well. But Archie had left to find his master yesterday, before the ceremony of oath taking. He'd made sure I knew he disapproved of my liaison with John.

He had been present when Radburn Blakely announced our marriage to the assembled household and diminished court.

I wished I could have told Hugh myself that the marriage was a sham and how much I regretted my liaison with John. I'd gained a little knowledge of magic, but nothing else from the encounter. Now I had fully severed my ties to the church and to Hugh. I doubted I'd ever trust another man with my body, my secrets, or my honor. The losses were not worth the gain.

I gulped back tears of sorrow lest I allow Blakely to see a weakness.

Chapter 34

"WHERE has he taken her?" Hugh bellowed to the knight wearing King John's device on his tabard.

The knight stood straight and firm, mouth closed tightly. "I am not privy to the king's plans," he replied. Each word came out slowly and distinctly as if it cost him dearly to utter each one.

Hugh scanned the walls of Kirkenwood for any sign of Ana's device of a red griffin on the wing with a black bear in each corner. All of the banners and guards' tabards bore the royal insignia instead. Cold dread began to creep through him.

"Be off with you, Fitz Chênenoir," the knight snarled. "You have no business here."

"You need not be impolite, my son." A tall, slender man enveloped in a clerical robe with the hood up drifted toward them, so thin he seemed more cloth and shadow than man.

"You!" the knight gasped. He stepped back and crossed himself.

"Yes, I was supposed to follow the king and my lady to Durham and then south to Winchester." The priest nodded. A smile shone through his voice. "Benedicte," he greeted them belatedly.

Hugh suddenly liked the man immensely—though he'd had little use for the church most of his life. Rather, the church had had little use for him, the bastard son of a Norman lord who drank himself to death.

"But—but I saw you walk out of that gate myself, not three days ago," the knight stammered.

"Just because you did not see me walk back through that very same gate several hours later does not mean I did not." Again the voice verged on the edge of laughter.

"To Durham and then Winchester, three days ago." Hugh confirmed the information.

The priest nodded in reply. "King John wished to usher me, a cleric in a land under Interdict, into exile along with several of his bishops. But my place is here, guarding . . . my flock. I can no longer offer them the solace of Confession and Eucharist, but a priest's work goes beyond the Sacraments."

"If I had known priests like you as a child, I might be more faithful in observing those sacraments," Hugh muttered.

"A blessing on your journey, milord." The priest placed his hand gently upon Hugh's head. A sense of healing peace invaded his entire body. He'd felt the same magical energy in Ana's hands.

The knight backed up, crossing himself again and again.

Hugh swallowed his smile.

"Might I know your name, Father? I will remember you in my prayers."

"Truman." The priest bowed slightly and walked toward the well where a raven perched. His dusty robe blended with the dirt in the courtyard and the molting feathers of the bird perched on the well. In a moment he was indistinguishable from the buildings, the dirt, or the other people milling about aimlessly.

"You—you are welcome to enjoy the hospitality of Kirkenwood Grange," the knight stammered. "Your journey has been long and thirsty. Join me for a mug of wine."

"Who are you to offer the hospitality of the grange in the lady's absence?" Hugh asked, affronted.

"King John appointed me, Sir Kendric of Southwark, head of the castle guard in the lady's absence." The man straightened his shoulders again, trying to look down his nose at Hugh. The ploy didn't work, they stood shoulder to shoulder, the same height.

"Southwark, eh?" Hugh tightened his mouth to keep a laugh from escaping. "Another dock rat mercenary bought by John's silver and loyal only as long as the money flows from the Exchequer." He turned and prepared to remount.

"Are you any different, Sir Hugh Fitz Chênenoir?" Sir Kendric sneered.

"I like to think so. I gave John my loyalty even before he paid me to fight for him. I saved his life because my honor demanded I do so, not because he paid me." He swung into the saddle and reined Orage toward the gate.

The sound of pounding hooves on the road halted him. His hand went to his sword instinctively. Sir Kendric did not react so quickly but stared at the gate with his mouth half open.

Archie burst through the portal. White foam flecked the horse's mouth and hide. Its sides heaved. Archie didn't look much better as he slid to the ground, clinging to his saddle on wobbling legs.

Hugh dismounted and ran to his sergeant at arms.

"You're a hard man to find, Sir Hugh." Archie drew a deep breath between each word.

"Ana? Is Ana safe?" Hugh asked. He kept a hand on Archie's back, helping him remain standing.

Archie snorted. "Nay, milord. I come from Bellecôte. Young John has taken ill again."

"Johnny?" Hugh's thoughts whirled. He had to find Ana. His son needed him. Where should he go?

"Aye, the bloody flux again. He took sick on the road from Wales. Two days of rest at home with no sign of getting better," Archie replied. "Met the messenger halfway here from Bellecôte and turned right around."

"Archie, where is Ana? You must go to her, protect her while I go to my son." Hugh ran for his horse.

"That strumpet!" Archie snorted again. "She won't need the likes of me to protect her. She's found her own methods. She married Radburn Blakely and became John's mistress."

Hugh's gut froze him half into the saddle. He thumped back onto the ground. Sharp pains ran up and down his thigh, setting fire to knee and hip. Meeting the Marshall in the lists couldn't have jolted him more.

"Not my Ana," he whispered.

"Lord Blakely announced to all of us the marriage by proxy, performed in Edinburgh, Sir Hugh." Kendric smiled lasciviously. "She likes the king so well she refused Blakely the marriage bed."

"I ride for Bellecôte, Archie. Join me there when you can." Hugh fought the darkness crowding his vision. "She betrayed me," he whispered.

"Do not judge her yet, my son. Her motives are more complex than stated. She needs you more than you think." The priest's voice echoed around Hugh's head. He searched the bailey for a sign of the tall, thin man. The priest had disappeared.

Hugh kept his eyes straight ahead, denying the verity of the priest's words.

Hugh bathed his son's brow with a cool cloth. The little boy moaned.

"Try to take a little water, Johnny," he urged.

The boy turned his head slightly toward the cup, mouth open a crack. He kept his eyes tightly closed against the light of a single oil lamp.

Hugh tilted the cup and spilled most of it. A few precious drops dribbled into John's mouth. He swallowed with difficulty.

"Thank you, Papa," Johnny whispered and fell back into his restless, fever dreams. He thrashed about clutching his distended belly but did not waken again.

Hugh sat back in his chair and buried his face in his hands. Tears burned at the corners of his eyes. So tired. He was so tired. He desperately needed sleep, a bath, a meal. He dared not leave Johnny's side.

"He can't survive, Sir Hugh," Sir Andrew said quietly from the shadows near the doorway.

"My son has recovered from worse," Hugh insisted.

"He has never been worse," Sir Andrew reminded him.

Hugh slumped, caving in upon himself. He hated to admit that his friend, his knight, was right.

"You know what you have to do, Hugh. You have to secure Bellecôte. You have to secure your right to guard the Welsh boys." The sounds of muted childish laughter drifted in from the Hall. The children had already made Bellecôte into a home.

"Not now, Andrew. I can't think beyond nursing Johnny."

"Let one of the women relieve you for a time. They will call if anything changes."

"No. No one will nurse my son but me. He fell ill because I took him to Durham and Wales. The journey wearied him too much. 'Tis my fault!"

"You could not have known, Hugh. We all thought him ready to grow into more responsibility. You have to think beyond this terrible moment. I know you hurt, Hugh. You have a right to grieve for your son. You love him. He was—is a wonderful little boy. Any man would be proud to claim him. But you have responsibilities beyond your love."

Hugh dipped his cloth into the basin of water again and mopped sweat from Johnny's face and neck. He lingered over bathing the boy's hands and wrists, caressing each finger.

He almost wished Ana were here. She could use her magic to heal the boy, as she did with her dog. Her gifts shouldn't be wasted on a dog when Johnny lay dying.

But he couldn't trust her. She had taken King John as a lover and married the black sorcerer, Radburn Blakely.

Johnny coughed. The spasms racked his too-thin body. Blood dribbled from his mouth and nose.

Hugh lifted his son's frail body into a sitting position. Still the boy choked and gasped, never waking fully to help himself breathe through the spasm.

At last Hugh laid him back down. His hands burned from the heat of Johnny's body.

"The priest waits in the Hall, Hugh. Johnny can't last long. He deserves last rites."

"I . . . I . . . bring him in. Pray for a miracle as I pray every minute."

The priest shuffled in, bearing incense and oil. The large bed-chamber seemed suddenly crowded, devoid of air to breathe.

Almighty God, look on this your servant, lying in
great weakness, and comfort him with the promise of life
everlasting, given in the resurrection of your son Jesus
Christ our Lord. Amen.

The priest made the sign of the cross over Johnny's body.

Hugh remained beside Johnny, holding his hand. The Latin words drifted through his consciousness. He took no comfort from the offer of peace and eternal life in heaven.

Sweet Jesu, he is so young. He had so much potential. Why do you deprive me of him when I have nothing, no one else? he implored over and over again.

God the Father,
Have mercy on your servant.
God the son,
Have mercy on your servant.
God the Holy Spirit,
Have mercy on your servant.
For the sins of my lips, forgive me.

The priest anointed Johnny's lips with a drop of holy water.

For the sins of my eyes, forgive me.

Another drop of oil on each eyelid. The priest continued with each of the five senses and added hands, heart, and feet as well.

Protect this your child, O Lord from the fires of
hell. May his body be free of demons.
Grant his time in purgatory short and light as
befitting his young years.
May the angels receive him with joy.
By your precious Death and Burial,
Good Lord, deliver him.
By your glorious Resurrection and Ascension, and by
the Coming of the Holy Spirit,
Good Lord, deliver him.

The litany rambled on, seemingly without end. At last the priest made the sign of the cross on Johnny's forehead with holy water.

Hugh clung to Johnny's hand, pressing his lips to the fingertips.

At the appropriate moment he dropped to his knees beside the bed and crossed himself. The priest touched Johnny's lips with the sacred bread and wine. The little boy's throat worked as if he had indeed taken the host into himself. His mouth trembled a little and turned up at one corner as if casting aside his pain.

Hugh bowed his head and held up his hands to receive his portion. If his son could find comfort in this celebration of Communion with the Lord, then Hugh must try to do the same.

The priest ignored Hugh's proffered hands and consumed the remnants of the host.

Hugh wanted to rise up, roaring his outrage. To deny a grieving father the solace of Eucharist at his son's deathbed . . .

"The Interdict," Sir Andrew whispered into his ear. At the same time he clamped strong hands on Hugh's shoulders to keep him calm.

"The Interdict," Hugh repeated. "What earthly good are these rituals and ceremonies if they exclude those most in need!"

" 'Tis not for us to question. The answers rest between our king and the Pope," Sir Andrew replied softly.

"Then the king must be made to see reason. He must reconcile."

"If only 'twere that easy."

At last the priest finished, making the sign of the cross over Johnny, murmuring a last benediction.

"I love you, Papa," Johnny said, almost clearly.

"I love you, Johnny," Hugh breathed, kneeling beside his son once more.

Johnny smiled. His body went slack, devoid of the tension of fever and cough and belly cramps. With one last shallow breath, almost a sigh, he closed his eyes.

"No!" Hugh shouted. "I won't let you die!" He shook his son violently. "I can't let you die."

"Enough, Hugh. He's gone." Andrew grabbed his shoulders and yanked him away from the bed. "He's gone."

"Forgive me, Johnny." Hugh collapsed onto the bed. Great sobs racked him. Nothing existed but the pain; the emptiness.

"Hugh?" Andrew asked after a time. "Hugh, you have to let the women in to prepare the body."

Body. Cold. All that remained was a limp carcass. Johnny, his Johnny, had passed beyond this mortal realm.

"Let him go, Hugh. He's in God's hands now."

"What did God ever do for me?" Hugh screamed. "What has His church ever done but ignore me, thrust me aside, or belittle me?"

He tore out of the room at a run. He had to get away. He needed to punch something, someone. His feet pelted up to the ramparts. Heedless of the wind and rain he ran the length of the curtain wall, skidding to a halt at the eastern tower.

Below, the walls merged with a cliff. Down, down, to the churning, muddy waters of the River Sence. An urge to plunge down into that water, to let the current rip the pain from his heart overtook him.

"That isn't the answer, Hugh," Andrew said quietly from behind him.

"Why are you still haunting me?" Hugh gripped the stone crenellations until his knuckles turned white and the rough edge cut into his palms.

"To protect you from yourself, Hugh. Grieve, storm, cry if you must. But think as well. Young John was Baron of Bellecôte. You but his guardian. This castle, all the honors of the barony revert to the crown. If we have any hope of protecting the Welsh hostages from the king's wrathful whims, you must secure the title and honors for yourself. You have to go to John and convince him to give you Bellecôte as he promised years ago. Maybe then you can influence him to reconcile with the church. Life can return to the way it was."

"Nothing will ever be the same again. My Johnny is dead. Ana has given her heart to another." He looked at the river one last time with longing, swallowed the lump in his throat, and turned back to his knight. "King John would not betray the rights of hostages. He has vowed to keep them safe."

"As long as their fathers keep the peace. But John continues to hound them. He presses them to go to war. How long before enough of their farms and castles are burned that they rise up in rebellion? How safe will those ten little boys be when that happens? One child has died this night—your child. For the sake of the others you must go to John and secure Bellecôte."

A knot of cold reason inserted itself into Hugh's mind. Andrew was right. John had proved time and again he couldn't be trusted. Especially not with those in his wardship—like Ana.

His mind jerked back to the Welsh woman offering herself to the knights in return for the safety of her daughters. Could Ana have done the same thing? She might very well have swallowed her pride and gone to John's bed in order to prevent the marriage to Blakely.

But John and his half brother had betrayed her anyway.

He needed to go to her, find out for sure if she had given her heart to another.

But . . .

"Not now, Andrew. I can't go yet. The hurts are too new. My son is not yet cold, not yet hidden away in a crypt." The burning ache gave way to a numbing chill. He felt nothing, knew nothing.

"Bury the boy in the morning, as is your duty. But then ride hotfoot to John. You need to be the one to carry the news and win the barony. Only you can do it. Evil minds whisper into John's ears. Make certain he hears sanity from you."

Once more the sounds of children playing in the Hall came to him. They had subdued their laughter and running out of respect for Johnny, but nothing could totally repress their youthful energy and vigor. The Welsh children thrived here.

"For the other boys, I'll do it. They are all precious. For them. But not for myself. I don't want anything but my son back."

And Ana.

Chapter 35

WE rejoined the court at Durham, then began the long trek south toward London. John planned to winter in Winchester. I wondered at the speed of this progress. Kings did not have a fixed home. They journeyed constantly, partly to preside in judgment, partly to collect their taxes in kind, partly to keep watch over the baronies. John's restlessness kept him on the road long hours after his retinue drooped with weariness. Rarely did he sleep two nights in the same bed, in the same castle, grange, or manor.

Two weeks into the journey, we bypassed York and found shelter in an old castle. The squat tower atop a crumbling motte, with only an old wooden palisade around the lower bailey, was a remnant of the civil war between King Stephen and John's grandmother Matilda. It has not been modernized and served more as a hunting lodge than a defensive structure.

The entire court squeezed into the Hall and minuscule solar. Anyone who could sought quarters in the wooden barracks in the bailey.

Queen Isabelle laughed out loud as we bumped into each other trying to find places for clothing, toiletries, and baths. The intricate dance of preparing for the evening meal became a game of laughter as Newynog nipped at heels and darted around feet.

Isabelle herself landed on her bum after one such encounter. Newynog claimed her prize by laving the queen's face with a wet sloppy tongue. She received a fierce hug in return.

Of course I had to dip my hands in the bathwater and splash Newynog. Of course the queen was in the process of ruffling the dog's ears at that precise moment and received most of the water in her face.

More laughter ensued and more splashing by one and all.

And so the ladies of the court joined the men in the Hall in bright spirits, ready to make our own entertainment this night.

Guessing games, drinking songs, and boasts kept us all laughing well beyond the last remove. My fears and depressions drifted to the back of my mind for a while. Since I could not escape and hope to regain Kirkenwood, I might as well enjoy myself.

One boast led to a challenge. The disputants arm wrestled to settle the issue. That challenge led to another. Arm wrestling led to full body matches at the center of the room.

Through it all Blakely sat slightly behind John, quiet, sullen, finding more wisdom in the bottom of his wineglass than in laughter. Truly, the man had no sense of humor.

A few brave souls attempted to include the king's half brother in the merriment. Each met with a rude rebuff that sent someone scuttling away and left Blakely more alone than before.

I preferred to ignore him. I'd had few enough opportunities to play with my peers in my life. I intended to make the most of this one.

And then someone took aim at one of the tattered war banners hanging on the wall with a sharp meat knife. It pierced the fabric three finger-lengths to the right of center and penetrated the wood paneling. Another knife followed almost immediately. This one went wide to the left, missing the banner altogether. The man who had thrown it dissolved in a fit of drunken laughter, rolling on the floor.

Quickly a lady drew a line in the rushes and decreed that the knife wielders must stand behind it.

"My tippet to the one who comes closest to the center!" I cried waving a scarf over my head.

"Sit and behave yourself, wife," Blakely snarled at me.

Defiance made me bold. I stood and held my scarf, prepared to drop it to signal the beginning of this tournament.

The knife wielders shuffled for position and turns at winning my favor.

Blakely stood and lunged across John to seize my wrist and the scarf before I could drop it.

I caught a glimpse of a shadow drifting away from the men at the side. For an instant Fantôme stood out among the crowd, a blade in his hand ready to throw. The next knife flew wide, aimed directly for Blakely's eye.

Time slowed.

A vision of darkness spiraling downward to death flashed before my eyes.

In that instant before time restored itself, I sent a silent bolt of magic into the knife, deflecting it to land in the planks of the high table, a hair's breadth away from Blakely's hand.

Had anyone seen me do that?

Fantôme blanched and took two steps backward, still visible and part of the group of contestants.

The crowd erupted in applause and more laughter. I saw the men slapping Blakely's servant on the back. Fantôme evaded them and drifted away, once more as insubstantial as a shadow.

"You saved my life," Blakely whispered. A little bit of awe colored his tone. His hand shook as he removed the knife from the table and examined it minutely.

"I revere all life, even yours. I could not let you die if I could prevent it."

"Would you die rather than kill?"

I stared back at him, stunned that he dared ask. All merriment left me. I sat heavily, wondering if indeed I would give in to death rather than kill and probably follow my victim in death as my talent forced me to share the experience.

"I'll remember that next time." The familiar sneer of contempt marred Blakely's too beautiful, too young face.

"You must kill her since we cannot find the evidence we seek," Radburn whispered to John as they prowled the battlements of Lincoln Castle several weeks after someone had tried to kill him. When he discovered the culprit, he'd have a new sacrifice for the magic that would end Resmiranda's control over John forever. He'd made gains since leaving Kirkenwood, but the lady still managed to make John smile and think logically.

No one dared interrupt their conversation on these windswept parapets. Radburn made certain no one came close enough to overhear.

Below them, that pesky knight Silvester prowled his rounds. Radburn had thought his prying eyes removed when he'd ordered him to castle guard here in Lincoln shortly after he caught up with the court between Durham and Kirkenwood.

Weeks had passed since Lady Resmiranda had saved Radburn's life. Weeks in which she taunted him hourly with her refusal to accept their marriage or bow to him. Her mind remained firmly close.

And yet John drew strength from her. She negated Radburn's seeds of discord within John's mind. Radburn saw himself aging daily in his mirror. He needed to get rid of her before his face and body caught up with the years he had actually lived.

In the distance, the cathedral bells rang Compline. "The priests ring the bells to order our lives, yet they deny us the solace of Mass, Confession, and Eucharist," John mused. He paused to look across the growing city until the resounding peal had finished echoing across the River Witham. A few fluffy clouds blazed bright pink as the sun dropped below the horizon.

"Perhaps the evidence that Arthur of Brittany lives does not exist," John said, raising his left eyebrow. "Perhaps Sir Brian de Griffin obeyed us and assassinated Arthur of Brittany as we ordered."

The cocky expression only fueled Radburn's anger and frustration. Weeks they'd been on the road. Weeks and not once had Lady Resmiranda spoken to him or allowed him near her. She also made a point of wearing a plain green cyclas over her bliaud while at court. Other ladies, proper ladies, wore their husband's emblems and colors on the overgown, much as retainers wore the same devices on their tabards. Lady Resmiranda pointedly proclaimed with her choice of clothing that she belong to no man.

Strangely enough the color green she had chosen matched her magical signature exactly. Few magicians, only the strongest, could see their own colors. Her potential chilled Radburn. He must possess her soon and control her magic, or she would outgrow him and possibly become strong enough to destroy him.

And that damned artifact of power remained as elusive as the evidence that Arthur of Brittany lived.

Until the marriage consummation was witnessed and recorded, their union existed only on parchment. She could have it annulled. His tenuous link to her that would lead to eventual control would evaporate.

And Radburn had no claim on the child he suspected she carried.

"The evidence that Arthur lives exists. I can smell it. She has hidden it with sorcery," Radburn said.

"Then seek it out with sorcery. You claim to be all powerful. We will not countenance her death until you show us whatever records she possesses. our crown will not be safe until those records burn."

"She has had no contact with her father in Normandy. He is the only one who could possibly supply evidence that Arthur lives. You killed her mother without hesitation when she tried to flee to the continent. You must destroy Resmiranda now, before she destroys you."

"Send your pet assassin to Normandy and have him slip a knife between Arthur's ribs. If Arthur has died as we ordered some years ago, then your Fantôme can dispose of Sir Brian de Griffin." John resumed his restless prowl through the mist rising from the river. The weather had not allowed him to hunt for days. The disputes brought before him at court had bored him. Petty matters of unjust fines imposed by the sheriff, or failure of just trial, of higher fines levied upon freemen and serfs than upon wealthy merchants. John did not like to deal with injustice, only the justice he imposed.

"I would trust the assassination of a lord or prince only to myself, Highness. And we both know that Philip of France would go to war before he allowed me to set foot on the continent."

"A war with Philip—hm," John said, looking thoughtful. "We would need to raise an army to be ready to sail right behind you. We could be poised and ready to win back the lands Philip stole from us."

John had hounded his barons relentlessly for four years for the means to renew his war with Philip. They had not supported such a move. Would they now?

Not bloody likely, Radburn thought. *These lords are more English than Norman. They like keeping their treasures close to home and their lands safe from royal encroachments. Since the Interdict, only two months ago, they have grown used to keeping their tithes and using them to boost their power and prestige at home—in England.*

"We do not need to wait for Griffin's death to remove his daughter," Radburn urged.

"I have no desire to see the lady removed from court."

"If you think she will return to your bed, forget it, Brother. She carries your child. Just like her great great grandmother who seduced your great grandfather, Henry I. She plans to use the child to enhance her line with more royal blood. Philip wants to use Arthur against you, to steal the crown from you. Resmiranda Griffin's child will be a more powerful focus for your *English* barons who have no love for Arthur of Brittany or Philip of France. If you allow that child to be born, the barons will rise up in rebellion against you. They will murder you and put her child on your throne—your son's throne. You are but a tool in her dynastic game." Radburn spun a tendril of compulsion into John. He had to be subtle about it. John resisted chaos these days, in favor of logic—Resmiranda's logic.

John whirled and paced back three steps to where Radburn stood. Fury creased his face and curled his lip. His eyes blazed pure hatred. The barb had struck home.

"Come with me. We will throw her into the oubliette together."

"Do not forget to take the prayer beads and cross from her first."

Chapter 36

I OPENED my leather trunk in the dark corner of the subterranean storeroom. I had to check Excalibur. No matter how often I looked upon the magnificent sword, I had to know it remained safe. I trusted my eyes more than my magic for this chore. I did sense the magic spell that still surrounded it. But I could see it. Who else could?

Again and again I asked myself why I had brought it along in my luggage. Other than as a mundane weapon, I had no idea how to use it. Perhaps it was nothing more than a mundane weapon. Arthur Pendragon had wielded the sword to save England from the chaos of foreign invasions. No rumor of his using magic filtered through the legends. Others used magic for and against him.

Radburn Blakely dogged my every step. Our confrontation could not be far off. I'd need Excalibur for that. The sword hummed in the back of my mind, waiting, ready to be used. I had but to lift it, and then . . . what?

Could I kill Blakely? Could I kill anyone? Since that night at Kirkenwood, when I had tasted betrayal by my lover and his half brother, I had lost much of the murderous rage that had engulfed me then. My reverence for life grew along with the child growing inside me.

Newynog would be little help. Pups grew large in her belly, too. She snapped and snarled at all of the dogs we encountered on the journey south. King John had ordered her muzzled on the road, kenneled at each stopping place. I missed her terribly.

Footsteps sounded on the turret stair to my left. I ignored them. Guards and servants pounded up and down the steps all day and all night. They'd learned to avoid this little storeroom, filled with sacks of grain, my luggage, and my pallet. I'd set wards at the doorway within moments of our arrival in Lincoln three days ago.

"She's made a rat's nest for herself over here," Blakely said quietly.

The wards muffled his words, and I had to strain to make certain I heard correctly. Before I could decide to replace Excalibur in the trunk, the door burst open. John and Blakely stood shoulder to shoulder. In back of them two grim-faced guards drew their weapons. Behind the guard, the low door into the deeper prison cells stood wide open.

"Excalibur!" John gasped reverently. He reached out as if he expected me to hand him my treasure. "That is a royal sword. Only we should possess it. Keep it at risk of our displeasure, Lady Resmiranda."

"Guards, take her! She'll kill the king with that sword!" Blakely yelled. A wicked, triple-edged blade slid from his wrist sheath. He flipped it outward, almost casually. His aim was true, directly at my heart.

Magic from the sword heightened my senses and quickened my reflexes. I ducked the blade. It bounced against the wall and landed on the floor. A speck of black on the tip had to be poison.

My heart pounded in my ears.

The guard advanced. No expression on their faces or in their eyes betrayed their next move.

What could I do?

Excalibur sang brightly in my mind and weighed heavily in my hand. I took a defensive stance, hampered by the elegant court gown John had given me. Then I raised the blade, gripping the hilt with both hands. It glowed faintly, ready. Power rippled through my blood. With this sword I could conquer the world.

If I wanted to. I had to remind myself, all I truly wanted was the safety of England from the likes of Radburn Blakely.

"What transpires, Highness?" I didn't dare take my eyes off Radburn or the guard to judge John's mood, or his motives.

"Where is the record of Prince Arthur's death?" John asked.

"I know not of what you speak, Highness," I lied. "I have lived most of my life cloistered. Dynastic politics have no place within a convent." I shifted my feet, seeking a more comfortable stance. The power trapped within Excalibur began to burn my hands, begging me to direct it.

A weapon of destruction. Arthur Pendragon had used it often to kill his enemies.

Could I?

"Your family records everything," John said. His voice took on the beguiling tone he'd used the day we lay together beside the pool in the forest. "You said so yourself, Lady Resmiranda. Our men found the storeroom full of scrolls and books, which remained hidden during all the years of your great-uncle's imprisonment. But nowhere is there a record of your father's inheritance of Griffin lands in Normandy. Nowhere is there a record of his part in the battle to capture Our nephew. Where is the record, Lady Resmiranda?"

John could not say more in front of the guards lest they know of his assassination orders. If these men were loyal to John only because of his royal blood, they would equally shrink away from shedding more royal blood no matter how politically expedient.

I girded myself against the seduction in his tone. He promised forgiveness. I knew his treachery.

"If such a record exists, I have never heard of it." Not exactly a lie. I hadn't heard of it. I'd discovered and read it myself.

"She lies, Highness. I can read it in her eyes." Radburn spat.

"I do not lie to my king—and my lover!"

"You lie. But you will not be able to spread your treason further!" Radburn said quietly. Too quietly.

A fiery magic spell left his hands as he stepped away from the doorway.

Without thinking, I shifted Excalibur. Green sparks bounced off the shiny metal blade. It hit the wall behind and above Blakely's head.

"Bitch!" he yelled and launched three more spells in rapid succession.

The sword moved faster than I could think. Faster than I could see.

One of the fiery magic blasts hit the drawn sword of one of the guards and bounced back, directly into Blakely's eyes. He staggered, crossing his arms before his face. He screamed. The sounds of his agony echoed and amplified among the stone walls. Blinded, he crashed into the solid wall beside the prison hatchway. His head hit with a terrible thunk. He slumped down, eyes wide and staring. His mouth opened into a surprised "O." Black smoke seemed to escape his mouth. Perhaps it was only his evil aura leaving him. Perhaps an evil demon fleeing his dead body. More black flames dribbled from his slack fingers, grounding harmlessly into the floor.

Echoes of his dying screams rang through my head louder than cathedral bells. My head grew numb from the sound of his death. Death at my hands.

The guards crossed themselves repeatedly as they raced up the turret.

"Radburn!" John screamed and ran to his brother's slumped form. "You've killed him," he sobbed. "You killed my brother." He stood up, hands clenched tightly before him. Torchlight reflected redly from his eyes. His wrath pulsed around his aura like shooting flames.

Fighting the darkness that crowded my vision, I threw Excalibur into the trunk. The lid slammed shut without my aid. Then I rushed to Radburn's side. I had to save him before I followed him into death. I knelt at his side, feeling for a pulse.

Nothing.

"You killed him!" John said. Grief aged him hideously. Deep wrinkles drew his mouth down and almost made his weak chin evaporate. His ears stuck out from the sides of his head almost like horns. I thought I saw a demon staring out of his eyes.

"He killed himself, John. His spell backlashed." I tried justifying my actions; tried to stave off the black tunnel that opened before me, drew me like a lodestone to iron.

"You killed him!" John screeched. He tore his hair and frothed at the mouth in near insanity.

I searched for an escape. From him. From the dead man.

John blocked access to the stairs. The only way out.

"Every person who works magic knows that a backlashed spell triples in intensity. He could have avoided it if he prepared properly." I tried reason. Somehow I must break through the chaos of his grief and reassert logic in his thinking.

"You killed him. And now you must die." His tone took on the authority of the finest judge in all of England. "I loved you, Resmiranda. I truly loved you. But I must abide by the law. You murdered. Now you must die."

I tried to run, tried to push him aside and run up the stairs.

My legs refused to move.

"He killed himself," I repeated. My knees wobbled as I stared at my king, my lover, the father of my baby. He couldn't do this to me. He wouldn't.

A coldness behind my heart told me I knew he would.

He'd hounded de Briouze and his family out of England for less. Threatened them with death if they ever set foot on English soil again.

"Your son carries royal blood," John said as if reciting a poisonous litany. Blakely's litany. "You carry royal blood. We are cousins to the third degree. You also carry the blood of The Pendragon of legend. The boy will be a rival to Henry, my son and heir. You must die, Resmiranda, before you use the child against me."

"No, John. I would never do that to you."

"You will. You will betray me, as everyone betrays me."

"No, John. If I carry a child, I will cherish it, raise it quietly at Kirkenwood. We will never acknowledge you as the father." My legs threatened to collapse. John blocked my escape.

"I must stop you from using your son against me. I must punish a murderer. You must die, Resmiranda. Here. Now."

His fist connected with my jaw. Stars burst before my eyes. Darkness swirled around me.

Half senseless, reeling, I staggered. I tried to move away from him. Instead I fell . . .

As in my dream of portent I landed with a bone-crunching jolt. Pain shot up from both ankles.

"John!" I screamed. "Help me, John."

"We are sorry, Resmiranda. We did love you." He slammed the hatch closed and slid home the bolt. The sounds of his plodding steps climbing the turret stair echoed loudly against my ears.

"Find me, Newynog. Bring help!" The stone walls of my prison absorbed my voice and my thoughts, preventing them from escaping.

No one else cared enough to even look for me when I did not ride out with John in the morning.

"I'm sorry, Hugh. Please forgive me," I whispered into nothingness.

Chapter 37

HOURS passed, perhaps days. I had no way of knowing. Hunger gnawed at me, passed, and became nausea. But thirst would not go away. I tried licking moisture from the clammy walls. But any movement at all sent long shafts of pain up my legs.

I screamed.

No one heard.

I tried to explore my surroundings. My fingers traced the stonework walls and floors. About four feet square. Not large enough to stretch out, barely enough room to curl up into a ball. If I could move at all.

Tears streaked my cheeks as I began trembling uncontrollably.

I thought I heard footsteps.

"Help me," I called. I'm down here."

Was that a low chuckle above me? John come back to taunt me?

"Why bother with the body? That one's dead. Throw 'im int d' midden!" a rough voice snarled.

"No!" I screamed, though little sound came from my parched throat. "He must be buried, grounded in ritual to keep demons from using his body."

"He was my master. I need to bury him." A quiet voice, slightly better educated than his companion. Fantôme?

"Such as he don't deserve burial. It's the midden fer 'im."

Footsteps retreated followed by the sound of something heavy dragging behind them.

Silence reigned again. Silence and emptiness in my mind, my stomach, and my soul.

Perhaps I slept.

Dream images formed before my eyes. Mama, Aunt Lotta, Uncle Henry, even my papa visited me. The light from their auras showed me the dank walls, rough dirt, insects, and stinking algae of my prison. The people of my past crowded the tiny enclosure, leaving little room for me. Hugh, the one person I wanted desperately to see, to apologize to, to beg forgiveness of, stayed out of my hallucinations.

"Don't let anything happen to Arthur," I begged my father, reaching a hand to him.

"Arthur lives or dies at my command, not yours," he said sternly, turning his back on me. As he had always turned his back on me and Mama. He cared nothing for us, lived only for war. He followed King Richard. They lived by a warrior's code. Home and family meant nothing to them.

But he'd said he loved me. Once in a letter.

"Uncle Henry, help me find the magic to get out of here," I begged.

"We are all prisoners of magic, Ana. Learn to live with it, or die learning that one grim fact," he replied and faded into the stonework.

"Mama, don't desert me again."

"You were never my child. You always belonged to *them.* I tried to save your soul. I left you with the nuns so they could beat the magic and Satan out of you. But Satan and the Griffin blood were too strong. Die unshriven as you deserve." She vanished in a sheet of flame and choking smoke.

I coughed and stared at the place in the wall where she had vanished until dream darkness claimed my mind again.

I woke startled, trying to rise. The pain in my feet and ankles brought new screams to my throat. Dryness kept the sounds inside.

I could try to heal myself at the cost of wasting my precious life energy, possibly damaging the baby in my belly. Which did I choose—comfort and fast death, or pain and pray for a miracle to save us both?

Aunt Lotta remained before me. Not the old woman I had known with white hair and care lines outlining the map of her life on her face and hands. She came before me a maiden, in the first blush of womanhood, younger than I. She wore her lustrous black hair in two thick braids that hung below her waist. Her blue-gray eyes sparkled with life and humor. Apple blossoms tinged her smooth cheeks. Her bosom showed above her simple gown, firm and proud. She laughed lightly.

"You think me a phantasm of your imagination, child. I come to you as Henry first knew me. As I always thought of myself, even when age and illness made my tits sag and my belly droop." She laughed again.

"Why have you come?" I croaked out the words around the dryness in my mouth.

"To teach you, of course. Teach you as no woman took the time to make you proud of your body, proud of the magic within you, and the life you give to the next generation."

"Why? Why now, when I am dying? My baby will die with me."

"Because now you will listen."

"I'm not going anywhere." I held out my hands to emphasize my prison.

"I loved my Henry the moment I met him. Oh, he was full of anger and violence when he came home from the Second Crusade. He hated with all of the intensity he later learned to love."

"That is not the Uncle Henry I knew."

"Of course not. This was more than fifty years before you knew him." Her laughter chimed like faery bells. "I had come from Wales to study the standing stones at Kirkenwood. I arrived the week before Samhain."

"A bad time to be traveling."

"Aye. The storms were fierce that year. Some say they portended the terrible events of that Samhain. Some say your great-uncle raised those storms with his fearsome anger."

"I can't believe my Uncle Henry would do such a thing."

"He could and did. He saw many terrible things in the Holy Land. He was the victim of some of them. He carried those seeds of anger with him everywhere. He needed to destroy things in order to convince himself he still lived."

"What happened that Samhain?" I thought I knew but the timing seemed wrong.

"The portals between worlds thin on Samhain Eve. Demons and faeries, devils and angels, pass easily into this world. Once loosed, they roam freely until the light of dawn sends them back where they belong. No one can banish them by mundane or magical means until then."

The scene came to life before me, as if I lived it. . . .

Henry Griffin galloped his horse down the processional way from Kirkenwood Grange. Aunt Lotta/I stood in the center of the stone circle, beside the tallest stone. Blackness and flame dominated Henry's aura. The burning rage and hatred he carried in his heart overshadowed the glimmer of magic and love he'd been born with.

"The most beautiful man alive, and he wastes himself on drink and acts of cruelty," we muttered as he skirted the circle of stones. They'd not allow him to enter the circle while possessed of such demons.

He spurred his horse to greater, more dangerous speed. The sun setting behind him cast a long and menacing shadow.

"Be careful, Henry Griffin," we cautioned. "Samhain comes hard on the heels of your shadow."

He raced past us, adding the goad of a whip to his spurs in the horse's flanks.

The darkness of his shadow swirled around and around the perimeter of the standing stones. It beat and howled at the solid barrier of magic.

And I knew that demons lurked at Henry Griffin's heels, waiting for the sunset to possess him.

What could we do? Had we enough magic within us to protect him?

All of the villagers huddled within their huts this night. They built their fires high and lit extra lamps and precious candles to banish the shadows where a demon might lurk. We'd find no help there.

Only we stood lonely sentinel beside the living stone at the center of the circle, staff in hand. Only we saw a young girl creep out of a hut near the edge of the circle.

"Go back," we pleaded. "Whatever your errand, it can wait for the dawn and safety."

"The sun is not yet set. I have time to fetch my laundry from the burn. 'Tis only a few steps," she called back to us. She shrugged her shoulders at our warning, too young in years and experience to understand the danger. She raced the sunset and lost.

We chased after her, desperate to enfold her with whatever protective spells we might conjure.

The last ray of sunshine shot a single arrow above the horizon and died.

Henry and his demon awaited the girl beside the little cascade and pool where the women gathered on sunny days to share the chore of laundry.

At the moment we spied him in the fading twilight, he opened his arms wide and embraced the black form. A riot of colors burst from his aura. He opened his mouth and grinned, wickedly pointed teeth gleaming in the eerie light cast by his own augmented life energy.

The sheer evil glowing in his red eyes beat at us, driving us away from the girl.

We threw the staff up before our eyes to counter the vicious light. Red glare crept around the old oak and nearly blinded us.

In those few moments of hesitation, the girl was lost.

Her screams forced us to open our eyes. She kicked and clawed at the naked man who lay atop her. He had shredded her simple gown to expose her breasts. As we watched he dragged a clawlike fingernail down her belly to her wispy thatch.

She screamed again.

We forced ourself to move out of the paralysis and run.

Too late.

Henry Griffin pounded into her, again and again. He laughed madly, nearly howling in triumph. He withdrew, dripping blood from his penis. Then amazingly he rolled back on top of the girl and entered her again. The demon gave him stamina beyond a true mortal's.

We stumbled over a rock and continued off-balance in our mad dash to help the girl; get her back within the protection of the standing stones. As he laughed again, grunting at the moment of his orgasm, we struck him with the seasoned oak of the staff. He collapsed on top of her, unconscious, still pumping his seed into her.

The horrible vision faded. I found myself once more in the dank oubliette facing the saddened vision of my dear great-aunt.

"What happened next?" I asked in a whisper, too shaken to remember that no one could hear me.

"I took the girl back to the village and nursed her hurts. She nearly went mad over the next seven months. She died giving birth to her premature child. Blood, so much blood. The demon child tore her to shreds from the inside." Sadness shadowed her beautiful face, and she faded into a matron. Her face was fuller, gray streaked her hair. The stark leanness of youth gave way to rounded hips and breasts. Pain and the mature patience to bear it shone in her eyes.

"A beautiful baby girl, full of sweetness and light that the entire village cherished and protected." I finished the story for her. "But Uncle Henry told me the man responsible went mad and drowned himself in the pool by the kirk. He said it had happened twenty years later. . . ."

"Henry tried to drown himself in the pool beside the kirk. He could not live with the knowledge of what he had done and nearly went mad. He tried to drown himself in the pool, but the Lady would not let him. She threw him back to me. The water cleansed him of some of his guilt." We both chuckled at the image of that cool and wise personality rejecting Uncle Henry's untimely sacrifice.

New guilt assailed me. I had failed to return Excalibur to the Lady. At least I had ended Blakely's black manipulation of our king.

"In a sense the man responsible died that day," Great-aunt Lotta continued, ignoring my silence and regret. "The man who lived from that day forward was a different person altogether, gentle, forgiving. Loving. I worked with Henry for more than a year before he could finally accept responsibility for himself and for the child." She faded a little into a misty form as her memories separated us from the here and now.

Then she heaved a sigh and reformed before my eyes. "Only when he acknowledged that responsibility was he strong enough to capture the demon and banish it to the netherworld. The spell required all my strength as well as his. Yet it still beats at the portal trying to break through the seal."

I roused myself from the endless loop of anger toward myself. Something about the story nagged at me. I knew I was hallucinating, but the detailed mind pictures Aunt Lotta wove for me seemed so real, so logical I could not discount them.

"Henry changed for the better after that. His violent ways ended. He embraced the light and learned to control his magic. Together we worked to perpetuate the light and lessen the influence of demons and other devils." Again my great-aunt changed. From maiden to matron and now a crone. Thinner, slightly bent, her fingers had turned to claws with the bone sickness. Wisdom and humor radiated from her entire personality, not just her eyes.

This was the woman I had known and loved through my childhood.

"That means that Radburn Blakely is Uncle Henry's grandson, first cousin to my father." I shuddered at how close he had come to being my husband by law as well as deed. "And he is closer to forty than the twenty he looks." Thirty now. He'd aged unnaturally since those days he'd ridden to Edinburgh to marry me by proxy.

"Forty-two. A year older than his half brother, King John." Aunt Lotta stared at me forthrightly. "King Henry II and his queen had not spoken to each other in a year. He rode the kingdom, never staying in one place more than a week, often with only a few knights as escort." Much as his son John did now. "Henry came upon our remote stronghold on Beltane. Henry's daughter was willful, determined to celebrate the festival in the old manner. She ran away from us, broke through the wards of the standing stones. The first man she encountered was King Henry. She stayed with him several months, then came back to us for a time. She never told us her lover's name. Like her mother, she died in childbed. Priests and armed men claimed the baby the next day. We never heard from the child again. We hoped that the church could mend his soul. But rumors persisted of a Black One. An evil man with an aura of pure black."

"And because Blakely wants people to believe he is only twenty-two or three, no one made the connection between himself and the Black One until he invaded Kirkenwood the night you died."

Now he lay dead. Dead by his own backlashed spell.

"Magic can work for good," Aunt Lotta said urgently. "Magic is neither good nor evil by itself, but its power can corrupt the wielder. Remember that and feel no shame for your talent, for your passions, for yourself. You still have work to do. Do it proudly, without shame." Aunt Lotta faded into mist, leaving behind only her smile and a feeling of peace in my heart.

You do not die unforgiven, my dear. Embrace the light. Embrace your place in the light. Her words lingered with me as I passed into oblivion again.

Awroooo!

I woke again to Newynog's mournful howls. The prayer beads cut my palm where I clutched them. I fingered the circled cross. My chin quivered and more tears washed my cheeks.

"Hush, Newynog. Hush, my beloved," I whispered into the darkness. Her howls receded to pained whimpers. "Go home, Newynog. Go home to Kirkenwood. Do not die with me."

Awroooo! She howled again in protest.

"Let me die in peace, Newynog." She pawed frantically at the bolted hatch. Her claws scraped at the wood without effect. Even if she could break through the thick planks, she could not raise me from the hole, and I could no longer help myself.

With the last of my strength, I conjured a little ball of witchlight on the chance that I might see her beloved shaggy face one more time.

"I will not die in the darkness. I will die in the light." I counted the beads one last time, thinking the prayers, no longer having the strength to speak them.

Awrooooooooooo!

Chapter 38

"WHERE has the king gone now?" Hugh asked wearily. He felt as if he'd been in the saddle for months instead of days. His aching grief still gnawed at him. Yet he had to push on; he had to secure Bellecôte and find Ana.

"Off to London Tower, Hugh," Lord Silvester said. He possessed a minor manor within Lincolnshire. As the authority summoned by the guards, Hugh presumed he served castle guard in lieu of knights' service in the absence of the earl. Otherwise he'd be with the king and Ana. He looked as tired as Hugh felt.

"You should have stayed with him, Silvester. I asked you as a friend to protect Ana."

"I could not disobey a royal command, Hugh. King John sent me back here within hours of catching up with him outside of Durham."

"Did the command come from King John or his half brother Blakely?"

"A written order delivered by Blakely's servant. Had to hunt for an hour to find a cleric to read it to me."

"A false order. John probably never knew you had joined the court."

"I could not disobey."

"I know." Hugh sighed wearily. "How long ago did he leave?" He barely had the strength for words. Still four hours of daylight remained. He needed to press on.

"Yesterday morning."

"He'll linger in London before moving to Winchester," Hugh muttered, gathering his reins to remount.

"I don't know, Sir Hugh. He rode out of here like all of hell's demons nipped at his heels."

"As long as Blakely whispers in his ear, that's likely," Archie muttered from the watering trough where he held both his horse and Hugh's.

Hugh and the local lord looked each other in the eye and nodded briefly, acknowledging the truth of the statement. They'd fought together in Normandy. Hugh had followed Blakely into the French sewer tunnels at the behest of Silvester's earl. Only a raging fever had kept Silvester from joining him. They both knew the depth of Blakely's evil.

Hugh wearily put his foot into his stirrup, not eager to continue his journey without a bath, a meal, and a full night's rest. He'd not sleep. He hadn't slept since Johnny died.

Awrooooo! A ghostly moan wailed through the castle, bailey, and demesne.

Archie raised frightened eyes to Hugh. He crossed himself and muttered something.

"What ghosts did Blakely leave behind this time?" Hugh asked, removing his foot from the stirrup.

"Not a ghost, Hugh," Silvester said. His eyes wandered away from Hugh's face toward the lower entrance to the keep.

Awrooo!

"It's the dog. Blakely ordered us to kill the beast. But she's pregnant and her pups valuable. My men wanted to wait until she whelps. But now she lies in the undercroft and moans like that. We may have to kill her after all. She's almost driven us to the edge of sanity."

"How long?" Hugh launched into a wild run for the tower keep. Desperation gave him the strength to shatter the door when the hinges and bolts resisted.

"She's been there most of the day. What does it mean, Sir Hugh?"

"Didn't you have the initiative to find out why the dog mourns the loss of her mistress?"

"The dog snarls and snaps at any who approach. We dared not come too close. Besides, Lady Resmiranda rode out with the king."

"Ana would never leave that dog behind. They are like two halves of one whole." Hugh pounded down the stairs to the lowest excavated level.

Newynog lay beside a wooden trapdoor near the far wall. An oubliette. A place where prisoners could disappear and be forgotten forever.

The dog raised her head and loosed another soul-shattering howl. The sound echoed around the stone chamber until Hugh's hearing felt bruised.

"Holy Mother, I pray we are not too late." He approached Newynog slowly, holding out his hand, palm up. "You know me, Newynog. You trusted me to rescue her once before," he said, forcing calm into his voice though his heart raced and leaped into his throat.

Awroooo! Newynog answered him, scratching at the wooden hatch.

"Let me lift it, Newynog." Hugh knelt beside the dog and reached for the bolts.

"Hugh, that is an oubliette," Silvester objected. "This a royal castle. We dare not open it without the king's permission."

"Damn the king to hell! You, too, if you interfere." Hugh threw back the hatch and peered into the black hole. A faint glow drifted across the opening, obscuring his view of the bottom.

"I cannot countenance this, Hugh."

"Then turn your back, go elsewhere, and leave me to this. A light, Archie. I need light and a rope."

Newynog leaned over the opening with him, snuffling and scrabbling to get down.

"If the witchlight glows even a little, she lives," Hugh reassured the dog and himself.

Archie produced a torch and a length of rope. He lashed one end to a torch bracket in the wall. Hugh tied the other end around his waist.

"How deep is this bloody hole," he asked Silvester who hovered near the bottom step, not a part of the rescue but not condemning it either.

"Eight feet, no more."

Deep enough to keep a tall man from reaching the top.

"I cannot believe King John would do this to a woman," Silvester muttered.

"Believe anything of King John as long as Blakely controls him," Hugh replied, testing his weight against the rope. "Let me down easy, Archie." He dropped over the side, bracing his feet against the stone wall and his weight against the rope. Archie let out the coil slowly. Hugh dropped below the glow of witchlight into the tiny prison. Ana lay in a crumpled heap, taking up most of the floor.

Gingerly he placed first one foot down behind her bent back and the other beside her sprawled arms. The sight of her swollen and misshapen feet and ankles sent chills through him. She didn't seem to be breathing.

"God's wounds, he'll pay for this, Ana," he said through clenched teeth. "I'm down," he called up to his comrades.

He bent and touched his fingers to her clammy throat, seeking a pulse. The faintest of flutters answered his quest.

"Does she live?" Silvester asked timidly.

"Barely." He took a deep breath for courage and touched her shoulder, shaking her lightly. "Ana, wake up. I'll get you to safety now."

"Let me die in peace," she croaked past cracked and dry lips. She fluttered her hands, tiny movements that suggested she flailed against him in thought if not deed.

"Not bloody likely. I'm risking rebellion against my king for you. You'd damn well better live." He gathered her into his arms, being careful not to jostle her feet against the walls.

"End this. Let me die." She waved at him again with half-clenched fists.

He barely felt the blows.

"Haul us up, Archie. Slowly, gently. She's hurt." He gathered her close against his chest, imprisoning her hands to keep them from thrashing against the close walls.

His breathing grew sharp and shallow at the thought of those stones closing in on him. He'd never feared small spaces before. He'd never accept them again.

"Oh, God, Ana. What have they done to you?" he moaned, burying his face in her hair.

Inch by inch he half walked up one wall, his back against the other. Ana lay still, no longer fighting him. Her breathing stilled. Her skin felt cold to his touch.

The stink of her own filth filled his head and gave birth to violent, rebellious, treasonous thoughts.

"I'll kill John with my own hands for this."

Newynog threw up another of her soul-shattering howls. The echoes stabbed Hugh's mind and broke all coherent thought. His right foot touched the rim of the hole. He couldn't think how to move next.

"Hold the rope tight, Archie," Lord Silvester barked, taking over the thinking. "I've got her, Hugh. You can let go now. Let go, Hugh. I won't let anything happen to her. Nothing more anyway. God's teeth, I can't believe John did this to her. Blakely, yes, but not John."

Moments later, Hugh crawled from the stinking pit and over to Ana's inert form. Silvester himself dribbled a few drops of water into her mouth. Newynog licked her face and hands. Ana stirred a little, moaning in pain.

"Why didn't you let me die?"

"Because . . . because . . ." *Because I love you.* Hugh couldn't say the words. The last person he'd said them to, Johnny, had died. He wouldn't let her die.

Lord Silvester coaxed more water down Ana's throat. She swallowed greedily now, resigned to the fact that she might live.

"Get some blankets, she's shivering. The cold and weakness can still take her. For the love of God, get her a blanket, Archie."

"There's a chest in that little storeroom," Silvester said. "It was left behind when John departed."

Archie scooted into the room

Newynog lay down beside her mistress, still washing her face with a long tongue.

Hugh took over chafing her hands and wrists, trying to get her blood flowing.

"Now what, Hugh? I can't keep her here. The king will have my head—yours, too. He personally entrusted this castle to me in the absence of the earl." Silvester held the cup for Ana again. "Not too much, milady. You'll bolt it if you take too much too soon. Then we'll be back to where we started from."

"Every castle, township, river, and field in this blasted country belongs to King John." Hugh almost pounded his fist into the stone flooring. "We barons merely hold our lands in custody for him in return for outrageous taxes and unending knights' service." He restrained himself before he damaged his sword hand with the useless gesture.

"No matter where you take her, John will find her and execute us all."

"He won't go to Huntington." Hugh half smiled at the inspiration. Once before he'd tried to send Ana to Huntington. This time she wasn't strong enough to fight his decision.

"Earl Robin Locksley and his people will feel no obligation to inform the king that his prisoner lives," Silvester confirmed.

"I'll need a woman to travel with us. One with a knowledge of healing and herbcraft."

"I'll send one to you. Best if you not appear above ground until after dark. I trust my people. But you never know who else might be watching."

"Uh, Sir Hugh?" Archie said quietly from the doorway of the storeroom. "I think you'd best see this trunk. We've got more trouble. I think I know what John and Blakely were looking for when they threw her into the oubliette."

Radburn opened his eyes, wincing at the pain in his head. Automatically he searched his body for the source of his hurts. His mundane senses told him only that light stabbed his eyes and his scalp burned at the touch of the rough blanket beneath him.

He found no trace of magic anywhere within him. NO! This could not be. How could he function without that extra sight-beyond-sight, the oversensitive hearing, his awareness of every living thing in his immediate vicinity, without his demon grandsire whispering truth into his mind?

He whimpered uncontrollably.

"So you decided to live," Fantôme said from a slight distance. Not far, not close enough to touch.

Where are you? his mind screamed. He opened his eyes again slightly to find the young man crouched before a fire. The light played across his features, trapped by walls of some sort rather than dissipating into the night. A spark rose. Radburn followed it with his eyes and detected the general shape of a rooftree and thatch.

"Do you call this living? How do you stumble through life with only these inept five senses?" Radburn moaned. He rolled to his side and nearly retched from the increased pain in his head.

"Who said I have only five mundane senses?" Fantôme brought a little ball of witchlight to his palm. It burned brighter than the true flames at his feet. The twin lights threw a mask of shadows onto the planes of his face. He suddenly became an older, taller man, full of power and ruthlessness.

"I thought there was something different about you." Radburn rolled onto his back again, covering his eyes with an incredibly heavy arm. "What an ironic twist of fate." The laughter bubbling in him turned hysterical. He gulped it back with difficulty.

"You are wondering how I, a mere peasant, have inherited powers to rival your own and the Lady Resmiranda's," Fantôme said. His eyes narrowed as if he peered into a murky darkness.

The murky darkness of Radburn's mind. *I don't have the strength to keep him out.* Merde, *I can't even tell if he truly is there, mucking about with my memories and secrets.* That thought brought a moment of panic. He fought it. His stomach churned with the effort.

He rolled back onto his side in case he lost everything in the struggle. He didn't want to die choking on his own bile.

When he could speak again without coughing up his insides, Radburn asked the question that hovered between them. "How?"

"Ever hear of a witch called Nimuë?" Fantôme fed another stick into the fire. Was he conjuring a vision?

"A legendary woman, consort to The Merlin or something. Long, long ago," Radburn replied, sorting through the stories and songs that told the tale of the vengeful woman trapping her lover, the magician Merlin, in an oak tree.

"She bore a child. My Gran says that when the ashes of Camelot were sifted through and sorted out, all the dead counted, including Arthur Pendragon, Nimuë's son had gone missing. Gran claims descent from him. We pass the talent from grandmother to grandson to granddaughter in a straight line of descent from him. We have sought to bring about the death of The Pendragon ever since. I came to see you as a servant because I knew you could lead me to her. The Griffin clan cannot be assaulted within the protection of Kirkenwood and the standing stones. They do not leave that protection readily. Even their staff won't gain me entrance to Kirkenwood by magical means." He clenched his hand as if he wished to hold the missing staff by his side.

"What did you do with it?" Radburn croaked.

"Broke it. Removed the cross. Wrapped it all in a moth-eaten and flea-infested blanket and threw it in the midden. Lord Silvester heard the splash and thought I'd tossed your body there."

"Have your family passed the knowledge of how to use the talent along with the family tree?" Radburn asked sarcastically. The beginnings of a plan niggled at his brain. He might not have magic at his fingertips but Fantôme was his servant, his shadow. Fantôme owed him his life as well as his loyalty.

"Of course my family preserved the knowledge. The knowledge is more important than the family tree. Nimuë consorted with demons. I could smell the demon in you when first we met. Now I can't. The Pendragon witch did more to you than backlash a spell." He stood up and loomed over Radburn's inert form.

Helplessness turned Radburn's muscles to water. He tried putting on a cloak of bravery. Maybe he could bluff his way back into control. If he held firm. If Fantôme's family had bred stupidity back into their peasant brains.

He should get up, loom over his servant with his superior height, superior lineage. His muscles refused to obey.

"I remember little beyond seeing an enchanted sword in the hands of my wife."

"You threw a spell to rob her of her magic and knock her unconscious. The sword caught it and threw it to the wall. It bounced around until it found a home in your eyes."

Memory of blazing pain nearly robbed Radburn of consciousness again. A backlashed spell tripled in intensity. He'd not recover his talents soon, if at all. "How did she die?"

Fantôme threw back his head and laughed, long and loud. "John thinks he killed her."

"That bumbler," Radburn spat. "He didn't have the guts to do it himself, so he gave the job to an underling who failed."

"Not quite. John thought you dead. He condemned the lady to death on the spot and threw her into the oubliette. She should have died. She would have."

"Let me guess. John left Lincoln, and the valiant Sir Hugh Fitz Chênenoir rode in and rescued her again. That man will be the death of me yet. What does it take to bring him low!"

"He is as faithful as a dog. Beat him, starve him, lie to him, cheat him, and he still comes back for more." Fantôme continued chuckling. "But he was too late. The lady had been in the oubliette two days. They did not revive her."

"You saw yourself?" Radburn had to know for certain that Resmiranda had died, taking her magic and her evidence with her.

"I have it from a very reliable source. She could not resist my compulsion. Or my charms." He fondled himself in lewd suggestion of how he had used his informer.

"Lady Resmiranda is dead. John believes me dead. I have lost . . ." He wasn't about to tell this servant he'd lost his magic, even if the disability only proved temporary.

"You've lost everything but me, Radburn Blakely. Including your magic." Fantôme's eyes narrowed in speculation.

Radburn recognized the malicious glint there. He'd seen it in his own mirror too many times.

"Now what?" Radburn asked warily.

"You tell me all you know about that sword. I carry the same magical heritage as the lady. I can handle it as well as she. I will have it. And then I will rule England with or without John. With or without you."

Chapter 39

HUGH stared down at the old-fashioned sword lying in the leather traveling chest. The bejeweled hilt glinted gold beneath the leather-wrapped grip. The blade itself shone in the weak light. Beside it, the golden scabbard was finely sculpted with ancient Celtic knotwork.

He ached to hold the thing in his hands.

"Magnificent!" Silvester breathed. He knelt beside the chest and reached in for the sword.

Jealousy flared inside Hugh. He should be the one to lift it, to cleave enemy necks with it, to know the glory of possessing such a magnificent thing!

Then he checked himself, realizing what drove his thoughts.

"Do you have any idea what that thing is, milord?" Hugh asked his friend.

"The most magnificent sword ever crafted. With this at my side, I could defeat the Plantegenet and rule Britain as it must be ruled, with an iron fist and just laws." Silvester reached in to claim the sword. "Yieee!" he squealed and jerked his hand back, sucking his fingers as if burned.

"Lady Resmiranda Griffin is descended from Arthur Pendragon. That sword could be Excalibur," Hugh said quietly.

"The sword of The Pendragon, returned to the Lady of the Lake upon Arthur's death. Yes! But what is she doing with it?" Silvester stood up, still nursing his red and blistered fingers.

Newynog ambled into the room to check on them. She walked up to the chest, snuffled at the sword, and returned to her mistress.

"Ana is The Pendragon. She wears the signet ring of the red dragon. Why wouldn't she have the sword?" Hugh countered. He needed to be with Ana now, not arguing over this antique artifact. She was cold and needed more water.

"But she is only a woman. She should name a champion to wield the sword for her. I shall be her champion." A strange glaze covered Silvester's eyes as he stalked back to Ana's inert and shivering form.

"She can't name a champion. She has to wield the sword herself," Archie said, loudly enough for all of them to hear. "That's why she had me teach her sword craft when she should have concentrated on archery or a staff or any weapon more suitable for a woman."

Silvester stopped short. "If that thing is indeed Excalibur, then none of us are safe as long as it is here. You have to leave Lincoln. Now. With the lady and the sword."

"The sun is almost set. Prepare a packhorse for the traveling chest. I'm not going to risk carrying it," Hugh ordered. He returned to Ana and lifted her in his arms. For a long moment he just stood there, cradling her next to his heart, cherishing her slight weight, gazing at her sweet face.

"I'll order a litter for her." Silvester mounted the first stair up to the main part of the keep.

"A litter is too slow. She'll ride with me." Hugh held her so tightly that she whimpered a little in her delirium.

"Again?" Archie asked, sounding more than a little disgusted.

Forever, Hugh thought.

"Again?" Silvester repeated.

"Tell him the story, Archie, while you prepare the horses. And don't forget to send a healer, blankets, some broth, and more water. We have to make certain she is as strong as possible before we ride to Huntington."

"I hope Earl Robin is crazier than you are," Archie muttered as he mounted the steps. "If he is even a little bit sane, he'll throw us all to King John's wolves."

"Hugh," Ana whispered. She reached a delicate hand to trace the shape of his chin, then dropped it as if the effort to move was too much. "Hugh, where did they bury Blakely? I have to perform a ritual over the grave to make certain demons do not raise him."

"What?" Silvester and Hugh asked together.

"I killed him. John condemned me for it. Where did you bury him?" She stared long and hard at the wall next to the open hatch. Black streaks Hugh had presumed to be mold but which now appeared more like scorch marks showed the rough outline of a man's head and body on that wall.

He did not want to think about the forces Ana controlled if she had made the man a living inferno.

"Blakely left with the king," Silvester said. He came back down the two steps to face Ana directly.

"He couldn't have. I killed him, with the sword. He's dead. John said so. I checked him and found no pulse, no trace of breathing."

"He's not here now," Hugh said quietly. He turned in a full circle, still holding Ana so they could both see that no body littered the ground.

"My men did not see the body when they tried to remove the dog from here," Silvester said. "They would have reported to me as royal steward."

"I heard a guard and Fantôme drag him away. The guard wanted to throw him in the midden, but he must be returned to the earth, and a ritual performed to keep him there."

"No one told me of this," Silvester protested.

"How long from the time King John left the castle until the dog began howling?" A cold knot formed in Hugh's belly. He prayed that Blakely truly was dead. That sorcerer on the loose, unchecked by John or the semblance of propriety maintained a court . . . there would be no end to the evil destruction he could loose on England.

"A full day," Silvester replied. "The dead body lay here a full day and no one knew."

"Someone knew. Someone spirited the body away. I can only guess at the evil use they will put it to." Ana made the sign of the cross and kissed the prayer beads she still clutched.

"You must go to King John and secure Bellecôte in your name, Hugh," I insisted nearly a week later. High summer was upon us, and I itched to go outside and bury my hands in clean dirt. Earl Robin's herb garden had been sorely neglected since the death of his beloved wife Marion. The plants called to me. I craved sunshine and fresh air. I could not heal indoors.

One broken ankle and one severe sprain kept me prisoner in my bed or whatever chair Hugh deigned to deposit me in. He wouldn't hear of taking me beyond the thick walls of Huntington Castle, not even into the bailey.

Earl Robin left us pretty much to ourselves, spending his days riding his lands and patrolling his borders. From the near continuous *thwack* of bow strings within the bailey, I suspected Earl Robin and his sons practiced with their legendary longbows and arrows fletched with feathers dyed Lincoln green.

I had another reason to encourage Hugh to leave me for a time. My monthly courses had not returned, even after the trauma of two days in the oubliette. The healer muttered soothing phrases about shock. I knew that a new life grew within me. I did not have the words or the heart to tell Hugh of my true condition.

I kissed him tenderly and caressed his dear face.

"Go to John before more time passes, Hugh. I shall miss you sorely, but you must go." My insides ached at the necessity of driving him away—perhaps forever.

"I won't leave you, Ana. The time has come for us to marry, beget a family. I've buried a stepchild, I'll not raise another. If I return to John, he'll press me to marry another widow. He said as much before he sent me to Wales. I want my own children."

His words cut my soul.

"I am not well enough to travel to Scotland. We cannot marry in England as long as we are under Interdict. You must go to John and secure Bellecôte." I repeated arguments we'd discussed a dozen times this past week. I could think of nothing new that would persuade him.

"I am in rebellion against my king," Hugh replied. He withdrew from me, crossing his arms and standing his ground.

"John doesn't know that," I countered. "You still have a chance to be John's adviser now that Blakely is dead. You can make John see logic and sense, push him to act for the good of all. He reacts to all opposition as treachery rather than advice. Only you can keep him from falling victim to another such as Blakely."

"She is right, Sir Hugh," Earl Robin said coming into the Hall. He smelled of leather and horses and fresh air. Wonderful, fresh air. The Hall seemed suddenly too small to contain the three of us. Robin Locksley dominated every situation with his height, his personality, and his twinkling green eyes. Though his auburn hair was streaked with gray, he still held himself as a young man, strong and lean, full of energy. Only the loss of Marion had diminished him from his glory days of rebellion against John as Prince Regent fifteen years before.

"I do not care to accept honors from a king who could do this to Ana." Hugh refused to back down. As stubborn as a cat, I knew he'd only give in to pure logic, minus any emotion.

"But you are in a marvelous position to keep the other disgruntled barons informed of John's intentions, alert us when his anger and distrust get out of control," the earl said quietly. "De Vesci, Fitz Walter, and I cannot openly go to court anymore. You can."

"You want me to spy on the king."

"Marion spied upon the Sheriff of Nottingham for me. Can you perform the task less admirably than she?" Earl Robin's mouth quirked up on one side as if he fought to swallow the taunting smile. At the same time, a hint of sadness made his eyelids droop. Marion had died. He had to continue living without her.

Hugh fumed at the entrapment of his personal honor.

I silently applauded my host's maneuver. I reminded myself never to play chess with him.

"What if . . . ?"

"King John will not discover that I live, Hugh," I replied before he could fully form his objection. "Huntington is the most secure place in England. John will not voluntarily cross its borders."

"None of my people will talk, Sir Hugh," Robin reassured him. "I pay my taxes on time, I send my knights for military service when required. John keeps other barons from trespassing on me and my rights. Other than that, we barely acknowledge each other's existence. So it has been for nine years. So it will be until we both die."

A flash of a death mask crossed his face. I blinked rapidly to banish the vision and could not. This beloved hero of England would die on the same day as his greatest enemy.

Silently I wept for them both. My real tears were reserved for the man I loved and must send away.

"We tire you, Ana. I will take you back to bed."

Hugh bent to scoop me out of the thronelike chair.

"I tire of that damned bed!" I retorted. I let anger fill my voice and posture.

Hugh reared back, startled.

Instantly I regretted offending him. "Please, Hugh, I need time and space to heal in my own way. Please just give me that time. Go

to John and secure Bellecôte so that you can protect those hostages."
I pleaded with him with my eyes well as words. I would not use my
magic to persuade or compel him.

He took my hand in both of his.

"I do not know why I am so reluctant to claim the barony I was
promised. But I know I must. It's just that . . . Never mind. I will do
what is necessary to gain John's confidence as well as the lands and
title that should have been mine six years ago. And I'll not allow him
to select a new bride for me. I'll marry none but you, Ana." He knelt
and kissed my palm. "Take care, Ana."

I cupped his dear face with both my hands and kissed him fully
on the lips. I leaned into him, holding him, to keep him close as long
as possible. His tenderness nearly brought me to tears again. How
could I betray him by not telling him I carried John's child?

In that moment I vowed that if the child lived I would foster it. I
would never burden Hugh with the child of his enemy—if he could
still love me when he discovered my betrayal.

Abruptly Hugh broke off our embrace and stalked out of the Hall,
hurling orders as if they were weapons aimed for John's heart.

"He doesn't know about the child," Robin said quietly.

"How did *you* know?"

"Secrets do not leak from Huntington, but they do circulate
within my lands. All of them come to me eventually. Some sooner
than others." He smiled enigmatically. "Marion gave me five children.
I recognize the symptoms. Primarily your inability to keep breakfast
within your stomach."

"What will I do?" Even if I could bring myself to use specific
herbs to abort the child, I did not know which ones I could take
safely. My injuries kept me from exploring the herb garden. Distance
from Kirkenwood kept me from Aunt Lotta's books and writings.

"You will do what you must. As must we all. I shall find ways to
keep Sir Hugh either with John or at Bellecôte for the next year. Now,
I believe some sunshine is in order. I will carry you to the garden for
one hour. Then you must nap before the evening meal. You may not
be hungry now, but you will be. You must eat for the sake of the
child."

"I care not for the child sired by the man who tried to murder
me."

"Trust me. You will think otherwise when you hold it in your arms."

"Never."

He merely cocked one eyebrow and carried me into the herb garden.

Fantôme stretched a horseshoe impossibly thin. It glowed with his characteristic orange/red magic. Radburn had to strain his eyes to see the magic at all.

With a flick of his wrist, before Radburn could react, or even see the movement, Fantôme snapped the metal around Radburn's neck into a binding collar. The iron should have burned Radburn through to the bone. All he felt was the weight of metal on his shoulders and his soul.

That was not all. A strange tingling made his mind itch. A cold knot of fear numbed his awareness of anything but the slave band. "Wh . . . what is this?"

"You do not recognize the mark of my ownership?" Fantôme laughed.

"I have made no vows of obedience, exchanged nothing with you that defines slavery. You are my servant. You made an oath of fealty to *me*." Radburn replied. He had to swallow around the thickness in his throat. This couldn't be happening to him. Fantôme was nothing but a short, stocky peasant, not even a decent bed partner. He couldn't read, owned nothing, could barely ride a horse, and yet he presumed his magic made him superior to a man who counted kings as well as powerful magicians in his lineage. Fantôme did not even have a real name, at least not one Radburn knew.

"Oaths mean nothing, slave. Only obedience to the stronger man. You will submit to me." Fantôme clenched his fist and twisted it as if cranking a wheel.

The slave brand shrank, pressing sharply into Radburn's flesh. He cried out with the pain, fearing his neck would snap under the pressure. The brand continued to shrink.

Fantôme smiled.

Radburn sank to his knees. He clawed at the collar. Nothing existed but the pain. His vision narrowed, his senses closed down. A low keening moan escaped him. A moan that sounded like little more than an animal's bewildered awareness of pain and imminent death.

"I am Radburn Blakely, Lord of Nigel Burn, son of Henry Plantegenet, second king of that name. King John Plantegenet is my half brother. Tryblith, the demon of chaos, is my grandsire." He uttered the litany that identified him to himself. The names of all those he held in esteem in his lineage streamed before him. Gradually he regained the strength to stand.

The pain from the band did not lessen, but he found he could endure. He could control his response to pain.

"Remember that I control the band, slave," Fantôme said. He opened his fist, and the collar slipped easily about Radburn's neck.

"I have a name, Fantôme."

"No, you don't. You are my slave and I am your master."

"Do you have a name?"

"A little late to ask. You may call me Master. I will call you slave."

Radburn gritted his teeth as the band tightened once more in reminder.

"I have a name," Radburn insisted loudly.

"You will answer to 'slave' until you have completed the task I set for you."

"And what is that?" Radburn refused to attach a "Master" to that sentence.

"You will teach me all you know of magic. And of the sword."

"That will take years." Years and years of bleak obedience to this petty tyrant. This . . . this peasant!

Never.

"I have patience. And while you teach me to replace you as the most powerful sorcerer in England, you will also teach me to replace you as John's adviser. I will replace you in all things, slave. All things."

"Never."

The band tightened again.

This time Radburn screamed his agony before his air supply diminished. He flailed with his mind at the fate the gods had handed him. The collar tightened until his vision reduced to red-and-black blurs.

After several agonizing moments, the collar loosened enough to allow him to breathe.

"If it takes the rest of my life, I will recover my magic and kill you most horribly, Fantôme."

"You will call me 'Master.' " The slave band tightened once more. Radburn grimaced and fought the cringing weakness.

"Now we will go find this cave of yours and consult the demon." Fantôme's brown eyes took on a glitter of malice much older than his actual years. An old soul dwelled in his body. A very old soul that needed violence and vengeance to survive.

Fantôme led Radburn out of the half-ruined hut west of Lincoln and began the long walk to the stone circle and barrow outside of Wells.

Chapter 40

SIR Hugh Fitz Chênenoir, guardian of the late Baron of Bellecôte burst through the doors of the Hall of the White Tower at the edge of the City of London. The massive stone keep held all of the dark chill Hugh harbored in his heart. He hadn't bathed, shaved, combed his hair, or changed from his rough riding leathers before interrupting the king's court.

Beside him strode Silvester of Lincoln, equally disheveled, tired, and filthy with road dust.

"Whatever you do, don't antagonize him," Silvester said quietly.

"I'll do what I must, but I don't have to like it."

Hugh almost hoped King John Plantagenet would exile him for his dishabille. At the same time, he knew he looked the epitome of the grieving father.

"A word with you, Highness." Hugh stalked through the semicircle of disputants gathered before John's throne on the dais. One of the litigants, a fat merchant who smelled of garlic and had grease stains on his fur-trimmed cotehardie, tried to block Hugh's passage. The Lord Mayor of London stood shoulder to shoulder with him. Probably the only time in their lives they would.

Ahead of them a lord pleaded that he had founded an abbey on his own lands. Since the Interdict, the abbot had removed himself and all of the brothers to the continent. The abbey stood abandoned. The lord wished to reclaim the land. Bishop de Grey, standing beside the king, refuted the argument, stating that the land still belonged to the church; would always belong to the church.

John leaned forward, chin on hand, elbow on knee, ardently interested in the arguments.

"Wait your turn," the merchant hissed at Hugh and Silvester, obviously not recognizing nobility, or perhaps he believed himself their equal.

Silvester swept him aside with a single sideways blow from his arm.

"Sir Hugh, this is most unseemly," protested John de Grey, Bishop of Norwich, John's secretary and candidate for Archbishop of Canterbury. He rose from his chair to John's right.

Peter des Roches, Bishop of Winchester, also rose from his chair to John's left. The king presented a picture of a man supported by the church even though the Pope had placed the entire land under Interdict for the king's disobedience.

Knowing the depth of evil John was capable of, Hugh considered perhaps that Pope Innocent III was right to insist upon Stephen Langdon as the next Archbishop of Canterbury. Having one of John's henchmen head the church in England could only lead to more abuses of power like the near murder of Lady Resmiranda Griffin of Kirkenwood.

Sitting just beyond the bishops, Brian Delisle, Hugh Neville, and William Brewer, the king's gaming companions, lounged with cups of wine. William Longsword, Earl of Salisbury, another bastard half brother to John, fingered a pair of dice idly. His mother had been noble, so Henry II had elevated him to the earldom. Blakely's mother had come from peasant stock and therefore he rated only a small barony. Nigel Burn barely produced enough revenue to support a single knight. Blakely's money and prestige came directly from John's purse.

These longtime cronies gave the impression that they bided their time in boredom until the king was free of his onerous duties to play with them. This group spoiled the image of solidarity with the church presented by king and bishops.

"Forgive my impulsiveness, Your Highness. I have urgent news that will not wait." Hugh bowed slightly, as deeply as he could manage without gagging. How could Earl Robin expect him to grovel at the murdering tyrant's feet?

"The Welshmen have rebelled again!" John shouted. He stood so fast, his throne rocked and nearly tipped over. "We must punish them."

"No, Highness," Hugh interrupted before John could jump to more drastic conclusions. "I left the Welsh provinces secure. My mission is one of personal tragedy. My son . . . my stepson has died. Bellecôte is without a baron."

"Took him long enough," Brian Delisle muttered.

John waved him silent with a brief gesture. "This is dire news indeed," John replied. He sat again, smoothing his robes. The mask of regal calm descended upon his features. "We grieve with you, Sir Hugh."

John's eyes strayed toward the back corner of the dais where the queen and her ladies did their best to restrain the toddling Prince Henry.

Sight of the boy opened new wounds of grief in Hugh. His stepson had been about that age when Hugh married Ardyth and took the boy under his wing. Johnny had never had the prince's robust and bouncing energy. But he was always sweet tempered and amiable, never throwing his toys or screaming when he didn't get his way. The prince did precisely that as Hugh watched.

"I suppose Fitz Chênenoir wants to claim the barony for himself now," William Longsword said in a deriding voice that carried to the farthest reaches of the vast Hall.

Hugh cringed. That was exactly what he intended to do, but not for the selfish reasons the earl implied.

"May I remind Your Highness of promises made six years ago when you gave the dowager baroness to me in marriage, as well as wardship of her young son." Hugh stood straight and tall, unwilling to grovel no matter how important his mission to court.

"Remain calm and self-assured. Don't let John see a weakness," Silvester whispered into his ear, barely moving his mouth.

"We would not wish to break a promise," John conceded. "However . . ." He paused, drawing out the moment. The entire crowd hushed, waiting.

Hugh dreaded the remainder of the statement. Almost like waiting for the executioner's ax.

"However," John cleared his throat and continued. "When we left Lincoln so hastily, an important artifact was left behind. We need you to retrieve it. When you return, we will invest you with the Barony of Bellecôte."

Ana! He sends me back to bring him Ana's dead body. Only she's not dead! Panic nearly sent him running from the Hall. All was lost. John would know of his rebellion within moments. Huntington hadn't had time to gather the barons and convince them to depose John.

For all of his problems with the church, John had been crowned and consecrated by a bishop. His blood was royal. Rebellion risked their souls as well as their lands and lives.

"He means the sword," Silvester whispered in Hugh's ear. "He wants the sword as a symbol of his right to rule with or without the church."

"Not the girl?" Hugh whispered back out of the side of his mouth. He was almost grateful for the immense proportions of the Hall and the press of bodies against him to muffle their quiet conversation.

"Only if he wants the world to know he murdered an innocent woman without benefit of trial."

Excalibur! Hugh sighed almost in relief. *John knows about Excalibur. But I can't retrieve it. It belongs to Ana, given to her by the Lady of the Lake. No one can wield it but the Chosen of the Lady. I carried the trunk to Huntington myself. I can't betray her again by stealing Excalibur from her.*

Hugh bowed to John and retreated. "Now what?" he muttered to Silvester, as they left the Hall to clean up for the evening meal.

"How good a look did he get at the sword? Would he recognize that specific sword? Or did he presume that any rich sword in the hands of the Griffin clan could only be Excalibur?"

Hugh stopped in mid-stride on his way to his horse and saddlebags. "Could we substitute another?"

"Know any local witches who could cast a glamour on another sword to make it temporarily shimmer in the light like Excalibur does?" Silvester chuckled and grinned broadly. "I like the idea of tricking the wily fox."

"So do I. I don't know any local witches, but I think I might know someone who does. Do you have a sword that might pass?"

"Not with me. But you have the Bellecôte sword strapped to that monstrous horse of yours. It has a jewel or two in the pommel, a rich scabbard and is about the same length."

"It's a ceremonial sword. I don't think it's been sharpened since the first baron hung it on the wall above his bed three generations ago."

"All the better. We won't be depriving you of a real weapon."

Together they walked through the gates of the castle into the city. A coin crossed the palm of an old crone who habituated a nearby tavern. Another coin to the innkeeper to say Hugh had not been there this day. Six silver pennies to the apothecary gave Hugh an introduction to his old mother. She, in turn, required only a little of his blood, three of his hairs, a vial of his piss, and some clipped fingernails to work her magic.

Hugh paced the herb garden behind the apothecary shop for over an hour until the old woman hobbled out to him, cradling the sword of Bellecôte as if she carried a tiny baby. The blade glowed with more than a good polishing and sharpening. Hugh took it from her as gingerly as if he held the genuine Excalibur.

Three hours later, scrubbed and dressed for court, Hugh and Silvester joined the king and his intimates, his servants and retainers for dinner. Hugh carried the heavy sword wrapped in a rich cloth of gold borrowed from one of the queen's ladies.

He approached the dais slowly, measuring his steps as if awed by the artifact he carried. In truth, he masked his limp. The stress and fatigue of the last weeks preyed upon his old wound as much as his conscience did.

John's face beamed. "At last! Even the church cannot defy me while I possess Excalibur." Only Bishop de Grey's restraining hand kept him from vaulting the table to grab the sword away from Hugh. "How did you bring this magnificent artifact to us so quickly?" His mouth twitched and he clenched his fists repeatedly as if they itched.

"When I stopped at Lincoln on the journey here, my Lord Silvester remembered the forgotten traveling trunk in the undercroft and decided to bring it to you. We had your treasure with us without knowing it, Your Highness." Hugh bowed low, as much to cover his conspiratorial smile as in reverence. The lord beside him made the same obeisance.

"Very good, Sir Hugh, Lord Silvester. You have both served us well." John escaped his bishops and moved around the high table to step off the dais. He took the sword from Hugh and ripped off the covering veil. He had to close his eyes against the sharp light radiating off the sword. Ancient runes rippled along the blade like fire imps.

Hugh stepped back, catching his breath. For a brief moment, he wondered if the old crone had indeed substituted Excalibur for the sword of Bellecôte. And he was bound to this blade by his blood, his hair, his urine, and his fingernails.

"Kneel, Sir Hugh, we would invest the barony of Bellecôte upon our most faithful servant with this very sword."

Hugh had to smile at the rightness of the gesture, considering the true nature of the blade.

"William Longsword, Earl of Salisbury, Brother. Join me in this ritual. Then you shall have custody of this most ancient and precious sword. You shall carry it before me in all solemn processions and rituals to proclaim to the world that I am the true descendant of Arthur of Legend, the one and only true king of England."

Hugh almost rose in protest. The sword was *his*. The sword of Bellecôte. Longsword had no right to it.

Silvester held him down with strong fingers digging into his shoulder. "Don't betray it now. You'll earn another sword," he whispered. "We have time."

John hesitated a moment, balancing the sword between his hands. "We cherish this artifact so well, we deem a higher reward fitting. Bellecôte is now an earldom, and you, Sir Hugh, as first Earl of Bellecôte must join our court as adviser and friend. We have never had cause to doubt your loyalty and love for us. We cherish you as we do this sword."

An earldom! Hugh could annex more land. He would become patron to more knights and men at arms. Joined with Lincoln and Huntington, he'd have the makings of a true army to depose this murderous tyrant.

If only he could keep his thoughts to himself and hide behind a mask of lies.

In that moment he hated himself almost as much as he hated his king.

Chapter 41

TIME hung heavy on my hands. My injuries healed slowly. Newynog grew fat with her puppies. Earl Robin and his oldest son, a strapping boy of fourteen, took turns carrying me from my bed to a chair in the Hall, to a bench in the garden, back to the Hall, and then back to bed. Robin's two daughters included me in their conversations, their needlework, and their dreams of marriage. The two youngest boys played with Newynog at my feet. Earl Robin made me one more member in his happy family. When I could hide my own pregnancy no longer, he treated me as if I would soon present him with his first grandchild.

The name of the baby's father never passed between us. He helped compose my terse messages to Hugh that kept him away. I worded them carefully, knowing that a cleric would read them to Hugh. That extra pair of eyes viewing my missives added a potential for betrayal.

I trusted no one.

Then one day a messenger arrived with a small scrap of parchment folded many times along with the normal rolls of news and gossip. The courier made a point of putting the private message directly into my hands.

I unfolded it layer by layer, being careful not to tear the fragile piece. The parchment had been used and scraped clean many times, making it as thin as an onion skin. Awkward strokes sprawled across the page.

ANA, JE T'AIME.
HUGH.

325

Ana, I love you.

My Hugh had gone to a great deal of trouble and time to learn to write those few words himself. A tear dropped on the precious message. Before the ink could dampen and run, I refolded the parchment and tucked it inside my breastband, next to my heart.

I should have expected our next visitor after that. Humidity weighed us all down. The sun looked as if it wanted to hide behind a thin veil of haze. The blue sky looked dull, almost metallic. We all waited breathlessly for a thunderstorm to release us from the heat and the weight of the heavy air.

Hugh arrived like a precursor of the bank of clouds building on the western horizon. He barged into the Hall unescorted by any of the Locksley family.

"Ana, I could not stay away any longer. I had to see you." He rushed forward.

"Hugh! I received your message. I love you, too." Surprised and delighted by the sight of him, I rose awkwardly from my settle in the Hall. I could stand on my own, but walking with a crutch was still so painful and slow that I could not rush to greet him as I wished. All I could do was hold out my hands, begging him to come to me.

Newynog lumbered to her feet as well. The bulge in my belly echoed hers.

Hugh stopped short, five paces away from me. He took one long look at the two of us. "So it's true. You carry the king's child," he said flatly.

"Hugh, please, we must talk about this. I have much to say. I hope you can understand."

"I told you once before. I will not raise another man's child again." Abruptly he turned and left the Hall.

"Wait, Hugh, please." I hobbled in his wake, each step a painful journey.

"You betrayed me as John betrayed both of us." He kept walking purposefully with long strides. His squire had not had time to unsaddle Orage. Hugh remounted and rode back out the gate just as the first clap of thunder echoed around Huntington.

I cried for several days. I composed a dozen messages and discarded them all. None of them expressed what was in my heart, especially not the ones written in vague language that would protect us both from the king and whoever read the missive to Hugh.

Earl Robin held me while I cried. And when I had no more tears, he washed my face and carried me out into the sunshine to heal, as if I were one of his children.

A few days later, Newynog settled into a corner of the stable and presented us with nine healthy puppies. Each one seemed to have been sired by a different dog; only one looked full wolfhound. "Newynog, you rascal." I fluffed her ears as she licked her babies over and over, cleansing them. "How many kennels did you visit?"

She grinned at me wickedly. I felt a thrill of excitement run up my spine at her memories. Mine, too. John had been a considerate lover, taking pleasure from my own enjoyment. I blanked those pleasant memories, concentrating on my hatred of the man who had condemned me to a slow and painful death in the oubliette. The man who had separated me from Hugh.

I lingered with Newynog long after she needed my affectionate company.

One by one, the rest of the Locksley family joined us to share in the wonder of new life. The younger boys, Toby and Will, squealed with delight and immediately claimed one puppy apiece. Newynog's possessive growls kept the boys from carrying the wiggling blobs of fur back to their pallets. So Toby and Will set up camp in a neighboring stall. I wondered how many nights they would linger before the next thunderstorm drove them back to the relative dry warmth of the castle.

I sat with Newynog a long time that first day. As I cradled a sleeping puppy in my arms, the wolfhound male, the earthy scents of fresh hay, horse, oiled tack, and stone damp filled me with a longing for Kirkenwood. My home was lost to me, as was the kirk with the crypt of my ancestors. I had a few books with me. And Excalibur. Nothing more of my home remained.

I did not even have the sanctuary of a convent where I'd found homes through most of my life.

Newynog nudged me to relinquish her babe. I placed it near her teats so that it might nurse, and left a heavy hand on my dog's head. Through our special bond I shared with her the immense satisfaction of motherhood. She didn't understand my determination to give my own babe away on the day of its birth. I barely understood it myself.

I would have trouble giving away Newynog's pups to people I knew when they were weaned. How could I give my own child, cherished under my heart for many months, to strangers?

How could I keep a child sired by a man I hated with every fiber of my being? A child that Hugh would never accept, never agree to raise.

Without the babe, perhaps in time he could forgive me.

Months passed. The pups grew. My own babe swelled my belly. I exchanged the crutch for a cane and gradually waddled about the castle on my own.

By the first autumnal storms I felt as if I had lived with this boisterous family all my life.

The day came when the weaned puppies became too frolicsome for Newynog and she pushed them away from the comfort of her teats. I waited another two weeks to be certain the pups would thrive on their own. Then I took the wolfhound male, near twin to Newynog in markings, wrapped him in a shirt I had made for Hugh—to replace the one he had ruined to bandage Newynog—and summoned a messenger. I had patiently embroidered the cuffs and neck opening of the shirt with love knots, rosemary for remembrance, and forget-me-nots. He'd know the message.

I cried as I hugged the puppy one last time and handed him to the silent man dressed in Lincoln green who carried a longbow and trod the rushes more quietly than a cat. Tears fell on the fine shirt.

Newynog nudged me with her nose, anxious about her baby boy. I held her by the scruff of her neck to keep her from following the messenger. The moment the great door of the hall closed behind him, she broke free of my grasp and dashed to the door. She whined and worried the worn planks with her claws.

"I'm sorry to separate you, Newynog, but Hugh deserves this pup. Your boy will bind us all together. I may have lost Hugh, but he will have the pup. He will remember us."

Another month passed. I heard that Hugh had received the pup safely. But he sent no return word.

I presumed he understood the message.

Then one day just before winter closed in on Huntington, I sat before the fire stitching the first seams of a shirt for Earl Robin—intended as a Yuletide gift. He wore out more shirts than I thought possible with his hours of practice with his longbow, and arduous rides about his lands seeing to every aspect of the lives of his people. The earl's daughters, Marion and Meredith, worked embroidery on the pieces that would become the cuffs for the shirt. Their stitches were finer than mine and I envied them the patience to sit for so long with their stitchery when the herb garden called me and the activity in the bailey drew my attention and I spent long hours staring at nothing, remembering Hugh and the closeness we had shared but could never rekindle. I had betrayed him.

I fought my tears again. They came all too readily, often for no reason other than a memory of the man I had loved and lost.

For once the two youngest boys, ages five and eight, had found other pursuits and didn't clutter up the hall with their tops and balls, their dogs, and their incredible energy.

Will, the eight-year-old, and his older brother Rob were both of an age to be fostered to other lords. The custom of fosterage cemented alliances among barons as well as giving the boys an education away from the loving tolerance of failure often found within the family. Robin kept his boys close to home and taught them with firm vigor. I had no doubt they'd make fine knights. Even Tobin, the youngest had begun carrying a tiny wooden sword in practice for the day he'd actually train with a larger one. They all excelled with the longbow, including the girls.

A chill draft fluttered the cloth in my hands. I stopped plying my needle until the air passed and I could control my stitches again. Something tingly in the air current made me look up. The girls continued their work, not noticing anything different about this draft. People came and went through the Hall all day long.

"Father Truman!" I cried. I nearly forgot my still weak ankles as I tried to rise. Lack of strength and off-centered balance from the babe made me sit down again quite abruptly. The swell of my belly remained hidden beneath the folds of my gown and the blanket wrapped around me.

"What are you doing here? Is everything well at Kirkenwood? What news?" My questions tumbled over each other like the remaining puppies that frolicked about Newynog.

"Benedicte, milady." The priest bowed stiffly. "I brought you a few of your great-uncle's books." His voice lacked the vigor I expected of him. Had he walked all the way from Kirkenwood, sleeping rough, eating rougher?

The grimoire? I asked with my mind.

He nodded in silent reply, patting a small bulge in his loose robe.

"Come, sit by the fire and warm yourself." I cleared a place on the adjacent settle for him. Marion and Meredith shifted their own stools to make room for Father Truman to stretch his long legs before the fire.

He dropped onto the bench heavily. He sighed and closed his eyes, leaning his head against the tall wooden back of the furniture. If his breathing hadn't remained uneven, I might have believed he'd fallen asleep.

"Father Truman." I jostled his arm a little. "Marion, Meredith, Father Truman is cold and weary. Could you please fetch him some mulled wine, bread, and cheese?"

The girls scampered off, chattering about the excitement of a visitor with gossip from afar.

When they had gone, Father Truman opened his eyes slowly and turned his head toward me. "Forgive me, milady. Travel is not easy for a priest these days. King's men and local bullies view us as easy targets." His voice rasped. I couldn't tell if a chill had invaded his throat or strong emotions. "This Interdict drags on too long. I fear for the health of all our souls."

"Why have you made this perilous journey?" I searched his face and form for overt signs of injury. He held his left shoulder a little higher than the other and cradled his left elbow. I couldn't search for the sore spots without reaching awkwardly across him.

"Kirkenwood belongs to King John. He has proclaimed you dead. You have no other family to inherit." He sighed and closed his eyes again.

"How did you find me?" I stared at my stitchery, willing my tears to dry before they fell and blotched the fine linen.

"I knew you lived."

"How?" My head snapped up. I darted looks about the Hall, searching for spies or armed men come to arrest me once again.

"I carry the same blood as you," Father Truman said quietly. "My gifts are not as strong as yours, but in my quiet way, I *know* how to find my kin, my flock, those I care for." He kept his eyes closed.

I had known the moment Uncle Henry died. In our years of separation I had a vague awareness deep within my heart that he lived even when imprisoned. I knew that if I truly wanted to, or dared, I could find him by looking long into a candle flame.

I had worked no magic since coming to Huntington. They must know of my talents. Everyone suspected the Griffins of magic. But we never mentioned it, pretended magic did not walk within the walls of Huntington. For their safety as well as mine, I wanted to keep it that way. Whoever had stolen Radburn Blakely's body might be able to follow my magic trail and betray us all.

"I sense unease in you, milady, more than the physical hurts." He turned and looked at me hard. His eyes seemed to penetrate every secret locked in my mind. Then his gaze strayed briefly back to my swelling belly. Before I could challenge his stare, he settled back and reclosed his eyes.

"John will not welcome news of this child," he whispered.

"Nor do I." I sighed and fought my tears once again. "What news sends you to me if you knew me alive and safe?" I whispered.

"King John has evicted all churchmen from royal lands, especially those of us who hold to the old ways and have a wife and children." He continued speaking very quietly. I had to strain to catch every word. "Kirkenwood is now a royal household, since you are officially dead. It is no longer safe for me there."

"What of your wife?" I gasped louder than I should. "And your sons?"

"The people of Kirkenwood shelter them. What is one more widow among the villagers? The king's men do not bother themselves with peasants." He grinned. I sensed a note of sarcasm in his tone. "Other priests' wives have not been so lucky. Some are beaten, others imprisoned and branded." He shuddered.

"Do King John's men mistreat my people?" I asked. My hatred for John built within me.

"No more than any distant landlord. His men are bullies but not the point of taking pleasure in inflicting pain. Our people are adept at surviving. They have done so for centuries."

"But not for a long time," I interjected.

"Not all masters are as benevolent as your great-uncle and -aunt. In his youth Henry Griffin resorted to senseless violence to ease his own hurts."

I stilled deep within me. Perhaps my vision of Aunt Lotta in the oubliette had been truth rather than hallucination. How else would I know of Uncle Henry's terrible soul-pain when he returned from the Second Crusade?

The girls bounced into the Hall. Servants carrying trays of food and pitchers of wine to heat by the fire followed closely in their wake. Earl Robin nearly trod on their heels.

Father Truman rose wearily to greet the lord of the castle.

"Sit, Father." Robin placed a firm hand on the old man's shoulder and pushed him back into the settle. "Members of the clergy are always welcome in Huntington. Interdict or not, I have always revered and supported the small churches and the men who serve them."

Did anyone else notice how the earl had omitted references to the Pope and his church in Rome or the king and the bishops he had appointed?

"Offering me shelter may well put you in perilous disfavor with the king." Father Truman kept his gaze on the earl, challenging him to withdraw his offer of hospitality.

Earl Robin threw back his head and laughed long and loud. "I have always been in perilous disfavor with John Softsword. He knows what will happen if he pushes me into open rebellion."

"And what will that be, milord?" I asked softly, almost afraid of the answer.

"The same thing that happened fifteen years ago in Nottingham. I nearly killed him. Only the intervention of his brother Richard saved his life."

"But this time, King Richard will not return to extricate you from hanging as an outlaw."

"Aye. But this time, I have the church to back me against a king in rebellion against the Pope. This time, I also have you, Lady Resmiranda. You and that precious sword of yours to rally every baron in the country against John. This time, John will not survive my challenge to his authority."

The baby kicked me hard the moment Robin's words left his mouth. Could I openly rebel against my child's father—seek his death as he sought mine?

Holy Mother help me if I willingly took another life.

Chapter 42

"TELL me the ritual again," Fantôme demanded. He traced pentagrams idly in the dirt before the fire with a stick.

Radburn shuddered at the man's casual use of such a powerful symbol.

"You must take the noose of a hanged man, burn it. Collect the ashes into a new clay vessel that has been fired alone in the kiln, untainted by contact with other vessels used for other purposes." Radburn replied as he huddled beneath a ragged blanket. The wind blew through the cave, howling around the demon door as if it sought to join the being trapped behind the sealed portal.

"Yes, yes, I have done that." Fantôme smudged his latest doodle in the dirt.

Radburn breathed a little easier. No telling what kind of magic Fantôme would raise with his uncontrolled scratches.

"If the hanged man was a murderer, you must take the hand that struck the fatal blow and burn it with the noose. If the man was a thief, then you must take both the hand that clasped his stolen goods as well as the supporting hand and burn them with the noose. If the man sodomized children or raped an innocent woman, then you must take his penis and testicles and burn them with the noose," Radburn recited as if reading a lesson in a book. The ritual he described would work, after a fashion. But it cursed the man named in the chant in Arabic that came later. The spell to open or close the portals to the demon world was similar, not exactly the same.

He alone would unseal the portal that trapped his demon grandsire. For the demon would be obligated to the opener. That must be no one but Radburn Blakely. But he could not do it until his magic returned. Nearly five months since Excalibur had backlashed his spell and negated his magic. Five months and not a bit of his talent had returned.

He felt so hollow, so empty.

And this pig of a peasant presumed to dictate to him.

"You did not tell me this before!" Fantôme screamed. He jumped up from the rock where he perched his bottom.

Radburn didn't rank a rock. He had to sit on the cold, dank ground.

"I do not have my books. I must search my memory long and hard for the spell."

"Books are but wasted tools. My family has never needed them. We remember everything."

"Then why do you need me to remember the details of the spell?"

That earned Radburn a solid blow behind his ear. He fell to the ground, nursing the hurt a few moments.

Fantôme resumed his seat until Radburn recovered enough to sit up.

"Sit up straight and do not pick your nose. You must learn to act a gentleman as well as a magician," Blakely admonished his former servant. The discussion of books seemed to have ended.

"Magic now. Manners later!" Fantôme broke his drawing stick over his knee. The wood crumbled to dust, sending out eldritch blue sparks.

Radburn could see that magic permeated Fantôme's entire being, but the former servant didn't have the control or the knowledge of ritual that would give him control of his power. He just might succeed in his quest before Radburn recovered his magic.

That must not happen.

"I must have my books. I cannot remember every detail."

"Books, bah!" Fantôme spat into the dirt. "No one in my family has ever needed to read. If Gran hadn't died early, taking her knowledge with her, I wouldn't need you. We do not leave this cave until I have demon magic at my fingertips."

"Then we will both rot here," Radburn murmured to himself. Then louder he lied, "I told you about the body parts. You did not listen." He'd deliberately left out key elements of every spell Fantôme demanded he teach. The man was bright—too bright for a peasant.

"You told me only about the noose, slave," Fantôme sneered. "I must punish you for this crime against me!" Fantôme closed his fist.

Radburn's slave collar tightened about his throat. He gasped, clawing at the hateful iron. Chill invaded his veins. Darkness crowded his vision. His lungs burned, and his heart beat too rapidly.

Fantôme's face blotched red. He slammed his right fist into his left. The iron collar tightened further threatening to sever Radburn's neck. He knew this time he would die.

Not yet, he pleaded with whatever powers might hear him. *I'm not ready. If this man is turned loose on the world now, he will do more than wreak havoc. He will totally destroy England.*

The pressure of the collar on his windpipe lessened.

Long after the collar returned to its normal looseness, he continued to gasp and struggle for air. Just like the spell he had used on Lady Resmiranda, making her cough long after he clenched his fist in her presence.

And just like the spell he used on the lady, his body weakened more with each use. If Fantôme did not remove the collar soon, Radburn would die of some other disease his body could no longer fend off.

He drew his fingers inward until his palm bled from his ragged fingernails.

In the back of his mind he heard a deep, bone-racking cough.

Perhaps it was only the wind roaring through the cave. Perhaps it was more.

His fight for air kept him from smiling.

I waddled into the Hall on the Eve of the Nativity, the last of the crowded household to take a seat.

As if they had all waited for my reluctant presence, the Lord of Misrule, the lowest of the scullery serfs, pounded his scepter on the high table.

"Let . . . let the revels begin!" he proclaimed in his harsh, lisping voice. His mother, the laundress, had to prod him to get him to speak clearly.

"How may I serve you, Lord of Misrule?" Robin Locksley, Earl of Huntington, bowed low to the young man. He kept his expression bland. But a muscle twitched in his cheek to belie his seriousness.

I half smiled, not really wanting to participate in the raucous mirth of the season, but truly entertained by the reversal of roles.

The Lord of Misrule giggled. He swung his scepter—a long stick topped with a cloth jester's head; a mockery of the staff I had inherited from Aunt Lotta and Uncle Henry but which was now lost—in his pudgy hands. His wide moon face and pinched eyes shone with delight. On this day of the Feast of the Nativity the lowest ruled the highest. Father Truman and I sat far below the salt on this night of revelry; as did the rest of the family.

"I . . . I bid thee fetch me . . ."

The Lord of Misrule's mother whispered into her son's ear again.

"I bid thee fetch me wine. Mulled wine. With lots of honey and spices!" The boy drooled a bit. He had a sweet tooth—not that he had many teeth left. He was young to have lost so many.

Widsyth, the wandering minstrel who knew more of what transpired in England than anyone, and his trio of musicians played a raucous chord in agreement with the Lord of Misrule's order. A juggler piled five splendid silver wine cups into a tottering tower, keeping them balanced on one finger while he threw three apples into the air, keeping them flying in a circle.

Earl Robin grimaced slightly in trepidation. Those five wine cups had cost him many silver pennies, and he reserved them for very special guests. Father Truman and I would not drink from those cups tonight. Nor would anyone else; the Lord of Misrule was a mite careless and clumsy to entrust with such wealth, even on this night of reversed roles.

Lord Robin presented the Lord of Misrule with a tray laden with the makings for mulled wine. Graciously he mixed the spices and honey—sparingly—with the rough red wine. Then he stuck a hot poker from the fire into the concoction.

The Lord of Misrule took the cup from his master and sipped a little. Then he smacked his lips in approval and downed the rest of the cup in a single gulp. He choked and sprayed red wine over his company of servants at the high table on the dais.

A shout of laughter rose from the assembly. That seemed to be the signal for all of us to dig into the piles of food set on the tables before us. Robin joined us shortly. He drank deeply from a mug of new ale before straddling the bench next to me. He draped his arm familiarly about my shoulders.

I smelled stronger spirits on his breath than the ale. He'd been drinking most of the day, as had everyone else. I had tempered my consumption. The baby didn't like ale or wine and upset my stomach if I indulged in more than a sip of anything stronger than watered wine.

The juggler put aside the silver wine cups and turned to acrobatics. Robin breathed a sigh of relief. If he had slipped and any one of the cups had been dented, it would require very costly repair. The musicians played a rather lewd song about a farm lad and a goose girl. They tempered none of the lyrics for the young ears crowded into the Hall. More than one woman had her buttocks pinched or her body groped by the juggler/acrobat as each chorus dissolved into more graphic descriptions of how the goose girl entertained the innocent lad.

Robin's arm grew heavier upon my shoulders as he urged me to lean closer into his broad, hard chest. The warmth of his body was different from the fatherly comfort he was wont to offer, not altogether unwelcome.

Immediately I remembered another man's strong arms cradling me gently as we rode together in flight from Mendip Mor Castle toward Worchester. A lump formed in my throat. *Oh, Hugh, I do miss you.* I straightened away from Robin and turned my attention back to the meal.

"Do not fear me, Ana," Robin whispered. His breath fanned my ear with erotic promises. "Unlike some of these drunken louts, I'll not press myself upon you without invitation." His thumb began a circular caress of my shoulder and nape.

A fistfight broke out between two servants over possession of a delicate morsel of venison. Widsyth struck up a rollicking song that perfectly matched the rhythm of the fight.

"Shouldn't you do something about that?" I asked Robin rather than reply to his suggestion.

"Not today. 'Tis the responsibility of our Lord of Misrule."

The Lord of Misrule seemed to think the fistfight had begun specifically for his entertainment. He clapped his hands together with enthusiasm.

"Marry me, Lady Resmiranda. The child will take my name. I'll raise it as my own. John will have no claim on it or you." Robin suddenly lost his air of drunken carelessness and became serious. "Gossip already links me to the child."

"Nobility may not marry without the king's permission unless they are willing to court his extreme disfavor." I held back a cough. The dry hacking always attacked me when I was weary, distracted, or nervous. It seemed to be a lingering remnant of the ailment that had plagued me at Bellecôte last spring.

But Blakely had induced that illness. Blakely had died. I had killed him. This . . . ?

Holy Mother, let this not be punishment for my sins. I could gain forgiveness from the church if I married and gave the child a name.

"I have never sought this king's permission for anything. I have never had his favor for that matter." Robin chuckled lightly as he renewed his caress of my shoulder. "Together we would lead a formidable opposition to King John. I need The Pendragon. You need a name for the baby."

"Are you forgetting the Interdict, my Lord Earl?" What else could I say? The proposition had its advantages. But he was not Hugh.

"I could arrange a fast trip to Scotland. Or there is always the honorable tradition of common law." He intensified his assault upon my senses as he traced the outline of my breasts with his inquisitive finger.

"I cannot forget the Interdict, milord." Nor could I so easily forget Hugh. Though I must. I had betrayed him and he did not easily forgive.

"Nor can you forget Fitz Chênenoir, I suspect." His hand lowered to cup my swollen belly. His words echoed my thoughts. He knew me well.

If only I had the solace of Confession, I could unburden my soul of my sins and embrace the future.

"Do you hear from Sir High?" I couldn't help but ask. I needed to know how he fared.

"He manages. His reports are frequent and terse. The messages all come by the same trusted courier. I doubt King John is aware of them."

"Has he asked after me at all?"

"Once. Before he discovered you carry the king's child."

"Why was that message not passed to me?" I still carried that fragile message of love written in Hugh's own hand next to my heart. I would cherish another equally.

"At first you were too ill. I hesitated to give you any reminder of the people and events surrounding your—your ordeal. Then I realized your true condition and knew why you sent away a man who loves you deeply. When he discovered the truth and stormed out of here, I feared his earlier inquiry after your health would hurt more than heal."

I bit my lip. I had betrayed Hugh. "He asked only that I not give my heart to another. I did not. I gave only my body as a ploy. I hoped to break Blakely's influence over the king. I hoped to convince John that he must not give me to Blakely in marriage."

"Fitz Chênenoir, any man, cannot separate a woman's body from her heart. He is lost to you forever, even if you give up the child."

A moment of sad silence enveloped us, separated us from the rest of the merry company.

"As Marion is lost to you."

"Aye."

I allowed the silence between us to linger. We had both lost a beloved. No one would ever truly replace our lost ones. We had that in common. A bond we could build upon.

"Think on this a while, Ana." He patted my hand solicitously, once more my friend. "I would prefer to travel to Scotland in spring or summer, but by then the babe will be here and adoption more difficult."

"I will consider the possibilities, Robin." Slowly I rose and bowed to the Lord of Misrule. "Have I permission to retire, milord?" I asked the scullery lad.

"Permission granted," the lad said. He waved me away in a gesture borrowed from the earl.

"Ana?" Robin rose with me. "I would enjoy your company in my bed any night."

"Even with this between us?" I patted the roundness of my belly. We both smiled at my awkwardness.

"There are ways. . . ."

"I must think on this."

Radburn watched the morning sun creep into the cave opening. It slid a few hairs' breadth past the small mark he'd made three days ago. By his reckoning forty days had passed since the Solstice. Warmth had not returned with the increasing moments of daylight. This cold cave kept the perpetual wind out—most of the time. He didn't ask for more.

Almost past caring, he watched a worm crawl across the small puddle of light rather than partake in Fantôme's most recent attempt to break the seal on the demon door. Every spell Radburn had given him had failed. As Radburn intended. Now Fantôme attacked the door with the sheer force of his will. He threw bolt after bolt of raw magic at the seal.

Briefly a blue/green light outlined the door. Something new.

Radburn watched more carefully. The seal should not glow any color but the bright green of new leaves—Lady Resmiranda's signature color.

"It comes. But slowly." Fantôme sagged with weariness. He rested one of his clumsy peasant hands on the dragon boss at the center of the door. More of the blue/green light glowed in an outline of his fingers.

"I need food and sleep," Fantôme continued, heaving himself away from the door. The outline of his hand remained a few heartbeats before fading into the door, as if the wood and metal absorbed the power—or drained it from him.

"You are close to the solution—Master." Radburn choked out the vile taste of the last word. "But we are low on food. I must go into the village and steal more."

"Very well." Fantôme wove his hands in a complicated gesture that loosened the slave collar on Radburn. He could wander a bit farther from the cave before the hated iron choked him. At the end of the gesture, Fantôme's shoulders slumped, and he hung his head as if it was too heavy to hold up any longer.

"Sleep, Master, while I fetch you food." And something tasty for himself as well.

"I just don't understand how Lady Resmiranda's seal could still be so strong. Isn't it supposed to fade after her death? That's what Gran told me. All spells dissipate after the wielder's death."

"Of course!" Radburn slapped his forehead. How could he have forgotten such a basic tenet of magic? His mind suddenly brightened.

He'd been so depressed by the loss of his magic he hadn't been thinking clearly. As if all the sharpness and clarity of his thoughts deserted him along with his talent. He'd succumbed to the very seeds of chaos that he had sowed.

"Of course 'what'?" Fantôme snarled. He stumbled to the pile of dried rushes and stolen blankets he used as a bed.

"The lady hasn't died. The spell holds fast because she lives and thrives." Radburn's thoughts whirled. How? Who? "Of course, Fitz Chênenoir must have rescued her. He lied to your trustworthy source, told her only what he wanted her to know. I wonder if John knows that my wife still lives?"

"Your wife, eh? She must still obey you, then. Women must obey their men. That was the only true thing my da taught me. We can force her to open the door." Fantôme sat up, suddenly more alert and energetic.

"We have to find her first." But not until Radburn had his magic back. If he could see the seal on the portal flare with each of Fantôme's assaults, then part of his talent still worked. The rest might return in full if he could just get rid of this damned iron collar.

"Where would she hide? Where could she hide from John?" Fantôme asked the crucial question.

"If I had my magic back, I could find her in the scrying bowl."

"I will seek her in the bowl. After I sleep and eat. Steal extra rations suitable for journeying. We leave at dawn to seek the lady." Fantôme lay back on his pallet. He was snoring before Radburn reached the barrow mouth of the cave.

"You won't find her. I won't let you, Fantôme. I'll find a way to cloud your vision. Somehow I must. Until I have all of my magic at my command, you will not find her. Otherwise she will defeat us both with that damned sword of hers."

She or Fitz Chênenoir. If the sword held true to other artifacts of power, it could only be wielded by the one who received it from its otherworldly custodian. But he thought the recipient could choose a champion. Resmiranda would choose Fitz Chênenoir over every knight in England.

"You die, Fitz Chênenoir. Your blood will fuel my spell to destroy Excalibur."

Chapter 43

HUGH stared out the narrow window at the blustery rain that melted snow by the handful. March winds signaled the end of the winter and a near frantic restlessness in King John. Hugh had suffered from the same need to pace, to ride Orage until exhaustion claimed them both, to pound his fist into someone's face, or drive his sword into someone's gut—preferably King John's.

London offered meager diversion this long winter. Hunting was sparse, tournaments nonexistent, and arms training sporadic. Legal disputes had diminished to near nothing throughout the land. Even the Lord Mayor of London did not protest every new tax, levy, or passage of troops through the city as a violation of ancient and inviolable rights.

Hugh wondered if the fact of the Interdict had begun to penetrate men's thoughts. Without Confession, Absolution, and Eucharist, they now feared to break the law as corporal punishment frightened them in a way it never had before.

Without the court, or hunting, John had become bored with the ladies, the jesters, and the minstrels with their gossip and news from both England and the Continent. He snapped at his councillors and paced the ramparts in all weather, always looking east toward the Continent.

Hugh paced as well, usually with Coffa the wolfhound pup at his heels. Much as he tried, he could not forget Ana, especially not with the pup named for remembrance at his heels. Her betrayal burned in his gut day after day. She invaded his dreams and robbed him of sleep.

Even now, both he and the king faced the winds and the rain on the ramparts. Coffa slept by the fire with the other dogs; he was afraid of heights. John stared in the direction of his foreign enemies. Hugh looked only into himself and did not like what he saw. He wished the rain could wash him clean.

John's usual gaming companions did not join him on the wall, nor did the two bishops who always hovered close by the king. Those two whispered to him in convoluted platitudes and logic twisted so tightly John could find any answer he wanted in their words.

Hugh heaved a sigh of resignation, drew his cloak tighter, and joined his king on the walls. He had a mission tonight. Robin had sent word that the barons, led by de Vesci and Fitz Walter, were as restless as the king after the long winter. They wanted a fight as much as the king did.

The thought of civil war did not sit easily with Hugh. He wanted John dead, deposed, exiled, something. But civil war would destroy more than it healed.

"This wind will break the ice on many of the inland rivers. Goods and troops can begin moving again," John said without looking at Hugh. He had that uncanny ability to sense the approach of others. Part of staying alive as a child among three older, more ambitious brothers and ruthless barons bent on kidnap rather than obedience.

"Horses and wagons will become mired on the roads. Your Highness will not be able to bring siege engines to Portsmouth for another month at least," Hugh replied. His mind worked along familiar pathways, thinking through the problems of launching an invasion of the Continent, though he knew in his heart as well as his head that he must persuade John away from it.

Huntington and Lincoln would welcome another fruitless expedition to Poitou as a reason to rebel.

Hugh would follow them into rebellion this year as he had not in 1204.

But he knew the time was not right. Most of the barons would refuse service and scutage. But civil war? Once the routine of spring planting and the beginning of tournament season came, they'd cease fretting and look at the problem with level heads.

" 'Twill take a month for the barons to muster their knights and men at arms," John continued. "They can put many of the supplies on barges and ship them to the coast. We have to set sail before Philip has a chance to rally his own troops."

"The Channel is not safe until well after St. Joseph's Day. Spring storms have claimed entire flotillas."

"A chance we will have to take. Philip of France sits on our land, commands our barons, grows fat on our resources." John pounded the parapet with his gloved fist. He radiated energy and purpose. "Our honor demands we reclaim our Continental heritage."

Dammit! Hugh liked John as a man, while he hated John the king. They had much in common, thought along similar lines, had familiar priorities, and had shared many adventures together on the field of battle.

"Your barons in England are English, Your Highness. They have divested themselves of all lands and interest in the Continent. . . ." Hugh certainly had. Not that he'd ever had much in Normandy. His fortunes began the day he saved John's life.

"Except for the Marshall. He refused to withdraw his oath of allegiance to Philip for his Continental lands. We have to admire the man's honor, though we deplore his flaunting a royal decree and a duly witnessed and blessed treaty. The Marshall still has the power to command men. If we recall him from exile in Ireland, our barons will follow his example."

"Eustace De Vesci of Northumberland has rallied the northern barons to refuse you men, arms, and money," Hugh reminded the king quietly. Would they follow him into war against the king?

"He still fusses about our lawful fish traps!"

De Vesci "fussed" about more than fish traps, but Hugh did not deem the time right to remind his king of that.

"Very well, then, I will take scutage in lieu of service," John continued. "I would rather use the barons' money to hire mercenaries anyway. Their loyalty is bought and predictable."

As Hugh well knew. He'd begun his career as a mercenary.

"You can only demand scutage so many times, Your Highness. Once a year, by law, at most. Beyond that you need the common consent of the assembled barons and bishops."

" 'Tis not a law. Only tradition. Show us where it is written that we cannot demand money from *our* barons whenever needed!"

Since the campaigns of '04 and '05, the barons had grown increasingly bold in defying their king. Five years ago, Hugh was new to commanding the resources of a baron and had felt obligated to obey his king with men and money. John had had to abort his plans every year since then.

Now? Everything Hugh valued was in England. Even Ana remained in England. She might flee to her father in the spring, but certainly not until she had given birth. If she survived the ordeal.

He pushed that thought away as he pushed away memories of her every day, every hour. He doubted he'd support an invasion of the Continent even to maintain the guise of loyalty he had so carefully woven over the course of the winter.

Without Ana, was the rebellion worth all of these lies?

The lives of ten Welsh hostages depended upon that mask of loyalty, he reminded himself. He had to think beyond himself. Many of the barons did not.

"Every other campaign in Normandy, Philip has had to fight a war on many fronts, keeping his enemies at bay from the east, placating the Pope, while dealing with your troops to the west," Hugh continued. "This year, the Pope will support any monarch who rallies against you, Your Highness. If you insist upon invasion, you give Innocent III an excuse to excommunicate you."

"Our bishops tell us differently. They insist that a reprieve from Innocent III can be bought if we but repossess our Continental lands. Everyone has his price."

"Is that the truth or what you wish to hear, Your Highness? Innocent III is known for his faith, his piety, and his incorruptibility. If he threatens excommunication, he means it." Hugh bit his lip at his own audacity in challenging the word of two consecrated bishops. He believed God knew what He wanted. His bishops did not always listen to anything but their own ambition.

John stilled his constant pacing. He had yet to look directly at Hugh. Nor did he focus on the horizon, or the parapet. Hugh hoped he looked deep within himself for the answer.

"You think this invasion ill-advised."

"Yes, Highness."

"Why should we trust you over our bishops?"

"I have never lied to you, Highness." But he had. Every day he professed loyalty when all he wanted to do was murder this man who had betrayed and ill-used Ana.

With that thought he acknowledged that he still loved her. Would always love her. He just was not certain he could forgive her.

John speared him with a hot gaze. Hugh returned it boldly. If he flinched or cringed in the least, John would know he lied.

"Do you speak for your own gain or ours?" John asked.

"I speak for England. You cannot afford to offend the Pope further. The soul of every Englishman is at stake should our king be excommunicate. The health of the land depends upon healthy souls. I never thought I would be the one to say this, Highness, but England needs the church, England needs a king at peace with the church. Make peace with Innocent III."

"And what of the barons? Do you speak for them as a whole?"

"I speak as a baron. Should the Pope excommunicate you, I must weigh my oath of loyalty very carefully. How will I answer to God if the Pope demands I rebel against you? I do not know how to answer that question. I doubt many of my fellow barons know either."

"I like you, Hugh Fitz Chênenoir, Earl of Bellecôte. I like your blunt honesty and your courage for remaining honest. Perhaps it is time for another campaign in Wales. Or how about Ireland? Those Gaels remain altogether too independent. Our barons will answer the call to arms for Ireland." John resumed a normal rhythm to his steps and headed for the turret stairs of the corner tower.

"Must you campaign this year, Highness? I would think a leisurely progress through England would serve you better. You must convince your barons that they owe you loyalty no matter what action the Pope takes." Hugh held the door open for John. The habit of deference to the man did not die easily. *Sacre bleu,* he liked and agreed with his king when he was reasonable.

"Nothing like a campaign to forge the bonds of friendship and loyalty. You know that, Hugh. You became our friend on the field of battle." John stopped to clasp Hugh's shoulder in affection.

If only I had not stopped that rogue knight from running you through all those years ago!

But if he had allowed John to be killed in battle, Hugh would not be an earl now. He would not have known the love of his son. Would never have met Ana.

I love you, Ana. I miss you terribly. But fate and King John had interfered and driven him away from Ana. He had only the wolfhound pup, Coffa—Remembrance—to remember her by.

"We have many good memories and bonds, Hugh." John paused on the top step and looked directly into Hugh's eyes. "Watch your back as closely as you watch ours. Our spies tell us there are those jealous of our continued good favor toward you. They seek to remove you from court, by lies, politics, or violence."

"Will you case this endless pacing, Father Truman. You make me nervous!" I said testily. My thread knotted, and I swore under my breath. Newynog prowled the confines of the Hall in his wake. March winds made us all just a little jumpy.

My cough returned with the stronger gusts.

Marion and Meredith looked at each other over their own sewing, exchanging silent confidences. I sighed at them in exasperation. They insisted upon making delicate baby garments for me, refusing to accept my decision to give the baby away at the moment of her birth. An older knight in Robin's service and his lady had lost all three of their own children. They desperately wanted to rear my unwanted babe, give it a name and a home with no taint of bastardy.

I stitched sturdy jerkins for Toby and Will rather than prepare for a baby I would not keep.

"I sense . . . something strange, milady." Father Truman paused beneath one of the high narrow windows and looked up at the shuttered opening. The wind battered the wooden barriers as if human hands tried to lift the latch.

"I sense nothing." Indeed, my magical talent had become centered in my baby. I knew its tiny heartbeat, the restless flutter of legs, the comfort of sucking a thumb. . . . Water no longer drew me. 'Twas the earth I sought as my element of choice. The hems of my bliauds were still dirty, but from walking endlessly through the herb garden and not from splashing in puddles.

I sent my thoughts and awareness elsewhere. I could not afford to become emotionally attached to my daughter. I must give her away.

The wind fluttered around my thoughts in a new draft, fierce and driven. I looked up, startled. Something different about this wind . . .

I coughed again.

"Have you renewed the wards about the castle?" Father Truman asked very quietly.

I jumped, not having noticed his return to my side.

"I never set wards." I hadn't wanted to taint my daughter with any contact with magic. Perhaps, growing up in a different household, she might escape the talent as I had tried to for so many years.

Restlessness and an urgency to hide twitched in my limbs. Something strange occurred.

"How could you be so careless!" Father Truman renewed his pacing. "We must set them now." Without apology, he hauled me out of my padded chair. My sewing dropped to the rushes.

I found myself following the priest before I could protest. He threw a cloak at me as he pushed me toward the bailey. I kept looking over my shoulder expecting to find someone watching me.

Only shadows and that prying wind. I held my breath lest I cough again.

Outside in the wind I recognized a questing mind behind its gusts. Someone sought me in a scrying bowl. The search triggered the remnants of the cough Blakely had planted within me. So far the search was vague and preliminary. We had to hurry.

"Gather kindling and lay it ready for the spark at each of the four corners of the curtain wall," Father Truman ordered.

I waddled toward the east tower. My arms and legs wanted to pump in rapid movement. My awkward bulk refused to move at more than a snail's pace. My back ached.

"Outside the curtain wall," Father Truman reminded me. "No sense letting the Seeker see the outside of the castle. He'll recognize it."

"Who?"

"I am not certain."

I thought I knew. The sorcerer who had stolen Blakely's body. The awareness of his malevolence sent me scuttling a little faster.

We separated for our individual tasks. I grabbed two double handfuls of twigs from the woodpile beside the stable and stuffed them into my sleeves. I should have gathered fresh kindling from the forest. I didn't have time.

A cramp along the right side of my belly plagued me the entire walk to the outside of the east tower. We had to work deasil, along the path of the sun. I doubted I could walk the entire circumference of the castle twice. So I laid the first fire and waited for Father Truman to join me. He mixed herbs in a pouch as he walked, cradling flasks of wine and oil against his body.

He sprinkled the herbs over the newly laid kindling while I poured three drops of wine, then three drops of oil. Together we recited an invocation to God to protect the castle and all who dwelled within from outside evil.

Then the worried priest looked at me, expecting me to light the fire from my mind.

"I don't know if I can," I protested. "Have you flint and iron?"

"You must do it with your mind, milady. 'Tis the only way to ensure that prying mind cannot penetrate. It is strong; growing stronger and more focused by the minute."

I knew that mind would rip apart any casually laid wards. These had to be strong and perfect, forcing that mind around them subtly enough that the watcher wasn't aware of an absence.

Resigned, I closed my eyes and mustered all of my strength. A new cramp started on the left side of my belly before I smelled smoke rising from the tiny fire.

When I opened my eyes, a pale shimmer of energy spread upward and outward from the fire. When we completed the circle, the entire castle would be enclosed within the protective barrier.

We couldn't finish fast enough to satisfy me. Already the questing mind sniffed the presence of magic.

Father Truman offered me his arm for support as we trekked to the south tower. Twice more we repeated the ritual. By the time the third fire flared from my kindling I swayed and nearly fell with exhaustion and pain.

Now I knew the cramps for labor pains. I needed to be inside. I needed the midwife and her birthing chair.

"You must finish this, milady," Father Truman urged. "If you abandon it now, the fourth ward will be weak, the circle incomplete. This enemy will find you all the quicker by sensing the presence of unfinished wards." He sounded desperate.

"I know," I gasped. "Just give me a moment to catch my breath." More a rapid panting, like a dog after a long run.

Newynog nudged me. I rested my arm across her neck, letting her take some of my weight. Never before had I appreciated her great height and weight as I did now. No other familiar could support me as she did.

Together we stumbled toward the north tower. Father Truman laid the fire, sprinkled the herbs and poured the water and wine. I placed my hand atop his as he performed the tasks so that I was a part of the ritual, but I had to put all of my concentration into remaining upright and breathing steadily as a new pain nearly felled me.

The wind increased in intensity, circling the castle, beating at us. Only if it succeeded in stopping or delaying us could it penetrate the shield we raised. Already the shimmering energy was taller, thicker, nearly complete.

"The chant, milady. We have to say the words together. Slowly. Say each word clearly and distinctly as I do."

Word by word we pushed the chant into the spell. Word by word we approached closure of the circle.

"Now the fire," he coaxed. "Light the fire."

This time I held my hand out and pointed toward the kindling. Too exhausted to think or care how or why the twigs ignited, I set the thing blazing. All my doubts about the sin of using magic vanished with my pain.

The wind howled its displeasure and renewed its assault upon my senses as well as the castle walls. But I did not cough.

"One more short walk, milady. We must close the circle."

"I can't," I gasped as I took one step and nearly collapsed. The pains were coming closer. Too close. Pressure built within me. The baby wanted to be born right now!

"You must walk. I can't carry you. Your steps and mine must complete the circle.

Give in to the pain. Give up this fruitless endeavor. I'll find you anyway, the wind whispered to me.

I recognized the rhythm of the words, the accent that claimed no single language as its root, the evil behind them. Radburn Blakely.

But he was dead!

I could not think the question through while the pains came so quickly, so strongly.

Fear gave me strength. I took each step as if driven from behind. With each step, the wall of power strengthened. With each step, the baby beat at me for exit.

At last, we rounded the east tower and came upon the wispy ashes of our first fire. We said some more words, sprinkled more herbs and poured more oil and wine.

I heard the protective wall snap closed in my mind. At the same moment, my thoughts mingled with those of my baby. She knew her warm, wet world intimately. The time had come for her to stretch, to breathe real air, to explore my world and my magic.

I had not the strength to sever the bond between us. As my knees gave way beneath me, I knew I could not abandon this child. She was a part of me that I could never—would never—cast aside.

I would accept Robin's proposal when the Interdict was lifted. I'd not marry him outside the church.

Waiting for Hugh's forgiveness was useless.

Chapter 44

NEWYNOG growled at Father Adrian, Robin's household priest, and Father Truman who stood behind him in the doorway to the solar. Three days and my dog took her duties as protector of my daughter as seriously as she did her role as my familiar. Three days and the bond among us, mother, daughter, and dog, had deepened beyond the realms of my imagination.

"I must baptize the child, milady," Father Adrian insisted.

Three days. The child thrived. Neither one of us seemed likely to succumb to the fevers that so often claimed both mother and babe.

"I will witness the Sacrament." I rose from my chair, still holding my daughter. Three days and I was reluctant to let another hold my baby, though Meredith and Marion vied for every opportunity to carry her away, show her proudly to one and all of Huntington, as if they were the proud mamas and not I.

Father Truman, standing behind Father Adrian, looked embarrassed a moment. Then he bowed his head.

Father Adrian stepped forward, reaching for my daughter. "I am sorry, milady." He did not sound sorry at all. "You have not yet been churched."

Father Truman did look sorry and . . . stubborn. He might not like Father Adrian's actions or attitude, but he would not contradict.

"Then I will endure the ritual of cleansing after childbirth before you christen my baby." I stared at both priests determinedly. "I will attend my daughter's baptism. She shall receive her name from me and none other!"

"Milady—" This time Father Truman had the grace to look away and shuffle his feet. "Milady, the Interdict forbids all Sacraments and rituals except baptism and last rites. You may not enter the chapel. You may not witness the ceremony."

"But the men of the household may?" I screamed.

Father Adrian nodded, reaching for my baby.

I snatched her out of his reach.

"Ridiculous. There is nothing unclean about childbirth. 'Tis the greatest miracle of the life God has granted us. Men should be churched after siring a child. They are the unclean ones." My heart pounded loudly in my ears, I broke out in a cold sweat. I clutched my baby far too tightly. Hysteria threatened to rob me of logic.

The baby cried in protest at my clasping fingers. Newynog rose to her feet and nudged my hands with her cold wet nose.

I breathed deeply, forcing calm to return.

"If the church denies me the right to witness my child's baptism because of a silly ritual conceived by old men—celibate old men hidden away in Rome—then I shall deny the church the rite to claim my daughter." I grabbed a cloak from a peg in the wall and shouldered the priest aside from the doorway. Father Truman steadied him with firm hands on his shoulders, also preventing him from following me.

"Marion, Meredith, come with me."

The girls followed, half gaping in awe at my audacity, half marching proudly in my wake. Their posture shifted back and forth between the two emotions; finally pride won and they stiffened their backs, snubbing the males of the household.

"We need an old woman," I said absently as we passed beneath the massive walls of the castle at the postern gate.

"Whatever for?" Meredith asked, still trying to march out into the world in defiance of society's view of life's priorities. She had never been the obedient one.

"A crone, a matron, and a maiden," Marion corrected her younger sister with a punch in the arm. "Mama told us about it. Don't you remember? Real magic needs a crone, a matron, and a maiden."

"Your mother knew of the old magic?" I asked quietly, pausing in the shadows of the walls. A hint of trepidation made me bite my lip. What was I doing? I had defied the church, the church I had been raised to revere above all else in heaven and on earth.

Not quite true. I should revere God, Jesus, the Holy Ghost, and the Blessed Virgin Mary before the church. But the church authorities often saw themselves as superior to the Holy Trinity and the Mother of God.

What was the Holy Mother but a different manifestation of the ancient Goddess of Life.

My resolve reasserted itself.

"Mama said that if we ever truly needed to work magic, we should go to the old herb witch who has a cottage by the stream that springs from the cliff." Marion pointed toward the base of the hill that rose in back of Huntington.

"A spring?" I asked. Delight and relief washed over me. Something about free-flowing water always made everything seem *right*.

We set our steps in that direction. A warm April wind promised showers later in the day. The air smelled fresh and clean. The earth beneath our feet pushed up new growth. Johnny-jump-ups bloomed in a carpet of sunny yellow. The fire of life glowed in our blood.

All four elements accompanied us on our journey.

The small circular hut of sticks woven together with withy reeds and thatched with sagging bundles of river grass seemingly grew out of the hillside that formed its back wall. A bent old woman, clad in black, devoid of wimple or veil, awaited us. Her thin gray hair hung in wisps about her face and down her back. She smelled of flowers and earth.

Beside the hut, a tiny stream chuckled over a fall of rocks.

"I've been waiting two days for you to come," the old woman said without preamble. "Should 'a done this first day after the wee one entered this world." She set her long walking staff in front of her and stalked to the streambed. Each step she slammed the staff into the earth more for emphasis than support. A fanciful fish adorned the top.

Suddenly I regretted the loss of my own staff. Perhaps I should carve a new one.

"I came as soon as I knew I should," I excused myself.

"Had your needs tainted by that mannish church, ye did." She stopped and looked over her shoulder. "Come along, then. Shed your clothes. Cain't connect to the elements with all them draperies on." Her own black garment dropped to the ground. I did not see her touch it. It just fell, like a snake shedding its skin.

Marion and Meredith looked away from the old woman's wrinkled skin and shriveled breasts in embarrassment.

"Do it," I whispered. I had half expected this from my readings of Aunt Lotta's rituals. She and Uncle Henry both placed a great deal of importance upon shedding barriers between themselves and the elements. The baby blinked and cooed in one of her infant chuckles. My mind brightened, and I lost the inhibitions imposed upon me by a lifetime of the church's view of modesty.

I dropped my cloak and fiddled with the side laces of my bliaud one-handed. The ties knotted and tangled.

Giggling all the while, the two maidens stepped out of their clothes quickly. Marion held the baby while I eased the knots and finally stepped out of the puddle of clothing.

"Her name is Deirdre," Marion said quietly. "She doesn't like introductions. She already knows everyone's names, and expects them to know hers as well."

"Deirdre, I am hopelessly ignorant. Will you tell me the nature of this ritual?" I asked.

The old woman already stood in the middle of the stream below the tumble of rocks. I placed one foot into the water and gritted my teeth rather than yank it back out at the first touch of the icy flow.

"Ye'll have to make your own comfort within the water, lass," Deirdre cackled. "Very little in life is comfortable. Get used to it."

"I know that, old mother." Resolutely I took up a position directly downstream from her. The water lapped at my legs mid calf.

Clutching their arms about them in a futile attempt to ward off the cold, the two girls splashed their way toward us.

"Now what?" I asked.

"We make it up as we go along," Deirdre replied.

"I am not used to devising my own rituals. I have always relied on the experience of others."

"Good for a start. But now 'tis up to you. Make the gestures, say the words that reflect you and your daughter and the special bond you share."

Newynog burst from the woods and leaped into the water. Streams of water shot up and drenched us all.

"Very well, Newynog. You shall be part of this as well." I ruffled her damp ears and received a soggy kiss on my hand in return.

"Three maidens," Deirdre pointed to the two girls and the baby. "Two matrons." She included Newynog and me in her gesture. "And one crone. A neat triad." She laughed again.

"A unique trinity of friendship," I agreed. "As friends and mutual protectors I bring this girl child to share in our lives and our friendship. May the bonds of love and our connections to Earth, Air, Fire, and Water grant us all peace of heart, love of life, and the wisdom of the ages."

I do not know where the words came from. But they reflected the moment and my relationship with the women about me.

"Give the babe a name," Deirdre said. She dipped the end of her staff in the water where it dropped from the rocks into the stream. Once thoroughly soaked, she held the carved fish so it dripped over the baby's head.

"Henrietta Carlotta of the clan of Griffins. Hetty among us."

"A good name. A good clan." Deirdre dribbled the water from the staff in a straight line from Hetty's brow, down her belly to her toes.

Hetty wriggled at the first touch of the chill water but did not protest. She stared up at me with wide and wondering eyes. Already the bluer-than-blue Griffin eyes shone through the misty light blue of infancy.

"Now, you girls, each of you say something." Deirdre passed the staff to Marion.

She dipped the staff into the water and repeated the drizzle of water on Hetty. "May you grow to be as wise and beautiful as your mother." She blushed and passed the staff to her sister.

"I hope you grow to find magic in all things," Meredith said forthrightly.

Newynog shook, spraying water from her fur onto all of us. She opened her mouth in a doggy grin. I knew that she promised one of her pups to become Hetty's familiar when the time came.

A bevy of faeries popped into view, swirling around us in delighted spirals, filling the little glen with giggles. they danced in and out of the little cascade and sang greetings to Hetty that sounded like a full choir of silver bells.

They blessed my daughter's baptism as they had not blessed her conception.

"Now off with you 'afore you catch a chill." Deirdre shooed us out of the water. "And remember, Resmiranda, your name means 'Wondrous Thing.' Your life is a miracle. All life is a miracle. Don't let those churchmen make you think otherwise."

"Thank you, Deirdre," I replied.

"Water is your element, Resmiranda. Water cleanses all it touches. So do you."

She scooped up her clothes and vanished inside her ragged hut.

The faeries took off on errands of their own.

Marion and Meredith had made no acknowledgment of the faery presence. Perhaps they could not see my friends.

"This was better than going to church," Marion said. "I went with Mama after Tobin and Will were born. I always felt dirty, as if giving birth were a sin."

"As Deirdre said, life is a miracle," Meredith asserted. "We don't need a church to change things around from the way they really are."

"We need a church, Meredith," I replied. "But perhaps not the one in Rome." I don't think I could have expressed my longing for the beautiful rituals of daily life, among them the bells ringing out the order of the day and the solace of prayer, heightened by incense, candles, and hymns. "The time may come when we English make our own church."

"But there is no other!" Marion protested.

"Many, many Christians in Greece and Constantinople, and even the kingdoms of the Rus would disagree with you," I mused as I wrapped Hetty in her blanket and dressed myself. Strange that I felt no chill and relished the sensation of freedom from the air bathing my naked body.

"The three of us cannot change the church," Marion said. She tangled her hands in Newynog's thick fur.

"No. Churchmen have too much political power as well as spiritual. The Interdict is perpetuated by politics—not by faith or a lack of it. Our lot is perhaps to keep alive the tradition we just celebrated and not let it get lost in politics."

Chapter 45

THAT night, Father Truman christened my daughter Henrietta Carlotta with Robin and his son Robert as witnesses. The two girls stood as godmothers. I watched from the doorway of the family chapel.

Father Adrian was not present.

Hetty stopped smiling and cooing at the moment the holy water and oil touched her brow. She screamed in protest as she had not when doused with cold water from the free-running stream. "She casts out devils," Father Truman proclaimed in triumph.

My bond with the baby told me she merely protested my absence from this most sacred rite. I snatched Hetty back from Father Truman the moment he emerged from the small sanctuary. She returned to her normal cheerful self the moment I touched her.

Over the next weeks and months, the Locksley family doted on my Hetty, especially Robin. He neglected his duties to spend hours staring at her in her cot, rocked her, and sang lullabies. His two daughters constantly vied for the right to hold her, change her, carry her to all parts of the castle. In order to snatch a few moments of privacy with my child I had to slip away from the castle.

As I walked with her, I told her my few memories of Kirkenwood and her namesakes. I had to gel those memories within me before they were replaced by newer experiences, newer relationships. Lessons in magic followed the personal memories. At the heart of each lay a reverence for the Earth as God's creation—indeed the first temple— and a firm connection to it as the foundation for dealing with the other three elements and God.

Water was my element. Earth was Hetty's.

Repeatedly my footsteps carried us uphill to a level clearing overlooking Huntington Castle. I could not see Deirdre's hut from up here. Indeed I never found it again in my wanderings. Perhaps I could only find it when I needed Deirdre.

Clear water sprang from triple boulders set in a rough triangle near the center of the clearing. The rocks offered me a convenient perch. From here I could watch the comings and goings around the castle, individuals identifiable only by the color of their clothing and their destination.

Cook always wore a bright yellow shirt and moved between his kitchen and the cold cellar. Owen, the head groom, wore dun brown and stood in the courtyard pointing and yelling at his underlings who scurried about like faceless ants. Robin always wore Lincoln green and strode purposefully about. His daughters in their bright purple and murrey gowns flitted from here to there and back again, seemingly without purpose.

From my observation post I knew myself apart from the men of this bustling household that rang with laughter and love. They welcomed me and my daughter, as they welcomed any refugee from King John's injustice. What did I need to do to become one of them as I had with Marion and Meredith that magical day we baptized Hetty ourselves?

I had promised to marry Robin. Would that make me feel as if I belonged? A hole in my heart told me I would never belong anywhere but Kirkenwood. Never belong to any man but Sir Hugh Fitz Chêne-noir.

You can belong anywhere you choose, a lilting voice giggled in my ear.

Hetty gurgled and reached for the flashing green insect that hovered over her head.

"Welcome, Willow!" I called to the green faery I had known in my youth. "You found me!"

Newynog nipped at the faery, prancing in a circle on her hind feet as the green mite easily eluded her.

We will always find you and the child. Come play! Willow swooped down and splashed a tiny spray of water at my feet.

Newynog bit a mouthful of water trying to catch Willow. She snorted and stomped heavily in the stream, spraying us all with her enthusiasm.

I heaved a deep sigh, regretting that Hugh could not be Hetty's father, could not share this moment with us.

The bevy of faeries flew a long spiral around me. Their circles grew wider and wider with each pass. I tried to follow them with my eyes. My gaze returned repeatedly to the verge of rough grass and broken stones ringing the level ground where the boulders sat and the stream burbled.

The faeries flew a perfect circle. The soft grass lay within their path. Outside it, the grass grew coarse and long, filled with wild endive, thistles, and stunted gorse.

I sat in the center of a faery ring! But where were the mushrooms or standing stones to define the edge?

Make the circle. Open yourself to the glories of our circle! The faeries flew faster, adding loops and whorls to their ring. Hetty's laughter bubbled up, adding a merry counterpoint to the bell-like giggle of my friends and the chuckle of water.

"This will be a lot of hard work," I said. I settled Hetty on a blanket in the triangle of sacred space at the center, a special place of protection, and walked to the mixture of broken stones littering the ground. Gingerly I picked up one that filled both my hands nicely. It didn't feel right. Why?

Newynog nudged one of the other nearby stones with her nose. I kicked at it. It rolled easily toward the place I suddenly knew it wanted to rest, but stopped short of the softer grass.

"Who tore this circle apart?" Who would dare?

The faeries did not answer. They did not need to. We all knew that only priests would have the audacity to challenge this ancient magic. Long ago, when Christianity was new to England.

"We must rebuild the circle," I said firmly to my faery friends.

Use your magic, the faeries urged. *The circle will be stronger if you set the stones with magic.*

"That is even harder work than doing it by hand," I protested.

We will help. Newynog's voice blended with the faeries. And was that Hetty's infant coos joining in?

I stared at the faeries as they skittered into a dozen different directions, each following a different pattern of spirals and swoops.

Newynog nudged another stone toward the place it wanted to be.

"How do we do this?" I demanded.

More giggles. A bright red female faery hovered directly in front of my nose. I had to cross my eyes to see her properly. Her perfectly formed breasts jiggled and her nipples tightened. The thatch of vermilion hair at the juncture of her thighs matched her tousled curls perfectly. I wondered if faeries mated in the same manner as humans. Was Willow as perfectly formed as John? What would it be like to mate with a faery?

I looked away in embarrassment at Vermilion's nakedness and my wanton thoughts.

Every one of the faeries stilled.

"I am sorry," I called to them. "I must not impose my own moral limitations upon you."

I sensed a slight easing of the tension among them, but they still hesitated between my world and theirs. If I valued their company, I must earn their trust once more.

Without thinking of the possible consequences if someone should observe me, I dropped my clothes and stepped into the stream where it exited the circle. I entered the faery domain ritually cleansed.

The faeries giggled and danced about.

A warm April breeze promised a hot summer. Moist grass tickled my toes. Every pore in my body opened to the sunshine and rejoiced. I raised my arms and turned in a circle, relishing the sensation of freedom, the removal of artificial barriers between me and the elements. My mind opened.

I had sensed this oneness of life, with life, before, all too rarely and quite by accident. Now I sought it.

I heard the tiniest insects twitter, felt the Earth move in its endless path through the heavens. In a dizzying moment I became one with all that existed.

The power of life hummed at the core of my being. The heavenly music of the spheres echoed in my spirit.

I could do this any time I chose.

Now the magic will be easy, the faeries reassured me.

Easier, certainly; easy had yet to be defined. I located the two stones that would define the eastern entrance to the circle first. They belonged on either side of the little stream that trickled toward the edge of the plateau. Anyone entering the circle would have to splash in the water—a ritual cleansing similar to baptism.

I laughed at the image and levitated the two rocks into place.

In another lifetime I might have waited for the summer Solstice dawn to choose the point of due east before setting a single stone. Today I knew without a doubt the precise point of each of the cardinal directions. With the help of my faery friends, I listened to the stones and let them find their proper resting places.

When north nestled into the grass. I saw a faint line of power skim the tops of the directional stones; akin to but not as strong as the ring of fire around the standing stones at Kirkenwood and before the barrow in the Mendip Hills.

A tremendous weariness settled into my bones and muscles. Sweat chilled on my skin and my teeth chattered. Even Newynog plopped down beside the stream, panting. She lapped up a little water and settled her head between her paws. In a moment she snored.

The power dribbled out of me, and that glorious sense of unity faded.

"Enough for today," I told the faeries. I clasped the remnants of today's experiences close to my heart.

The faeries agreed with a giggle and left us with a slight popping sound.

"I'll come back tomorrow," I said as I donned undergarments. My teeth stopped chattering as I slid chainse and bliaud over my head.

At the moment I settled my girdle about my hips, Hetty let loose with a yowl of hungry displeasure. My own stomach growled in response.

I sat with her between the central stones, dabbling my toes in the spring and nursing my baby while extreme contentment swept over me.

Building the circle of stones took many days of hard work. Sometimes I carried Excalibur up to the hill along with Hetty. I listened to the sword hum quietly in the back of my mind while I worked. The sword and I needed contact with each other to forge the bonds that would bring our magics into unity when the time came to use the weapon.

I had no doubt that one day I would have to wield Excalibur as a magical and a mundane weapon against a mighty sorcerer. Perhaps not today or tomorrow, but one day. The magician who had sought me in the scrying wind on the day of Hetty's birth would seek me and the sword eventually. I suspected Radburn Blakely's mind was behind the magician. Quite possibly it was Blakely himself. How? I did not know. But he was a part of it still.

I worked on the faery ring in the nude, rain or shine. My physical and mental muscles developed. I lost the last of the pregnancy flab around my belly. My breasts remained tight and firm despite the milk that filled them for Hetty.

April ended. On the first day of May, St Joseph's Day, I watched the bustle of preparation for celebrations from my perch on the central boulder. I had left Hetty in Marion's loving arms today. The baby was restless and fretted. She seemed a little feverish. So I mixed a mild, soothing potion for her and climbed the hill with my magical sword. Newynog had planted herself at Marion's feet, refusing to leave "our" baby.

Soon the faeries and I would place the last four small stones.

As I watched the men raise the maypole in the center of the castle village, a small troop of strangers rode out of the woods. I recognized their leader immediately. Only one man could master that arrogant, high-strung, dun-colored horse.

'Tis the feast of Beltane! the faeries shouted with glee. *'Tis a celebration of new life. We must share the joy, male and female.*

"Male and female," I sighed, wishing for what might have been.

It can still be, Willow and Vermilion insisted. They held hands as they flew about. Their shoulders brushed against each other. Their feet tangled as they hovered near me. They smelled of heady musk. Clearly they would mate today.

"How can Hugh and I be together? I betrayed him. He can never trust me again."

You must forgive and trust yourself first. Finish the circle. Then ask yourself the same question again. Call him to you. Tonight is all that is important.

"Tonight," I promised them and myself. "Tonight I would say good-bye to him properly." But first I had to slip into Huntington unobserved and nurse my baby.

Chapter 46

HUGH searched the bailey of Huntington Castle, desperately seeking a glimpse of Ana. Afraid he would see her. Disappointed that he did not.

"She wanders the hills most days," Earl Robin said before Hugh could voice the question. "Gathering herbs and minerals, she says, but she sits atop that hill and broods more often than not." He shrugged his shoulders. "You won't see her unless she wants to be seen."

Hugh bit his cheeks rather than show his disappointment and his relief. "I thought she'd be ready to celebrate with the rest of you." He pointed to the now erect maypole in the village commons with its still green crown of branches. The lower branches of the evergreen tree had been distributed to the village homes as symbols of good luck and hospitality. Last year's boughs already formed the basis of the huge bonfire beyond the houses and garden plots.

"Since the Equinox, she does not join us for more than meals." Earl Robin shrugged again. "I am not one to force her to remain within the castle. She has the freedom of my lands."

Given the man's youthful experiences as an outlaw, Hugh understood his need to allow another refugee from John's tyranny more freedom than conventional.

Hugh nodded. He wanted to ask after the babe. Had it lived? Had Ana fared well at the birth?

Robin shouted some directions to his people, clearly not willing to part with more information unless asked directly.

Hugh would ask no more. "I have messages for your ears alone, Earl Robin." His eyes strayed to the hilltop. He couldn't see the crest of the rise, a trick of the formations. But he was sure anyone sitting

364

up there could see all that transpired below. If Ana sat up there brooding, as Robin said, she would know Hugh had come.

His messages were brief, and he needed to be at Bellecôte as soon as possible. Best if he did not linger long enough for her to seek him out.

Inside the tower keep Newynog raced out of the solar and slid to a stop before Coffa. The two dogs sniffed each other eagerly. The younger male nipped his mother's ears and received a snarl and a huge paw on the back of his neck in return. Coffa rolled onto his back, ears back, tail tucked. Authority established, the two trotted off together.

What transpired that Ana had left Newynog here rather than take her on her rambles? She needed the dog as protection. Or did they all lie about her whereabouts and she did actually hide within the castle?

Hugh looked to Robin for an explanation. Robin merely shrugged and ordered ale for them both.

They discussed at length John's latest attempts to raise an army. Hugh lingered, wishing for the courage to leave and never see Ana again.

Sunset approached. Hugh finally made his excuses and ordered the horses saddled and his men away from the dancing with pretty and eager maids. Ale flowed too freely and inhibitions flew with the wind. Even Robin and his older children participated in the ancient revelries. Hugh expected Ana to join them as well. She had already proved herself a wanton and a witch. The pagan overtones of the celebration repulsed and fascinated him at the same time.

Could it be that Rome had withdrawn the church from England because these pagan rites invaded so many aspects of life here? Was England unredeemable?

Hugh set his spurs to Orage and rode out of Huntington, Coffa running eagerly beside him. His men followed a little sluggishly. He'd ridden ahead some distance when Orage halted abruptly, flicking his ears in rapid circles. Coffa stopped as well, sniffing the air and yipping excitedly.

Then Hugh heard it, a quiet song of joy drifting on the breeze. He kneed Orage to follow the song, not knowing why, only realizing something inside him felt incomplete without that song. Without the singer.

The horse found the path up the hill. It wound around, switching back on itself a dozen times or more. Frequently, Hugh could not see

where it led next. But Coffa did, or the wolfhound followed an instinct so old, Hugh did not know how to trust it.

She waited for him just outside a ring of stones. Slightly larger
matching stones sat on either side of a small stream.

Ana's whiter-than-white chainse clung to her in near transparency
that alternately hid and revealed the shapes and shadows of her femi-
nine secrets.

Hugh almost turned around. Ana had betrayed him once. She
would do so again. As had everyone else in his life.

But she was so very beautiful his heart ached to gaze upon her.

Slimmer than he remembered, but rounder, too. Her months of
healing and pregnancy had added a new blossom to her cheeks and a
light to her eyes.

He slid to the ground, dropping the horse's reins. He ordered
Coffa to remain outside the circle with Orage.

Ana held out a hand to him. "I knew you would come. I knew
you would find me," she said quietly. Her shining eyes never left his
face.

"Oh, Ana." He kissed her fiercely, branding her as his own. He
pulled her tight against his chest. Her body molded to his. They clung
together for a long, nearly endless moment.

He grew hard with a soul-deep longing. She did not back away.

"Ana?" He tried to push her away. Uncertainty plagued him. He
had waited for this moment for so long, dreamed of it, he could not
believe it real. Perhaps he held some faery sprite wearing the mask of
his beloved. 'Twould be fitting on this night of bonfires and dances,
of cleansing and fertility.

She reached up and touched his cheek with her open palm. He
turned his face and kissed the hand that caressed him so gently.

"How could you betray me, Ana? You slept with John. You married Blakely. You promised to give your heart to no other."

"Hush. We will talk later if you insist. For now, we have only the
night, only ourselves. Tonight we belong together. Tonight we will
celebrate the Mayday feast as lovers have celebrated for more generations than we can count." She led him by the hand through a gap in
the stone ring. She stepped into the center of the little stream, barefoot and as always heedless of dampening her hem. Hugh could only
follow regardless of any damage to his boots.

His doubts be damned. He deserved one night with her. He'd

worry about John and her bastard child later. Tonight she belonged only to him.

Inside the circle he spotted dozens of brightly colored night insects flitting around the tiny lanterns she had set beside the slightly larger stones at the cardinal directions.

"Give me tonight, Hugh. Give me tonight if nothing more."

"I loved you, Ana. How could you?" He brushed a tendril of golden hair from her face.

"I love you, Hugh."

"You hurt me terribly."

"Hush," she whispered and held a finger to his lips. He kissed the tip and flicked his tongue over it. She shivered and pressed her body closer. He wrapped his arms around her. Her body molded to his as if made to fit. She belonged to him. Belonged with him.

"We know our hearts, Hugh. We need nothing more tonight. No promises of tomorrow. No pledges. No forgiveness. Only tonight. Trust me. Trust yourself." She reached up on tiptoe and kissed his lips lightly.

He deepened the kiss before she could pull away. Her tongue flicked across his, lightly, teasing him to follow. His hands found her round bottom and tucked her up against his growing desire. She wiggled a little until the full length of him nestled against her belly. Her breasts felt so very good pressed against him.

He sighed, fanning her ear with his breath. They stood there a long moment until her hands wandered up to thread through his hair. Her fingertips against his scalp sent tingles down his spine. She traced the surges of sensation downward to his hips where she spread her hands to cover him.

"We have too many clothes on," she giggled. Her voice rasped huskily, rousing his passions further. One deft movement and her shift slid off her shoulders revealing the enticing roundness of her breasts.

He gasped in wonder at the primal beauty she revealed to him. He cupped her full breasts with both hands, rolling the tight nipple into a dark rosebud. The large, dark aureole invited his mouth to suckle.

The sudden release of his sword and belt dropping to the ground distracted him. Her anxious hands pulled at his cotehardie and fumbled with his braies. It pleased him that she seemed unfamiliar with men's clothing. He needed to teach her some things about men that John had not. He needed to banish all thoughts of John from her mind and his own.

Moments later their clothing lay in a heap at their feet. Hugh gazed longingly at every inch of Ana's body as she lowered her chainse slowly from her waist to the ground. She returned the favor as eagerly, wetting her lips seductively in anticipation.

He reached for her. She clasped his hand and led him to the sheltered area within three boulders at the center of the ring.

So this was to be a ceremonial bedding only. So be it. He did not need to forgive her, return to her again. They had tonight. She owed him that.

"Ana, I . . ."

"Hush. We have tonight. Cherish it forever." She knelt before him, dragging her hands along his hips and legs as her mouth found the moist tip of him.

He groaned with pleasure as she kissed him lightly and flicked her tongue along the length of him. Thankfully, regretfully, she did not take him into her mouth. He'd not have been able to contain himself long if she had. Gentle pressure on the back of his knees brought him to the ground. Her breasts invited his touch.

She explored his body with hands and delicate kisses. Flame followed the path of her questing mouth until the itch deep within him demanded attention.

Gently, he guided her to the ground, kissing her deeply, allowing his manhood to press against her belly, easing a tiny bit of his urgency. He found her thatch and tangled his fingers in the curly golden hair, testing her. One fingertip strayed deep inside her. She twisted her hips and arched her back to accommodate him.

"Lie still, or I won't be able to wait any longer," he groaned.

"Then don't." She guided him with her hand until he plunged deep within her. Where he belonged. Where he could never go again.

Waves of hot, moist need washed over him. He thrust deep and pulled out, needing to prolong their union, needing to establish his claim on her.

She lifted her hips to meet his next thrust and his next.

Wild arrays of colors showered through his mind, filling every fiber of his being.

"Ana!" he shouted as he exploded within her and collapsed on top of her. "Ana, my love," he whispered as his body stilled.

"Hugh," she breathed. Her body spasmed and held him tightly a moment longer. Then she, too, relaxed.

Tiny giggles like the chiming of fine glass bells roused him. He looked around hastily for unwanted observers and saw only the bevy of night insects.

Outside the circle of lamplight within the ring, darkness overtook the twilight.

Ana rolled from beneath him. She grabbed her chainse and darted a few steps toward the circle's entrance.

"Ana!"

"Good-bye, Hugh. I know you cannot forgive me. I can barely forgive myself. But I will cherish this night forever." Tears streaked her face.

"Ana!"

Orage nickered, Coffa yipped, and all was silent.

Except for the scent of crushed grass where they had lain, and the acrid scent of his own musk, she might never have been there.

And then a chorus of voices chiming like glass bells proclaimed, *The circle is sanctified!*

Hugh crossed himself as he placed Coffa across his pommel, jumped onto Orage and pelted down the hill.

She had betrayed him again. Used him in her pagan rite.

He could not ride away fast enough.

Chapter 47

Late autumn, in the Year of Our Lord 1209, tenth year of King John's reign, at a tournament outside Winchester.

HUGH steadied Orage with a brief pressure from his knees. He shifted the balance of his lance and leaned into his saddle. The noise of the tournament crowd faded into the distance. He lost track of the gay, fluttering banners that ringed the lists. The pungent smells of too many people packed together, or roasting meat and steaming vegetables, of eager horses pissing, and men fighting the sweat of fear ceased to exist.

He shifted uneasily, unable to concentrate. His gaze wandered from the crowd in the viewing boxes and galleries to the collection of knights at each end of the field. Something was out of place. Prickles climbed his back as they did before a battle.

"Concentrate," he admonished himself. He narrowed his vision to the length of the field he and Orage must charge and the man who would meet him in battle at the center.

His young opponent, clad in the blue and black of some small holding up north, had weathered many tournaments but had never known true battle. Battle never followed the orderly rules of tournament. Skills learned in tournament only slightly increased a man's chance of surviving the chaos of battle.

This was only a tournament. Why did he feel as if he faced a host of enemy soldiers?

He faced only one man in a controlled duel. If young Sir Egbert survived this joust, he'd most certainly go down in the melee tomorrow. That knowledge did not soothe Hugh. He had to unhorse this cocky knight. His honor depended upon it. He'd unseated four men already today. Victory had not tasted sweet so far.

The prickles on his back rose to his nape and rang in his ears.

He needed to win this tournament to enhance his reputation as a warrior among the barons. Winning today would give him their ears tomorrow in council. Then when the time came to dethrone John, the barons would heed his arguments and follow him into rebellion.

Hugh did not question the logic, only knew the facts of reputation and honor among his peers.

With John dead or defeated, he'd reclaim Ana. He'd plunge into her again and again until all trace of John's memory vanished from her mind.

What of her child? He'd heard nothing. Wanted to know less. He had a life and career totally separate from Ana now.

But he missed her sorely; still ached at her betrayal.

A flutter of movement off to his left broke his concentration and snagged his eyes off of Sir Egbert's every shift in posture. A man wearing bright blue and black pranced among the crowd. Sir Egbert's jester, no doubt, whipping up the crowd to cheer for his master.

Then the dancing man turned and stared at Hugh. His pale, almost colorless eyes seemed to lock Hugh's gaze and demand attention. A slight afternoon breeze fluttered his silvery blond hair. The sharp planes and angles of his features stood out in the bright sunshine.

"Radburn Blakely!" Hugh said quietly, exhaling sharply. Every muscle in his body stilled. "Why are you alive? Why are you come now?"

The man had grown thinner in the year of his absence, and aged deeply, looking closer to forty than twenty. His cheekbones and nose cast shadows beneath the crag of his prominent brow. This last year had not been easy upon him.

The jester twirled in place, hiding his face within the jagged points of his sleeve. When he turned again, he wore the face of an ordinary man.

Hugh blinked and looked again. No trace of Blakely remained in the jester's face or posture. The energy and precision of his movements had faded into the muddled dance of an aging jester. The crowd of commoners surrounding him lost interest and no longer laughed at his jokes. They had eyes only for the men waiting to entertain them with violence as they pounded down the lists and crashed into each other, with horse, lance, and shield.

Hugh turned his attention back to Sir Egbert, studying him for any sign of weakness among his many strengths.

Before he could decide if the young knight overcompensated for the weight of shield and lance by leaning backward, a lady in bright red fluttered her silk scarf at Hugh. She stood in a pavilion directly across from the royal box. He couldn't tell if she offered the scarf as a tippet for Hugh to wear in this joust or not. His squire didn't seem to think so. The lad looked at the woman and returned his attention to lining up the spare lances.

Another squire held Coffa tightly leashed. He, too, ignored the lady in red.

The scarf waved again in a bolder, wider movement. Hugh followed the pattern of the flutter, cursing that he could not concentrate on his opponent or the challenge before him.

The lady wore Radburn Blakely's face!

"*Sacre bleu!* I don't know what trickery you play, but I'll not be distracted again." Hugh concentrated his vision through the narrow visor of his full head helm.

Consciously he shifted the lance a fraction. He gambled on Sir Egbert's slightly backward posture.

Trumpets blared. The crowd hushed. Queen Isabelle dropped a white scarf. Orage plunged forward.

High melded with the steed's gait, relishing the weight of his weapons, the heat of his armor, the smell of conflict.

Forty yards, twenty, five. Hugh kept his eyes on Sir Egbert's shield and the tip of his lance, watching, waiting for the slightest waver to betray him.

Sir Egbert's chin lifted, as if his eyes shifted to a point beyond Hugh's left shoulder. Hugh couldn't tell for sure. The nosepiece of the boy's open-faced helm effectively shadowed his eyes.

Hugh ignored the ploy and lifted his lance a fraction.

Horses screamed. Wood and metal screeched. Pressure and then spine-numbing vibrations slammed into Hugh's arm and shoulder. He fell backward from the impact. His knees gripped Orage in fierce defense of his balance. His fist knotted on the shield grip.

The horses thundered forward. And he was past Sir Egbert. Hugh drew in a ragged gulp of air. Quickly he assessed his condition. A sharp muscle ache in his shoulder. A trembling in his legs just above the knees. A little short of breath. Nothing broken. Not even his lance.

Tournaments aged a man rapidly. War aged him faster. He'd felt like an old man at fifteen. Now, in his thirties, he was ready to retire.

But he couldn't. Not while the fate of England sometimes hung on his advice to the king.

He wheeled Orage around and discarded the lance. No sense taking a chance on a weakened or split weapon. A squire handed him a replacement. He tested the weight and balance as he assessed the now reeling Sir Egbert.

The knight still sat his horse, but his torso wavered from side to side. His helmet rested at a decided list, and he gripped his reins with both hands much too fiercely. At the opposite end of the list he sat still for many long moments before turning his horse and accepting a new lance. Outwardly he looked composed, sitting his horse firmly, with no sign of trembling muscles or twitching nerves.

But he clung to his reins still. He no longer had the confidence or balance to rely on his knees to communicate with his horse.

Behind the full helmet, Hugh smiled. He knew precisely where to place his lance against Sir Egbert's shield. He prepared himself to lunge forward with Orage for one last charge.

The image of Radburn Blakely's face flitted across his memory. No time to think on that. Queen Isabelle dropped another scarf. The horses lunged forward. The crowd surged to its feet.

Hugh heard the crash, felt a slight tingle in his arm, and cast aside his splintered lance before he realized that Sir Egbert lay unmoving in the center of the field. He drew his sword as he dismounted, keeping his shield at the ready.

Sir Egbert remained immobile. Hugh approached cautiously. He'd been fooled by a seemingly dead enemy on the field of battle only once. He still bore the scar on his thigh.

"Arise and draw your sword, Sir Egbert," he commanded loudly.

The young knight stirred slightly but did not rise.

"Arise and draw your sword, Sir Egbert," Hugh repeated the ritual challenge to combat afoot.

"Ughhhhhhhhh," Sir Egbert moaned. His shoulders came off the ground a bare handspan. They dropped back onto the packed dirt with an audible thud.

Hugh knelt beside him and removed the dented helmet. He discarded it along with his own. Then he checked for bleeding anywhere about Egbert's body. Seeing no signs of overt injury, he looked more closely at his opponent's face, assessing his skin for color and clamminess that might indicate internal injury.

Radburn Blakely stared back at him, grinning like a fool. His pale skin and hair reflected the sunlight. His narrow, colorless eyes peered at him with malice.

Hugh blinked and pinched the bridge of his nose with his left hand. When he had the courage to look again, only Sir Egbert's normally ruddy skin and muddy brown hair showed lying in the dust. The young man moaned again and rolled slightly away from Hugh. He disgraced himself, vomiting his breakfast.

"That's a normal reaction, boy. Don't be ashamed. Did it myself the first time I faced armed men in battle, before the charge even began." He offered Sir Egbert his hand and helped him rise.

"I suppose you'll want my horse and armor as ransom," Egbert muttered.

"Keep them, boy. I'd rather have your friendship and loyalty." Together they approached the royal box.

As Hugh bowed to King John and Queen Isabelle, a strange silence swept through the crowd. He turned full circle searching for a view of what threatened.

John sat very still staring at a rolled parchment. Isabelle held his hand. The two pet bishops crossed themselves repeatedly as they worked prayer beads.

Hugh vaulted the railing into the box. "What ails you, Highness?" He grabbed John's other hand, not caring that he presumed upon the royal personage.

"Innocent III excommunicated him," Isabelle whispered.

In the back of his mind, Hugh heard Radburn Blakely laughing long and loud. The wicked humor stabbed his mind.

He had a reason to rebel now. Could he take the risk?

For Ana's sake, he must. For the good of the kingdom, he must remain at John's side. Felling John would leave a vacuum of power that the ghost of Radburn Blakely wanted to fill.

Chapter 48

The twenty-first day of June, the Year of Our Lord 1212, thirteenth year of the reign of King John Plantagenet. The Mendip Hills.

"I AM master here. I will not soil my hands with this mundane chore," Fantôme announced. He waved a seemingly bored hand at a tethered goat beside the demon door. Then he shook his hands at his sides as if ridding them of water droplets. In the last four years he had acquired many of the haughty mannerisms of a minor lord, including a bored whine in his voice, a disdain for doing anything himself, and a total disregard for anything but his own comfort and ease. He even wore clothes stolen from a knight. But he would never lose the peasant drawl in his speech.

Radburn had to kill the knight for Fantôme and mend the tears in the clothing and wash out the blood.

Fantôme had no idea that the death had flooded Radburn with power. Enough power to send the illusion of his face and form dancing around the lists on the day John's excommunication arrived. The power had lingered and grown—gradually—until today. Moon, sun, and stars all fell into alignment today. He felt their power singing in his blood.

Four years he had nursed that power, playing mind games with the people who had cheated him of his life, his power, his influence. Four years he had watched them in the scrying bowl and plotted his revenge. But he had not found Lady Resmiranda. Nor had he seen her sword in the bowl. But soon. Soon he would have them all back in the palm of his hand.

"Go ahead, kill the thing, as you described in the ritual," Fantôme ordered.

Radburn laid a small fire in the center of the cave before the demon door. Then he drew a large pentagram in the dirt, enclosing the fire, the bleating goat, Fantôme, and himself. Technically, Fantôme should not have been within the central core of the sigil since he would not perform the ritual, but Radburn needed him trapped within easy reach.

Fantôme handed his slave a knife. Radburn held it high over his head, hilt in left hand, blade in right, and chanted words in an obscure dialect of Persian He implored ancient and nearly forgotten gods to accept the sacrifice of blood and fire, and acknowledge his reverence with magical power. Fantôme had learned the words by rote, but had no sense of their true meaning. As Radburn gripped the blade tighter and tighter, the edge sliced his palm. Blood oozed across his hand and dripped down his sleeve. A burning tingle followed its trail. The tiny pain warmed his veins and sent the first surge of power into his mind.

Quickly, Radburn finished the chant and lowered his hands before the arrogant son of a bitch beside him noticed the blood. He pointed the blade at the kindling. Flames erupted from the wood, herbs, goat wool, and bird feathers. Pungent smoke rose above the flames and circled the participants, eerily following the lines of the pentagram. In the same gesture, Radburn yanked the goat's tether and pulled its neck within inches of the flames.

The goat bleated once more, lolling its tongue. A blast of grassy bad breath mingled with the smoke.

"That is the last time I will listen to your ill-mannered complaints," Radburn told the goat and Fantôme. He slashed the goat's neck in one quick movement. Blood gushed, nearly drowning the fire. He drank in the warm coppery smell as if he'd been holding his breath a long, long time. Smoke invaded his lungs, making him cough. He held in the itching need to expel the foreign element from his body.

With each heartbeat, the power within the smoke infiltrated every crevice of his body. His skin burned and glowed. Magic crackled within his blood like lightning across a hot summer sky. The cut across Radburn's palm healed, leaving a pulsing dark blue scar; a blue so dark it appeared almost black; the same blue as his magical signature.

Behind the door, the demon panted in anticipation.

At the peak of the intensity, Radburn reached up and grabbed hold of the hated iron slave collar. The cold metal had never warmed to his skin. He let the dark blue scar on his palm linger on the cool iron. As his magic invaded the essence of the iron, he sought out the seal Fantôme had used to keep the collar in place all these years. The joining burned hot within his mind as he broke the control it had over him. Never again would it rob him of air and dignity.

"This is the end!" he screamed as he yanked the collar apart at the seal.

Fantôme's eyes opened wide in fear. He tried lifting his feet to run from Radburn. The pentagram trapped him. Panic made his muscles twitch. He broke out in acrid sweat. The scent of his fear fueled Radburn's growing magic.

He stripped off his stinking, bug-infested rags and dropped them into the fire. The fire blazed anew with the added fuel. The crackle of hundreds of insect bodies incinerating made Radburn laugh. The symbolic freedom of ridding himself of things lightened his mind and his body. He could have floated about the cave!

Instead he extended his hand. Dark blue lightning shot from his fingertips. The snakes of eldritch light became fetters on Fantôme's hands and feet. Fantôme froze in place, knowing just enough to avoid aggravating the otherworldly chains.

"Now you shall know the weight of my displeasure about your throat," Radburn snarled. "You shall have the collar of your own fashioning choke the life from you."

The iron collar flew from Radburn's hand and encircled Fantôme's throat. It snaked around into a perfect circle and snapped closed in a seal that Fantôme would never be able to break because he had not bothered to learn the essence of his tools.

Then Radburn slowly closed his fingers into a tight fist. The collar also closed tighter and tighter around Fantôme, crushing his windpipe.

"D—don—don't—kill—me, Master," Fantôme implored.

"I see you revert to peasant habits a lot easier than you learned the ways of your betters," Radburn sneered. He stopped the closure of the collar but did not ease the pressure. He wanted Fantôme silenced.

His control over the fearful young man sent waves of lust coursing through Radburn's loins. His erection throbbed.

"I—will—serve you without question," the young peasant gasped, staring wide-eyed at Radburn's obvious arousal. His voice came out a harsh croak. He knew what portended.

"As you should have served me in the beginning." Radburn tightened the collar a fraction as he ripped Fantôme's clumsily mended cotehardie and shirt from his thin shoulders, exposing his sunken, hairless chest.

Fantôme clawed at the collar, bug-eyed with panic.

"Remember this lesson next time you try to think for yourself."

Radburn kissed the lad hard on the lips, running his hands down the pale skin of arms and belly. A thought shredded Fantôme's belt. His braies slid to the ground over narrow hips and quaking knees. His cock shriveled and his balls shrank and knotted.

And still he clawed at the chokingly heavy collar.

Radburn laughed as he slapped the boy on the back, forcing him to his knees. Without preparation, he drove himself into Fantome's backside. Thrust after thrust made his victim scream in pain and humiliation. Thrust after thrust built power within Radburn until he screamed with his own release.

Radburn withdrew his now bloody penis and stood up, satisfied and hungry for more victims. Sex with a man or a woman was about control and domination; pleasure and possible procreation were minor side benefits only.

"Prepare the goat for roasting," he ordered. "I will make a meal of her, and gain more power. You shall dine on gruel. Then you shall steal me some proper clothes. At dawn we begin the journey to regain control of England."

July, in the Year of Our Lord 1212, Chester Castle, near the Welsh Border.

Hugh lounged in a tall chair in the solar of Chester Castle. Boredom made his legs twitch and his hand itch for something to do. He scratched Coffa's ears. The dog opened one eye but did not lift his head from his paws. Across the room, John and his favorites rolled dice and chatted idly. Hugh could not see the amusement in gambling. Yet he had a feeling he should not leave the king's presence today. Something nagged at him. The army camped outside the city wall should have comforted any unease. King John had brought troops north to assist King David of Scotland in ousting a pretender.

Something almost physical made Hugh wary of every flutter of breeze, scurry of rodents, or sigh of the dogs by the hearth.

Why today? he asked himself over and over. This unease was more typical of his feelings right after he came back to court from Ana . . . Ah, Ana. Three years he had mulled over their dilemma. Three years and he still did not know what he truly felt about her. Every time he thought he could not go on without her, a reminder of her betrayal knotted his stomach and clouded his mind.

He had heard nothing from her or about her. His communications with Earl Robin had become sparse and infrequent. He corresponded with de Vesci and Fitz Walter more regularly.

In these three years since John's excommunication, the king had been most cooperative with his barons, dispensing justice and largesse with a wise hand while keeping his taxes and demands as reasonable as possible.

The rebellion had no focus.

Several successful campaigns in Wales had done much to mend John's relations with his barons as well. But since he had defeated his former favorite, William de Briouze in battle, hounded him into exile, and imprisoned de Briouze's wife and family, he kept his other barons at arm's length. Even Ranulph, Earl of Chester, their host on this campaign, was not welcomed at the gaming table with John and his common-born friends. Of the barons, only William Longsword was privy to John's private quarters or knew aught of his thoughts.

Hugh had to glean information from council meetings and gossip overheard at the gaming table.

The barons had no need to rebel now. Not while John behaved himself and the contentious Welsh gave them a common enemy. They didn't like the Pope and his demands to control England through his appointed archbishop any more than John did. The kings of England had always appointed key bishops, especially Canterbury. Why should they relinquish that right just because one Pope wanted more power?

And yet—the absence of Mass, Eucharist, and Confession in these men's lives preyed on their spirits. Hugh saw it in their eyes, in their hunched shoulders, in their long hours of private prayer. Many had taken common law wives since they could not say their vows before a priest. The possible illegitimacy of their children also weighed heavily on their minds.

In many ways, Hugh hoped, prayed, that Ana had given him a child after their one tryst within the faery ring. No word of a baby— his or John's—had reached him from any of his sources. In many other ways he was glad an illegitimate child born of a pagan rite, conceived within a magic circle had not happened.

Hugh watched the king and his companions warily. He listened to the clatter of rolling dice, the idle chatter of men engrossed in the game of chance, the snoring of the dogs. Years on the battlefield had taught him to trust his feelings. Somehow Coffa's reaction to minute changes in the air told him to be wary. With the dog's silky ears in his hands, he never doubted himself, almost as if Ana whispered in his ear and made him feel whole as she had done so often during those days on the road together. He petted Coffa again in hopes of recapturing some of the vivacity and honesty of those days.

One of the dogs by the hearth perked its ears and raised its head. Coffa followed suit. He sniffed and pointed his sensitive nose toward the door. A low growl of warning rumbled through him. All of the dogs instantly leaped to their feet and bared their teeth.

Hugh drew his long dagger and took a defensive stance between his king and the door. As much as he wanted John dead, the blame for negligence must not land on his head if he hoped to shape the new regime.

The door flew open by unseen hands. The sunlight from the open windows framed a glistening figure in white in the doorway. Hugh blinked rapidly, trying to dissipate the luminescent glare from the brightness of the figure's clothing. White cotehardie with exaggerated points on the sleeves, white shirt, white boots, white-blond hair. All in white including the penetrating eyes that looked almost as pale and colorless as the man's clothing; eyes that trapped men into the deepest, darkest hole of their own secrets.

"Blakely," he breathed.

"Radburn?" John reared back in his chair, shying away from the ghost of his half brother.

"Highness." Blakely bowed low. Some of the whiteness around him dimmed. He looked almost human now.

Hugh shifted his balance, wishing he had his sword—a weapon no man was permitted within the presence of the king except his

Marshall and that formidable warrior remained in exile in Ireland. What good was a mundane weapon against a shade from the otherworld?

Not a shade. Hugh wished for something to shield his eyes against the blinding whiteness of the man.

"You live," Hugh stated. Why not? He'd rescued Ana from certain death. Why couldn't someone else rescue the sorcerer?

But where had he been hiding these last four years? Which lord would shelter him? Surely John on one side, or Huntington on the other would have heard of his continued existence. They had known every move de Briouze made until his lonely death in exile. Blakely could not have been living secretly in the hills or caves, not wearing those rich clothes illuminated by magic.

More important, did Blakely know that Ana lived and he might still legally claim her as his wife? Hugh had to send a message to Huntington quickly. Better yet he'd break his code of silence and ride there posthaste.

He might see Ana again. Could he bear that?

"Highness, I am returned to your side at last, healthy and vital once more after the near fatal blow the Griffin witch dealt me. You did burn her at the stake, didn't you?" Radburn said in his hated drawl that held just a hint of an odd accent—as if no single language shaped his speech.

"Radburn," John repeated on a breathy whisper.

Blakely stepped forward into the king's private chamber.

The pet bishop, des Roches of Winchester—the only one left in England since the excommunication—crossed himself repeatedly. His prayer beads clanked together loudly in the hushed room.

Hugh angled himself between Blakely and the king. This is what his gut and the dogs had alerted him to.

"I would embrace you, Brother." Blakely sounded surprised and disappointed at the same time.

"Do you truly live, Radburn?" John asked, still not moving from where he pressed himself against the back of his chair.

"I do, though for many months I hovered near death, nursed back to life by my faithful servant." He'd regained some of his youthful bearing, but still looked older than four years of hardship should have inflicted.

Blakely never lowered his eyes from John.

Hugh wanted to break that eye contact, knowing Blakely must seek to control the king's mind with that direct gaze. Amazing how much knowledge of magical tricks he had picked up over the years.

More amazing that he had come to accept the occult as normal.

As if a puppet on Blakely's string, John rose in one long, awkward movement. He continued off-balance, but he never dropped back into his chair. Nor did he look anywhere but into his half brother's eyes.

Hugh tried again to step between the two men and break the connection. No matter how many steps he took in any direction, Blakely seemed to be elsewhere—without moving.

John took three steps toward his brother. Blakely took four steps closer to his king. The correct number for John to maintain his superior position and yet welcome his brother back from the dead.

Hugh had no doubt that Blakely choreographed the entire scene. At last, Hugh stopped trying to interfere. He had no power here.

Ana, I need your help. But I must keep you away from this man, I must perpetuate the myth that you have died.

"I bring you sad news, Highness," Blakely said, while still clasping John tightly. "Llewelyn has incited Wales to revolt. Your castles burn, your men are slaughtered."

"How dare they! We took thirty more of their sons hostage last year." John broke the embrace, resuming the haughty posture of outrage that had dominated him three years ago but which he had put aside in favor of cooperation since the excommunication.

"Highness, no," Hugh protested. He could almost see John's mind working, his umbrage at the presumption against his divine right to rule, his need to lash out violently against those who opposed him; the destruction of logic in his mind.

"You must punish them, Highness. You must show these insolent princelings that they cannot rebel," Blakely urged. His eyes narrowed their focus into the king's.

Hugh almost saw a flash of midnight-blue light pass between the two men. He shook his head free of the illusion.

"We have no choice." John said. "The hostages must hang. All of them. Earl Hugh, see to it."

Chapter 49

Huntington Castle

MY mundane practice weapon clanged against Robin's. The echoing rings filled my ears, blotting out the sounds of a crowd watching me cross swords with Robin. I met his next blow a little low, throwing me slightly off-balance. To recover, I spun in place, shifting my grip to parry his next thrust at shoulder level.

His eyes widened in surprise and a hint of respect at my unexpected maneuver. A smile spread through me. His superior height and weight gave him the advantage. I hoped only to defend, as he had taught me. A month ago he'd have disarmed me by now. A month ago I sparred with smaller men, less skilled men. But now Robin had deemed me worthy to challenge him.

I ignored the sweat on my back and brow. Soon I would have to confront a much fiercer enemy. I knew not how or when, but since the Solstice Excalibur hummed louder in the back of my mind all the time, even while I slept. An enemy awaited.

I pushed myself to meet the next thrust off to my left. Robin sought to upset my balance with that blow, to wear me down and then surprise me with a quick flip of his wrist. His men at arms and knights had broken my two-handed grip on my sword with the same tactic many times over the last three years. This time I had held my own longer than either of us expected.

Suddenly a child's laughter rang through my mind. Hetty leaned over the staircase that led to the first floor Hall of Huntington Castle. Through her eyes I saw Robin tense his back muscles in preparation for raising his sword in an overhead blow.

I caught him in mid swing. He stepped back a little awkwardly. Not much. Just enough for me to step forward. I initiated the next move.

Hetty laughed again. The last barrier in my mind broke apart. I *knew* Robin's next move, saw it before he began it.

I no longer felt the weight of my weapon. It melded with my hands and arms, becoming an extension of my thoughts, moving in a design I saw in Hetty's mind but did not yet feel in my muscles.

The world hummed in harmony with the presence of Excalibur.

The last barrier of reticence crumbled within my mind. No more would I merely defend, allowing victory to those who sought to protect me—if they could. No more would I depend upon others. When the time came for me to use Excalibur, I would be on my own. If I hoped to survive, if I ever hoped to win Hugh's forgiveness, if I wanted any of this, then I had to become the aggressor.

Parry, thrust, swing, dance forward, duck, thrust again. Backward I drove my sparring partner. Robin fought to remain upright under my assault. He parried my moves and lost ground with each defense.

I leaned into my next thrust, shifting at the last moment to a twist. With a ringing clash, Robin's sword flew from his right hand. Before it landed in the dust, I leaped to plant my right foot squarely in the center of his chest.

He went down heavily. I landed astride him with the tip of my sword at his throat.

Both of us panted and sweated, waiting for the other to move.

"I yield, milady. I yield!"

Hetty laughed again. I joined her.

"Mama, we did it!" Hetty cried as she pelted down the semi-enclosed steps into my arms.

"Yes, Poppet, we did it." I hugged my daughter lightly. Then I whispered, "But your part must remain secret. We talked about this before."

Henrietta Carlotta nodded seriously. I ruffled her blonde curls and set her down again.

"Thank you, Robin, for a lesson well taught," I said as I extended a hand to help him up.

"I never taught you that last move," he replied, dusting off his clothes. Bright sunlight shone on the gray streaks in his auburn hair. His eyes shone with pleasure and speculation. "Where did you learn it?" he asked. He stooped and caught Hetty into his arms. When the three-year-old rested comfortably against his shoulder, he draped his other arm around me in a familiar gesture.

I had accepted long ago that I would marry this man. Only the church, or rather the lack of one, kept me from his bed. I liked him, enjoyed his company, even found him attractive. But I did not love him. Not like I loved Hugh. Would I ever be comfortable making love with Robin?

This I knew for certain: Never again would I succumb to my passions outside of marriage. I would gladly die for Hetty, and I wanted more children—many more children. But not out of wedlock, not until the church allowed me to confess my sins and partake of Eucharist at a nuptial Mass.

Secretly I hoped that Hugh would return and forgive me. But that was a fantasy I cherished only in the dark moments between midnight and dawn when Excalibur nearly shouted with alarm and nothing else could push aside my fears.

"Ahhem!" A newcomer cleared his throat.

I tore my loving gaze away from my daughter and the man who behaved as if he had fathered the child.

Hugh Fitz Chênenoir, Earl of Bellecôte sat astride his massive, ill-tempered warhorse, just inside the gate. His wolfhound Coffa stood beside him, relaxed and laughing but still guarded. Hugh gathered his reins and made as if to return whence he had come. A black scowl covered his face and shadowed his aura.

"Hugh, come back." Ana's voice rose over the sound of Hugh's break-ing heart. Why had he expected anything from her but more betrayal, this time with Robin Locksley.

He reined in Orage. He couldn't do anything else. Coffa pranced around Ana's legs as if greeting a long-lost friend. The traitor.

"Coffa, come," he called impatiently. The dog sat on Ana's foot and looked at him strangely, as if questioning his sanity. Maybe he did.

"Your mission must be important if you came yourself," Earl Robin said.

Resigned, Hugh heaved himself off the horse, signaling his men to do the same. He would not linger here. He needed to ride to Belle-côte. Now. Before John could follow him with troops and warrants and more murder in his heart.

"Blakely is returned, and the king listens to him," Hugh said. "John has ordered the murder of his Welsh hostages in retaliation for their fathers' rebellion." None of his churning emotions colored his tone. He longed to fling himself back atop Orage and gallop out of here. Away from the intimate family scene he had interrupted.

The sight of Ana kept him frozen in place. Three years had added roundness to her figure, removed some of the worry lines from her eyes, given her an air of purpose and strength. Her barbaric Saxon braies and jerkin showed her long legs and luscious breasts to advantage. He'd forgotten how tall she stood, always thinking of her as petite and vulnerable. She'd stare King John in the eye and stare him down with stubborn courage and strength now.

Jesu! How he longed to hold the length of her against him one more time.

He loved her more than he thought possible with each passing moment.

She had betrayed him. She had borne John a daughter and kept the child close. She had used him in a disgusting pagan rite. She betrayed his love again by becoming Robin's mistress.

How could she? The cold knot in his gut turned to burning rage. Heat flooded his face and his fists balled.

The little girl laughed again. Her infectious mirth rang around the bailey. The muscles in the back of Hugh's neck and shoulders loosened. His stomach eased. The toddler turned her brilliant smile on him. He knew the urge to answer her grin with one of his own.

He fought it while he studied the child. Blonde curls as golden as her mother's and the Griffin midnight-blue eyes betrayed only half her heritage. Her chubby arms and legs gave no clue to her eventual height and bone structure. A sturdy and happy child, so unlike his Johnny who had been sickly and thin from birth.

His heart ached anew for his lost boy. Why should Ana and John be blessed with a healthy bastard daughter when he had lost so much?

His fist balled again. Why should Robin embrace her as if he truly belonged at her side, as if they were lovers, or worse, *married?*

"I'm Henrietta Carlotta Griffin. Who are you?" The child

squirmed for release from Robin's arms and ran the last few yards to greet Hugh without ceremony.

"I am Sir Hugh Fitz Chênenoir, Earl of Bellecôte." Hugh crouched down closer to her level.

She bobbed a clumsy curtsy. Hugh refrained from steadying her as she wobbled on the upward movement. He remembered Johnny's easily injured pride at that age.

"Mama says you are a friend." Henrietta studied him with a frank stare.

"Yes. I do believe I am a friend to this house." In that moment, the anger burned out of him.

"I see Hetty has worked her magic on you, Hugh." Ana smiled, just like her daughter, and held out her hands in greeting. "Dear Hugh. Welcome. Even if you bear sad news, you are very welcome here."

Hugh rose slowly, taking the few moments of stretching his muscles to regain his emotional balance. Ana welcomed him as if she were the chatelaine. What was her position in this unusual household? Mistress? Wife? Honored witch?

"Aye, welcome," Earl Robin echoed Ana. "I am remiss in my duties as host. It seems milady usurped more than my dignity in that little skirmish." Robin rubbed his backside.

"You have trained her well," Hugh admitted. "She anticipated your every move."

"She learned that all on her own," Robin replied. "Come, you must be thirsty. We will have your news over ale, then a bath before we sup." He gestured for the crowd to disperse to their duties. The entire household scurried away.

Except for Ana. She looked at the ground, at the walls, at Orage, but not at him.

"May I pet the horse, Mama?" Henrietta asked. Her gaze seemed glued to the massive destrier.

"You must ask the horse, Hetty. If I remember correctly, he likes his chin scratched," Ana said lightly.

"He's foul-tempered . . ." Hugh began.

"He's a bully who needs to think he's in charge. But like all bullies, he has his weaknesses," Ana reassured Hugh.

Hetty stared at the horse a moment in absolute concentration. Miraculously, Orage dipped his head and consented to be scratched on the chin, the only part of him Hetty could reach. Ana paid attention to the horse's ears in the precise spot Hugh used to persuade the animal to cooperate. He'd suffered many bites and kicks learning where Orage would tolerate being touched.

Coffa finally consented to come to his side. Hugh scratched the dog's ears a moment; felt their pricking beneath his fingers at the same moment a deep-throated growl erupted from the dog's throat.

Newynog erupted from the stable in a mass of fur and drool and bared teeth.

Hugh used to think Ana's dog huge. Now Coffa topped his mama in height at the shoulder by several inches as well as in breadth of chest.

Coffa spread his legs, bristled his neck ruff, and growled again, asserting his dominance over the female. He'd never done that before. Usually Coffa assumed a dominant position among lesser dogs by simply ignoring them. In the three years Hugh had the dog, Coffa had never challenged another dog. Only another wolfhound would dare attack his mass.

Newynog launched herself at Coffa, neatly wrestling him to the ground with her jaws fitted loosely on his throat. Coffa rolled onto his back and whined like a puppy, submissive and . . . and happy about it judging by the grin on his face and the near frantic wagging of his tail.

"Well, that issue is decided," Ana laughed. The two dogs stood and shook. Drool flew in a dozen directions. Then they pranced off together, mother firmly in control of son.

"Come, we have much to discuss, Hugh. We'll leave the ladies to their pets," Robin urged Hugh toward the keep. A young knight, a near mirror image of Robin, joined them.

"I will join you," Ana announced. "Meredith, see that Hetty stays out of trouble."

The young woman who rushed to gather Hetty into a tickling embrace also bore a strong resemblance to Robin.

"Begin with the return from the dead of the king's half brother. Are you certain 'tis him and not an imposter. After four years, memories dim, people change." Robin directed Hugh to the high table.

Ana followed, not exactly meekly but not imposing her presence upon them either. Hugh's confusion over her place in the household grew.

" 'Tis Radburn Blakely, a little older. Other than that, precisely as I have seen him a thousand times over the decades. He never aged before. But he has now. The years have been hard on him."

Ana crossed herself. He caught the glint of gold-and-ivory beads around her neck, beneath her shirt. She retained the prayer beads and cross of Arthur Pendragon. "Blakely's demon blood keeps him looking younger than his true years. Something must have occurred during the last years to interrupt the flow of energy from the demon. Perhaps it is a weakness we can exploit." She sat, straddling a bench like a man, and crossed her arms atop the table. Her face scrunched as if she thought long and hard.

"Tell me John's orders about the hostages precisely. Perhaps we can intervene before . . ." Robin began.

"The deed is done." Hugh allowed the silence to stretch between them. He needed time to keep the lump in his throat under control. "John ordered me to do it. I refused and earned the king's extreme disfavor. Now I must ride posthaste to Bellecôte to secure my castle and the hostages I protect."

"Who . . . who carried out the hanging?" Ana choked out.

"William Longsword, John's half brother and the only earl who sits in council with him now." And keeper of the Bellecôte sword. Hugh was glad he and Lincoln had pulled off the deception, making the king think the blade Excalibur, but he chafed that *his* sword rested in another man's hands. He touched the hilt of his father's sword, his battle sword. No one would ever take that from him.

"And John has only one bishop. The rest of his intimates are commoners, mercenaries, and servants. They command few if any troops," Robin mused. "The Pope will rally to our cause. We must issue the call to arms now. Time to dust off Excalibur, Ana. You demonstrated today that you are ready to handle it. We'll have the church back and a new king. This time the barons will have a hand in the selection. This time we will control England."

"And who will control the barons when the barons control England?" Ana asked.

Chapter 50

THREE days later, seven barons had assembled at Huntington to plan the end of King John's reign. They waited only for Eustace de Vesci of Northumberland and Robert Fitz Walter of Dunmow in Essex. Not once in those three days did Robin comment that with the potential lifting of the Interdict, we would marry. Clearly, I held less significance to him than the demise of his old enemy. I was but a tool to him, as I had been to Blakely and King John.

Either that or he recognized that with Hugh returned I could not marry another.

But a stony wall of silence remained between Hugh and me.

In those three days of waiting, Hugh avoided me, as much as anyone could avoid another in the cramped quarters of a castle. We danced around each other, never speaking of the questions that rose to our lips every time we looked at each other.

He learned that I had always slept with Meredith and the other ladies in the solar. That knowledge did not seem to weaken the barriers between us.

The scrap of parchment with his simple statement of love crackled beneath my breastband every time I moved.

At last I cornered him in the stable, where he spent most of his time. He groomed Orage so frequently, the horse's hide was due to develop ripples in the pattern of the brush's bristles. His tack gleamed and still he oiled and cleaned it. His squires, who should have tended to these chores, had been dismissed. They practiced with Robin's sons at the archery butts, or trained with the knights, leaving Hugh in solitude.

Hetty chatted gaily to Hugh while he brushed his horse yet again.

She filled the stall with her laughter. Hugh smiled and nodded but remained stoically silent.

"Henrietta, time for your nap," I called softly. At least I wore a bliaud today, light linen the same color as my eyes. Hugh had heard and surmised enough about me to disapprove without the unflattering Saxon clothing I adopted during training. The court would label me barbaric for wearing braies of any kind. Civilized men and women wore robes.

"But, Mama, Sir Hugh is lonely. He needs me. . . ."

"How did she know?" Hugh asked, whirling to face me.

Orage nickered at the sudden lack of attention.

"I will keep Sir Hugh company for a while, Hetty. Meredith is looking for you in the solar."

Marion had married the previous year and moved to one of the smaller estates in Huntington. Both young women had spent nearly as much time mothering my daughter as I had.

Hetty looked as if she would protest her temporary exile from Hugh's company. I touched her mind with my own. She yawned and shuffled out of the stable without further protest.

"She is your daughter. That is how she knows my moods before I do. She has your magic," Hugh said quietly. He turned away from me rather than face the questions between us.

"She is also the daughter of King John." I swallowed my pride and spoke of things I had buried deeply and hidden from all but Robin. "I allowed myself to be seduced by a powerful man who promised to destroy the betrothal agreement between Blakely and myself. I also sought to break Blakely's controls over John through magic. A magic that can only be achieved by—intimacy.

"But when Blakely took matters into his own hands and married me by proxy in Scotland without my knowledge or consent, John applauded him for his boldness and agreed to let the marriage stand. My magic wasn't strong enough to counteract Blakely's. Anyone else would face trial and execution within the hour for flaunting the king's orders so blatantly."

A huge weight left my shoulders. A storm might follow between us. I could weather that. As long as I kept the truth between us, I could withstand his fury and his distrust.

Hetty had already wormed her way into his heart. Dare I hope he would put aside his previous vow never to raise another man's child?

"King John, the child, I might learn to forgive you those in time. But you used me in a pagan rite in that faery circle. I meant nothing to you that night. . . ."

"You meant the world to me that night. Yes, I used you. I used you to grab a few happy memories to cherish in the long lonely nights that followed. Whatever else, I had that night to hold in my heart." I fought the tears of regret and loneliness that threatened to choke me. I needed to be strong now. If we forged a bridge across our hurts, I needed to know he forgave me truly and did not merely rush to rescue me once more.

"What of Robin? When did you become his mistress?" He turned his back on me, resuming his vigorous strokes of his horse.

"If you must believe that, then we have nothing more to talk about." I turned on my heel and marched back toward the hot July sunlight. Thunder and driving rain would ease the heaviness in the air tonight. But nothing could lighten the heaviness in my heart.

"Ana."

The simple sigh beneath his call stopped me in my tracks.

"Where did we go wrong, Ana?"

"I'm not sure that we did go wrong. The fates conspired against us."

"Can we talk."

"We just did."

"Talk in earnest about what is in our hearts. About the why behind our actions. About what we can do to be together always."

I flew into his arms, holding his heart close to mine until they beat together in the same rhythm.

"Somehow, we must keep other men from falling in love with you, Ana," Hugh said around a huge smile.

"They do not love me, they love my sword, my name, my connections, and my land," I replied. I could not keep the bitterness from my voice. His grim expression made me amend my statement. "Except for you, Hugh. You loved me when you thought me a nameless peasant fleeing the fires at Mendip Mor Castle."

He smiled again and kissed me. The lonely ache I'd carried inside me since those brief days together at Bellecôte four years ago dissolved.

We kissed. We laughed. We talked.

My heart swelled to near bursting with love for him.

As his hand dropped to cup my bottom and draw me close against him, I stiffened. "We mustn't love. Not yet. Not until . . ."

"Mama! Mama." Hetty hurtled into the stable. That child could not move slowly or with less than her full energy. "Fitz Walter and his friend is come. They need you in the Hall," she proclaimed at the top of her lungs.

"I have let her run wild too long," I groaned. She knows nothing of manners or discretion.

"She is delightful, what every child should be. She is what I wished my Johnny to become, what our other children will have to live up to." Hugh crouched to stop Hetty's lunge by entrapping her in a playful hug. They fell into the straw together, laughing and tickling each other.

"Hetty, let Sir Hugh up. We are needed in the Hall," I said as sternly as I could, though I wanted nothing more than to join them in their affectionate tussle. Even Orage moved aside, with a disdainful snort. He looked at me with a condescending sigh.

Good thing the dogs were elsewhere or we'd never get to the conclave of barons.

The three of us walked back to the Hall holding hands. Hetty swung between us, making a game of all in her life's encounters. I wished her entire life could be as carefree; that she could afford to trust as innocently as she did now.

Instinctively, I fingered the chain of prayer beads in my pocket as I made my wish. Perhaps the Holy Mother would listen to my prayer for my daughter, if not for myself, sinner that I was.

The cool dimness of the Hall brought instant chill to my flushed face and skin. Hetty sensed more than just the cool air trapped within the massive stone walls. She loosed Hugh's hand and clung to my leg, impeding my walk toward the dais where the barons hunched over the high table consulting maps. Few of them could read or cipher, but they had learned maps along with battle tactics almost before they could walk.

Once more I touched the cherished scrap of parchment within my breastband. Its familiar crackle made me smile at Hugh. He returned my wondrous grin.

He had sacrificed much time and effort to produce that simple message from his heart.

Robin looked up at our approach and signaled us to join them. He did not reach to hold me against his side as had been his wont a few days ago. I had lost importance to him now that he had a war to plan. I had fooled myself into thinking any woman could replace his beloved Marion.

Best I end his plans for our marriage as soon as possible. But in private.

"John has diverted his planned expedition from Scotland to Wales," one of the two newcomers said, Eustace de Vesci, the stern northern lord who resented every move John made. "Softsword will cross the pass here. Blakely was most certain of this plan." He pointed to a chain of mountains indicated on the map.

Blakely! Was I the only one in the room who had heard him? No one else seemed overly concerned that the king's half brother gave information to the king's enemies.

"We will go with John and ensure he dies when Llewelyn ambushes him," Fitz Walter, the second newcomer, said. He raised his gaze to each of the men around the table. A fanatical gleam in his eyes chilled me more than the room. The source of the unease Hetty and I both sensed came from him.

"What makes you so certain Llewelyn will attack at this pass, Fitz Walter?" Robin asked. He held the man's gaze, challenging his fervor with practicality.

"My spies are the best in the world," Fitz Walter replied. He did not back down from the earl's challenge.

"More like, Blakely has kept them both informed of when and where," I whispered to Hugh. "Blakely thrives on generating chaos. Fitz Walter's fanatical hate of John makes him vulnerable to Blakely."

"I do not fully trust him either," Hugh muttered back. "But he commands great resources in London and Essex, as well as large numbers of men and arms. Do I sense you believe Blakely orchestrates both side of this campaign?"

I nodded. Hetty scuttled off to a far corner with Newynog and the newest batch of puppies. Coffa now stood defensively at Hugh's side. They did not trust Fitz Walter any more than I did. So much for my prayers.

The other barons cheered and promised each to be the one to deliver the killing blow to John.

"We need a core of dedicated men to remain behind," Eustace de Vesci said quietly. "They will have the most important job."

Silence met his words.

"I will lead the men who seize the treasury at Winchester and eliminate John's heirs," Fitz Walter continued outlining the plan. "Blakely will meet us there. He plans to become regent, but we will leave no minor heir for him to rule for."

"No," I breathed. "You cannot murder innocent children." *You cannot trust Blakely!*

"John murdered innocent children," Fitz Walter replied. He stared at me as if I wore the rags and bells of a leper.

"The Welsh boys were hostages. Their fathers violated the treaty. The fathers forfeited their sons' lives. John has the law on his side no matter how hideous his version of justice. To murder more innocents as punishment is a hideous mockery of justice! It is anathema to God and to men." Anger rose up in me. Power tingled in my fingertips. I could blast them all with a bolt of witchfire. Instead I curled my fingers inward, pressing until my fingernails drew blood. If I ever hoped to stop these men, I must retain their trust.

"John violated every rule of chivalry when he murdered twenty-eight innocent young men and boys," de Vesci insisted. His eyes gleamed with the same fanaticism as Fitz Walter's. They both nearly frothed at the mouth with their vehemence. "We cannot allow John's bloodline to continue. We will have no more Plantagenets on the English throne."

Hugh and Robin both stared directly at Hetty. John had other bastards, known to all and married honorably and parents of more Plantagenets.

"And you do not violate those same rules of chivalry by cutting down your king from behind!" I shouted.

"The Pope has nullified our oaths of fealty. John is no longer our king. We owe him nothing. We owe England a king who governs with his head and not with his cock!" de Vesci replied hotly.

"Ana, you of all people must know the necessity of assassinating John," Robin argued. He alone remained calm.

Blakely's chaos ran rampant among the shouts and arguments around us.

"John has robbed us of Holy Mother Church, he has corrupted our wives, and driven us deeply into debt with his obsessive and useless campaigns to regain territory on the continent." Fitz Walter leveled his burning gaze upon me.

I dared not flinch, though I sensed his condemnation, because I, too, had been "corrupted" by King John.

"I understand your need to murder John," I replied as calmly as I could. "God knows he has earned our wrath. But I cannot countenance the murder of his queen and children."

"Nor I," Hugh echoed my sentiments. I almost sagged with relief that he stood with me on this vital issue.

"You have no choice but to agree, milady. We will do the deed. We do not ask you to wield a weapon." Fitz Walter pounded the table with his mailed fist. "We ride to war against our king tonight."

"You ride without Excalibur or the blessing of The Pendragon of Britain." I stood firm, twisting the signet ring on my thumb so that all could see the dragon rampant. John must be warned. The queen and her children must be protected. I harbored rebellion in my heart, not murder. Even John made a better king than these bitter, violent men.

"Ye'll do as ye're ordered, woman," de Vesci spat at me, drawing his sword and holding it level with my throat. His men at arms crowded close to me.

I smelled the blood lust on their sweat. They needed to kill someone, anyone. Now.

Blakely's accent colored their thoughts.

In the blink of an eye, I grabbed a sword with my mind from the nearest man. Hugh unsheathed his own weapon. We stood back to back ready to defend ourselves.

Newynog, get Hetty to safety and do not leave her no matter what happens to me!

Coffa took up a defensive stance over the pups as my dog grabbed Hetty by the back of her gown and dragged her screaming toward the bailey.

Parry, thrust, lunge, shift grip, kick out, parry yet another man crowding in on the first.

Hugh and I fought our new enemies together.

My skirts hampered my movements, keeping them shallow, primarily defensive.

I opened my mind to the man I engaged. He overcompensated for a bruised rib from a tavern brawl. Three blows and I had maneuvered him to expose that vulnerable side. Slash, thrust. Blood sprayed my midnight-blue bliaud. The hem was already dirty.

My opponent's pain slashed through me with equal intensity.

Behind me, Hugh lunged and ran his man through.

His death clouded my perceptions, dragging me into darkness with him.

I gagged, nearly doubling over in my shared agony.

De Vesci disarmed me with a laugh.

Hugh dropped his guard and stooped to support me.

"Tie him up. Get her out of here, lock her away," Fitz Walter ordered.

De Vesci half carried me to the solar and dropped me onto the stool beside the loom. "Stay where you belong, woman," he sneered.

He slammed the door and bolted it behind him.

Chapter 51

I SAT and shook for quite some time. I had sorely wounded one man. Hugh had killed another. I could not divorce myself from their pain and their passing.

Eventually my mind stopped circling. My vision cleared a little, and at last I was able to think through the situation.

Blakely had returned. I had known he would. Deep down, I had known that he did not die four years ago in the Lincoln cellar. My own reaction to wounds and death just now reminded me sharply that I had felt nothing when Excalibur backlashed Blakely's spell. He'd been stunned, had the wind knocked out of him, robbed of his magic probably, but he had not died.

I had accepted John's pronouncement as truth. I would not make the same mistake again. Next time I would make certain I killed Blakely myself.

If I could kill anyone. How could I play God and steal another person's life? I wanted to roll into a fetal ball and hide from the real world for the rest of my life.

I had to go on. For my daughter, for Hugh. I had to work to make England safe for my daughter. Fitz Walter and de Vesci had pushed me onto a new course of action.

Before I dissolved into a puddle of tears and trembling whimpers again, I shed the bloody bliaud and threw it into the fire.

I chose my clean clothing with care for what I must do next.

A tap on the solar door roused me from my concentrated packing. The persistent hum of Excalibur in the back of my head almost drowned out the true sound of knuckles on wood.

As long as I put all my effort into folding clothes into a saddlebag, my hands did not shake and I did not waver from my resolve to warn John of the rebels' plans.

"Enter," I called, kicking my bag behind the loom. Beneath my clean linen chainse and bliaud I wore my hose and braies. I'd only need a moment to shed the skirts and don a jerkin.

Meredith entered with a tray. The smell of savory food preceded her into the room. My stomach grumbled in response to the aromas. How could I be hungry? I had wounded a man, and Hugh had killed another.

Behind Meredith, Father Truman slipped into the room, not much more substantial than a shadow. I nodded briefly to him and turned my attention back to Robin's second daughter.

"I brought you supper," she said quietly, keeping her eyes on the floor. She flipped the cloth away from the bread, cheese, ale, and mutton stew on a trencher. The stew and ale alone would make a hearty meal for a big man. She'd packed the extra bread and cheese for a journey. Her idea?

I raised one eyebrow at her, but she did not reply. "Thank you, Meredith. I did not think they," I jerked my head toward the Hall where men still argued loudly, "would remember to feed their prisoner."

"Does this mean you will not marry Father?" she asked shyly.

"Aye. I'll not marry him now." No need to tell her I had made that decision before defying the rebellion.

"I'll miss you, Lady Resmiranda." An hour ago she had called me "Ana." She deposited the tray on a low table and fled, not bothering to hide her tears.

"I'll miss you, too, Meredith," I whispered my reply.

With the door solidly closed behind her, and bolted again, I looked up into Father Truman's steady gaze. "You are supposed to be at Kirkenwood."

"Benedicte, Lady Resmiranda." He smiled at my total lack of greeting or manners. "I am but recently returned. I go back again tonight. At full dark. Hetty will be safe there with me and my family." He walked to the arrow-slit window and examined the stonework with minute care.

"Hugh?"

"Tied to a chair and yelling his opposition to every plan they put forth until they gagged him. Hugh is a capable tactician and finds flaws in their proposed actions as well as their motives. They muzzled his dog as well. Robin persuaded them not to shoot it with a crossbow."

"Do they need Hugh?"

"Some do. Fitz Walter and de Vesci listen only to their own inner demons. They have plenty of their own reasons for craving John's death. If Radburn Blakely is manipulating them, he does not have to work very hard. The disputes among them almost guarantee disaster."

"Earl Robin?"

"Mostly silent. Thinking. Something weighs heavily on his conscience. For all his rebellious youth, he always stopped short of murder."

"Hugh and I will need fast horses, saddled. Outside the postern after full dark. Newynog and Coffa will guard them until we can claim them." At the end of July, the nights remained very short. We'd need every minute of darkness to make our escape. With luck we'd be in Coventry by noon, Chester by midnight tomorrow. If we pushed our mounts and ourselves to the limits. Newynog would not want to leave her pups. But they were nearly weaned. No danger in leaving them.

"I'll see to the horses. Archie and Hugh's other men are locked in the cellar. They already plan their escape. I will direct them to Nottingham and thence to Chester. How will you deal with the bolt?" He looked meaningfully at the closed door.

"I am a Griffin. No lock ever invented could keep one of my clan prisoner. Too bad we can't lift our own bodies as easily as a bolt. I'd have escaped John's oubliette a lot easier."

"And what of you and Sir Hugh?" Something about his tone, the wariness in his eyes told me something was amiss.

I raised my eyebrows and let him think what he would.

Father Truman smiled. "I look forward to presiding at your wedding, milady. When the Interdict is lifted, of course. And you have settled the matter of the marriage by proxy to Radburn Blakely and bought off Earl Robin's betrothal contract . . ."

"Blakely," I said flatly. "I'm not certain I can deal with him. With luck, John will see sense and make peace with the church. That should divert some of the energy behind this rebellion. I'd rather annul the marriage through the church than . . . than . . ."

"You must counter the influence of Radburn Blakely with our king no matter the cost."

"I know. I don't know how to do that yet. I do not know if I can kill him, or any man. But I know that only I—with the aid of Excalibur—can kill the demon spawn."

"Then you must find political ways to stop him."

"I need help. Will you join me in Chester once my daughter is safe?"

"You will know what to do when the time comes. My presence will only attract unwelcome attention to Kirkenwood and Hetty. Trust your instincts, Resmiranda. Trust your heritage. Trust your magic." With those final words he stared at the closed door.

I heard the bolt shift once more. He escaped as silently and unnoticeably as he had entered.

Radburn Blakely caressed Fantôme's cheek with a delicate finger. The boy shuddered and flinched from the light touch. Radburn's loins grew hard relishing the boy's humiliation and disgust. He'd fight being penetrated again. A few lashes from the whip would make him scream but accept Radburn's ministrations.

Poor Fantôme. He lusted after women. Perhaps the time had come to allow the boy a tryst with one of the scullery serfs. That way he'd not likely forget his true manhood. Possibly sire a child to pass his talent on to a future generation. Then he'd fight Radburn all the more.

"Tonight, my boy. Tonight you shall be my lover," Radburn whispered. He kissed his fingers and passed the caress onto Fantôme's lips.

Fantôme spat into the rushes.

Radburn laughed out loud.

King John lifted his head from his maps and his supper. The campaign to invade Wales progressed ponderously. Radburn savored every moment of John's final days as king. Not long now. The rebellion was progressing nicely, better than the campaign against Wales.

He sipped lightly of the fine wine Ranulph of Chester provided. After four years of rough living in a cave, eating and supping only the most meager supplies he could steal, he relished every mouthful.

Warming to his game with Fantôme, he allowed the boy a small mouthful of wine, presenting the cup so that his slave must drink from the precise place that Radburn had.

"We will split our forces and cross the border here, here, and here." John stabbed the parchment map with his greasy table knife. "My daughter tells me that Llewelyn is holed up here." John nodded to his illegitimate daughter Joan.

Strangely, her husband, the rebellious Llewelyn himself, had sent her home to Papa for safekeeping. She was supposed to travel on to Winchester to join the queen's household. John kept her close at his side, never trusting her out of his sight.

Radburn made certain John trusted no one. His extreme fear of betrayal pushed him into more radical actions.

"There is a narrow defile here. A few men traveling single file could penetrate all the way to Llewelyn's stronghold undetected," the Earl of Chester said. He traced the route with his own knife. By the end of the meal, the parchment would be unreadable.

"I would meet mine enemies in open battle," John stated firmly.

"Oh, come now, Brother. Don't lose the war on a matter of chivalry and honor. Go for the kill and be done with the problem," Radburn said airily. "You did it with the hostages."

Joan blanched and sobbed into his kerchief.

John tapped his teeth with his knife tip, clearly contemplating the possibility of quick assassination over open battle.

"I need a clear victory to suppress the other princelings," John said decisively.

As Radburn knew he would. His other set of plans needed that battle to end John's tyranny over England and begin the more chaotic tyranny of the barons. Radburn planned to be in Winchester with the queen and the next king of England before the battle even started. John's son and heir, Henry, would need a strong regent. The first man on the scene to grab the treasury and the heir had the best prospects of continuing to rule in the boy's name. Especially if Fantôme and his magical talent with fire took care that Queen Isabelle did not interfere with the new government.

John had used the same ploy in 1199 to keep Arthur of Brittany from grabbing the throne. Good thing Ranulph of Chester had divorced Arthur's mother, Constance, dowager Countess of Brittany, or the formidable earl would have opposed John instead of supporting him. Now he made a business of selling his loyalty. John and Ranulph both knew the conditions and terms of their alliance. They dealt well together.

Radburn wondered where, besides the Exchequer he could put his hands on the enormous sum necessary to buy Chester's loyalty away from John.

The herald pounded his staff against the flagstones at the entrance. "Your Royal Highness, my Lord Earl, Gentlemen and Ladies, Sir Hugh Fitz Chênenoir, Earl of Bellecôte, and Lady Resmiranda Griffin seek audience," he proclaimed with a very smug smile.

"Resmiranda!" John shouted. He stood so quickly his throne tilted backward.

Radburn leaned back in his own chair, eager to watch the show.

"You are dead!" John added. He crossed himself twice, paused, and repeated the action. "You are dead."

"I live, Your Highness, as does the man you accused me of murdering. And I bring you dire warning of a rebellion. Those who hid me these past four years now plan to slay you from behind in battle and murder your queen and sons. They may already be in Winchester, carrying out their schemes." Lady Resmiranda stalked to the high table as she spoke. Her long and determined strides matched her masculine clothing. She radiated strength and purpose.

Radburn lusted after her more than he did Fantôme's slim body.

Joan, the king's bastard daughter and wife to Llewelyn of Wales burst into tears—again. She ran from the room sobbing uncontrollably. Her actions gave credence to Resmiranda's words.

"Wife, I rejoice that you are returned to me!" Radburn rose and held out his hands in greeting. He had to get her out of here and deflect her truthful statements.

Radburn's words and gesture checked her forward movement, as he planned. She shut her mouth with an almost audible snap. The fool, Fitz Chênenoir, almost bumped into her. The foul dog that always followed her growled deeply and bared her teeth. As did the twin monster at Fitz Chênenoir's heels.

Radburn bared his teeth and growled back. The dogs retreated behind mistress and master.

The Hall erupted into chaos.

John stood silent and still, staring at the woman.

"If you wish my goodwill, the goodwill of The Pendragon of Britain, and my continued loyalty, you will deny the validity of that man's claim upon me and mine," Resmiranda spat. She flashed The Pendragon's ring on her thumb. The venom in her voice would have poisoned a lesser man. Radburn's magician senses detected the crackle of energy in her aura.

She'd lost none of her magic in the last four years. Indeed, he suspected she'd practiced and honed her talent. Victory would be all the sweeter when she succumbed to his powers and he sacrificed her to the ancient gods of blood, war, and death. With her death, the demon door would open and he'd allow Tryblith, the demon of chaos, to feed upon her wonderfully firm flesh.

"For now, the rebels ride without the blessing of The Pendragon of Britain." She stood tall and proud, facing her king, challenging him. She stepped closer and touched John's hand, the barest whisper of contact but enough. John's aura was cleansed of Radburn's control.

"Swear on the bishop's Bible that what you say is true!" John said at last. "Swear it, and we will see that the marriage by proxy in a foreign land, without our consent, is declared illegal by the laws of man and God." He gestured his pet bishop forward.

Des Roches nodded vehemently as he proffered his missal, the closest thing to Holy Writ in his immediate possession.

"Highness, no. You promised her to me. You promised." Anxiety made Radburn's hands tremble. The weakling would ruin everything by making his own decisions. He shouldn't be able to. Radburn had to reestablish eye contact with his half brother, now, before he succumbed to the witch's spells.

"Highness, I will swear on the relics of the saints, in any cathedral, or on any Holy book you choose. Only move quickly. You must protect the queen and your sons. You must protect yourself." She knelt before the bishop and placed her hands upon the missal.

"She's a witch, Highness. She'll lie," Radburn whispered into the king's ear. "She is my wife. You promised me that."

"Oh, shut up, Radburn. Chester, take Fitz Chênenoir and your men to Winchester, now. Tonight. Ride all night. Save my sons from the assassin. Save my boys. And now Lady Resmiranda, you have a lot of explaining to do. In my privy chamber."

John took Resmiranda's hand and led her to the small chamber behind the dais. As she left Fitz Chênenoir's side, their hands touched, fingers lingering as long as possible. A poignant display of their love.

"You die, Sir Hugh," Radburn muttered. He stalked in John's wake toward the solar. John must make no more decisions without him.

The dog tangled in his feet, slowing him down.

John slammed the door in Radburn's face, bruising his nose.

Chapter 52

"YOU survived, Ana. We prayed that you would. I prayed that some-one would find you." John clasped me close and placed his head on my shoulder. He wept.

I did not return the embrace, though a perverse part of me longed to hold him, share his thoughts and his body. I had loved him in a way.

He fathered my child. My beloved Hetty who even now giggled inside my mind.

"You may have prayed that someone found me, but you ordered my dog killed and you told no one what you had done to me. You just let me disappear, along with Radburn," I said without inflection.

John lifted his head but did not release me. "You have every right to hate us, Ana. But you have returned to us, hale and whole. You must love us a little to break with the rebellion."

"I was one of them until they decided to murder innocent chil-dren. Bad enough that you hung twenty-eight Welsh hostages. You had political reasons." I nearly spat my words. Politics. I hated the manipulations of politics.

"You had the law on your side," I continued. "But for the rebels to murder your sons, not in retaliation or even legal or moral punish-ment, but as a means to eliminate opposition to their own candidate for the throne . . . I could no longer follow them." I kept my hands at my sides and my emotions buried deep within me. I stated facts only.

"You have come back to me. That is the important thing." He dropped the royal "we" and became once more, the funny, intelligent, likable man I had almost fallen in love with. "Did you bring me the sword, the magical sword?" He squeezed me tightly again.

Any longing I had for him froze. He only wanted my sword and my blessing as The Pendragon. I would use both in my quest to bring peace and unity back to Britain. I did not have to give myself as well.

"I thought you gave Excalibur to William Longsword of Salisbury."

"A carefully perpetuated hoax. We knew Fitz Chênenoir could not have brought the true sword to us. He would have returned it to the Lady of Lake. But we had to make a show of claiming Excalibur and the right to wield it on behalf of England." His hands ran up my arms to my shoulders. His thumbs caressed the underside of my jaw.

I stared at him blankly, feeling nothing at his intimate caress.

"You could not touch Excalibur yourself," I corrected him. "That is why you left it at Lincoln. The sword was not given to you by the Lady of the Lake. Only I can wield it, and the sword will determine which battle I will fight."

His hands returned to my arms and shoulders, testing the muscles I had built over the last three years.

"Who leads the rebellion, Ana? Who must we fight to regain the safety of our kingdom? Together, you and we make a formidable pair. The King and The Pendragon, riding together with Excalibur. Who could doubt the righteousness of our cause?"

"Pope Innocent III." I avoided naming the conspirators until I knew John would do what had to be done to unite England behind the crown and the church once more.

John released me and paced to the window and back, hands behind his back, once more the restless tactician.

"The rebels shout their loyalty to Holy Mother Church as the justification for their war against you and your family. You can defeat them in battle, but you can only win this war if you reconcile with the church," I said.

"We cannot, Ana. The struggle has gone on too long."

"You must. You and your pride must bow to the church. One by one, every monarch in Europe will bring war against you. One by one, every man in England will welcome them. At first, they did not miss the church. But now, after four years, they feel the loss. They need the Sacraments. They need the church. They need a king at peace with the church."

"You believe this will end the rebellion?" John turned troubled, vulnerable eyes on me. I could fall into the depth of those dark eyes.

I could believe the myths he wove behind those eyes. I knew the truth, not the myths.

"The rebellion will wane for a time. But the barons chafe under your authority. They want more control over their lives and their fortunes. Use the time God and the church grant you to bind them to you once more."

"What more must we do? We need all our barons loyal. We need to keep Wales under control. Ireland is near going up in flames again. Our lands on the continent remain in French hands. Advise us, Pendragon—Ana, my love. Tell us what must be done."

John's reversion to the royal "we" convinced me that he truly asked for advice as a king, and not just as a prideful and suspicious man.

"Recall the Marshall from Ireland. Send emissaries and gifts to the Pope. Seek council among your barons—and heed it."

He swallowed deeply, closed his eyes, and sighed.

"We would meet with the leader of the rebels. Privately. Can you arrange it, Ana? We need to know what they desire of us. We need to know if we can set these matters straight."

"It is possible." I thought furiously. "This may take a little time. Messages cannot go directly. There must be an intermediary or two. Widely distant."

"Do it. Do whatever you must to arrange it. But make certain the meeting is private."

I nodded.

"Stay with me, Ana." He held out his hand to me.

"No. I will stay at court, but I will never warm your bed again."

He opened his eyes and stared at me. "Was I so unpleasant a lover?" A sensuous smile replaced the worry lines around his eyes.

I returned his gaze, steady and calm, not the least interested. "I ask your blessing to marry Hugh Fitz Chênenoir. I *will* remain faithful to him because I truly love him. To you I must remain only the Baroness of Kirkenwood and the heir to the Griffin heritage." I inspected the Pendragon signet ring I wore on my thumb. We both knew the ancient significance of the dragon rampant.

"We must first annul Radburn Blakely's presumptuous marriage by proxy." John resumed his pacing, hands behind his back, head jutting forward in belligerence.

"More reason for you to reconcile with the church."

"While We await these momentous events, you must promise us that you will bed no man. I will not have the issue of your marriage clouded by a consummation of the marriage or an affair with Fitz Chênenoir."

"Or an affair with you."

After a long pause he nodded his head once, decisively.

I closed my eyes and swallowed my regret. *Soon, Hugh. We will be together soon. But first we must wait a while longer. What is a few more months when we have waited three years and more?*

"Very well, Highness. I will abide by the laws of the church and take no man to my bed until the truth of this travesty of a marriage to your half brother is settled. But you must do all in your power to reconcile with the church and make peace with your barons."

"Tell me, first, were you truly pregnant four years ago as Radburn hinted? Did you bear me a child?"

"Will you reconcile with the church?"

"You may help us write the petitions."

"Will you swallow your pride and work with the barons?"

"We have already requested you arrange a meeting."

"I miscarried a few hours after Sir Hugh rescued me." A bright chiming laughter echoed in my mind. Hetty was truly safe.

"Stay," I commanded Newynog as I dismounted outside the faery ring above Huntington Castle. Mists surrounded this hilltop refuge. The sounds of three horses munching on the rough grass, of bridles chinking, and two other riders shifting uneasily in their saddles distorted eerily in the fog.

Only King John and Hugh accompanied me to this clandestine meeting. The court had been left in Nottingham. Another horse and rider had followed us and secreted themselves farther up the hill. I intended for Radburn Blakely to hear what transpired here. But he would not be able to interfere. I must ensure that.

I took a deep breath and stepped between two stones, slightly larger than the majority of those making up the ring, taking care to place both feet in the little stream of water that ran between the rocks. Immediately, my skin began to tingle with power. A faint green line of energy touched the top of each stone. I proceeded to the triangle of boulders at the center and the source of the creek.

Carefully I climbed atop the flattest of the trio and stood facing the entryway. In my barbaric Saxon braies and chausses, with a hooded jerkin and my hair unbound, a sense of freedom accompanied the power that built within me as I made mental contact with each of the stones.

"Highness, you must enter by the avenue at the east," I said softly.

"And if We do not?" John shifted his shoulders and stiffened his spine. He had solicited this meeting, yet he fought me every step of the way.

"If you step over the stones at any other point, this cloak of isolation will tear. Every man, woman, and child in England will hear the words spoken here today." An exaggeration.

I heard him dismount and hand his reins to Hugh. He placed his feet carefully on the slippery bank of the stream. He slipped and landed heavily in the water, bathing a lot more of himself than just his boots. He cursed and passed into the ring. I directed him to stand before one of the boulders in front of me.

Moments later the sounds of a man walking up the indirect path from Huntington Castle whispered to me on the breeze. I recognized the stride of a man practiced at moving silently through forest and field. Robin, Earl of Locksley.

Hugh and John made no indication they heard Robin's approach. They both jumped and reached for weapons as he stepped out of the mist.

"The eastern gateway, milady?" Robin asked as he bowed ever so slightly in my direction. His gaze never strayed to John.

I realized that I presided here in the role of priestess of this pagan circle of magic over two lifelong enemies. A role Uncle Henry and even Deirdre of the fading hut had prepared me for. I lacked only a staff, but I did not think I would comfortably use one again.

"Aye, milord."

Robin looked at the creek and sighed heavily. He splashed into it and moved up beside me impatiently.

"You will both lay your weapons upon this altar. I will have no armed conflict."

John looked at me, mouth half-open, as if to protest. Then he glared at Robin.

The Earl of Huntington unbuckled his sword and lay the sheathed weapon across the top of the boulder by my right foot. He added the longbow he habitually slung across his shoulders. John mimicked his action on the twin rock.

"And the daggers." The men eyed each other warily before pulling blades from concealed sheaths beneath their cloaks.

Newynog sat up, ears alert. I snapped my fingers impatiently. Newynog lay down, head up and ears alert but no longer on guard. Coffa did the same.

"And the rest," I commanded.

Boot knives, wrist knives, an ax and a crossbow—a crossbow beneath John's cloak?—joined the growing pile of weapons.

Hugh chuckled in the distance, and I sensed he relaxed, no longer concerned for my safety with these two volatile men. Newynog rested her head on her paws.

Only when I believed the two men naked of lethal weapons did I raise my arms and whisper an ancient prayer in Welsh—I had studied that language more closely these last three years. I turned a complete circle as I murmured: "Blessed creator of life, grant these men peace in their hearts as they come together, seeking peace in the land."

Green fire shot from my fingertips to each of the stones, connecting me to them and them to each other in a glowing chain of magic. The mists outside the ring rose up in a solid wall, blocking out the rest of the world.

I could not find Hugh or Newynog with my mind and almost panicked. Bright, chiming laughter whispered across my mind. Hetty. Fear flowed away, replaced with a unique double vision of the inside and outside of the circle. I caught a hint of Newynog joining the joke of illusion within the fog that the three of us shared and the poor mundanes could never understand.

John and Robin gasped as the mist thickened and swirled. Faces seemed to form in the fog, the faces of watchers of old who presided over this meeting as much as I did.

Both men crossed themselves anxiously.

"You have nothing to fear," I said, jumping down from my altar stone. My voice echoed strangely in my ears as if the dozen watchers all spoke through me in a single voice.

Robin and John crossed themselves again. They stepped a little closer to each other, seeking comfort in the solid presence of another earthly warrior against forces they did not understand. I smiled at the first hint of accord between the two men in two decades of hostilities.

Since 1194 when Richard returned from the Crusades and sent regent John running into temporary exile, John and Robin had met only once, on the day Robin swore fealty to John as king, reluctantly, and then only when all hope of putting Arthur of Brittany on the throne had failed.

"You have both agreed to this meeting."

John nodded.

"I did not like that you used my daughter as an intermediary, Lady Resmiranda. I would keep my children free of this conflict," Robin stated forthrightly.

"Meredith was a willing participant. Indeed, she suggested this meeting place, at this time," I reprimanded his complaint. She probably watched the proceedings within a scrying bowl in Deirdre's hut.

Did Blakely have a scrying bowl with him as well?

"What do you rebels want?" John cut through the preliminaries. "What will bring your loyalty back to us?"

"Your death."

I allowed a moment or two of heavy silence before speaking. "I do not expect compromise from your coconspirators, my Lord Earl. I do expect *you* to be reasonable."

Robin sighed. "The barons of England want their rights restored, as you promised in your Coronation Charter." He avoided addressing John by title, name, or honorific.

"Where is this charter written?" John asked. " 'Tis not law, but merely suggestions to gain the support of those who would divide England with opposition."

"We want the rights that have always been ours and you whittle away with each tax, each fine, every levy of scutage for campaigns we find useless."

"Who decides which war is useless? Always the king and only the king. You all swore loyalty and military service to us!"

"We have rights!"

Impasse.

"Your Highness, you wish for a written copy of promises?" I intervened.

John nodded, knowing full well that the only written copy of his informal address to the assembled barons on his coronation day thirteen years ago would be in the hands of chroniclers; men who could and often did change the petitions to suit their own prejudices.

"After thirteen years, men remember only what they want to remember. Who is to say what I promised?"

"Another charter exists."

Both men stared at me in stunned silence.

"An older charter. The one made by Henry I upon his coronation." Frantically, I reviewed the books and scrolls I had read from Uncle Henry's lair. Such a document existed. What did it say?

"I have heard of this charter. The barons were most enthusiastic about it when *his,*" Robin gestured toward John with a vague wave of his elbow, "great grandfather assumed the throne upon the death of William Rufus," Robin said quietly.

"If I can produce such a document, will you and the other barons who rebel against King John's authority accept it?"

"I do not know," Robin replied sadly. "This rebellion has taken on a life of its own. Men join the ranks for no reason other than to satisfy their restlessness and vague unease over events."

"Why do you seek compromise, milord?" John asked. For the first time I noticed a parting in John's firm refusal to compromise.

"In all the times you and I have clashed, I have never countenanced murder. Theft, bribery, trickery, yes, even poaching when I and my men were starving. But never murder, especially the murder of innocents."

"We remember a time when you would have cheerfully murdered us. We still bear the scar of your blade on our throat," John sneered as he tilted his chin to reveal a thin white line beneath his ear.

"You held Marion hostage, threatened to hang her."

"Not us. The Sheriff."

"You were always one to cast the blame for your mistakes on others. Fitz Walter may be right. . . ."

"Fitz Walter betrayed us. He surrendered our castle prematurely, without permission. He had the supplies, weapons, and men to hold out another week until we could relieve the siege. Why should we ransom a traitor from our enemies? 'Tis his own fault if his ransom beggared him for a time."

"I trust Queen Isabelle, young Henry, and Richard are safe?" Robin replied.

"Aye. They thrive, no thanks to you. They are hidden and heavily guarded lest you and Fitz Walter and the others try again to murder."

"I will not countenance murder!" Robin nearly shouted. "Your wife and sons live because I managed to delay Fitz Walter and de Vesci until Ana had a chance to warn you and take defensive action."

"For that I thank you." John's eyes softened a tiny bit. He replied as a husband and father, not as an affronted king.

I jumped into the argument before they could find more to disagree upon. "Are we agreed, that if I can produce a copy of Henry I's Coronation Charter, you, King John, and you, Robin Locksley, will seek compromises based upon those ancient rights *and responsibilities* of barons?"

The two opponents glared at each a moment then replied almost in unison, "Aye."

"We shape our future for the better," I assured them.

"I fear, Lady Ana, that some men will never seek the future when past glories, that exist only in their own minds, seem more attractive." Robin bowed his head sadly. "Some men will never compromise."

"You must make them see wisdom in compromise, Robin." I touched his arm in genuine affection. If I had never met Hugh, never let my heart weave a pattern of love and life with him, I could have been happy with this man.

He placed his hand over mine and squeezed it.

I clasped John's fingers with my free hand. For the moment I bound the two rivals together in common purpose. How long would it last?

"Trust each other!" I ordered them as if I could erase a lifetime of distrust between these two men and centuries of distrust between the barons and their kings.

"Trust yourselves," I implored them, as well as myself.

Chapter 53

Sunday, the ninth day of July, the Year of Our Lord 1213, fourteenth year of the reign of King John Plantagenet. On the road to Winchester.

THE clash of my sword against the blade of my enemy sent shock waves up my arms to my shoulders. The ring of metal hacking at metal drowned out the hum of Excalibur meeting its destined challenge.

A peculiar brightness tinged the edges of my vision. Radburn Blakely's blue/black aura reached out to drown my own life energy. Sweat poured from my brow despite the coolness of the demon cave. Fatigue weakened my knees.

I tried to disengage my blade from his. He laughed and tangled my dying weapon tighter. He drew me closer, closer. His foul breath, tainted by demons and carrion filled me with nausea. I had to break free. He laughed again.

Every fiber of my being froze.

Tryblith, the demon of chaos, gibbered into my ear. My thoughts spun. My body quaked. My soul withered.

I woke with a scream choked off by my sudden awareness of other women in my pavilion. The sparse light of glowing embers in the brazier gave me a point of focus.

My shoulders ached as if I had truly engaged Blakely in mortal combat.

My dream had not yet come to pass.

I still had a chance to remove Radburn Blakely's influence from King John's council by political means and compromise. How long before the dream came to pass? How long before I was forced to choose between killing another human being or being killed by him?

I wrapped my arms about myself and clenched my teeth. I had never been able to change the essence of a dream of portent before.

I rose from my pallet and drifted silently to the ewer and basin. The cold water on my face banished the last tendrils of the dream fabric and replaced them with cold logic.

Blakely's fetid breath still permeated my senses. He slept in another tent close by. He whispered into John's ear through his dreams.

Each morning during this last year John awoke determined to contradict every compromise he had reached the previous day with Papal Legate Pandulf and Archbishop Langdon.

Every morning I forced myself to touch John with my bare hand. He gazed into my eyes, and I watched the cloud of anxiety and betrayal fade. His warm gaze would engage mine.

I risked falling in love with him again when he did that. But I could not forgive him for what he did to me. I did not trust him with my life or that of my daughter.

But these were emotions I kept hidden behind a smiling face and political expediency.

John had made progress toward reconciliation with the church this past year. We had made progress toward ending the rebellion led by Robert Fitz Walter and Eustace de Vesci. Earl Robin had backed away from the other leaders. I suspected he still supported them with men and arms and money while remaining quietly away from them.

When the rebels declared their followers the army of God, John countered by promising to go on a Crusade, making England a papal fief. Any rebellion against him risked excommunication from the church.

The rebels countered by seizing a shipment of new minted coins that would have helped fund the Crusade. They could only have known of the shipment if someone on John's council had told them the time and the route. John declared them outlaw and placed a huge reward on their heads. They demanded the right to choose their own regent during John's proposed journey to the Holy Land.

I knew they would choose Blakely—he'd compel them to do that.

And while I must remain close to John's side, I could not escape to Kirkenwood to search for Henry I's Coronation Charter or to see my daughter.

During all this, the negotiations with the church continued in an equally volatile nature. John offered the Crusade in return for the right to nominate the Archbishop of Canterbury. Innocent III accepted the Crusade and offered absolution for the murder of hostages, but not the royal right to select bishops.

Each time the dispute with the rebels came close to ending, the one with the church would flare. The last year had passed in tumult and lonely despair. John had to swallow his pride too many times. He needed my cleansing touch more and more frequently. I wondered how long it would be before he ended all of the talks and responded with a call to arms.

I threatened to retire to Kirkenwood, taking Excalibur and the symbols of The Pendragon with me every time he considered initiating civil war. John backed away from aggression under my threats. But he refused me permission to leave court. When I reminded him that he had confirmed Kirkenwood and me as baroness independent, he turned a deaf ear and continued to hold possession of the barony hostage. The last time I packed to leave him, he issued an edict of Praecipe—Kirkenwood was forfeit until the dispute of possession was settled.

I almost left court for good that day without permission. But I could not. England needed me to keep John sane and logical. As Pendragon of Britain, I had to stay by his side, countering Blakely's black influence.

So I pressed John with logic. I wrapped him in protective charms against Blakely's sorcery. I touched him often.

The Marshall came back from Ireland and assessed the military situation with sighs of resignation and rolling eyes. He set to work without delay.

It all came down to the morrow. Tomorrow in Winchester John must settle the final agreement with the church or lose everything. The papal legate and the archbishop threatened to return to Rome unless John complied on the morrow.

And through this all, I watched Blakely gnash his teeth at each hint of progress. He could not allow John to reconcile with the church and succeed in his plans. His eyes betrayed his frustration. His attempts to get me into his bed became more blatant.

I never told Hugh of the three times Blakely had tried to ambush me with rape in mind. Every time I had managed to escape, with

Newynog's help. One time I had screamed so loudly, physically and mentally, I summoned three armed guards who owed me favors.

As Blakely backed away, he warned me that my refusal to consummate the marriage was my death warrant.

I feared that if ever Blakely did manage to rape me, his sorcery would negate every bit of good I had accomplished so far.

I refused to contemplate the consequences if he managed to poison my soup or stab me in the back with his wicked vorpal blade.

Next Sunday, Archbishop Langdon would formally accept John back into the church in a solemn ritual at Winchester Cathedral—provided John made the final concessions tomorrow.

Yesterday, Robert Fitz Walter and Eustace de Vesci had rallied their troops and attacked a royal stronghold north of Winchester, between the king and his meeting with the archbishop in the cathedral. Hugh's timely intervention with troops kept the delay minimal. We would arrive in Winchester on time, but would John sign the agreement? Hugh and the Marshall chased the rebels westward even now, keeping the road safe for the king and his rendezvous with the church authorities.

Hugh had spent most of his time this last year in the field, hounding the rebels, trying desperately to counter the forces that worked toward tearing England apart.

I saw him for a few hours each month and little more. If we had any more time together, I was not certain I could honor my vow to stay out of his bed.

With each passing day I missed Hugh more, ached for a glimpse of him, the sound of his voice, a hint of his unique masculine scent.

I still kept the cherished scrap of parchment he had written next to my heart.

In all this long year, I had not seen my daughter at all. But every time I missed her, I had only to reach out with my mind and hear her bright laughter. I knew she was safe. That had to be enough.

Archbishop Langdon and Papal Legate Pandulf refused to hear my petition for annulment until after John's official reconciliation and the return of the church to England.

My dream of portent pounded in my head. Had I seen my own death in that dream? Had I seen my own death before next week's ceremony and my chance to be with Hugh forever?

More likely I had seen my death before John signed the final agreement. If I did not cleanse his thoughts in the morning, Blakely's influence would win.

I splashed more water on my face. The fetid stink of Blakely's breath seemed to permeate the air. I was surprised none of the other ladies in the pavilion had roused to protest the stench.

I pulled on a plain white bliaud and a plainer green cyclas, my normal court dress. I would not wear the colors or crest of any man, not even the griffin rampant with bears at each corner, for Blakely wore that crest openly. He claimed Kirkenwood as well as me.

Never.

Perhaps if I immersed myself in one of the scrolls or books I kept with me for study, I could banish the lonely sense that I faced my own death. Soon.

I opened a huge tome at random. Aunt Lotta's neat writing in the margins drew my attention.

> *Burn the entire rope of a hanged man within a pot of newly fired clay. The pot must be fired alone, without being tainted by pots to be used for other uses.*
>
> *When the rope has been reduced to ashes, dilute with my own urine and the blood of the demon's victim. Stir three times widdershins with a silver spoon.*
>
> *Use this paste as a medium to define the pentagram of both the working space and the place of containment.*

The spell went on to define a long list of herbs to burn as incense, the number of drops of water, how to light the fire, and a chant that would seal a portal against all but the strongest of magics.

Beside these precise notes, the text of the book listed demon after demon, its characteristics, attractions, weaknesses, and preferred prey.

Tryblith, the demon of chaos was underlined in blood.

I stared at the black/brown smudge of dried blood beneath the name for long, endless moments.

Tryblith.

Aunt Carlotta and Uncle Henry had devised this spell to contain the demon that had invaded Uncle Henry's body on the night of Samhain so many years ago. They had locked it behind a dragon portal deep in the Mendip Hills within a cave that was fronted by an ancient barrow.

Blakely's grandsire was the demon Tryblith. He thrived on chaos. A very strong and determined demon.

I should have known. I should have seen the clues every time we met. Blakely would never allow John to reconcile with the church or the barons. He would never stop his campaign to gain power by keeping England in chaos.

I shuddered, knowing Blakely would murder John and seize the heirs rather than allow this reconciliation. Once firmly established as regent, he'd murder John's sons and crown himself king.

King of Chaos.

Under his reign, civil war would prevail, leaving England open to invasion from France, from the Holy Roman Empire, from the Vatican.

The King of Chaos would preside over blood and death and torture.

I saw it all clearly, as if the events played themselves out before my eyes in a scrying bowl.

If exiled, Blakely would return again and again. If imprisoned, he'd break free. No oubliette was deep enough to contain him.

No compromise. No logic. No choice.

Blakely must die. Only a person with strong magic and stronger determination could prevent him from following through with his plans.

I had to take Excalibur and murder Radburn Blakely. Or die trying.

Today. For the kingdom, I had to challenge Blakely today.

But first I had one last thing I must do.

Hugh stalked the perimeter of his camp. He nodded to each of the pickets and greeted them by name. On the far eastern edge he directed his men to move closer together for a better view of a thicket one hundred yards away. A few words brought three more men to patrol and watch. He listened to the song of insects and nightbirds as twilight dimmed to full dark. The moon was only a day or two short of full on this July night. He could see shadows within shadows. Any flicker of movement stood out in sharp contrast to the soft silvery light.

He wondered what Ana was doing at this moment at court in Winchester. In nearly a year of negotiations with Pope Innocent III, Ana had not left the king's side. Nor had Radburn Blakely.

Papal Legate Pandulf had arrived in England last February to negotiate John's reconciliation with the church. And still Eustace de Vesci and Robert Fitz Walter rebelled. Huntington had gone to ground, never leaving his lands.

Hugh had harried the rebels from one end of England to the other in the course of that year. Better to live in the field with other fighting men than to sit idle at court, watching letters being written, clauses argued, and nothing happening. Better to be in the field than watch Ana every day touching the king with her gentle cleansing touch and not be able to touch her himself. Better to dream of her rather than burn with jealousy as John and Radburn vied for her attention. Both sought to claim her influence and her body. Hugh had to trust her to keep them at arm's length. Their brief times together only made him long for her more.

Meanwhile he kept the rebels on the run. Tomorrow he would spring his trap. Tomorrow de Vesci and Fitz Walter would either make new oaths of fealty to John or sail from England into exile.

"I miss you, Ana. I miss your smile, your laughter, your logic, and your warmth. I want to be with you and Hetty forever," he whispered to the stars. He'd seen Ana's daughter last month when his trail of the rebels had taken him north. Her laughter had dimmed a little. She missed her mama as much as he did. But she still bounced around the village of Kirkenwood, delighted with each new day and discovery.

The familiar night noises of three hundred men settling down to supper and campfires and bedrolls, soothed Hugh. This was where he belonged. He'd lived the life of a warrior since he'd turned fourteen.

He'd had many regrets since leaving his father's castle that day. The loss of Johnny was chief among them. But his deepest, most painful hurt was that he and Ana could not be together. Not yet anyway.

Next week perhaps. After the return of the church to England.

"I miss you, beloved."

"I am here, Hugh."

His incredible longing for her must have ignited his imagination. He had not really heard her.

"Look at me, Hugh. I am real. I am here."

Hugh whirled in the direction of the voice. Hope nearly choked him. "Ana?" he breathed. "How did you get through my pickets? What are you doing here, so far from Winchester?"

"No one can see me when I choose invisibility, you know that. What you really need to know is why am I so far from the king." She smiled bitterly with only half her mouth.

He opened his arms to her. She clung to him with fierce hands and muffled sobs. He couldn't hold her close enough. He wanted to cry, too.

"I could not stand our separation any longer, Hugh. So I ran away with only Excalibur and Newynog as companions." The dog trotted into the circle of light cast by Hugh's campfire. She plopped down, panting. Coffa snuffled her ears, then joined her on the ground.

Longing sent fire to Hugh's loins. He cherished a moment longer the possibility of finally loving her.

"Archbishop Langdon has arrived in Winchester," Ana continued. "He will not hear my petitions for annulment from Blakely's unorthodox marriage by proxy until after the ceremony of reconciliation. He will not acknowledge that he or the Pope received my earlier petitions. I fear that you and I will never be able to marry."

Something else troubled her. He could see it in her eyes. Something more dire.

"Hush, beloved. Tears will do nothing but make you more beautiful and irresistible than before. My patience is strained, too." He forced himself to hold her away from his body. Her warmth ignited fires he dared not allow to burn unchecked.

They must wait.

"Must we wait any longer for the ponderous wheels of the church, Hugh?" Her breasts strained the jerkin she wore over her chainse and braies. He longed to bare them to his gaze and his hands.

Hugh closed his eyes and gulped. " 'Twas your decision, love. I agreed. We want the blessing of God and the church a well as the king upon our union."

Something odd penetrated his senses. If only Ana did not swamp his awareness of the camp with her scent, her voice, her presence. She opened her mouth to speak again.

He hushed her with a finger to her lips.

Damn! She sucked his fingertip. How was he supposed to listen, to seek whatever seemed out of place? He watched Newynog and

Coffa. The dogs should sense an unauthorized presence before he did. Newynog pricked her ears and wiggled her nose. She growled.

Coffa echoed her.

They warned but did not attack. Someone they knew and distrusted but had been taught to accept.

Blakely?

A rustle in the underbrush that did not belong on this still night. The scent of a man sweating heavily with acrid overtones. Hugh opened his eyes to study the outlines of twigs and bracken that had not been this close to camp ten minutes ago. One branch protruded oddly.

Not a branch.

"Duck!" he said even as he pushed Ana to the ground and drew his sword. Time seemed to slow, each instant passed in agonizing clarity.

A stinging burn penetrated his left shoulder. His mind registered an arrow sticking out of his upper arm even as he heard the whir of it flying.

Then the force of the bolt almost knocked him to the ground.

"Intruders! Alarm!" he cried as the pain began to numb his mind. He stumbled back to his feet and charged the tangle of shrubs. His sword met air and wood.

The assassin had fled as silently as he had come.

Men swarmed around him in noisy pursuit. He gritted his teeth against the pain and resheathed his sword. "Ana!" He had to make sure she was safe. "Ana!"

"Here," she called, rushing toward him as his knees collapsed. He fell into her arms and safety.

Chapter 54

"DRINK this." I handed Hugh a large mug of brandywine with a dose of distilled poppy juice. He had nearly passed out as his men moved him into his tent. Blood soaked his shirt, his blanket, the ground where he had lain. I had to work fast to remove the arrow and end his blood loss.

My mind had gone cold and logical. When this was over, when I knew Hugh to be safe I'd tremble and cry.

I trusted no one else to see my love safe and well. I gathered the two camp medics close to assist.

"What is this?" He looked at me skeptically.

"Something to deaden the pain." To demonstrate how much he needed the drink, I ripped his shirt away from the arrow shaft.

He bit his lip through rather than yell. I daubed his bloody mouth with a clean cloth. "I have to take out the arrow. Fortunately it has penetrated the fleshy part of the upper arm. I do not believe it has touched the bone or any of the major arteries. Your quick actions saved us both."

"I've had numerous wounds over the years. I need none of your concoctions," he muttered.

"I love your stubbornness," I said, kissing his mouth. "But this is going to hurt a lot. Don't be a martyr, Hugh."

Live and go on when I am no longer here. Make sure Hetty grows into her potential.

"I want to be awake. I need to think. Someone followed you through my guards, in the wake of your shadow." His skin grew paler, more clammy. "He was well cloaked. The dogs barely detected him."

I knew who, the moment he said the words. "Newynog did not

raise the alarm. She has grown used to the man's scent." I barely heard my own voice over the hum of Excalibur. It had grown louder since Langdon's arrival. Louder yet since my dream of portent. My final confrontation with Radburn Blakely neared.

"If you won't drink the brandywine, then bite this." I handed him a wooden block.

"Only brandywine?" His eyes took on the glazed quality of a man fighting for consciousness. "I do not wish to demoralize my men. They must not hear me scream."

I nodded rather than lie about the poppy juice I had added to it. He gulped the mixture down and took the wooden block that should keep him from biting his tongue. "Save the fletching," he murmured sleepily.

"I recognize the pattern of feathers." Four years in the Locksley household had taught me more about archery than I thought possible. "Four feathers rather than three. The blue/black feathers of a raven. It came from a crossbow. The assassin could crawl on his belly and remain hidden." Radburn or his shadowy servant? Either could have crept unseen through the picket lines in my wake. Either could have shot the crossbow at Blakely's command.

He and I both knew that one of us must die before John's final meeting with the church leaders in the morning.

How many nameless, faceless, people had fallen to his vorpal blade since that scene beneath the streets of Paris? How many more would die if he won the coming duel?

At least two a year. Blakely's voice laughed in my mind. *A death to celebrate each Solstice. A death to give me life and youth and power. The next death will be yours!*

If the forces of Chaos triumphed, de Vesci and Fitz Walter would make sure John died. John's will specifically named William Marshall regent for his son Henry. Blakely and his demon guide would not survive long under the rule of the Marshall. The greatest knight in Christendom would have to die as well.

My dream had told me that Blakely planned to kill me. Soon. He'd just tried once and failed. He was less likely to fail next time.

I drew a deep breath of resolve, knowing what I had to do.

I poured more wine over the wound. Blood mingled with the wine and ran freely into the pallet beneath Hugh.

Hugh blanched and clenched his teeth on the wooden block. Before he or I could lose our courage, I rolled him to his side. I probed the wound with my mind and found what I feared most. The arrowhead had penetrated bone. I needed to divert it to the side or risk cutting it out of him. Neither option pleased me. I needed all of my strengths for the tasks ahead of me.

Newynog leaned against me. Her own strength and blind faith in me gave me an extra measure of confidence. Coffa whined at Hugh's head, out of the way but still present and worried.

"This is just like opening a lock. Move the arrowhead up and to the left with your mind," I told myself. At the cost of trembling limbs and a blinding headache, I let my mind "See" the movements more precisely than my fingers could feel. Moving metal through flesh was not like shifting lock mechanisms through air. More blood spurted from the wound. Too much blood. Hugh moaned loudly and almost lost the wooden block in his mouth.

I leaned on the arrow shaft until it broke free of his body.

Hugh passed out.

The camp medic rushed forward to break off the arrowhead. The moment I heard the wood snap, I withdrew the shaft in one long smooth movement. Another medic doused the entry and exit wounds with more wine while I grabbed a white-hot iron from the fire.

If I stopped to think what I must do, I would never have the courage. Hugh did scream as I touched the wounds with the poker. The smell of burning flesh nauseated me. I wanted nothing more than to crawl into a corner with Newynog and vomit. But I had to watch, had to judge the precise moment when the bleeding vessels became cauterized, before I burned too much flesh.

If only I had a stronger healing touch! I could dissipate bruises, strengthen soft tissue, give vitality at the cost of my own. Nothing but white-hot metal could stop the bleeding of major vessels. Nothing but time and immobilization could mend broken bones.

If I had a maiden and a crone to help me? No time to search them out.

No time for regrets. I had to recover my senses and follow Radburn Blakely.

"Give him more poppy juice when he rouses, along with lots of watered ale. Fluid and sleep are what he needs most. And immobilize the shoulder in a sling," I told the medic. I needed Hugh asleep and not interfering with my task.

Good-bye my love. Remember me kindly and raise my daughter with love. I kissed his lips one last time and slipped out of the pavilion.

Radburn slapped Fantôme soundly. "How could you have missed!" he screamed. "You had her heart in your sights. Miserable fool." He slammed his fist into his slave's gut. The boy doubled over, gagging.

His wretchedness did nothing to alleviate Radburn's anger.

"Fitz Chênenoir is sorely wounded. He won't be able to spring his trap tomorrow. The rebels have another chance to disrupt John's ceremony in Winchester," Fantôme choked out.

"That is no excuse. His men know the tactic. They'll follow through with the plan. Resmiranda has to die. She has to die tonight. Otherwise she'll convince Langdon to annul the marriage. She'll make sure John goes through with the reconciliation. How can I create chaos with her interfering every step of the way? How can I serve my grandsire while her life seals his portal? I must serve my grandsire." Lightning crackled from his fingertips. He set fire to a tree just to release some of his pent up energy.

The old oak exploded with flames. The heat drove him backward. He drew more of the energy of destruction into himself.

"There is nothing for it. I must kill her myself. Make certain she follows me to the demon cave. I want to be there to absorb the demon the moment she dies and the portal seal dies with her." He threw the last order over his shoulder as he mounted his horse. He never questioned that his faithful slave would obey him. He'd set the chains of fear and humiliation deeply into place.

"Where is she!" Hugh bellowed. He searched the tent for signs of Ana's presence. Not even a whisper of Newynog's scent said they had been here. He struggled to sit up. His shoulder burned, ached, and shot sharp pains into his neck and back all at the same time. "Breathe deeply," he commanded himself. "Slow deep breaths to control the pain." He repeated the chant over and over until he could bring himself upright without passing out again. Coffa pushed against his bare chest with his cold wet nose.

Hugh fell back again, too weak to resist his dog's orders. After three deep breaths he struggled upright again.

"Milord, you must remain still. The wound still seeps," one of the medics said. He rushed to Hugh's side and tried to force him back against the pallet.

"The wound be damned. I have to go after her." Hugh batted him aside. He had to put his head between his knees to keep the black stars in his vision at bay.

He met the stony stare of an outraged dog.

"The—the lady—uh—merely seeks rest and privacy," the medic stammered.

"I know her better than that. She's gone after the assassin." Hugh dared raise his head a few inches. Dizziness swirled around him but did not overwhelm his senses. He reached behind him for the remnants of his shirt. Useless with one sleeve slit from neck to cuff. But a clean one lay in the chest four long paces away, on the other side of the pavilion.

"Help me dress. Order my horse saddled. I'll take Coffa. He's the best tracker in camp." He staggered to his feet and across the tent. A table supported him until he had the stability to open the chest.

What seemed like hours later, he heaved himself onto Orage's back. The beast must have learned a few manners over the years. He actually stood still long enough for Hugh to mount with the aid of two squires and a mounting block. His sword rode comfortably at his hip once more. He didn't trust Ana's magic or her magical sword. Hugh trusted himself and his own expertise.

Chapter 55

I DIDN'T need daylight to track Radburn Blakely. I had Newynog. I also had Excalibur. The magic within the sword nearly shouted with glee as I turned my horse west toward the barrow and the demon cave outside of Wells. Blakely needed the demon of chaos to disrupt the ceremony of reconciliation next week. "Why hasn't he absorbed the demon before this?" I asked Newynog.

She just turned her head back at me and laughed. Her drool flew from her beard as we raced through the night. Something in her manner told me I should know the answer to my question.

I touched the mind of my mount with my urgency. He sped onward through the night without faltering. Dawn glowed pink on the horizon before I sensed the horse's true fatigue. I eased my control over it and allowed it to walk along the Roman road until the rooftops of Wells met my gaze. In the distance I heard voices raised in song. The cathedral canons practiced for Sunday's ceremony and the official return of the church to England. They could finish building their glorious cathedral, a soaring hymn in stone to match the beautiful voices they cultivated.

Five years had passed since Hugh and I had ridden through here after fleeing Mendip Mor Castle. Did I dare take the time to beg a meal and a fresh horse from John Howard's inn?

I halted the horse and sat a long moment, thinking. What kind of preparations would Radburn need and how long would they delay him? He'd need food to fuel his body; something—or someone—to sacrifice to the demon; fire, a pentagram . . . I did not know what else he'd require.

I needed food and rest myself. Better that small delay and a tiny chance of survival than walking into a death trap exhausted and depleted.

Oh! Why had I allowed that man to live all those years ago as I stood naked over him with a sword at his throat? I should have killed him. Or let him die rather than divert the knife that nearly took him in the eye.

But if I had killed him or let him die by another's hand in my presence, I would not have been true to myself, I would never have learned the true value of life. Could I take that same life now?

I had to.

Could I prevent my soul from following my victim's into death?

No matter. His death had become more important than my life.

Best I prepare myself as fully as I knew my enemy would prepare for me.

John Howard remembered me. He fed me and offered me a bath. I was just about to refuse when Hugh rode into the courtyard, reeling and cursing.

"Give him something to drink, and rebandage that wound. He's bleeding again. And keep him here!" I ordered John Howard. The moment Hugh dismounted, I threw myself onto my own horse. He'd not climb aboard Orage's tall back soon.

I couldn't leave him like this. My dream had been too vivid.

"I love you too much to let you come with me, Hugh," I said as I dismounted beside him.

"Let me protect you, Ana." He held my face between both of his hands.

I looked up, memorizing every feature, scar, and worry line. "Take care of my daughter, Hugh. Father Truman can teach her about the Griffins and magic and history. But I trust you to love her as your own." I rose up on tiptoe to kiss his cheek.

"You will live. *We* will live, Ana. I'll not raise another man's child by myself," he whispered with the hint of a wry smile.

He shifted at the last moment, capturing my lips with his own. We lingered together, long and bittersweet. One last moment of bliss.

"Archie and I will go with you. As we began this adventure," he said firmly.

"Forgive me, Hugh." I slammed my fist into his jaw, knocking him into Archie's outstretched arms. "Take care of him. He'll know when it is safe to come for me, if I do not return on my own."

Coffa licked Hugh's hands solicitously.

"Stay," I ordered Newynog.

She whined and paced an angry circle. The look of bewilderment and hurt in her eyes nearly made me relent.

"Guard him, Newynog. I need to know that you will live, that you will give one of your pups to Hetty." Without looking back, I kicked the horse into a gallop. If I looked back, I would relent and keep my love and my familiar close at my side. If I looked at them again, I'd give up my quest and allow Blakely victory.

If I looked at him one more time, he'd see my tears and nothing would keep him from coming with me to his own death and mine.

"Today, Grandsire. I promise she will die today." Radburn caressed the dragon boss on the demon portal. A familiar gibbering in the back of his mind reassured him. Success was at hand. Four years he had waited for this day. Four years of knowing that Resmiranda lived and countered his every move.

No more. Today she died at his hand.

"Gather firewood, Fantôme. Enough for a bonfire." He dismissed his slave while he sorted through the chunks of obsidian he had imported at great cost from Constantinople. Impatiently he chipped the largest into an edge sharper than any metal knife. When he cut his finger just testing the edge, he smiled in satisfaction.

"With my blood I bind thee to my will," he murmured in Greek. Best he use the language native to the stone, though Greek was the language of logic and weakened the seeds of chaos in his spells. He squeezed his finger until his blood covered the edge. Dizziness teased at the edges of his perceptions.

Good. His magic grew strong enough to challenge the inherent power within the stone.

"Cut deeply, my friend, cut into the rocks. Bind me to the Earth that formed you, give me the power of the Earth." He knelt before the demon door and made the first stroke of his pentagram. Sparks of blue/black fire flared as the obsidian scraped the stone floor of the cave. A miasma of deepest black smoke followed the sparks.

He continued his preparations for battle hidden within the shadows of Earth and Blood.

The bright green seal around the demon door dimmed.

"Control. Chaos robs me of control," I muttered as I tethered the horse outside the ring of standing stones at the ancient barrow. I could mold the power of the stones to my control, just like I did the faery ring at Huntington. The barrow was the lair of chaos. I could not allow Blakely to draw me into the barrow and cave.

If I died today, I would do so out here in the fresh air and sunshine.

The sun had already reached its zenith and moved toward the horizon. My strength would wane with the light as his grew strong with the coming dark. For good or for evil, the struggle would end by sunset.

By now, John should have signed the documents required by the church for the formal reconciliation ceremony on Sunday.

If I failed today, Blakely still had time to send England back into chaos.

"Come forth and meet my challenge," I called as I unsheathed Excalibur. The sun caught the bright metal of the blade and radiated outward in a glorious shower of whiter than white light.

But nothing could outshine the outline of Radburn Blakely standing beneath the barrow capstone. His white clothing was shrouded in a deep black aura that absorbed all light.

Excalibur became heavier in my hands as Blakely absorbed its light and its power.

I swallowed my fear and stepped into the ring of stones. Excalibur flared brightly again. I held it up as a beacon brighter than the sun.

"I challenge you to ritual combat, Radburn Blakely," I spoke the ancient words in the Gaelic, the language of the land and my people.

A shiver of elemental powers in conflict rocked beneath my feet. Blakely had invoked the power of the Earth. I knew he would use blood in his preparations. His bond would be greater. But having used blood, he could not now call upon the other three elements.

A mist began to fall upon my head and shoulders. I gathered my element of water into my powers and took a long, slow breath. "Holy Mother, let the combination of all your graces overcome this force of evil. Help me vanquish this foe so that Your church may return to the land." Earth in the stones of the circle, Air moving in and out of my lungs, Water in my blood and in the air, and Fire in my sword. All four elements pulsed together within me.

"Come and get me, Resmiranda," Blakely snarled, lowering his sword. But not in submission.

I had to stay within the stone circle. Once inside the cave, I'd lose logic, and control; I'd succumb to my emotions and fears and let them rule my magic. Five years ago I'd had no control over myself or my life. I trusted nothing, not even God. I'd grown in many ways since then.

Did I dare succumb to the lure of simple fury?

"I can wait in here forever, Resmiranda. I can wait for sunset. Can you?"

I observed his posture closely. He stood slightly off-balance, not used to the weight of his sword. I had trained with sword and long-bow nearly every day for over three years. My body was as strong as I could make it. My magic blossomed with the full moon. Two days hence I would peak and be able to battle him day and night.

I did not have two days. I had today.

Keeping Excalibur at the ready, I approached the barrow entrance.

The two swords fairly leaped at each other of their own volition. Thrust, parry, shift my grip. I engaged him in opening moves to assess his powers and his weakness.

Suddenly fire lanced up my arms. The hilt of my sword grew hot, as white hot as the poker I had used to cauterize Hugh's wound.

"Illusion. You seek to startle me with mere illusion," I sneered as I forced myself to tighten my grip.

He backed up one step. The hilt grew cool again where I gripped it.

I took the next step beyond the barrow uprights into the cave proper.

Immediately I sensed the difference in the air.

"Holy Mary, Mother of God, grant me grace and peace."

"Your prayers mean nothing in here, Resmiranda. In here my grandsire, the demon of chaos, rules," Blakely taunted. He withdrew deeper into the cave.

"Not quite, Blakely. The demon remains behind his portal. Why haven't you broken him free in all these years. Surely you could have murdered your servant if all you need is a blood sacrifice." I had to keep one eye on my footing.

Instinctively I sought the puddles. With each wet step I was cleansed of the chaos inherent in the cave.

If only I could keep one foot in the water, I might have a chance.

A blast of blue/black magical energy shot from Blakely's outstretched hand.

I blocked it with Excalibur. The sword absorbed the magic, sending shock waves through my hands and arms. I nearly dropped the weapon. My knees threatened to collapse.

Gritting my teeth, I took three steps back toward the entrance and the light. Onto dry ground.

Panic gibbered in my mind like a demon fighting its chains of logic and control.

Blakely followed me. He moved his left hand in a ritualistic pattern while he muttered something. I caught the cadence of Greek but did not recognize the words. I waited and watched until the moment he extended the sword to channel the next blast.

Greek? A logical and precise language, alien to the demon of chaos. Why?

At the moment his sword point leveled in the region of my heart I dropped and rolled, coming up under his guard within inches of him. I aimed my blade for his neck.

"Kyrie eleison. Christe eleison." Lord have mercy upon us. Christ have mercy upon us. Greek. Logic.

He slowed, taken aback, but was still too fast for me. His sword caught mine. Grinning in a feral snarl, he forced my blade down, down, down with his superior height and leverage. I dropped to my knees. My shoulders ached. Fire burned in my lungs.

I hadn't loosed a single spell yet.

My knee touched a puddle.

Gathering the last of my strength, I willed all the light and fire in my veins into my sword. Years of hatred for my childhood of separation from my family, of fleeing for my life every time I grew comfortable, boiled within me along the course of the blade into his.

"Kyrie eleison, Christe eleison!" I shouted. Logical precise. A weapon against chaos.

"Yieeeeee!" he screamed, dropping his sword. He staggered back, landing on the demon door. The seal glowed bright green. He bounced off it into the opposite wall.

My legs wobbled too much to stand. Excalibur seemed molded to the floor as iron held by lodestone.

Blakely recovered faster than I. He picked up his weapon and stalked the five steps toward me. He raised his weapon for a killing blow. I hadn't the strength or will to counter him.

The demon gibbered louder. My thoughts skittered about the cave like rats fleeing a sinking ship.

"Sweet Jesu, protect my daughter," I prayed. Automatically my hand reached for the prayer beads with the ancient circled cross. I held up the talisman, wanting the cross of Arthur Pendragon to be the last thing I saw in the life.

"Kyrie eleison. Christe eleison."

The blow did not come.

"*Merde,* put that thing away," he hissed.

I held it up higher.

"Kyrie eleison. Christe eleison."

Blakely backed up. His shadowy servant, nameless, nearly faceless popped up out of the darkness. In a movement too quick for me to see, he wrapped a knotted cord around Blakely's throat and pulled . . .

Excalibur leaped into my hands. I lunged upward, running Blakely through.

Blood sprayed over my hands, my face, my chest.

"May the lord have mercy upon your soul."

"You can't kill me," Blakely gasped, clawing at the garrote. "I do not give you permission to kill me, slave!"

I clung to Excalibur and pressed it deeper.

Through Blakely into the Fantôme.

The slave slumped. His hands went slack on the cord.

Blakely breathed his last one heartbeat before his servant. The nameless man died with a satisfied smile on his face.

I collapsed upon both of their fallen bodies. Blackness pulled my consciousness down, down into a spiral of death. I had taken two lives, I must pay with my own.

"Kyrie eleison. Christe eleison."

Chapter 56

ORAGE shied and refused the bit at the edge of the stone circle. Hugh nearly fell off the horse. He jabbed the beast with his spurs. Orage merely reared and pranced in place. Clearly he would go no further.

Both dogs stood at the entrance to the barrow, noses working, distressed whines in their throats. But they waited for Hugh.

The sun kissed the horizon. Deep twilight spread across the land, throwing long shadows of darkness across the path.

Hugh dropped to the ground. Archie had anticipated his movements and caught him as his knees wobbled and his head reeled.

"Why in hell did she come back here?" Archie crossed himself as soon as Hugh stood on his own.

"Because Radburn Blakely chose the place of their confrontation." Hugh bit back a nasty comment about Archie's stupidity. He didn't like the tactical situation. The hair on his nape stood up straight in atavistic fear.

The last time they had been at this barrow and cave Ana had made him face a demon. Granted the demon was only memories of his father and brother buried deeply behind his spleen. Still the situation had been uncomfortable.

They crossed the open circle in six long strides. The dizziness stayed away for a moment. At the barrow entrance, Hugh paused while his eyes adjusted. Ana, someone, had lit torches leading deep within the silent cave. Too silent. Not so much as an insect squeaked inside. Hugh swallowed a moment of cold dread.

He looked for a hint of faeries flitting about and saw only natural shadows flickering in the torches.

"Ana?" he whispered, not daring to startle her or her opponent. The sound echoed around and amplified. "Ana, ana, an, na, na, na. . . ."

Then all was preternaturally quiet again.

Archie held back.

Hugh forced himself to move forward. The torchlight spread only as far as one step carried him. All seemed dark ahead until he took the next step and the next torch showed him another small area.

He kept his left shoulder and the wounded arm next to the wall and drew his sword with his still sound right hand. Hesitantly, he proceeded forward one careful step after another.

At the split in the cave he saw deep scuff marks on the floor, a scrape where metal had hit the stone walls with force, a downed and dying torch.

"Ana!" he said louder. The walls absorbed his sound as if made of heavy wool.

Three steps farther he found the tangled heap of bodies and pools of blood. Lots of blood.

"Ana!" He dashed to her side, feeling for a sign of a pulse in her neck. No sign of life fluttered against his fingers. "Ana! Don't leave me yet, Ana," he sobbed.

Archie examined the other two bodies and shook his head. "Both dead. Bodies still warm. What about her?" He turned his attention back to Hugh and Ana.

Ana's eyelids fluttered as if dreaming. Or was it merely the flicker of torchlight?

Checking for signs of injury, Hugh gathered her in his arms. "Ana, my love, what ails you?" Hard to tell under the torchlight if her cool skin was unnaturally pale and clammy indicating internal bleeding. She continued a dead weight against his arms. Alive or dead, he had to get her out of this demon cave.

Newynog bounded up and licked Ana's face. She whined pitifully and looked up at him, imploring him to do something. Anything to save Ana.

"Let me carry her outside," Archie said. "You're in no shape to do it. You're in no shape to be here," he muttered.

"Careful," Hugh warned. "She may have internal bleeding."

"I'll be careful. I just need to put as much distance as I can between me and that demon behind the door." He glanced furtively at the dragon head in the center of the door.

Hugh caught no sound or sense of a presence behind the sealed portal. That frightened him as much as Ana's continued stillness.

Had Ana managed to permanently seal the portal or had the demon escaped?

"I'd want to die, too, if I was trapped in this godforsaken cave," Archie muttered as he slung Ana over his shoulder.

Hugh stumbled after them, barely able to stand upright from pain and blood loss and fear for Ana.

"Into the stone circle," he ordered Archie as his sergeant at arms rested Ana within the arches of the barrow.

Outside the sun passed below the horizon. Twilight lingered. Between light and dark. Between life and death.

"Come back to me, Ana. I don't want to live without you."

A tiny glimmer of light beckoned me onward through the black spiral of death that tossed me in its downward progress.

An end to this endless churning.

The light of life or the light of an angel offering me an end to this pain?

I hoped to find an angel holding a star in his hand. If I lived, I'd relive the moment I took a life over and over until I died. I'd never truly live again.

The light grew brighter. A shining beacon of hope in this endless nothing.

I reached for it.

A strong hand clasped mine and pulled me—up—out of the darkness into the fading light of sunset. Death or life?

Loving arms enfolded me. A love so great it could only come from God.

"Come back to me, Ana. I need you, my love. I cannot live without you."

"Hugh?" My eyelids fluttered briefly, then scrunched closed. The first moments past sunset seemed so bright after the darkness of death that my eyes felt stabbed by tiny knives.

"Hush, Ana. I've come for you." He smoothed damp tendrils of hair off my face.

"Blakely?" I asked, though I knew. My last glimpse of him in the flickering torchlight had shown him staring up at me with the blankness of the dead. The great sword, Excalibur pinned him to his servant beneath him.

"Excalibur? Where is it? I must return it to the Lady. I have to ride to Kirkenwood now."

"Hush, my love. You'll not be riding anywhere for a while. You need rest, and food. All the blood dulled the blade, I guess."

"No, the magic is gone from it," I choked. My throat felt as if I'd walked the deserts of the Holy Land without water. "The moment Blakely's eyes went dim, the sword lost its magic. It is silent now. My head is free of the buzzing." I shook my head and slapped my ear lightly. Then I opened my eyes wide and truly looked around.

"Lie still a moment, Ana. You may be hurt." He held my shoulders against his lap.

"No, Hugh, don't you see. The sword has died. Its task here is finished. That's what my dream meant. Not that I would die, but that the sword would. I must return it to the Lady." I rolled to my knees. He was still too weak from his wound to hold me back. "And the demon portal is intact. It is quiet, too. The demon of chaos has retreated." I stood before the barrow uprights, one hand held up, palm out, feeling for any trace of Tryblith or his grandson.

"The demon itself may have retreated, but the seeds of chaos and mistrust are deeply sown among the barons. Its evil still walks the world." Hugh sighed and struggled to his feet.

"They always will. 'Tis my job as The Pendragon to counter those seeds whenever possible." I faced him, the beginnings of a smile tugging at my lips.

I lived. I *lived!*

"How can you, one woman in possession of a minor barony, counter chaos? The barons clamor for a return of their rights outlined by Henry I's Coronation Charter. John insists upon his rights as king by Divine Right. The church wants control of all the rights, to dispense them as they see fit." Hugh shook his head and clasped my hand as if he feared I might run away from him.

Never again.

"What we need is a new charter that outlines everyone's rights as well as responsibilities. Something written and signed so that it becomes part of the fabric of the law," I said. Somehow we would work it all out. Somehow.

What mattered now was that I lived and I loved Hugh and he loved me. My dog and my daughter were safe. In the next few days England would be set back on the road toward a safe future.

"John will like a written charter. He loves laws."

"A charter," I mused. "A great charter that no one can dispute."

"They will dispute it, though."

"Then we must work to make it happen, make it work. I think Archbishop Langdon should be the one to propose it. Both the barons and John will listen to him." I took his arm and led him toward the horses.

"Then we ride for Winchester tonight?" Hugh asked. He looked askance at his horse. "I'd rather rest here a while before riding that beast again."

"I'd rather be back at the inn before a bright fire with a mug of ale and a trencher full of John Howard's stew," Archie muttered. He positioned Orage beside a rock that Hugh might be able to mount from. With help.

"Hugh, I think you and I will set up camp here among the stones of the faery circle. Archie can go back to the inn by himself. With the dogs as escort, of course."

Hugh grinned as a flurry of brightly colored dots of light danced around them. He nodded in acceptance of their presence. "Just like last time, Ana."

Epilogue

WE married short hours after John reconciled with the church. A hasty ceremony with only the king and queen and a few retainers as witnesses. Father Truman assisted Archbishop Langdon at the nuptial mass.

I retired to Bellecôte during a seemingly endless pregnancy. Hetty joined me there. Our reunion was joyous, and laughter returned to my life.

I found a copy of Henry I's Coronation Charter and sent it and numerous copies I penned to everyone I thought would study and use it in settling the civil war that alternately simmered and raged.

Hetty stayed with me through the long and difficult labor until Hugh's son burst into the world screaming his displeasure.

Hugh thrust into the room at that moment, certain the midwife had murdered us both. He did not leave me or his son all that night as we slept.

Robert Fitz Walter and Eustace de Vesci continued to rebel against John for another two years. Many of their compatriots signed John's charter—the Magna Carta. Hugh and I worked closely with King John and Archbishop Langdon in writing the great document, seeking compromises on both sides. The king gave much and received little in that document. Not even peace. Fitz Walter and de Vesci would settle for nothing less than John's death.

Robin Locksley, Earl of Huntington, did not sign the Magna Carta. Neither did he join the rebellion that followed.

I sent a long letter to my father. His reply showed evidence of surprise as well as warm welcome. He begged me to come to him. But I could not leave Hugh. I could not leave England without a

Pendragon—though Hetty will follow me with confidence, talent, and laughter. She already uses a staff more comfortably and confidently than I ever did. Papa and I continue to correspond, making up for the lost years as best we can. Mama did not flee to his side after she left me with the Holy Sisters at St. Dyfrig's. I sought her in a scrying bowl and found nothing. Papa and I can only conclude that she has died. I wish I could have spoken to her one more time, shown her that magic was not evil just because she did not understand it.

Civil war erupted again within days of John meeting his barons in peace on the field of Runnymede on June 15, in the Year of Our Lord 1215. William the Marshall and Ranulph, Earl of Chester, fought valiantly for John. Hugh joined them in battle.

But no army could guard the king against dysentery.

Late one night in the middle of October, Anno Domini 1216, a messenger arrived at Bellecôte with a written missive for me.

Expecting a report from Hugh on the progress of this battle or that negotiation, I tossed it onto the table to read later. Something in the courier's eyes made me look at the small roll of parchment a second time.

"John asks for you. He sickens and is near death." The Marshall signed it with his bold signature that took up more of the page than his message.

My heart leaped to my throat. John. Dying.

My first lover, Hetty's father. He tried to murder me. In the end, he almost became my friend. A tear trickled down my cheek. De Vesci and Fitz Walter might well win this war yet.

Moments later, a second courier arrived, this one wearing Lincoln green and carrying a longbow across his back. I barely recognized Robert Locksley, Robin's oldest son. "Da was in Wakefield on business," he said, short of breath from his long trek.

I cocked my head and raised an eyebrow in question. Robin leave Huntington?

"Since you worked your magic and made him compromise with King John, he does get out a bit more," Rob explained.

We both smiled at the almost compromise the two enemies had worked within the faery ring above Huntington.

"His horse hit a sinkhole in the forest at full gallop. He broke his shoulder and . . . and hit his head. We took him to Kirklee Abbey. The prioress is noted as a healer. But I do not trust her. She's related to Fitz Walter. He never forgave Da for backing out of the rebellion. He's dying. He asks for you, milady." Robert choked out the words. I knew what the effort to speak cost him.

My vision darkened around the edges. I was too late to save Robin. Before I could reach him, his lifelong friend would shoot one last arrow into the air. He would bury Robin where it landed.

A sob choked me for a moment.

I could have loved him.

The other messenger cleared his throat.

Could I do aught for John?

Doubtful. I could give him strength, possibly lessen his discomfort. But God called him, as He did to Robin. At the same time. Neither would triumph over the other by outliving his enemy by even a few hours.

For a moment I thought my heart would break at the loss of either, let alone both.

"Saddle my horse. Journey rations. Newynog!" I leaped into action.

"You'll come with me?" Robert's eyes lighted with a small measure of hope. I had listened to his woes as he struggled through adolescence into manhood. I pressed his suit to his beloved when she resisted his first clumsy attempts at courtship. I helped midwife his first child. Now he stood before me, a man ready to inherit his responsibilities as Earl of Huntington, yet grieving for his beloved father.

"I'm sorry, Rob. I must go to the king. Tell him . . . Tell Robin that I will miss him and that I will keep the faery ring safe for him. He can join his beloved Marion at last."

"You loved them both, John and my father," Rob replied, not bothering to hide his tears of grief.

"In a way. They are both special men. They both knew where my heart truly rested. Hugh and I will miss them both."

Moments later I galloped into the wind, Newynog running at my side, eager for the adventure.

We arrived at Lincoln two days later, exhausted, filthy, and grateful John still lived, though not for long.

Hugh held me tight as I dismounted. I drank in the strength he offered me once again.

"He asked that you come to him directly," Hugh said. His words came out hesitantly. We might never be able to forgive John, but we had learned to respect and value him as a king.

"I need a bath, clean clothes."

"His life hangs by a thread, beloved. You must go to him now, as you are." Reluctantly he released me and led me into Lincoln Castle, the place where John had nearly killed me in the oubliette.

I shuddered at the hideous memory. Hugh squeezed my hand in reassurance. When all else in my life crumbled, Hugh was at my side, then and now.

"Hugh." I held back.

He turned and put his arm around my waist, tucking me against his side. "There is not much time."

"Hugh, Robin Locksley lies dying as well. I had to choose between them." The lump in my throat grew and my chin trembled.

"You had to do that once before, *ma petite*. You made the right choice both times."

I crept into John's bedchamber. A hundred candles attempted to banish the encroaching darkness. Three braziers heated the confined space. Incense and smoke and the odors of sickness and death assaulted me. I almost retreated to the cooler, fresher air of the Hall.

"Ana." John's feeble cry of greeting drew me to his side.

I clutched his hand, instantly assessing his condition. Dehydration from the diarrhea, blood loss, high fever, and a weakened heart. Even if I had the knowledge of the ancient healing magic my family had sought for so many centuries, I could not heal him. He'd waited too long to call me.

"I am here, Highness."

"You still splashed through every puddle between Bellecôte and here, I see." He attempted a smile as he gazed at my drenched cloak and hair. "Stay with me, Ana. Stay until I pass into God's hands."

"Aye, John, I will."

"I loved you, Ana. I know I hurt you beyond measure. But I did love you. I only wish our child had lived." All pretense, the arrogant use of the royal "we," and his pride had been stripped away by the illness.

"I lied to you, Highness. Our daughter, Henrietta Carlotta—Hetty—grows strong and beautiful. She will represent the Griffin clan proudly."

"Named for my father." He smiled blissfully.

"Named for my great-uncle and his wife. She is a Griffin, through and through."

"And what of her Plantagenet blood?" A hint of his old smile and charm shone through his grimace of pain.

I bathed his brow with water and my own special cleansing. His features eased a little.

"You have two sons and three daughters by Isabelle to carry on your legacy, John. Leave me our daughter to carry on mine."

He squeezed my hand briefly before doubling up in pain. When his moaning ceased and I mopped his brow with a cool cloth again, he closed his eyes.

"In the chest beside the prie-dieu. I have rescinded the order of Praecipe. You may fully claim Kirkenwood. You must pass it to our daughter. She, her husband, and her heirs will take the name Kirkwood since she is not entitled to my name. The plague of Griffins will die with you."

"Was I such a terrible plague on you?"

"Aye and more. Trouble from the first time I saw you and you so boldly defied me. No one but an arrogant Griffin would do that."

"I will teach our daughter about the good you accomplished as king. Not just your failures, John."

"Cherish our daughter, Ana, as I cherish you."

My tears touched our joined hands.

"Robin of Locksley lies dying as well, John."

"Fitting. Perhaps in heaven we can meet in peace at last."

"You did that once—in the faery ring above Huntington."

"But only because you kept the peace between us." He sighed and fell silent so long I thought he must have slipped away. Then he roused a little. "I have asked to be buried at Worcester, Ana. Have them put me in monks' robes. Perhaps I can slip into heaven in disguise," he chuckled bleakly. "I have confessed my sins many times and yet I still feel guilt. I may never be cleansed of the evils I performed under Blakely's influence. Thank you for cleansing me of his presence, and making me seek the compromises that brought the church back."

I could not reply. The lump in my throat choked me as my tears blinded me to all but our joined hands, joined lives, joined hearts.

"Strange that you are the only one I trust to carry out my wishes, Ana. I have never trusted easily. But you gave me and my barons an instrument of trust. I wish I could live a little longer to learn to use it. Make sure my son learns how to find honest people like you and Hugh. Make sure he learns what trust is about."

"I will, John. I will carry your trust to the next generation and the next."

Crying openly, I gathered him into my arms and held him close until his life passed into another realm.

I followed him a little way into the tunnel of light. But he did not need me anymore. He trusted God.

𝔐agna 𝔠arta 1215

𝔍𝔬𝔥𝔫, by the grace of God, king of England, lord of Ireland, duke of Normandy and Aquitaine, and count of Anjou, to the archbishops, bishops, abbots, earls, barons, justiciars, foresters, sheriffs, stewards, servants, and to all his bailiffs and liege subjects, greeting. Know that, having regard to God and for the salvation of our soul, and those of all our ancestors and heirs, and unto the honor of God and the advancement of holy church, and for the reform of our realm, by advice of our venerable fathers, Stephen archbishop of Canterbury, primate of all England and cardinal of the holy Roman Church, Henry archbishop of Dublin, William of London, Peter of Winchester, Jocelyn of Bath and Glastonbury, Hugh of Lincoln, Walter of Worcester, William of Coventry, Benedict of Rochester, bishops; of master Pandulf, subdeacon and member of the household of our lord the Pope, of brother Aymeric (master of the Knights of the Temple in England), and of the illustrious men William Marshall earl of Pembroke, William earl of Salisbury, William earl of Warenne, William earl of Arundel, Alan of Galloway (constable of Scotland), Waren Fitz Gerald, Peter Fitz Herbert, Hubert de Burgh (seneschal of Poitou), Hugh de Neville, Matthew Fitz Herbert, Thomas Basset, Alan Basset, Philip d'Aubigny, Robert of Roppesley, John Marshall, John Fitz Hugh, and others, our liegemen.

In Chapter 8 Hugh Fitz Chênenoir and innkeeper John Howard discuss some of the following issues. The Interdict upon England and King John's excommunication stemmed from this problem.

1. In the first place we have granted to God, and by this our present charter confirmed for us and our heirs for ever that the English church shall be free, and shall have her rights entire, and her liberties inviolate; and we will that it be thus observed; which is apparent from this that the freedom of elections, which is reckoned most important and very essential to the English church, we, of our pure and unconstrained will, did grant, and did by our charter confirm and did obtain the ratification of the same from our lord, Pope Innocent III., before the quarrel arose between us and our barons: and this we will observe, and our will is that it be observed in good faith by our heirs for ever. We have also granted to all freemen of our kingdom, for us and our heirs forever, all

the underwritten liberties, to be had and held by them and their heirs, of us and our heirs for ever.

In Chapter 9 Hugh faces the problem of nearly unending debt to the crown for his stepson's inheritance. As young John's guardian he is responsible for the debt.

2. If any of our earls or barons, or others holding of us in chief by military service shall have died, and at the time of his death his heir shall be of full age and owe "relief" he shall have his inheritance on payment of the ancient relief, namely the heir or heirs of an earl, 100 pounds for a whole earl's barony; the heir or heirs of a baron, 100 pounds for a whole barony; the heir or heirs of a knight, 100 shillings at most for a whole knight's fee; and whoever owes less let him give less, according to the ancient custom of fiefs.

If Hugh pays off the entire death relief for young John's inheritance will there be anything left for John to inherit when he comes of age?

3. If, however, the heir of any of the aforesaid has been under age and in wardship, let him have his inheritance without relief and without fine when he comes of age.

Hugh Fitz Chênenoir is a responsible guardian of a minor heir. Many were not and raped the land before the heir could come of age.

4. The guardian of the land of an heir who is thus under age, shall take from the land of the heir nothing but reasonable produce, reasonable customs, and reasonable services, and that without destruction or waste of men or goods; and if we have committed the wardship of the lands of any such minor to the sheriff, or to any other who is responsible to us for its issues, and he has made destruction or waste of what he holds in wardship, we will take of him amends, and the land shall be committed to two lawful and discrete men of that fee, who shall be responsible for the issues to us or to him to whom we shall assign them; and if we have given or sold the wardship of any such land to anyone and he has therein made destruction or waste, he shall lose that wardship, and it shall be transferred to two lawful and discreet men of that fief, who shall be responsible to us in like manner as aforesaid.

King John assumes Lady Resmiranda Griffin's wardship when her great-uncle dies. But he does not relinquish control of it even after she marries.

5. The guardian, moreover, so long as he has the wardship of the land, shall keep up the houses, parks, fishponds, stanks, mills, and other things pertaining to the land, out of the issues of the same land; and he shall restore to the heir, when he has come to full age, all his land, stocked with ploughs and "wainage," (carts and wagons) according as the season of husbandry shall require, and the issues of the land can reasonably bear.

In Chapter 27 King John agrees to Radburn Blakely's unorthodox marriage to Resmiranda when no one has been notified or given the opportunity to object—not even the bride.

6. Heirs shall be married without disparagement, yet so that before the marriage takes place the nearest in blood to that heir shall have notice.

One of the court cases addressed in Chapter 7.

7. A widow, after the death of her husband, shall forthwith and without difficulty have her marriage portion and inheritance; nor shall she give anything for her dower, or for her marriage portion, or for the inheritance which her husband and she held on the day of the death of that husband; and she may remain in the house of her husband for forty days after his death, within which time her dower shall be assigned to her.

See above.

8. No widow shall be compelled to marry, so long as she prefers to live without a husband; provided always that she gives security not to marry without our consent, if she holds of us, or without the consent of the lord of whom she holds, if she holds of another.

This problem is not specifically addressed. But since the land was the source of all wealth, many greedy bailiffs would rather seize the land and its continuing opportunity to supply wealth than just enough of the furniture, plate, and jewels to pay off the debt.

9. Neither we nor our bailiffs shall seize any land or rent for any debt, so long as the chattels of the debtor are sufficient to repay the debt; nor shall the sureties of the debtor be distrained so long as the principal debtor is able to satisfy the debt; and if the principal debtor shall fail to pay the debt, having nothing where with to pay it, then the

sureties shall answer for the debt; and let them have the lands and rents of the debtor, if they desire them, until they are indemnified for the debt which they have paid for him, unless the principal debtor can show proof that he is discharged thereof as against the said sureties.

Hugh briefly considers borrowing from the Jews to be free of his debt to King John in Chapter 12. All Jews were under the protection of the king. But not necessarily protected by the king.

10. If one who has borrowed from the Jews any sum, great or small, die before that loan can be repaid, the debt shall not bear interest while the heir is under age, of whomsoever he may hold; and if the debt fall into our hands, we will not take anything except the principal sum contained in the bond.

See above.

11. And if any one die indebted to the Jews, his wife shall have her dower and pay nothing of that debt; and if any children of the deceased are left underage, necessaries shall be provided for them in keeping with the holding of the deceased; and out of the residue the debt shall be paid, reserving, however, service due to feudal lords; in like manner let it be done touching debts due to others than Jews.

Feudal society was based upon an intricate network of duties and responsibilities of military aid. By the time of King John, this web had become so complex, some lords owing service to both sides in a war, John preferred to hire mercenaries than trust his barons. England was also moving away from a strictly barter economy and becoming more dependent upon coinage. Therefore exchanging military duty for money became a plausible alternative. See Chapters 11 and 38.

12. No scutage (money paid instead of feudal service) nor aid shall be imposed on our kingdom, unless by common counsel of our kingdom, except for ransoming our person, for making our eldest son a knight, and for once marrying our eldest daughter; and for these there shall not be levied more than a reasonable aid. In like manner it shall be done concerning aids from the city of London.

Chapter 38 mentions the long unresolved problem of London. The citizens recognized the importance of their city. No monarch could hope to rule long without their support. Therefore they held out to maintain independence. For

many centuries no monarch could enter the city—as defined by the ancient city walls—without the permission of the Lord Mayor.

13. And the city of London shall have all its ancient liberties and free customs, as well by land as by water; furthermore, we decree and grant that all other cities, boroughs, towns, and ports shall have all their liberties and free customs.

The very beginnings of a kind of parliament or rule by common assent among barons, church officials, and the monarchy. A brief mention for the need for this in Chapter 38.

14. And for obtaining the common counsel of the kingdom anent the assessing of an aid (except in the three cases aforesaid) or of a scutage, we will cause to be summoned the archbishops, bishops, abbots, earls, and greater barons, severally by our letters; and we will moreover cause to be summoned generally, through our sheriffs and bailiffs, all others who hold of us in chief, for a fixed date, namely, after the expiry of at least forty days, and at a fixed place; and in all letters of such summons we will specify the reason of the summons. And when the summons has thus been made, the business shall proceed on the day appointed, according to the counsel of such as are present, although not all who were summoned have come.

If the king cannot levy scutage without common consent, then neither can the barons. Robert Fitz Walter had to resort to this to pay his ransom from the king of France and never forgave John for not bailing him out.

15. We will not for the future grant to any one license to take an aid from his own free tenants, except to ransom his body, to make his eldest son a knight, and once to marry his eldest daughter; and on each of these occasions there shall be levied only a reasonable aid.

I did not specifically address this issue. But then there is always bootlicking. The king just can't make it mandatory.

[1]16. No one shall be distrained for performance of greater service for a knight's fee, or for any other free tenement, than is due therefrom.

This occurs throughout GUARDIAN OF THE TRUST. John may have been

---

[1] In a later issue of this document petitions #16 & 17 are eliminated

an admirable judge, much sought after by disputants. But there were other justiciars who could settle a case in the home county rather than have minor and
strictly local cases follow an itinerant king.

17. Common pleas shall not follow our court, but shall be held in
some fixed place.

**Lady Resmiranda tries twice, in Chapter 12 and Chapter 26, to sue for
redress for the murder of her great-uncle. In Chapter 48 she tries to regain
Kirkenwood from John's control. John will not allow her to bring suit. This
clause also allows for regular court sessions four times a year in every county,
precursor to the right to a speedy trial.**

18. Inquests of *novel disseisin* (a legal procedure to provide redress for those who have had their freehold unjustly taken), of *mort
d'ancester* (a legal procedure to provide redress for those who have
been denied an inheritance), and of *darrein presentment* (last presenta-
tion), shall not be held elsewhere than in their own county courts and
that in manner following,—We, or, if we should be out of the realm,
our chief justiciar, will send two justiciars through every county four
times a year, who shall, along with four knights of the county chosen
by the county, hold the said assize in the county court, on the day and
in the place of meeting of that court.

So logical a provision I did not address it.

19. And if any of the said assizes cannot be taken on the day of the
county court, let there remain of the knights and freeholders, who were
present at the county court on that day, as many as may be required
for the efficient making of judgments, according as the business be
more or less.

See Chapters 7 and 9.

20. A freeman shall not be amerced (punished by fine, punished
arbitrarily) for a slight offense, except in accordance with the degree of
the offense; and for a grave offense he shall be amerced in accordance
with the gravity of the offense, yet saving always his "contenement;"
and a merchant in the same way, saving his "merchandise;" and a
villein shall be amerced in the same way, saving his "wainage" (wagons
and carts)—if they have fallen into our mercy: and none of the aforesaid amercements shall be imposed except by the oath of honest men
of the neighborhood.

A jury of his peers. Note this applies only to the nobility. The common man did not have this right at this time.

21. Earls and barons shall not be amerced except through their peers, and only in accordance with the degree of the offense.

See Chapter 8. This is one of the issues that John argued with the church throughout the period of Interdict and Excommunication.

22. A clerk shall not be amerced in respect of his lay holding except after the manner of the others aforesaid; further, he shall not be amerced in accordance with the extent of his ecclesiastical benefice.

See Chapters 23 and 29. Building and maintenance of bridges was expensive. Tolls did not always meet those needs.

23. No village or individual shall be compelled to make bridges at river-banks, except those who from of old were legally bound to do so.[2]

Serious crimes had to come to the crown and not be settled arbitrarily by lesser courts.

24. No sheriff, constable, coroners, or others of our bailiffs, shall hold (try) pleas of our Crown.

Let's hear it for rent control! However, due to inflation, at times the crown nearly went bankrupt because of it. Brief mention in Chapter 38.

25. All counties, hundreds, wapentakes, and trithings (except our demesne manors) shall remain at old rents, and without any additional payment.

The ever present problem of collecting debts after a man died and his relatives tried to hide his true wealth.

26. If any one holding of us a lay fief shall die, and our sheriff or bailiff shall exhibit our letters patent of summons for a debt which the deceased owed to us, it shall be lawful for our sheriff or bailiff to attach and catalogue chattels of the deceased, found upon the lay fief, to the value of that debt, at the sight of law-worthy men, provided always that nothing whatever be thence removed until the debt which is evident shall be fully paid to us; and the residue shall be left to the executors to fulfil the will of the deceased; and if there be nothing due from him

---

[2] Petitions #23 & 24 are also eliminated from the version reissued by King Henry III

to us, all the chattels shall go to the deceased, saving to his wife and children their reasonable shares.

Let's keep the paperwork in order. John loved having everything spelled out, signed and filed.

27. If any freeman shall die intestate, his chattels shall be distributed by the hands of his nearest kinsfolk and friends, under supervision of the church, saving to every one the debts which the deceased owed to him.

Previous kings had been in the habit of collecting taxes and tithes in food and goods rather than coin. But as coins became more available and the economy shifted people had to make certain they were not double taxed in coin and goods. There was also the ongoing problem of feeding troops during war, foreign and civil. Who paid for it? See Chapter 18.

28. No constable or other bailiff of ours shall take corn or other provisions from any one without immediately tendering money therefor, unless he can have postponement thereof by permission of the seller.

Briefly mentioned in Chapter 24 when Silvester is ordered away from court to stand guard at Lincoln Castle. He probably could have bribed his way out of the duty if he had the cash, or assigned the task to another if he trusted anyone.

29. No constable shall compel any knight to give money in lieu of castle-guard, when he is willing to perform it in his own person, or (if he cannot do it from any reasonable cause) then by another responsible man. Further, if we have led or sent him upon military service, he shall be relieved from guard in proportion to the time during which he has been on service because of us.

See Chapter 19.

30. No sheriff or bailiff of ours, or other person, shall take the horses or carts of any freeman for transport duty, against the will of the said freeman.

See above. Again John is dotting "I's" and crossing "T's".

31. Neither we nor our bailiffs shall take, for our castles or for any other work of ours, wood which is not ours, against the will of the owner of that wood.

See Chapters 32 & 33 for Lady Resmiranda's problem. John confiscated the lands of his enemies, primarily William de Briouze who seems to have committed no crime other than to invoke the king's extreme displeasure. De Briouze died in exile after his family was imprisoned and probably died of starvation in an oubliette.

32. We will not retain beyond one year and one day, the lands of those who have been convicted of felony, and the lands shall thereafter be handed over to the lords of the fiefs.

Eustace de Vesci makes this point in Chapter 26.

33. All kiddles (a barrier in a river with an opening fitted with nets etc. to catch fish.) for the future shall be removed altogether from Thames and Medway, and throughout all England, except upon the seashore.

Chapter 48 Lady Resmiranda has forfeited control of her lands and cannot regain them until her dispute with John is settled. The matter is not settled until John's death.

34. The writ which is called *praecipe* (The order of forfeiture when title to land is in dispute) shall not for the future be issued to any one, regarding any tenement whereby a freeman may lose his court.

See Chapter 18. We have John to thank for standard weights and measures.

35. Let there be one measure of wine throughout our whole realm; and one measure of ale; and one measure of corn, to wit, "the London quarter;" and one width of cloth (whether dyed, or russet, or "halberget"), to wit, two ells within the selvages; of weights also let it be as of measures.

Disputants often had to pay a fee for the right to take their case to court. See Chapter 7.

36. Nothing in future shall be given or taken for a writ of inquisition of life or limbs, but freely it shall be granted, and never denied.

Another issue that attempts to untangle the complex relationships in a feudal society.

37. If any one holds of us by fee-farm, by socage (feudal tenure of land involving payment of rent or other nonmilitary service to a supe-

rior), or by burgage (tenure of land in a town on a yearly rent), and holds also land of another lord by knight's service, we will not (by reason of that fee-farm, socage, or burgage) have the wardship of the heir, or of such land of his as is of the fief of that other; nor shall we have wardship of that fee-farm, socage, or burgage, unless such fee-farm owes knight's services. We will not by reason of any small serjeanty which any one may hold of us by the service of rendering to us knives, arrows, or the like, have wardship of his heir or of the land which he holds of another lord by knight's service.

See Chapter 10.

38. No bailiff for the future shall, upon his own unsupported complaint, put any one to his "law," without credible witnesses brought for this purpose.

See Chapter 5 for Lady Resmiranda's problem and Chapter 12 for a reference to William de Briouze.

39. No freeman shall be taken or imprisoned or disseised or exiled or in anyway destroyed, nor will we go upon him nor send upon him, except by the lawful judgment of his peers or by the law of the land.

Briefly mentioned in Chapter 7, also in Chapter 26.

40. To no one will we sell, to no one will we refuse or delay, right or justice.[3]

We encounter this with a foreign merchant in Chapter 10.

41. All merchants shall have safe and secure exit from England, and entry to England, with the right to tarry there and to move about as well by land as by water, for buying and selling by the ancient and right customs, quit from all evil tolls, except (in time of war) such merchants as are of the land at war with us. And if such are found in our land at the beginning of the war, they shall be detained, without injury to their bodies or goods, until information be received by us, or by our chief justiciar, how the merchants of our land found in the land at war with us are treated; and if our men are safe there, the others shall be safe in our land.

[3] Petition #40 also received the ax in the later version of this document

Lady Resmiranda tries repeatedly to leave the country but cannot obtain permission from King John. Chapter 7 and Chapter 12.

42. It shall be lawful in future for any one (excepting always those imprisoned or outlawed in accordance with the law of the kingdom, and natives of any country at war with us, and merchants, who shall be treated as is above provided) to leave our kingdom and to return, safe and secure by land and water, except for a short period in time of war, on grounds of public policy—reserving always the allegiance due to us.

Hugh Fitz Chênenoir should not have to pay a death relief for Bellecôte because the previous baron—his stepson—died without heirs. The land and title should have been a free gift from the king to the new baron. Chapter 35.

43. If any one holding of some escheat <the reversion of property to the State or to a lord on the owner's dying without legal heirs> (such as the honor of Wallingford, Nottingham, Boulogne, Lancaster, or of other escheats which are in our hands and are baronies) shall die, his heir shall give no other relief, and perform no other service to us than he would have done to the baron, if that barony had been in the baron's hand; and we shall hold it in the same manner in which the baron held it.

Robin Locksley, Earl of Huntington probably had a hand in this petition.

44. Men who dwell without the forest need not henceforth come before our justiciars of the forest upon a general summons, except those who are impleaded (parties in a plea), or who have become sureties for any person or persons attached for forest offenses.

Chapter 10. Sir Arundel was more typical than we like to believe.

45. We will appoint as justices, constables, sheriffs, or bailiffs only such as know the law of the realm and mean to observe it well.

The church can't have it all. See Chapter 35.

46. All barons who have founded abbeys, concerning which they hold charters from the kings of England, or of which they have long-continued possession, shall have the wardship of them, when vacant, as they ought to have.

Robin Locksley again.

47. All forests that have been made such in our time shall forthwith

be disafforested; and a similar course shall be followed with regard to river-banks that have been placed "in defense" by us in our time.[4]

See above.

48. All evil customs connected with forests and warrens, foresters and warreners, sheriffs and their officers, river-banks and their wardens, shall immediately be inquired into in each county by twelve sworn knights of the same county chosen by the honest men of the same county, and shall, within forty days of the said inquest, be utterly abolished, so as never to be restored, provided always that we previously have intimation thereof, or our justiciar, if we should not be in England.

During the civil war of 1213–1215, John continued the honorable tradition of taking hostages. In Chapter 43 we saw how John sometimes treated his hostages dishonorably.

49. We will immediately restore all hostages and charters delivered to us by Englishmen, as sureties of the peace or of faithful service.

In Chapter 10 we saw briefly some of the mercenaries specifically mentioned in the following petition. In Chapter 9 we encounter some of the problems resulting from John's reliance upon mercenaries to fight his battles. In Chapter 4 I made one of the raiders a relative of the specifically named mercenaries.

50. We will entirely remove from their bailiwicks, the relations of Gerard Athee (so that in future they shall have no bailiwick in England); namely, Engelard of Cigogne, Peter, Guy, and Andrew of Chanceaux (or Chancell in a different translation), Guy of Cigogne, Geofrrey of Martigny with his brothers, Philip Mark with his brothers and his nephew Geoffrey, and the whole brood of the same.

See above.

51. As soon as peace is restored, we will banish from the kingdom all foreign-born knights, cross-bowmen, serjeants, and mercenary soldiers, who have come with horses and arms to the kingdom's hurt.

Again this addresses those like Lady Resmiranda who have been dispossessed. This type of claim must be decided by 25 barons, the beginnings of a Parliament.

[4] Petition #47 was also considered invalid in the later version.

52. If any one has been dispossessed or removed by us, without the legal judgment of his peers, from his lands, castles, franchises, or from his right, we will immediately restore them to him; and if a dispute arise over this, then let it be decided by the five-and-twenty barons of whom mention is made below in the clause for securing the peace. Moreover, for all those possessions, from which any one has, without the lawful judgment of his peers, been disseised or removed, by our father, King Henry, or by our brother, King Richard, and which we retain in our hand (or which are possessed by others, to whom we are bound to warrant them) we shall have respite until the usual term of crusaders; excepting those things about which a plea has been raised, or an inquest made by our order, before our taking of the cross; but as soon as we return from our expedition (or if perchance we desist from the expedition) we will immediately grant full justice therein.

A continuation of petitions #47 & 48.

53. We shall have, moreover, the same respite and in the same manner in rendering justice concerning the disafforestation or retention of those forests which Henry our father and Richard our brother afforested, and concerning wardship of lands which are of the fief of another (namely, such wardships as we have hitherto had by reason of a fief which any one held of us by knight's service), and concerning abbeys founded on other fiefs than our own, in which the lord of the fief claims to have right; and when we have returned, or if we desist from our expedition, we will immediately grant full justice to all who complain of such things.

This seems to speak directly to Lady Resmiranda and her attempts to sue for redress from the wrongful murder of her great-uncle.

54. No one shall be arrested or imprisoned upon the appeal of a woman, for the death of any other than her husband.

Correcting past wrongs, but allows for a committee to oversee the process. Again, an early form of what became Parliament.

55. All fines made with us unjustly and against the law of the land, and all amercements (arbitrary punishments) imposed unjustly and against the law of the land, shall be entirely remitted, or else it shall be done concerning them according to the decision of the five-and-twenty barons of whom mention is made below in the clause for secur-

ing the peace, or according to the judgment of the majority of the same, along with the aforesaid Stephen, archbishop of Canterbury, if he can be present, and such others as he may wish to bring with him for this purpose, and if he cannot be present the business shall nevertheless proceed without him, provided always that if any one or more of the aforesaid five-and-twenty barons are in a similar suit, they shall be removed as far as concerns this particular judgment, others being substituted in their places after having been selected by the rest of the same five-and-twenty for this purpose only, and after having been sworn.

Making a gesture of peace toward Wales.

56. If we have disseised or removed Welshmen from lands or liberties, or other things, without the legal judgment of their peers in England or in Wales, they shall be immediately restored to them; and if a dispute arise over this, then let it be decided in the marches by the judgment of their peers; for tenements in England according to the law of England, for tenements in Wales according to the law of Wales, and for tenements in the marches according to the law of the marches. Welshmen shall do the same to us and ours.

See above. Other versions of this document break up the following into five more clauses that lump together a number of political issues.

57. Further, for all those possessions from which any Welshman has, without the lawful judgment of his peers, been disseised or removed by King Henry our father or King Richard our brother, and which we retain in our hand (or which are possessed by others, to whom we are bound to warrant them) we shall have respite until the usual term of crusaders; excepting those things about which a plea has been raised or an inquest made by our order before we took the cross; but as soon as we return (or if perchance we desist from our expedition), we will immediately grant full justice in accordance with the laws of the Welsh and in relation to the aforesaid regions. We will immediately give up the son of Llywelyn and all the hostages of Wales, and the charters delivered to us as security for the peace. We will do toward Alexander, King of Scots, concerning the return of his sisters and his hostages, and concerning his franchises, and his right, in the same manner as we shall do toward our other barons of England, unless it ought to be otherwise according to the charters which we hold from

William his father, formerly King of Scots; and this shall be according to the judgment of his peers in our court. Moreover, all these aforesaid customs and liberties, the observance of which we have granted in our kingdom as far as pertains to us toward our men, shall be observed by all of our kingdom, as well clergy as laymen, as far as pertains to them toward their men. Since, moreover, for God and the amendment of our kingdom and for the better allaying of the quarrel that has arisen between us and our barons, we have granted all these concessions, desirous that they should enjoy them in complete and firm endurance for ever, we give and grant to them the underwritten security, namely, that the barons choose five-and-twenty barons of the kingdom, whomsoever they will, who shall be bound with all their might, to observe and hold, and cause to be observed, the peace and liberties we have granted and confirmed to them by this our present Charter, so that if we, or our justiciar, or our bailiffs or any one of our officers, shall in anything be at fault toward any one, or shall have broken any one of the articles of the peace or of this security, and the offense be notified to four barons of the aforesaid five-and-twenty, the said four barons shall repair to us (or our justiciar, if we are out of the realm) and, laying the transgression before us, petition to have that transgression redressed without delay. And if we shall not have corrected the transgression (or, in the event of our being out of the realm, if our justiciar shall not have corrected it) within forty days, reckoning from the time it has been intimated to us (or to our justiciar, if we should be out of the realm), the four barons aforesaid shall refer that matter to the rest of the five-and-twenty barons, and those five-and-twenty barons shall, together with the community of the whole land, distrain and distress using all possible ways, namely, by seizing our castles, lands, possessions, and in any other way they can, until redress has been obtained as they deem fit, saving harmless our own person, and the persons of our queen and children; and when redress has been obtained, they shall resume their old relations toward us. And let whoever in the country desires it, swear to obey the orders of the said five-and-twenty barons for the execution of all the aforesaid matters, and along with them, to molest us to the utmost of his power; and we publicly and freely grant leave to every one who wishes to swear, and we shall never forbid any one to swear. All those, moreover, in the land who of themselves and of their own accord are unwilling to swear to the twenty-five to help them in constraining and molesting us, we shall by our command compel the same to swear to the effect aforesaid. And if any one of the five-and-twenty barons shall have died or departed from the land, or be incapacitated in any other manner which would prevent the aforesaid provisions being carried out, those of the said twenty-five barons who are left shall choose another in his place according to their own judgment, and he shall be sworn in the same way as the others. Further, in all matters, the execution of which is entrusted to these twenty-five barons, if perchance these twenty-five are present, that which the majority of those present ordain or command shall be held as fixed and established, exactly as if the whole twenty-five had concurred in this; and the said twenty-five shall swear that they will faithfully observe all that is aforesaid, and cause it to be observed with all their might. And we shall procure nothing from any one, directly or indirectly, whereby any part of these concessions and liberties might be revoked or diminished; and if any such thing has been procured, let it be void and null and we shall never use it personally or by another. And all the ill-will, hatreds, and bitterness that have arisen between us and our men, clergy and lay, from the date of the quarrel, we have completely remitted and pardoned every one. Moreover, all trespasses occasioned by the said quarrel, from Easter in the sixteenth year of our reign till the restoration of peace, we have fully remitted to all, both clergy and laymen, and completely forgiven, as far as pertains to us. And, on this head, we have caused to be made for them letters testimonial patent of the lord Stephen, archbishop of Canterbury, of the lord Henry, archbishop of Dublin, of the bishops aforesaid, and of Master Pandulf as touching this security and the concessions aforesaid. Wherefore it is our will, and we firmly enjoy, that the English Church be free, and that the men in our kingdom have and hold all the aforesaid liberties, rights, and concessions, well and peaceably, freely and quietly, fully and wholly, for themselves and their heirs, of us and our heirs, in all respects and in all places for ever, as is aforesaid. An oath, moreover, has been taken, as well on our part as on the part of the barons, that all these conditions aforesaid shall be kept in good faith and without evil intent. Given under our hand—the above-named and many others being witnesses—in the meadow which is called Runnymede, between Windsor and Staines, on the fifteenth day of June, in the seventeenth year of our reign.